To Kiss a Thief

Susanna Craig

LYRICAL PRESS
Kensington Publishing Corp.
www.kensingtonbooks.com

LYRICAL PRESS BOOKS are published by

Kensington Publishing Corp.
119 West 40th Street
New York, NY 10018

First Electronic Edition: August 2016
eISBN-13: 978-1-60183-615-1
eISBN-10: 1-60183-615-5

First Print Edition: August 2016
ISBN-13: 978-1-60183-616-8
ISBN-10: 1-60183-616-3

Printed in the United States of America

*To my mom,
for teaching me to love books.
And in loving memory of my dad,
who was my first hero.*

ACKNOWLEDGMENTS

All authors incur debts of gratitude, but a first book racks up more than can ever be repaid. So if there's a debtors' prison for writers, that's surely where I'm headed.

Many thanks to my agent, Jill Marsal, who saw a sparkle in a rock and was endlessly patient while I chiseled it out, and to my editor, Esi Sogah, whose enthusiasm and guidance made the final polishing of it (almost) a pleasure.

Jenni McQuiston has been an extraordinary mentor and friend, providing much-needed encouragement, offering advice, and answering odd questions at even odder hours.

Other writers also offered helpful feedback. Thank you to the anonymous contest judges whose comments on the early chapters of this book made me want to keep going. A $1 raffle ticket won a priceless critique from Sarah MacLean, who generously gave a master class in character development.

I could not have done this without my dear friend Amy, who has read more drafts of this book than anyone should have been subjected to and who always found something to praise, even when there wasn't.

And finally, thank you to my husband, Brad, who has supported me through the tears and the fears, too much take-out, too little house-cleaning, early mornings, late nights, and all the other tortures writers put their loved ones through. I'm blessed to have you for my biggest fan, and I hope you know I'm yours.

Prologue

Mayfair, June 1793

Sarah Pevensey Sutliffe had never before noticed how much light was cast by candles thrust into a darkened room.

It seemed two wax tapers were more than sufficient to illuminate her total humiliation.

As the library filled with light and people, Sarah leapt to her feet and immediately made two more regrettable discoveries. First, the glass of wine she had drunk—or had it been two glasses?—made the floor pitch rather alarmingly, and second, her gown felt oddly loose about the bodice. Clutching the ivory silk to her breast with one hand, she waved the other behind her back, searching for something against which she might steady herself.

But Captain Brice, on whose knees she had been so precariously perched just moments before, was no longer within arm's reach. He had stood in the presence of ladies.

The Marchioness of Estley. The Honorable Miss Eliza Harrington. Mama.

Ladies—among whom she was no longer to be classed, if the expressions on the faces now confronting her were any indication.

Five sets of eyes took in the disorder of her gown and the darkness of the library and drew the inevitable conclusion. Only Mama looked away, her face turned into Papa's shoulder. Beside Sarah's parents stood her father-in-law, the Marquess of Estley, a thundercloud darkening his brow. Lady Estley's wide eyes darted to and from the fan she was fiddling with, as if she had witnessed some horrific accident and was trying to make herself look away. Next to the marchioness, Miss Harrington clutched the brass candelabra in a steady hand; the flickering candlelight danced across her deep red curls, flame against fire.

Sarah's startled gaze fell last on the impassive face of St. John Sutliffe, Viscount Fairfax. Her husband of just two weeks. His pale blue eyes betrayed not even a glimmer of surprise.

It had only just occurred to her to wonder what could have brought them all there at once when Captain Brice spoke. "Lady Fairfax felt a bit faint. I was merely offering her some assistance," he drawled in a tone that quite clearly said he expected no one to believe such a preposterous tale.

Horrified that she had allowed Captain Brice to set the tone of her defense, Sarah closed her eyes. But rather than settling her nerves, she was instantly assaulted by the memory of the scene that had sent her scurrying for safety.

> *The leaf-screened alcove outside the ballroom. Eliza Harrington's long, pale fingers spread possessively over her husband's chest. Plump red lips curled in a wicked smile against his ear. Whispered words Sarah longed to unhear.*
>
> *"Your father may have made you marry her, Fairfax. But he cannot make you do more."*
>
> *"No. She will never have my heart." Her husband's hand coming up to clasp Eliza's where it lay. "And you know why."*
>
> *A throaty, suggestive laugh. "I do."*

Captain Brice had found Sarah fumbling blindly with the stubborn knob on the library door, although it had proved to be unlocked. The wine he had offered had been cool and crisp, a balm to her hot, angry tears. His whispered consolations had been more welcome still. *"Who would dare to distress the bride at her nuptial ball?"* he had murmured, drawing her against the breadth of a shoulder made somehow broader by his regimentals.

Sarah jerked herself back to the present and met her husband's scrutiny. She suffered no illusions that his indiscretions would excuse her own. As their eyes locked in mutual distrust, her field of vision narrowed and everyone else fell away. For a moment, it was just the two of them. She stretched out her hand, grasping for words of explanation. "My lord, I—" But the wine seemed to have hobbled her normally quick tongue.

"Lady Fairfax." So cold, so formal. Had she ever heard his voice sound otherwise?

"This is not what it seems, my lord," she insisted. "I swear I am innocent."

St. John cut his gaze away.

Forgetting the state of her gown, Sarah took a step toward him. Her slipper caught the hem and jerked the neckline even lower.

"*Innocent?*" Lord Estley's eyes—ice-blue, like his son's, and capable of freezing the object of their stare with a single glance— darted over her rumpled skirts and gaping bodice. "Not precisely the word I would have chosen."

Sarah felt a traitorous blush stain her cheeks.

Just then, Miss Harrington whispered something in the Marchioness of Estley's ear. That lady's eyes grew wider still, and she gave a soft, shrill sort of scream. "My sapphires!"

Sarah swept her hand across her throat, expecting to brush against the heavy, old-fashioned collar of gems her father-in-law had placed on her neck earlier that evening, proof to the dazzling assemblage of titles to which he had been about to introduce her that this merchant's daughter was now one of their own. *"Presented to my ancestor by Queen Elizabeth herself,"* Lord Estley had said proudly, drawing her attention to a portrait of a man in doublet and hose, posed with one foot on a globe and a cache of blue gems spilling from his hand. *"Only a Sutliffe lady wears these jewels."*

Sarah's icy fingertips encountered nothing but an expanse of gooseflesh.

"Those sapphires have been in my family for eight generations. Where are they?"

Try as she might, she could not remember when she had felt the gems last. "I d-don't . . ." she stammered, shaking her head.

"That necklace is not something one could simply *lose*, like a—a handkerchief, or a hairpin, for God's sake," Lord Estley ground out. "No matter the distraction."

He flicked a disparaging glance toward Captain Brice, who stepped nimbly away from her, merging into the crowd of her accusers. "I say! Come to think of it, she wasn't wearing them when I found her—trembling like anything, she was. Said she had to get away . . ."

Sarah started. *Had* she been wearing the necklace when she had entered the library?

Her memory felt strangely fuzzy around the edges. She recalled gasping, choking, nearly fainting for want of air. Captain Brice had loosened her gown to help her draw breath—had he not? How much, if at all, had the stones at her throat contributed to the sensation that she was being smothered?

At the time she had been conscious only of the leaden weight in her chest.

Lady Estley was the first to shape her thoughts into an accusation. "Gone? Why, there must be three hundred people in this house tonight," she cried, snapping open her fan and speaking behind it to Eliza Harrington. "She might have passed that necklace to anyone."

The candlelight jerked and fluttered as Lady Estley's fan stirred the air, lending Miss Harrington's expression a menacing cast.

Sarah turned beseechingly to her parents, but shock had drawn shutters across her father's eyes. Her mother stared fixedly at the floor.

Was there no one who believed her innocent?

Surely St. John did not believe she had been unfaithful. Surely her husband did not think she was a *thief.* She shifted her gaze to him just in time to see his dark blond head disappear through the doorway.

Sarah watched the sky reflected in her dressing table mirror as it lightened, gradually but inexorably, from a darkness that was not quite black to a gray that was not quite dawn. Unwilling to allow the memories of the night before to overwhelm her again, she refused to close her eyes, although they burned with fatigue and unshed tears, and her head felt as if it might split in two. She understood now why the only wine she had been allowed to taste at Papa's dinner table had been watered down—unlike the wine she had so rashly drunk last night.

God, what a fool she was. A fool to believe that the marriage her father had arranged might grow to be something more than a business agreement. A fool to have thought that by virtue of her upbringing, her education, her marriage—and the title that had come with it—she could ever belong in the Sutliffes' world, in their house, in their family.

A fool to have fallen in love with her husband.

She turned toward the door when she heard the latch *click* and watched the knob turn. She had not bothered to lock it. Anyone who would want to come to her now had a key.

Lady Estley bustled into the room. "Hurry, dear! We haven't much time."

"Time? Time for what?"

The marchioness, who seemed always to be in motion, stopped and regarded Sarah with a puzzled look. "Lord Estley is on his way to escort you down to the library. The public rooms have already been searched, and your rooms are to be next. If the necklace isn't found, he intends to send for the Bow Street Runners."

So she was to report to the scene of her supposed crime, in order that this room, which was not yet her room, and these things, which were not yet her things, might be searched by strange hands, and all in an effort to uncover what? Proof of her guilt? But everyone already knew she was guilty—guilty of foolishness, and naïveté, and marrying above her station.

Theft seemed a trivial matter in comparison.

"I didn't steal it," Sarah gritted out from between clenched teeth, fighting back the desire to proclaim her innocence with a scream.

Lady Estley tilted her head to the side, as if considering the matter. "But you must have done. Everyone says so."

"And does everyone—or anyone—say why I would have done such a thing? Am I generally thought to be mad? Or in want of money?"

"Why no, dear. Until last night, you seemed quite levelheaded, and everyone knows you're a great heiress, even if the money isn't as old as one would like. No, I believe the general consensus is that you passed them to someone who was in more straitened circumstances— a friend, perhaps." With a tittering laugh, she hurried toward the dressing room. "Or a lover."

Sarah felt her face heat again. "Ma'am, I assure you . . ."

But Lady Estley continued as if Sarah had not spoken. "I confess myself rather surprised," she said, poking her head around the door-jamb. "I had thought that the middling classes objected to such arrangements, even for married women. And really, it is customary to wait at least until the heir has been born." She clucked her tongue and ducked back into the dressing room. "But Captain Brice is a dashing one. I do love a red coat."

Sarah opened her mouth to protest once again but shut it just as quickly, certain her words would fall on deaf ears.

"The sapphires, though—a priceless family heirloom—that was going a bit too far, I fear," the marchioness piped from the next room. "Lord Estley is really quite furious."

"If everyone is sure I passed the gems to Captain Brice, ma'am, then why isn't he the object of this investigation?"

Lady Estley reappeared in the doorway and looked pointedly at Sarah. "He was—at first. His commanding officer was even called in to search his person. But nothing was found, and we could not prevent him from leaving the house after that. I have no doubt but he'll make himself scarce," she said, handing Sarah a pair of kid gloves and a wide-brimmed bonnet. "And that's when I began to think that if he could disappear, why shouldn't you?"

"D-disappear?"

Lady Estley nodded. "Oh, I suppose there ought to be *some* punishment for what you've done, but I cannot abide the thought of you in Newgate, or sent to Botany Bay, or any such nonsense."

Prison? *Transportation?* Surely Lady Estley was mistaken. Even if Sarah *were* guilty of a crime, a nobleman could stand between his wife and the law—if he chose. And she was, after all, the Viscountess Fairfax now, for better or for worse.

For worse. Decidedly for worse.

Sarah tried to shut out every distracting thought, to focus on her mother-in-law's words. But nothing made them clearer. "I don't understand. If you believe I am guilty, why would you help me evade punishment?"

Lady Estley's voice took on an edge Sarah had never heard in it before. "Because Fairfax is miserable about this—this mésalliance his father insisted upon."

Sarah had known it, of course, but it stung nonetheless to hear that truth spoken aloud.

Her marriage was not all that Sarah had hoped for, either, come to that. A title had been her parents' dream for her, not hers.

She had dreamed of being desired for more than her dowry.

But really, what had she expected? She was no beauty—certainly nothing on the order of Miss Harrington.

Still, she had dared to dream of a love match.

Where had such a preposterous notion come from? Some book, perhaps, for she had no model for it in life—certainly not her parents' marriage, which had been arranged by their parents for the sole purpose of joining her father's burgeoning wealth with her mother's good breeding, to produce sons who might someday pass for gentlemen. The sons had never materialized, so the responsibility for elevating the family had fallen to their only daughter. Fortunately, impecunious noblemen were never in short supply.

Believing that love could grow under even the unlikeliest of circumstances, Sarah had nursed her dream through a perfunctory courtship, through a stilted exchange of vows, through a wedding night with a man not unkind but hardly brimming with passion for his new bride. Without conscious thought, she cut a glance to the door that separated her apartment from St. John's, the door through which he had entered her bedchamber and dutifully come to her bed every night of their married lives. Every night but the last.

Sarah, too, had been brought up to know her duty where marriage was concerned, and she had tried very hard to be the kind of wife she had been told Lord Fairfax would expect.

But now she knew that he had no intention of being the kind of husband of whom she had dreamed.

Lady Estley followed her gaze. "You'll get no help from that quarter, you may be sure."

"I—I was not looking for help," she replied with a bravado she did not feel. "But to leave, without any explanation—why, it would be tantamount to a confession."

"Yes, dear," Lady Estley agreed. "Everyone will assume you have run away with the jewels—and your lover. I believe that will enable my husband to arrange an annulment, or a divorce, or some such thing. Fairfax will be free."

The image of him in Eliza Harrington's embrace rose in her memory. *Free?* It seemed in all essential ways, he imagined he already was.

"You are not the bride *I* would have chosen for him. But I like you, Sarah. So I will help you by telling a little fib, and I will salve my conscience with the knowledge that he is happy and you are not rotting away in a cell or hanging from a gallows."

Sarah winced. Could such things really happen? And to her? She knew that thieves were sometimes put to death. And the consensus seemed to be that she was a thief . . .

At the moment, though, she could think of no worse punishment than staying put.

"Where would I go?" The whisper crossed her lips without volition.

"I know the perfect place. In Devonshire. By a stroke of good fortune, Miss Harrington put me in mind of it just last night—"

Eliza. Of course. If she were out of the way, St. John and Eliza could live happily ever after on the money Sarah's father and grandfather had worked lifetimes to earn.

"My parents?" Sarah interrupted.

"Your mother was unwell. Your father took her home. He offered to return, to sort things out, he said, but Estley insisted that would not be necessary. You must understand, Sarah, if you wish my help to leave, you must cut all ties with them, with everyone you know. Forever."

Sarah felt one hot tear slip down her cheek. Did her parents believe her guilty, too? She thought of Mama's downcast eyes, Papa's sagging shoulders. Even if they did not, in Lord Estley's world they were powerless to do anything to help her.

"It will be for the best," Lady Estley insisted. "If you could have seen your mother's face . . . The scandal will destroy her, I fear. This way, your parents can go back to Bristol and begin to put this unfortunate episode behind them."

Her parents, her husband—although Sarah had never been one to run away from her problems, it was difficult not to conclude that everyone would be better off if she simply disappeared.

Perhaps it would even be best for her.

She could live for herself. Choose for herself. Dream a different dream.

"All right," Sarah whispered. "I'll go."

Although Lady Estley had asked no question, Sarah's reply obviously pleased her. "Very good, my dear. I'll see that you have what you need. Come this way."

As Sarah took a last look around the room, she spied something on her dressing table. Almost against her will, she laid her gloved hand atop the small object, curled her fingers around it, and followed her mother-in-law down the servants' stairs to the rear of the house.

Lady Estley had had faith in her powers of persuasion. A hired coach and four were waiting in the mews, and her small trunk was already loaded—how long ago it had been packed, Sarah could not bear to guess. She stepped into the carriage without assistance and felt it sway into motion almost before she was seated. The coachman clearly had his orders.

For the first time, she allowed herself to look at what she held in her hand. In the half light of early morning, the leather miniature case lay dark against her palm. Lady Estley had been showing it to her just the day before when preparations for the ball had called her away. Doubtless she would miss the picture before long.

What, then, had possessed Sarah to take it?

With her thumb, she flicked the clasp and St. John's face was before her: aquiline nose, pale eyes, and hair the color of ripening wheat. It was an undeniably handsome face. Young. Arrogant. Almost a stranger to her.

And yet her stomach did a curious flip-flop when she saw it.

She snapped the case closed, leaned her head against the squabs, and resigned herself to the necessity of closing her eyes at last.

Chapter 1

Three years later

"But why did you leave, Fairfax? I still cannot fathom it!"
Because I was afraid.

God knew it was the truth, although he was not a man who liked to admit feeling fear—who liked to admit feeling anything. In any case, it was not an answer to satisfy his stepmother, who had asked some version of the same question a dozen times since his return.

"Because dueling is illegal," St. John offered instead, not for the first time.

She waved an impatient hand. "Oh, pish posh. One hears of duels being fought forever."

He glanced out the window of his stepmother's sitting room at the pallid September sky and the nearly empty London street below. "There was also the small matter of believing I might have killed a man. And the death of a military officer is no insignificant thing."

"But he didn't die," she protested.

"Three witnesses swore to me that Brice would be gone in a matter of days," he said. "I could only act on the information I had in front of me in the moment. This house had been overrun by the boys from Bow Street, and I had a man's blood on my hands. I felt it would be best if I left for a time."

It had seemed like bravery to call out a man of considerably greater experience and skill. It was what dishonored husbands did. But as he had faced Brice across a misty field in the uncertain light before dawn, St. John's sword had trembled in his hand.

"I did not take you for the jealous type, Fairfax."

St. John had cultivated a pose of studied indifference to the world for so long, he had forgotten that something might still lie beneath it. But he could not deny the truth of Brice's taunt. A duel was not the act of an indifferent man.

So when the duel was over, he had left, not out of fear of the law or of Brice, but fear of himself, of the strength of his reaction.

And he had stayed away until he was sure he felt nothing for his wife.

Nothing at all.

Not even regret at the discovery he need never have left.

"Well, even so," his stepmother clucked, "I certainly cannot fathom why you ran off to the West Indies, of all places."

"I had little choice in the matter. Ganett drove me to the docks. There was a packet in port bound for Antigua." The ship's destination had sounded interesting, exotic. The sort of place that offered just the escape he sought. It had been all of those things.

And none of them.

"I was . . . fortunate to secure a place," he concluded.

"But to stay away so long—?" She shook her head and patted the settee in invitation. After almost twenty years, his once-obnoxious behavior toward her had settled into a sort of cool politeness, but she seemed determined even now to pretend there was real affection between them. Reluctantly, St. John left his post at the window to sit beside her.

As she studied his face in the afternoon light, she raised one hand to trace her fingers down his left cheek. "I do not like to see a gentleman so brown," she chided. What bothered her most, he knew, was the curling scar left by Brice's blade, silvery-white against his tanned skin. "Although the color in your face sets off your eyes rather handsomely. Miss Harrington remarked upon it to me after dinner yesterday."

St. John covered his stepmother's hand with his own and returned hers to her lap. "She is most kind."

Her desire for him to court Eliza Harrington was almost a palpable thing. And he had to admit, it had been something of a shock to find Eliza still unwed after all these years. But he was the very last man to do anything about it. She was beautiful, yes, but an old friend, nothing more. Besides, it was impossible to imagine his own thoughts straying toward marriage again. Especially after—

"Is there nothing more you can tell me about Sarah's death?"

His stepmother stiffened. "Honestly, Fairfax. It's hardly a fit subject for a lady to discuss. Everything was a blur—Sarah disappeared, you went missing. Lord Ganett refused to reveal where you'd gone. Then the constable came to the door and announced that a woman's body had been pulled from the Thames. You'll have to speak to your father if you want the gruesome details—he identified her. Though after five days, one imagines it was difficult to be certain."

Despite her protests, she told the story with a certain relish.

Had he been in town when Sarah drowned, he would have been called upon to do the grim task his father had performed. Now, after so much time, he could no longer call her face to mind. He remembered mousy brown hair, gray eyes, and an upturned nose. But try as he might, the collection of features would not be formed into a whole.

Perhaps that was for the best. He had seen firsthand what heat and water could do to the human body. Although he had no intention of engaging the man in conversation about either the matter or the manner of his wife's death, when he imagined the scene with which his father had been confronted, he shuddered.

"Don't think on it." His stepmother patted his hand consolingly. "What matters is that you're free now—free to bestow your heart where you wish."

His *heart*? His stepmother of all people should have known he had no heart to give.

Love was for the weak and the foolish. He had learned that long ago. Even had he been prone to such weakness, such foolishness, what had his heart to do with his marriage? How could he allow himself to fall in love with the wife his father had all but forced upon him? Sarah Pevensey had been too meek by half, undeniably plain, utterly passionless.

In their two weeks of married life he had been tempted at times to believe he might have misjudged her. And in the end, she had proved him right. The woman he had thought he'd known had lacked the nerve to do what his wife had done. Brice had seen something in her, known something of her that he, her husband, had quite overlooked.

At the time, the revelation of her true nature had been oddly liberating. Her behavior on the night of the nuptial ball had confirmed both his father's poor choice and his own belief that love was a risk not worth taking. It had provided the perfect excuse for St. John to keep himself at arm's length from his wife. Now, Sarah was gone and, as his stepmother said, he was free. Free to do as he pleased.

He jerked to his feet and began to pace.

Why didn't he *feel* free?

"Oh, bother." His stepmother was rummaging through her lap desk. "Would you be a dear and fetch me some paper? I'll send 'round a note to Eliza and invite her to tea."

It seemed an unlikely bond had formed between the two women in his absence. As Eliza apparently came for tea every day, he very much doubted she required an invitation. But he strode across the room to his stepmother's escritoire, if only to put some distance between them.

"Middle drawer," she called after him.

The morning's post was strewn across the desktop. A stack of bills caught his eye: winter ball gowns, feminine fripperies, a new chaise for a sitting room where no one ever sat. None of it was surprising. Money had always run through his stepmother's fingers like water.

What rankled now was the knowledge that those were the sorts of uses to which Sarah's dowry was being put.

As he had married only to secure the family estate, St. John had willingly turned over the money to that purpose. The mistake had been ceding the management of it to his father in his absence. He shuddered to think what might have been made of those thirty thousand pounds in the hands of a man with a head for business—someone decidedly unlike his father, who had allowed his wife to squander a fortune and then informed his son and heir it was his duty to marry the daughter of a cit to save his family from drowning in their debts.

His hand curled around the carved rail of the escritoire's delicate chair until he heard something crack. His time under the Caribbean sun ought to have burned off some of his anger toward the man, but clearly live embers still crackled in the darker recesses of his soul.

"Fairfax, dear, I'm waiting."

"Coming, Mama," he said, pushing the address past a clenched jaw—although to be fair, she had never been the one to insist upon it. Did his father regret even *some* of the choices he had made?

He fingered the teardrop-shaped pull and tugged gently, but the drawer gave at best half an inch. More force made little headway. He jiggled the drawer from side to side, hoping to dislodge whatever obstructed its movement. After three tries, a small strip of crumpled paper fluttered to the floor at the back of the desk. He knelt to snatch it up, then opened the drawer, which slid easily now, and pulled out several sheets of writing paper to take to his stepmother.

"I'd forgotten all about that sticky drawer. Did you discover the problem?" she asked, reaching up for the foolscap he had brought.

"Just this," he replied, smoothing the torn edge of the slip of paper between his thumb and forefinger.

> *Memorandum.*
> *Midsumr. £500 — S.*

His stepmother's copperplate made the cryptic message even harder to decipher. Five hundred pounds was an enormous sum for a lady to spend, even one such as her, and the reference to the quarter day made it seem as if it might be some recurring expense. Rent? But for what? Or whom?

St. John read the note through twice more before handing it to his stepmother. "A record of payment, I'd say. Who, or what, is 'S.'?"

Coloring, she folded the paper and tucked it into her lap desk. "No one with whom you need concern yourself now, dear."

S. *S.?* "Not—!"

Although he had not finished the thought aloud, she looked away and bit her lip.

He tried to persuade himself that Sarah's name had leapt to mind because they had been speaking of her. But the guilty look on his stepmother's face told another story. What was it she had said about the body Father had identified? *It was difficult to be certain.*

St. John had always thought his stepmother woefully inept at telling fibs and keeping secrets.

Until now.

Grasping her by the shoulders, he lifted her from the settee, conscious that his fingers bit into her flesh, yet unable to restrain himself. The lap desk clattered to the floor, and in the awful silence that followed, he could hear the steady drip of ink trickling onto the carpet.

"My God. *Where is she?*"

* * *

Sarah stepped to the doorway of the vicarage to see that the afternoon's intermittent downpours had shifted to a steady drizzle, spattering against the boldly colored autumn leaves.

"Are you sure you won't borrow an umbrella, Mrs. Fairfax?" the vicar's wife asked, coming up beside her.

"No need, Mrs. Norris," Sarah answered with a laugh, tying the strings of her bonnet. "The houses down-along sit too close together to let a drop of rain pass."

With a wave she set off on the footpath that ran from the old Norman church and Haverty Court to the vicarage, and from the vicarage to the lane of wattle-and-daub cottages that was Haverhythe. In just a few steps she was at the top of the street, looking down the narrow, winding roadway to the sea.

She picked her way over cobblestones slick with rain, paused in a doorway halfway down the steeply pitched street to wait out a heavier shower, and caught a glimpse of the bay stretched out below.

Had Lady Estley known when she chose this place that Sarah would arise every morning to a view of the Bristol Channel? The sorrow Sarah had first felt at the sight had eventually been replaced by something like comfort: comfort in the knowledge that these same waves lapped the docks where Papa's warehouses stood, that this same sea breeze wound its way through Bristol streets to stir the draperies in Mama's sitting room.

Sarah was pulled from her bittersweet reverie by the sensation of something brushing against her ankles. She glanced down to see an orange tabby with four white socks looking up expectantly.

Sarah bent to stroke her. "Good evening, Meg!"

The cat chirped a greeting then ambled off down the street, her tail curled in a question mark and her bulging belly swaying from side to side.

"See something that tempts your sweet tooth, Mrs. F.?" The baker came to the door of his shop, his head dusted with white where he had run a floury hand over his balding pate.

"Oh, Mr. Beals, I shouldn't. I'm late for tea as it is, and Mrs. Potts will have my head." Sarah nevertheless cast a longing glance at the wares displayed in the shop window. "Do you suppose, perhaps, a currant cake would appease her?"

Mr. Beals's face split into a grin beneath his bushy moustache, and he stepped back into his shop to fetch an already-wrapped parcel.

Another few steps brought Sarah to the end of the lane. She ducked under a low archway and skipped up the stairs to the kitchen door of Primrose Cottage.

"There now," Mrs. Potts clucked as she lifted the sodden bonnet from Sarah's head. "And how was the lesson?"

"Oh, fine. Susan Kittery shows all the signs of musical giftedness that an eight-year-old girl who would rather be playing cricket with her brothers usually does, and Mrs. Norris is a saint for allowing us the use of her pianoforte," Sarah answered, setting the cake on the table and turning to warm her hands at the fire. "She sits and sews just as if she weren't being tortured. I suspect she stuffs her ears with wax before we arrive."

Mrs. Potts knelt to brush the damp from Sarah's hem. "I see you met Bright Meg along the way," she said, plucking a tuft of orange fur from Sarah's dark skirts.

"Oh, yes. If those kittens don't come soon, she'll not be able to squeeze her way down the street for that belly."

"Mr. Beals promised one to Clarissa, you know." Mrs. Potts sounded disapproving.

Sarah smiled. "Yes. I expect he thought she'd forget. Little does he know."

Mrs. Potts gave a chuckle and resumed fussing over Sarah's dress. "I don't know why you don't leave off wearing these widow's weeds, mum. It's been more'n three years, and this black will show the dirt like anything."

"A new wardrobe would be an entirely frivolous expense," Sarah chided.

"What about that trunk o' things molderin' away upstairs, then?"

Sarah flicked her skirts away from Mrs. Potts's fingertips and pretended not to have heard her. "Black suits me. I have it on the best authority."

"Oh? How's that, then?"

"The twinkle in Mr. Beals's eye whenever I step into his shop," Sarah teased, breaking off a corner of the currant cake and popping it into her mouth.

Mrs. Potts shook her head. "Beggin' your pardon, mum, but I think it's your tuppence he sees comin', afore the dress."

"Be that as it may, Mrs. Potts, he's going to sell those divine tea cakes of his at the bazaar next week and he's generously agreed to donate all his profits to the Fishermen's Relief."

"Humph," was Mrs. Potts's only reply as she turned to lift the boiling kettle, but Sarah knew the woman was reluctantly impressed. "Oh, Lawks!" The kettle clattered back onto the hob. "I forgot! There's a gentleman to see you, mum."

Sarah smoothed a distracted hand over the damp hair at her brow. "A gentleman? Did he have a card? Or give his name?"

"No, mum." Having been born in Haverhythe, Martha Potts had little experience with strangers. She had obviously not thought to ask the man's name, but equally bothersome was his failure to supply it. "He's in the parlor."

Sarah smiled inwardly at Mrs. Potts's insistence on such a grandiose label for the small cottage's plain sitting room, but curiosity quickly redirected her thoughts. The only strangers who called at Primrose Cottage were those seeking some kind of assistance. Her own means, albeit meager, were still beyond many in the little fishing village. But if Mrs. Potts described him as a gentleman, he was unlikely to be a vagrant begging alms or an itinerant laborer looking for work. "I'll see what he wants," she said. Three steps took her down the narrow passageway that ran beside the staircase. She stopped in the doorway to the parlor to observe her visitor.

The stranger stood looking out the window toward the sea, his back to her. He was tall and well-dressed, his dark blue riding coat and snug buff breeches hugging broad shoulders and well-muscled legs. Puddles had collected around the soles of his boots, and his greatcoat had been flung unceremoniously—almost proprietarily—over a nearby chair. Mrs. Potts had indeed been most remiss in the duties of a hostess.

Sarah stepped forward. Soft as her footsteps had been, the sound evidently attracted the man's notice. As he turned his head, the fading light struck a momentary sheen of dark gold.

Her vision blurred as the blood rushed from her head to her pounding heart. The handsome, blond-haired gentleman offered a stiff bow. "Ma'am."

"My lord," Sarah whispered. She curtsied automatically, though a moment's reflection would have forestalled the gesture. As she felt her knees bend, she very much feared she was going to go right on sinking to the floor.

She had no desire to display such weakness to the man who stood before her.

St. John Sutliffe, Viscount Fairfax.

Her husband.

Chapter 2

S t. John had no intention of allowing emotion to color his handling of this situation, but he could not entirely deny the little stab of pleasure he felt at seeing the extent to which three years in the back of beyond had humbled his false-hearted wife.

He stood motionless as she scrambled to her feet unaided. She looked older, of course, and she was. Twenty-one? No, twenty-two. Her jaw had gained a certain firmness. And did her wretched black dress impart that color to her eyes, or had he simply not known them capable of such steeliness?

"What are you doing here?" she whispered fiercely, as if afraid of being overheard.

St. John felt certain that her shock at seeing him was genuine. He had traveled alone and with all possible speed so that no one could have warned her of his approach or given her time to escape. "I would ask you the same, but I believe I had enough of the story to know what your answer will be."

Sarah's chin lifted defiantly. "Oh? And what—"

The door swung inward, cutting her short. A woman well past the middle years of life, dressed in a serviceable gown and wearing a plain cap, entered bearing a tea tray.

"I thought I'd just leave this and step out to Mrs. Thomas's, mum."

"Thank you, Mrs. Potts," Sarah replied. He marveled at the speed with which she could assume at least the appearance of calm.

The woman laid the tray on a low table in front of the window and went out, closing the door behind her.

Sarah took refuge behind the tea table, perching on the edge of one of the two worn but comfortable chairs that flanked it. With deliberate motions, she began to arrange cups and saucers. "Tea, my lord?"

"'My lord'?" he echoed, unwillingly recalling the note of desperation in her voice the last time she had addressed him so. "A wife may use her husband's given name when they are private, Sarah."

She flinched, but whether at the sound of her name on his lips or at the hardness of his voice when he said it, he could not hazard a guess. "A *wife* may, yes, but I am not certain what manner of relation I bear to you now, my lord."

St. John took one long stride toward the tea table. "What manner of relation? Are you not my wife?"

"I understood from Lady Estley that your father would arrange to have our marriage dissolved—annulled."

"Annulled?" He slapped one hand onto the table, rattling the teacups in their saucers. He rested the other on the back of her chair and leaned toward her, so that he was close enough to see her hands trembling in her lap. She did not raise her eyes. "Though our honeymoon was brief, I assure you there are no grounds for an annulment, Lady Fairfax."

His murmured words found their mark, dislodging some intimate memory that passed through her with a shudder. Revulsion? Fear? He watched a flush as it fanned along her cheeks and down her throat, saw her breasts rise and fall as she drew a steadying breath. Then, much to his surprise, she turned and faced him, her eyes just inches from his own. "A divorce, then. But please, do not call me that."

"You have cast aside my title?"

"I have cast aside everything—*everything*," she insisted, her voice cracking with intensity. "No one in Haverhythe has heard me addressed in such a way, and I would prefer to keep it that way."

"I see." He pushed himself away, having intended to discomfit her with his proximity and having been disquieted by hers instead. "But a divorce would have required proof of your infidelity, you know," he remarked, flinging himself into the chair opposite.

It would also require an Act of Parliament and thus his father's assistance, which he could not think he was likely to get and for which he had no desire to ask in any case. Divorces were messy, public, expensive things, just the sort of scandal his father would want to avoid.

But then, his father had gotten him into this fix . . .

Sarah resumed her study of the teacups. "What proof there was, you had," she said quietly.

He had expected her to proclaim her innocence. What reply could be made to the answer she had given? He watched her pour with a none-too-steady hand and then lift the tongs to drop three lumps of sugar into his cup, as if she remembered that he liked his tea sweet.

"In any case, your demise seemed to render such a step unnecessary," he observed as she handed over the saucer. No doubt a faked death had been part of Sarah's plan from the beginning, the better to escape with the gems.

But she did not blush at that reminder of her duplicity. Instead she paled and cut a sharp glance toward the bay. "My . . . *demise*? Yes, I suppose it would have." After a moment, she turned back to the table and closed her hand around a knife. "Bread and butter?" she asked, as calmly as if they were discussing the weather. "Or"—her hand hovered over the tray—"or currant cake?"

"No, thank you," he said, fighting the sardonic smile that had risen to his lips.

"Something amuses you?"

He took a sip of the scalding tea in an attempt to drive down the uneasy laughter that was rising in his chest. "I confess I find this charming domestic scene a bit at odds with our situation," he said with a nod toward the knife.

But Sarah did not seem to find any humor in it. She paused in the act of slicing the cake and laid the knife aside. "May I ask again why you've come? And why now? Only Lady Estley could have told you where I was, and I would very much like to hear the story that has brought you here after all these years."

"Very well," he said, placing his cup and saucer on the table and leaning toward her. "She told me that you came to her in the night after the ball and professed yourself in love with Captain Brice. You admitted to having the Sutliffe sapphires, but refused to reveal their whereabouts unless she helped you disappear. A few days after you ran away, a body was dragged from the Thames and identified, quite conveniently, as yours. Death by drowning. No more questions." He watched her profile, the delicate turn of her jaw, as he spoke; her gaze was once again fixed beyond the window, somewhere far out to sea. "And although Mama had done just as you asked, you kept the necklace and have been using it to extort money from her, money on which you have been living ever since."

A mantel clock ticked loudly in the silence. He could hear greetings called from nearby cottages as fishermen returned home. Beneath it all rumbled the steady sigh of the waves against the shore.

"I see," she said at last.

"You do not deny it?" he pressed.

The light was fading and no lamp had been lit. When she turned to face him again, her expression was unfathomable. "Would it matter if I did, my lord?" She began to gather the tea things and stack them carefully on the tray. "But you still have not told me why you waited more than three years to seek me out."

He debated whether to tell her where he had been and what he had been doing since she had seen him last, but he could not think it any concern of hers. "A happy accident, one might say. Just two days ago, I found a record of Mama's last payment to you. She was reluctant to explain what it meant, but I persuaded her that no good could come of keeping secrets."

"I see."

When she rose, he stood, too, out of habit. As if her hands were not quite steady, the cups on the tea tray chattered in their saucers, and she paused to collect herself before leaving the room. Making no move to help her, St. John listened to her footsteps as she walked down the hallway and into the kitchen. He heard a rattle, and in a moment she returned with a lamp, driving the darkness into the corners of the room. "This room is rarely used," she said, as if to explain the lack of comforts. She crossed to place the lamp on the mantel, where a mottled mirror doubled its light. "We usually pass our evenings in the kitchen, to save a fire."

She settled into the chair she had vacated, arranging her skirts about her with precise movements of her slender hands. He half-expected her to take up some bit of needlework. But her ladylike composure was almost certainly put on. How could it be otherwise?

"And what do you intend to do now?" she asked, her voice as calm and deliberate as her actions.

"Now? Why, I intend to take you back to London, of course, and settle this matter once and for all."

She gave an enigmatic half smile. "Oh, I think not. I do not choose to leave."

"Do you think I wait upon your choice, madam?" he asked, taking a step toward her and inwardly cursing as he did so. How could he allow himself to be rattled by a woman who meant nothing to him?

"I think you will find that if you attempt to remove me from Haverhythe without my consent, I have friends here who will . . . put themselves in your way, shall we say."

"They may try," St. John shot back, more sobered by her quiet threat than he cared to admit, and suddenly regretting his decision to go haring off to Devonshire alone. He had seen enough of the local fishermen to know it would be folly to test them.

Not half an hour past, he had been standing by the empty fire-place, cold and wet and impatient, entertaining thoughts of carting off his guilty wife, bound hand and foot.

If that particular dark fantasy was to be denied him for the moment, he would have to come up with another way of getting what he wanted.

"Very well, then," he began again, crossing to her. "I will stay here." What better way to discover everything she was hiding—including the whereabouts of a certain necklace?

For the Sutliffe sapphires were the key. If he recovered that damned necklace his father loved so much, he would not need to beg the man's assistance in procuring a divorce from Sarah.

He would have the means to make his father offer it.

Her throat worked. "Stay *here*?"

Her reaction—equal parts guilt and fear—told him all he needed to know. "Here. In this house," he insisted, his voice soft. "You are my wife, Sarah."

Another small smile. "My husband is dead."

It was a sharp, quick blow—as she had no doubt intended.

"Dead?"

"Yes. As anyone in Haverhythe will tell you, I am a widow," she said, smoothing a hand over her inky skirts. "My husband, a junior officer in Colonel Grayson's regiment, died abroad. Grief robbed me of my health, so I came to the seaside to recover."

"A clever ruse."

She nodded in acknowledgment, as if the compliment had been

genuine. "I was two days and a night in a carriage coming from London. It gave me ample time to think."

He recalled the torturous weeks at sea, the years abroad. What could she possibly know about time to think?

"Whatever you may choose to believe, I live a quiet life here," she insisted. "And a respectable one. It would never do for the Widow Fairfax to allow a strange man to share her—roof."

Mrs. Fairfax. He was inordinately pleased to discover that she had kept some small part of him alive—and inordinately frustrated at his pleasure. "I am not a stranger, ma'am. I am your husband."

"The house is small," she continued, fumbling for excuses now, "and Mrs. Potts has had trouble enough. It would give me pain to cause her more."

"You'll see me on the street before offending your maid?"

"Mrs. Potts is not my maid," she retorted sharply.

"Your housekeeper, then."

"She is my *friend*. And this," she said with a slight wave of her hand, "is her home."

St. John started and looked again at the half-empty room. "What of *Mr.* Potts?"

"He died at sea many years ago," Sarah said. "She took me in when there was nowhere else to go. She has shown me nothing but kindness, kindness I can never hope to repay."

"A very affecting story." St. John glanced toward the water, but he could see only the two of them and the empty tea table reflected in the darkened glass. "After we've gone, perhaps your time can be put to good use, setting it all to paper. You might support yourself tolerably well thereby."

But the insinuation did not appear to frighten her. Her eyes flashed with that unfamiliar spirit. "I have no intention of leaving Haverhythe."

"Nor do I, *Mrs.* Fairfax. At least, not without getting what I came for."

She rose and crossed the room to the spindle-backed rocking chair on which his greatcoat lay. "And what would that be, my lord?"

"Satisfaction."

"Then I fear you are doomed to disappointment." She walked to the doorway still holding his hat and stood there looking expectant.

"But you are welcome to make your way up-along to Mackey's Pub while you wait."

"Mackey's." He had passed it on his way through town. "The sign of the fish?"

"The Blue Herring, yes. They have rooms, although I cannot speak for their quality." She cast a glance at his mud-spattered boots. "You rode?"

"When the mailcoach could take me no farther."

"And your horse?"

"Tethered at the top of the street." He did not like to admit that he had stood for a long moment looking down the steep lane, uncertain how best to manage it, even on foot.

"Mackey's has stables in the back," she offered. "For the donkeys, mostly, but there might be room for a horse."

Donkeys? He rather felt as if he had fallen into an alien world and was struggling to maintain a foothold on some unfamiliar surface. He did not enjoy the sensation.

"Don't think of trying to leave," he ordered as he shrugged reluctantly into his greatcoat.

"Where on earth would I go?"

The rattle of the door latch appeared to startle her. She turned toward the sound of someone entering the house.

"That will be Mrs. Potts returning, I suppose."

"Yes."

He thought he caught a note of hesitation in her voice, but it was drowned out by Mrs. Potts's call. "Here we are, mum."

A whirlwind of light brown ringlets and dirty pinafore tore through the room with a squeal and buried herself in Sarah's skirts. "Mama! Mama!"

Chapter 3

Sarah passed her hand over her daughter's head. "And were you a good girl for Mrs. Thomas, Clarissa?"

But the girl had already been distracted by the presence of a stranger and toddled over to inspect him.

Sarah watched St. John study the child's features in return, no doubt searching for some sign of family resemblance—as she herself had done all too often. Clarissa had Sarah's brown hair, although sea, sun, and a passionate dislike of bonnets had turned it more golden than her mother's. The girl's eyes, blue at birth, had been Sarah's best hope, for no one would have denied that St. John was Clarissa's father if she had had his pale eyes. Over a matter of months, though, they had shaded to violet. Beautiful, yes.

But not Sutliffe eyes.

It would have been painful to have had that daily reminder, to see his reflection in her child's face, but she could have borne it, as she had borne so many things, to have had just that small security. It would not have proved Sarah's faithfulness entirely, of course, but it might at least have ensured that the girl would have some future—albeit a future spent far away from her mother, Sarah feared.

Now, however, she felt a peculiar gladness that Clarissa's paternity could not be so easily identified. It made the child hers—always and only hers.

"Who dat is, Mama?"

Sarah opened her mouth, although no reply was forthcoming, and watched in shock as St. John lowered himself to one knee to meet his daughter eye to eye.

"Clarissa, is it?" He extended his hand, and Clarissa placed her chubby fingers in his palm. "I'm called—" He paused, evidently searching for some suitable alias and landing, to Sarah's astonishment, on his given name. "I'm called St. John."

Not *Fairfax*? He must have feared his title would tip his hand. Even a child as young as Clarissa could recognize *Fairfax* as her mother's name, and her own. Convenient that his given name could pass for a surname—but then, it likely *had* been someone's surname once, a nod to the family of some other young woman who had traded her identity, or perhaps something more, to become a Sutliffe.

"Sijin?" Clarissa's two-and-a-half-year-old tongue struggled to frame the unfamiliar name, a name so intimate even Sarah had never ventured to utter it outside the marriage ceremony.

"Just so. I knew your mother many years ago. Pleased to make your acquaintance, Miss Clarissa."

Clarissa cast a backward look at Sarah and smiled in obvious satisfaction at being addressed like a grown girl, not a baby. Sarah set her free hand on the child's shoulder and pulled her gently away from St. John, fighting with every fiber of her being the instinct to snatch up her daughter and run as far and as fast as she could.

He rose to his feet and nodded stiffly to Sarah. "I'll bid you good evening, Mrs. Fairfax. But I'll be back tomorrow. It would seem we have one other little matter to discuss." She could not read his expression as he cut a glance toward Clarissa. "Mrs. Potts," he added with a nod in her direction, and was out the door before Sarah could speak.

Or even hand him his hat. "Uh-oh," Clarissa piped, tugging on its black brim.

Sarah looked down, startled. "No, no, dear." She lifted it gently from the child's reach and hung it on a hook near the door. And then, for good measure, she shot the bolt in the latch, a thing she had never done before in this house.

Mrs. Potts raised an eyebrow. "Everything all right, mum?"

"Perfectly, Mrs. Potts," Sarah replied with a calm she did not feel and ushered them into the kitchen. "Have you had your tea, then?"

If she hadn't already known the answer to the question, the quantity of gooseberry jam on Clarissa's pinafore would have told the story.

"Yes, of course. Mrs. Thomas wouldn't hear of us leaving without it," answered Mrs. Potts, just as Clarissa demanded milk. Absently, Sarah picked up the small jug from the tea tray, poured its contents into a cup, and handed the cup to her daughter. "Forgive me for saying so, but you don't seem yourself. Are you sure that gentleman didn't—?"

Sarah shook her head sharply, glancing at Clarissa. "As he said, we knew each other briefly, years ago. It gave me a start to see him again after all this time, that's all."

Mrs. Potts appeared to consider this explanation. "I 's'pect your head still aches from that music lesson, and that's what's got you looking peaked. Why don't you let me put the child to bed?"

Clarissa clapped sticky fingers. "Story," she sang out. "Story 'bout a cat 'n' a fish!"

"'Course, wee one," Mrs. Potts crooned, going to fetch a cloth to wipe the child's face.

"I do have a touch of the headache, Mrs. Potts. I believe I will lie down. Thank you." Sarah knelt in front of Clarissa. "Give Mama a kiss."

With a child's unconcern she leaned forward and brushed Sarah's cheek, her puckered lips cool and wet with milk. "'Night."

"Good night, dear one. Mama loves you." But Clarissa had already resumed her pestering of Mrs. Potts. Sarah mustered a smile. "Good night, Mrs. Potts." Mrs. Potts nodded in return and handed Sarah a rushlight so she could make her way to bed.

Sarah passed St. John's hat hanging on the wall as she walked to the stairs. How strange to see a man's things in the house. Would he come for it in the morning?

Would he come for his child?

Pressing her knuckles into her lips to keep from sobbing aloud, she forced herself to go up the steps at a measured pace, not to run or to slam the door of her bedchamber or to throw herself onto her bed as if she were no more in control of herself than Clarissa. Instead, she knelt near the foot of her bed, placed the rushlight on the floor beside her, and opened her trunk, lifting the lid slowly, as if its contents were something to fear.

Beneath a small pile of carefully folded clothing lay the miniature. She had not looked at the picture for a long time, months perhaps, but she had not always been so circumspect. The leather was worn near the clasp and dark from the sweat of her palms. With trembling fingers, she flicked the case open.

The boyish face that looked up at her confirmed how much St.

John had changed. The portrait was old, of course—painted when St. John was not yet one-and-twenty—but three years past, it had looked very like the young man she had married. Neither the artist nor her imagination had anticipated the ways that visage would change to become the face of the man she had confronted tonight.

The boy who had sat for that portrait had not needed to shave, she was sure, but this evening the lamplight had caught the shadow of a two days' beard along St. John's jaw. It had highlighted a long, thin scar, as well, running almost from his temple to his chin. She wondered what had caused it. A mistress's jealousy, perhaps—or that mistress's husband's.

The artist had given his subject a suitably aristocratic pallor. Tonight St. John's skin and hair had looked as if they had been bronzed by the sun. Promenades in Hyde Park? A curricle race through the countryside? Those had been the pursuits of the frivolous young man she had known. Were they his pastimes still?

There were other changes, too, changes the miniature could not show. He carried himself differently, and she did not think the broad shoulders beneath his coat had been put there by his tailor. She shivered again, as she had in the sitting room, and cursed her body for its betrayal. How could she have felt the slightest attraction, the slightest longing, after so much time and after so many hurts?

Yet feel it she had—the heat from his body, his breath on her ear—as she had felt it years ago, when he had lain with her, when she had not yet known whether it was pleasure or pain.

When he had given her their child.

Sarah snapped the miniature case shut, latched the trunk, and blew out the feeble light. Rising from the floor, she readied herself for bed and lay down atop the counterpane, staring into the darkness, clutching the picture to her chest, remembering.

Only his eyes—blue and piercing and cold—had been unchanged.

With strength born of both fear and fury, she threw the miniature from her and felt something like satisfaction when it struck the sturdy oak door at the foot of her bed. The clasp must have come loose in midflight, for she heard the small oval of glass shatter when it crashed into the wall and tinkled onto the floor.

In the silence that followed, she lay still, fighting tears and wondering whether one of those shards would be sharp enough to cut out her traitorous heart.

* * *

St. John ducked beneath a sign bearing a picture of a gaudily colored fish with the words *Colin Mackey, prop.* underneath and entered the pub, intending to get thoroughly foxed.

A half-dozen pair of eyes watched him cross the threshold and then returned to their mugs and their companions. By their weather-beaten skin and coarse clothing, the customers looked to be mostly fishermen, clustered in groups about square tables. Some played at cards, while others ate. One man, a hefty sort with a balding head and a bushy moustache, sat apart reading a broadside.

The pub looked respectable, although it was dimly lit and the white-washed walls had yellowed with age and the smoke of innumerable clay pipes. St. John made his way across a rough-hewn floor so ancient that in places it appeared to have become one with the soil beneath. Behind the bar, a man with brawny forearms and unkempt ginger hair was pulling drafts.

"Can I help you, sir?" he asked without turning.

St. John snapped a coin onto the bar. "A room for the night and a pint, if you please."

"Aye," the man replied as he set a foaming mug of ale before him.

"Have you a boy who can fetch my horse from the top of the lane and take it 'round to the stables?"

"Aye. Colin!" he barked. A boy of perhaps twelve or fourteen poked his carroty head around the door behind the bar. "Go up-along and get the man's horse."

"Right away, Pa," the boy replied and darted back from whence he'd come.

St. John had hardly needed confirmation that the pair were father and son, but the boy's address brought home a fresh stab of panic at the memory of the little girl, Clarissa. Perhaps she, too, shared her father's face, his features? He could not say. Even as he had been looking into her eyes, his mind had been racing to estimate the child's age—counting, adding, subtracting.

Mental arithmetic had never been his forte.

"Keep the pints coming," he said as he turned to face the small taproom.

The big man with the moustache lowered his paper and caught St. John's eye. "Have a seat," he said, pushing out a chair with the toe of his boot.

Gesturing his thanks with his mug, St. John levered himself away from the bar and took the offered chair.

"Beals," the man said, extending his hand. "I'm the baker hereabouts."

"Pleased to meet you," St. John replied.

"Been traveling far?"

He thought of the thousands of miles he had logged in the past weeks and nodded. "I left London the day before yesterday."

Beals raised one brow. "What brings you to Haverhythe in such a hurry?" he asked, just as Mackey came to the table juggling another pint, a rusty key, a bowl of steaming fish stew, and a hunk of crusty bread.

"Comes with the room," Mackey said, jerking his chin toward the food as he placed it on the table.

"Much obliged," St. John replied as he bit into the fresh bread and found himself surprisingly hungry. "Yours?" he asked the baker.

Beals's chest puffed with pride. "Aye." He folded his paper and laid it aside, then carefully removed his steel-rimmed spectacles and tucked them into the pocket of his waistcoat. "Sit, Mackey," he ordered the proprietor. "The boys'll soon have drained the dregs and then they'll be ready to head home."

Mackey cast a look over his shoulder at the handful of customers remaining and reluctantly drew a chair toward Beals's table, straddling it as he tossed his bar rag onto the table. "Somethin' to say, then?"

"Why, just that this gentleman's come all the way from London, and it behooves us to make a stranger feel welcome."

Mackey turned curious eyes on St. John. "How's that?"

He considered his reply carefully, straining to recall every word that Sarah had spoken. What she wouldn't tell him, surely the locals could. He had only to ask the right questions.

"I've come on behalf of a family looking for a young woman who disappeared several years ago. New information came to light recently, suggesting she might have come here, to Haverhythe."

Beals and Mackey exchanged a glance. "How many years ago?"

"Oh, two or three," St. John replied, affecting uncertainty.

Mackey shrugged, but Beals leaned back in his chair and folded his arms across his chest. "And if we knew of such a woman, why should we tell you?"

"Why, because her family is gravely concerned. She left under the shadow of an unfortunate—misunderstanding, shall we say." He shook his head somberly. "Everyone involved would like to see the wrong righted."

"What'd she look like?" Mackey asked, drawn in by the possibility of a tale of woe.

St. John paused, appearing to consider the question. "Brown hair, gray eyes. Slender build. Tallish, for a woman."

The baker and the publican looked at one another again. "Sounds like it could be Mrs. Fairfax," Beals offered at last.

"Mrs.—Fairfax, did you say?"

"'Course, that could be a, a whad'y'call? An assumed name," Mackey suggested, nudging Beals with his elbow.

"Well, she stayed right here at the Herring when she first arrived in Haverhythe, didn't she, Mackey? What do you recall?"

Mackey scratched his head, further disordering his ginger hair. "I dunno. Said her man was a soldier, killed in foreign parts. That was . . ." He paused, lips moving slightly, appearing to count. St. John half-expected him to begin to draw in the air, as if sketching out a particularly challenging arithmetic problem. Having himself been in that predicament a short while ago, he felt oddly in charity with the man, even as impatience gnawed at him. "Must be more'n three years ago now," Mackey decided at last. "I say that on account o' the child."

"A child?" St. John widened his eyes in astonishment only slightly feigned and lifted his drink to his lips, looking expectantly from one to the other.

"Oh yes," Beals chimed in. "A little girl. Cute as a button, she is."

Mackey nodded soberly. "'Tis pity she's a bastard."

Caught in the act of draining his mug, St. John sputtered.

"Now, we don't know that," Beals corrected mildly.

"No," Mackey conceded. "But when a woman says she's a widow, and then a baby comes along too many months after that, 'tis pretty certain the father weren't her dead husband. More'n likely," he concluded gravely, "she weren't never married."

"Perhaps her husband had died recently," Beals insisted, "but she did not wish it known."

"Or perhaps he isn't dead after all."

St. John did not know why he had said it, but once the words were out, it was clear to him how he had to proceed. Surely the men of the village would not stand against a wronged husband who had come to take his wife home? If he crafted his story with care, they might even prove allies to his cause.

Both Beals and Mackey jerked sharply to look at St. John. "Are you sayin'—?"

"I'm saying," St. John interposed smoothly, "that the circumstances under which the young woman left her family—"

"Ran away, you mean."

"The circumstances were less than ideal," he concluded, with a nod of confirmation for Mackey's words. "If your Mrs.—Fairfax, is it?—is the woman I seek, and especially if she has given birth to a child, her family deserves to know, don't you agree?"

Mackey nodded excitedly, as if awaiting the next scene in some cheap melodrama, but Beals was more circumspect. "But perhaps our Mrs. Fairfax is *not* the woman you seek. We ought not to be telling her story to a stranger. We do not know your motives, sir."

St. John hesitated. Were they seeking a bribe? Or some other kind of reassurance altogether? He decided on the latter and leaned toward them, lowering his voice. "I have been charged by the young woman's family to carry out a very delicate mission. If your Mrs. Fairfax is not the woman I seek, then her story is of no interest to me. I shall certainly tell it no further."

"And this woman's family—they'll take her in, take her back?" Beals asked.

"My good man, something precious to them simply vanished three years ago. You can have no idea how eager they are to see what was lost restored." St. John was pleased with his carefully worded answer. It was, after all, the truth.

But Beals seemed only slightly mollified by his response. "Mrs. Fairfax and her daughter have grown dear to me. I would not want to see them hurt."

It was a novel experience to find himself the object of suspicion where Sarah was concerned. Novel, and entirely disagreeable. "Where can I find this Mrs. Fairfax?" St. John demanded, more gruffly than he had intended.

"She lives with Mad Martha in Primrose Cottage, down-along and to the east, almost to the quay," Mackey revealed before Beals could silence him.

"'Mad Martha'?"

"Martha Potts. Her husband was a fisherman—"

"Smuggler, belike—" Mackey inserted.

"Who drowned right off the quay," Beals finished as if he had not been interrupted. "She watched it happen. It drove her to distraction for a time, and some people hereabouts"—he turned toward Mackey with hard eyes—"still see fit to call her 'Mad Martha.' "

"I see," St. John answered, picking up the key to his room from the table and moving as if to rise. "Much obliged to you for the information."

"One moment, if you please, sir," said Beals quietly, laying his broad palms on the table. "I don't believe I caught your name."

St. John hesitated a moment. Should he go through with it? Could he? But he had come all this way, and he knew no better way to get what he wanted. Determinedly, he cleared his throat.

"I'm Fairfax."

Chapter 4

A childish shriek of delight roused Sarah from a fitful slumber, and she dragged open her eyes to find midmorning sun slanting across her bed. She had fallen asleep shortly before dawn, having gone over her conversation with St. John so many times that the echo of their words had begun to blend with the dull, melancholy roar of the waves outside her window.

For long, dark hours, she had prayed desperately for something to dispel the haunting image of his eyes boring into her own. But when that something had finally come, she found she could not be grateful, for her traitorous mind had called up in its place the memory of the last time she had seen her parents, and it was to that same terrible vision it returned now.

For weeks—no, months—after her arrival in Haverhythe, Sarah had held out hope that her parents were searching high and low for her, believing her innocent; now she realized no such search had taken place, because they believed her to be dead.

Had they mourned her? Did they mourn her still?

Or had they washed their hands of even the memory of the daughter who had betrayed all their hopes?

She rose and went slowly about her ablutions before donning the same simple black dress. Then she carefully picked up the broken pieces of glass and returned the battered miniature to her trunk. As she descended the stairs to the kitchen, she spied St. John's hat still hanging from the peg by the door. So she had not slept so long as to have missed his visit.

Damn.

Sarah clapped a hand across her mouth in astonishment, although she had not spoken the unladylike word aloud. Already this encounter with St. John was changing her in ways she did not like.

When Clarissa spied her mother through the open kitchen door, she scrambled from her chair and ran toward her with outstretched arms. "Kitties, Mama! Kitties!"

"What's that, poppet?" Sarah asked, swooping in for a kiss.

"Mr. Beals were here bright and early," Mrs. Potts explained, nodding toward two loaves of fresh bread on the table. "Bright Meg had her kittens last night."

"Go see 'em, Mama?" Clarissa begged.

"Yes, dear," she agreed readily. "But I also promised to drop in on Mrs. Norris at the vicarage this morning. Are you sure the walk won't make you too tired? Can you be good as gold for your mama?" Clarissa solemnly nodded her head as Sarah returned her to her chair and accepted the cup of coffee Mrs. Potts was proffering. "Thank you. Goodness me, I must already be late. What time is it?"

"Half-ten," Mrs. Potts answered soothingly. "I was just about to wake you. That headache must've done you in."

"Yes." Sarah nodded, sipping her coffee. "But it's a beautiful morning, and I'm determined it won't plague me again."

"Well," Mrs. Potts began, sliding her gaze to Clarissa and back again, "I hope you're right, but I've had some news—"

"'Rissa go. See kittens," the child announced, slipping from her seat once again.

Heart pounding with dread, Sarah knelt. "In just a moment, dear one. Run to the shelf by the door and fetch your bonnet."

Clarissa's lower lip popped out, but after a moment of deliberation, the prospect of the outing won out and she toddled off in search of the dreaded headgear.

"Well?" Sarah demanded as soon as the child was out of earshot.

"That gentleman?" Sarah nodded encouragement to Mrs. Potts. "He went to Mackey's like you told him. And the boys got to talking..." Sarah's eyes dropped closed. Why did men accuse women of gossiping when they were by far the worse offenders? "Mr. Beals were there, you see. And, well, he brought more'n that bread this morning. He told me that gentleman said you run away from your family, and he's come to bring you home. He's sayin' he's your—your husband."

"*Damn.*"

But this time, she did say it aloud.

"Mrs. Fairfax!" Mrs. Potts sounded surprised, but not shocked. The wife of a fisherman had doubtless heard worse.

"I'm sorry, Mrs. Potts. It seems I'm not myself this morning, after all."

"Is it true, then?" Mrs. Potts's voice had sunk to an uncharacteristic whisper.

Sarah's mind raced. Had he told them who he was? Who she was? What everyone believed she'd done? It had been difficult, as a stranger, to find her place in a little village where everybody knew everyone else, and always had. The people of Haverhythe were warm and loyal. But it had not been easy gaining their trust. Once lost, it would be lost for good.

"Is what true?" she asked hesitantly.

"Is that gentleman your husband?"

Sarah's jaw stiffened, but she forced herself to nod.

Mrs. Potts's eyes widened. "And Clarissa's pa?"

At just that moment, Clarissa came through the doorway dragging her bonnet by its strings. Mrs. Potts cast a doting eye in her direction. "You'll have to tell her, you know."

"Tell what, Mama?"

"All in good time, dear one." Sarah sent Mrs. Potts a speaking glance. "For now, let's see about those kittens, shall we? Remember, though, you must not touch!"

Just as she knelt to tie the child's bonnet, a sharp rap came at the front door, echoing through the house like the report of a pistol. The two women jumped. Both knew who it must be.

"Go," Mrs. Potts insisted, taking the bonnet from Sarah's hand and ushering her toward the back door. "I'll take care o' him."

As Sarah scooped up her daughter, Clarissa lay her bare head against her mother's throat. Sarah buried her nose in the girl's tousled curls and inhaled deeply.

She could not—*would not*—lose the one thing that had made the last three years worth living.

Once they were out the door, Sarah set the child on her feet. Clarissa darted down the steps and into the alleyway, pausing at the archway that led to the lane. Catching up with her, Sarah saw a team of gray donkeys drawing a heavily laden sledge up the steep street, carrying cargo that had been off-loaded on the quay and was now bound for some Haverhythe cottage, Haverty Court, or perhaps points beyond. Although it was a regular sight, Clarissa clapped with delight and watched the donkeys pick their way carefully up the cobblestones, the kittens momentarily forgotten.

Yesterday's rain had given way to the kind of intensely blue sky unique to autumn. A light breeze gave the air a certain crispness, fluttering the ribbons of Sarah's bonnet and teasing loose a few strands of hair beneath it. It was a morning that ought to have called Britons of every sort to come out of doors to soak up the last rays of sunshine before the gloom of winter set in. The street was nearly deserted as they made their way up-along, however.

They made a game of guessing what the sledge carried and followed the donkeys slowly up the street, waving them on their way when they came to Mr. Beals's door. Having finished the morning's deliveries, the stout baker had just opened his shop and was sweeping off the oddly shaped wedge of a step that brought the shop's floor in line with the sharp angle of the street.

"And a good morning to you, Mrs. Fairfax!"

"Meg?" Clarissa cried out.

Mr. Beals smiled. "Why, there's my girl," he said, ushering them inside as he lifted his dusty apron from a hook and tied it around his ample middle. "Bright Meg's just back here, where it's warm. But I do believe she's ready for callers."

Clarissa darted past the counter and toward a basket in the corner nearest the oven. Sarah glanced around the shop and was relieved to see it otherwise empty. "Remember what I said, Clarissa. You must not touch. Do you hear me?"

"Yes, Mama," she said, throwing herself onto her hands and knees so that her chin was level with the edge of the woven container that held the stuff of all her dreams.

Inside a basket lined with scraps of soft fabric, Bright Meg was a circle of orange fur, her whole being seemingly wrapped around her four precious babies. Sarah envied the mama cat's contentment.

And her claws.

"Here."

The door to Primrose Cottage opened to St. John's knock just enough to allow his tall beaver hat to be passed through the gap. The disembodied hand that held the brim was most certainly not Sarah's.

"Mrs. Potts?"

"Take it," she insisted, giving the offending object a shake, "afore I let the wind have it."

Reluctantly, St. John lifted the hat from her grasp and placed it on his head. "Much obliged." Mrs. Potts tried to push the door closed behind it, but he had prudently wedged the toe of his boot in her way. "Please, ma'am, may I come in?"

"Mrs. Fairfax isn't here."

Knowing Sarah could not have got far, St. John held his ground. "That's quite all right. I had hoped to have an opportunity to speak with you."

The door opened a crack wider. "And what would you want wi' me? I won't tell you where she's gone, if that's what you're after."

"I would never ask you to betray the confidence of a friend, Mrs. Potts." He paused. "Mrs. Fairfax is your friend, is she not?"

At that, the door swung wide. "None better. And I won't stand by and see her hurt by the likes o' you."

Although she was surely not five feet tall, "Mad Martha" Potts cut an imposing figure in her gray serge gown, the knobby fingers of one hand clutching a broom handle as if it were a weapon. St. John had no doubt of her ability to use it as one. He raised his hands in a gesture of surrender, hoping to persuade her to relent.

But he did not move his foot, just in case.

"I deeply regret whatever I may have done or said that gave you the impression I meant Mrs. Fairfax any harm," he replied, laying a hand across his chest in what he hoped was the appearance of sincerity. "Do you know who I am?"

Her dark eyes narrowed and were nearly lost in the wrinkles of her weathered visage. "Word's abroad you're claimin' to be her man."

"And what does Mrs. Fairfax say?"

Mrs. Potts made no reply, but the answer was written on her face.

"So she has told you I am her husband. I expect you're wondering how I came to be here."

"Couldn't care less. What I'm wondering is how your wife came to be here without you."

"Fair enough." When pressed, he had given Beals and Mackey a simple story, one on which he could embellish as necessary. Based on their reactions, he knew it had the essential ingredients for success: misunderstood lovers, insurmountable distance, and broken communication, sufficiently probable that Sarah would find it uncomfortable to contradict him.

With Mrs. Potts for an audience, perhaps he could begin to refine it.

"But may I come in? I know how swiftly gossip will fly in a country village." With the right word in Mrs. Potts's ear, he suspected it might travel even faster.

She stepped back and allowed him to enter, setting aside the broom and gesturing toward the sitting room, where he and Sarah had spoken the night before. The morning light did not improve its appearance. It was neat and clean, but strikingly barren, not even a carpet for the scuffed wide-plank floors. Faded paper covered the walls, and what had seemed in the lamplight to be comfortably worn chairs, the light of day revealed as threadbare. Whatever the late Mr. Potts had done to support his family, legal or otherwise, he had been none too successful at it.

Mrs. Potts seated herself in the chair closest to the fireplace, so St. John took the other, the one he thought of as Sarah's. He laid his hat on the table between them, and at Mrs. Potts's encouragement, he began to speak, modulating his voice to suit his tale and donning a grave expression. "Mrs. Fairfax and I were married three years ago last June, against my family's wishes. But we believed our love could sustain us in the face of their disapproval."

The sentiment drew a sad smile from the woman. "As young people are wont to do," she acknowledged.

St. John gave a nod of abashed agreement.

"At my request, my father had purchased a commission for me, and I had received notice just a month before our wedding that I was to be stationed for a time in the West Indies. We thought of going out together—"

Mrs. Potts frowned. "You didn't mean to take my girl across the sea?"

"As it turned out, it might have been for the best," St. John averred, noting Mrs. Potts's maternal possessiveness and considering how best to put it to use. "But my mother professed to be of your opinion and would not hear of it. She insisted she would do her duty by my bride."

As if she suspected what was to come, Mrs. Potts leaned toward him and shook her head. "But she didn't."

"No, indeed. You cannot imagine my astonishment and anger when I returned just last week to discover that my wife had disappeared. I believe my mother and sisters must have driven her from the house shortly after I set sail. How she happened to come here, I do not yet know, but my mother had received one letter from her in all those years, and in it Mrs. Fairfax made mention of Haverhythe. So it was here I began my search."

"And her tellin' everyone—even me—that she were a widow."

"She might well have thought she was. If she wrote, I received no letters. I cannot say what became of those I sent her."

"Folks didn't always believe she was tellin' the truth, you know. Especially after Miss Clarissa came. Did you have any inklin' about the child?"

"None at all until you brought her home last night."

"And her never knowin' her pa." Mrs. Potts clucked disapprovingly. "But for a' that your missus don't seem too happy to have you back."

As if her observation had struck a nerve, St. John rose and strode toward the fireplace, studying its rustic mantel as he continued. "I did not expect a warm welcome, Mrs. Potts. If she did not think me dead, she must have thought me the worst scoundrel in existence for abandoning her. I left her with those who ought to have cared for her." He turned back to face the old woman. "I am responsible for her suffering."

It was the perfectly pitched confession of his guilt—so perfect, in fact, that he almost believed it himself.

It had been one thing to imagine Sarah living a life of depraved luxury on the profits of her theft or under the protection of her lover, and quite another to discover her in this ramshackle cottage on the edge of the sea, raising a child widely believed to be born on the wrong side of the blanket, and evidently relying on the generosity and good opinion of people so poor they had little of either to spare.

Was it possible he had been wrong about her?

Before sentiment could overwhelm his good sense, however, an image rose in his memory: a darkened room, his wife in Captain Brice's arms, her bodice gaping, skirts hiked up, and that other man's hands nowhere in sight.

He must not forget why he had come here. Sarah had escaped her punishment once, disappeared into the ether like the string of priceless gems she'd stolen. Her apparent poverty was a pretense. If it was freedom from this damnable coil he wanted, it was up to him to see her laid low in earnest.

"Will you help me, Mrs. Potts? Please?" he asked, his voice soft and his heart hard.

Chapter 5

"Excited, is she?"

St. John's voice came from the doorway behind her, and Sarah froze. With a perfunctory bow of his blond head, he strode toward the counter and squatted beside Clarissa.

"And which is your favorite?"

Clarissa lifted one chubby finger toward the kittens, no bigger than mice, wriggling against Meg's side. Sarah thought it likely that Clarissa had woken them, for their mouths were open in silent *meows* and they were groping blindly for their mother's milk.

"Ah—" Sarah prepared to reprimand Clarissa, but a sharp glance from St. John silenced her.

"Dis one," Clarissa said, pointing at but not touching a gray-striped kitten with pink feet that would one day be covered in dainty white socks like its mother's.

"A fine choice," St. John said. "And what would you name him?"

"Thomas," Clarissa replied without hesitation.

"But if he should prove to be a girl instead?"

"Thomas," she repeated, as if she suspected St. John were a trifle hard of hearing.

"Of course." St. John stood so quickly that Sarah had to step back to avoid him brushing against her breasts as he rose. He smelled of some cologne that she did not remember: spice and citrus and the heat of a tropical summer.

"Good morning, Mrs. Fairfax," he said. "I hope I'm not intruding, but our friend Beals was insistent that I stop in first thing."

Our friend? Sarah pressed her lips into a thin line, as she turned and made her way back to a small table flanked by two chairs, a place where the bakery's customers could wait in comfort or even enjoy some light refreshment.

"Have you had breakfast, Mr. Fairfax?" Mr. Beals asked, rubbing his hands together. At St. John's distracted nod, he said, "Cuppa tea, then," and disappeared into the kitchen through a swinging door.

Sarah wasn't fooled. "He thinks we will want to talk."

"And don't we?" St. John asked as he seated himself opposite her, tugged off his gloves, and tucked them inside his hat.

"Whatever about, *Mr.* Fairfax?"

"Oh, let me cast about for some suitable subject of conversation." He drummed his fingers against the tabletop. "How you came to live in Haverhythe, perhaps."

"I should think you would already know the answer to that."

"Nay. Although I'm given to understand Haverhythe is a haven for smugglers and thieves. Was it Captain Brice's idea, then?" His jaw clenched as he spoke, and the long, thin scar stood out white against his tanned skin.

"Captain Brice?"

She dredged up a name buried under the silt of time. She had long ago decided that Captain Brice must have followed her into the library with the intention of stealing the sapphires, and when confronted, had seized the opportunity to pin the blame on her. But too much had happened over the past three years to allow her to dwell on his bad behavior. He had simply been a dashing young officer who took advantage of a naïve girl—hardly the first such story, or the last. She could not even recall his face.

"I know nothing of Captain Brice, my l—er, Mr. Fairfax," she insisted, catching herself in the nick of time. She was quite certain Mr. Beals was listening from the kitchen, and heaven only knew what he would do if he overheard her address her husband as "my lord." "You must ask your mother why I am here."

"You mean my *step*mother, I presume."

The disdain in his voice and the sharpness of his correction caught her off guard. "Oh. I did not realize . . . I always heard you address her as 'Mama.'"

A curt nod. "My father's wish. I was still a small child when my mother died."

A token courtship and two weeks of marriage had afforded Sarah very little opportunity to observe St. John's interactions with his parents, but she had gathered that the marquess's "wishes," up to and including the choice of his son's bride, were meant to be obeyed. The tension between Lord Estley and his son could not be overlooked, but Lady Estley had spoken to and of her son—stepson—with open, almost fawning affection. If St. John had reciprocated with coolness, Sarah had simply thought of it as his nature.

Now she felt a sort of unexpected sympathy for Lady Estley, a fellow sufferer in Lord Estley's misguided attempts to dictate his son's affections. Uncertainty etched a frown into her brow. "I . . . I see. Well, in any case, I accepted the destination Lady Estley chose. I had no notion of where I was headed beyond Devonshire, but the coachman clearly did, because in two days' travel we stopped only to change horses."

"And you expect me to believe his orders came from my stepmother? What a bounder! She despises the country. What would she know of Haverhythe?" he scoffed.

Sarah shrugged.

When she first met Lady Estley, she had found her rather silly, an empty-headed woman skilled at little more than the sort of social lying that kept London's West End humming. Over the years, she had tried to imagine how the marchioness could have kept the secret of her involvement in Sarah's disappearance.

Evidently, she had underestimated her mother-in-law.

Lady Estley had been the first to insinuate that Sarah was a thief. Then she had swiftly spun a threatening tale to frighten her daughter-in-law into leaving. And another to convince her stepson that what he had seen the night of the nuptial ball had been only a glimpse into the blackness of his wife's character.

Clearly Lady Estley was a better liar than Sarah had given her credit for being.

I like you, Sarah. So I will help you by telling a little fib.

Infidelity. Theft. Drowning. Extortion.

Yes, in fact, Lady Estley was an excellent liar.

And Sarah could not say she was sorry for it. After all, Lady Estley's lies had made it possible for Sarah to keep Clarissa to herself all these years.

She brushed an imaginary speck of lint from her dark skirts. "She said Miss Harrington mentioned something that gave her the idea."

"Eliza?" he whispered, and Sarah's stomach lurched with the discovery that her name on his lips still had the power to cause pain. His gaze drifted away, as if he were trying to recall a story heard long ago. "Lady Harrington *was* from the West Country, I believe." Sarah closed her eyes for a moment. *Oh Lord*. She could almost hear the wheels spinning in Mr. Beals's bald head. "I suppose there might have been some visit to the coast, some holiday—there's a family here, I take it?"

"There are many families here, Mr. Fairfax. But you mean the family at Haverty Court, I gather?"

"Yes. That is, I suppose I do. How odd . . ." He sounded nothing short of incredulous. "And you've been hiding here all this time?"

Mr. Beals entered and laid a tray on the table with a flourish.

"How lovely, Mr. Beals," Sarah enthused. "Won't you join us?"

"Well, if that don't beat all. I forgot the currant cake, Mrs. Fairfax—and it your favorite." He shook his head and darted back into his kitchen. "I won't be a minute," he called back over his shoulder.

Sarah repressed a sigh. What had St. John said to win him over? But then, her husband had always had a reputation for being charming—even if he had never troubled himself to shower that charm on her.

"Not *hiding*," she insisted, even as a small voice inside her head chirped its agreement. She withdrew into the comfortable ritual of pouring out, wondering even as she did so how many times she would be forced to enact this pantomime of hospitality with a man who wished her nothing but ill.

Handing St. John his cup with a forced smile, she asked, "Sugar?" knowing the answer quite well but conscious of how it must have seemed when she had *not* asked the night before. But then, she did not remember whether he had even tasted the tea she had poured him. Perhaps he had not noticed that she had sweetened it just to his taste.

"Thank you, yes," he said, taking the tongs himself and dropping three lumps into his cup.

"You may find it difficult to believe, my l—love," she hastily substituted, forcing the word from between clenched teeth. "But I chose to stay. It may have been your stepmother's suggestion to go, but I quickly realized it would be for the best. I have made a new life here. I swore I would cut my past ties, and although it was not easy, I kept my word."

His lips twisted into something that was not quite a smile. "How refreshing to discover you are capable of upholding at least some of your vows."

"Cannot you just leave me—leave us all—in peace?" She dropped her gaze to the fraying edge of the checked tablecloth and drew an unsteady breath. "If there's someone else you want," she whispered, "just go to her. Marry her. I'll make no stir."

Her desperate offer hung on the air between them for a long moment.

"Someone else?" he echoed, clearly shocked by the proposal. "You seem to forget that we are still married, ma'am. To marry another now would be a crime—and I, at least, will not stoop to law-breaking." He shook his head. "No, I cannot 'leave you in peace.' However much I would wish it otherwise, I must keep you in my sight." St. John snared her wrist in his long brown fingers and drew her close enough to speak low in her ear. "And know this: When I leave, I won't go empty-handed."

She followed his eyes as they looked toward Clarissa, who was still lying on the floor with her head near the kittens' basket, rapt. "No," she whispered.

"No?" His eyebrows shot up. "You should not have kept the child's birth a secret from my family. You are my wife. By law she is mine, you know."

"Not only by law," Sarah averred.

Her narrow-eyed glare seemed to give him pause. Seizing the opportunity, she jerked free of his grasp, whisked up Clarissa from her place by the counter, and swept out the door before the child could muster even a howl of protest.

Beals pushed through the swinging door, bearing a cake on a plate. When he spied the vacant place across from St. John, one bushy eyebrow shot skyward.

"Mrs. Fairfax, er, recalled an appointment," St. John fumbled for an excuse.

"*Humph*," was the baker's skeptical reply. He left the plate on the counter and made his way to the table, seating himself in the empty chair and filling the empty cup. "So, how's the weather today?"

Perplexed, St. John glanced toward the doorway at the cloudless sky and back to Beals's face again. "The weather?"

"Aye, the *whether*, man—tell us *whether* or not Mrs. Fairfax'll have you in again!"

"Oh, that." Beals and Mackey had kept him until the early hours of the morning, plying him with pints and pressing him for details he had been reluctant to give, fearful he might later contradict himself. After three nights with very little sleep, he was feeling decidedly out of sorts and in no mood for wordplay. "I couldn't say."

"'Couldn't say'?" Beals laughed. "It's just like Mrs. F. to keep you waitin'."

"Think you so?" St. John asked softly. "But perhaps I am not such a patient man."

Beals appraised him with the same eye of suspicion he had cast over him the night before. "Mayhap not. But you best be prepared to cool your heels a bit, lad. She's not one to go back on a promise, and she's made one to the whole village."

Inwardly, St. John scoffed at the baker's assessment of Sarah's faithfulness. "A promise? Of what sort?"

"She and Mrs. Norris, the vicar's wife, have got together and planned a sort of festival on Michaelmas—folks sellin' their wares, and food and drink, of course, and a dance."

"A festival?" He was struck afresh by the contrast between Sarah's plain looks and her frivolous desires. Had his father known of the latter, he hoped the man would never have been taken in by the former—enormous dowry or no. Surely his second marriage had taught him something about the folly of making such a bargain. And Michaelmas? That was six days off. He had no intention of wasting a week in Haverhythe.

"Aye. I suspect that's where she got off to. She and Mrs. Norris likely had somethin' to chat about this morning."

Of that St. John had no doubt.

"Mr. Beals, I have a rather delicate question—one I very much regret having to ask," he said, drawing one finger along the edge of his saucer. "How has Mrs. Fairfax managed to support herself all this time?"

"Well, I reckon she had a bit of something from your folks when she arrived," Beals said, sounding as if he expected the information to provide some reassurance. "But like most hereabouts, she makes do on very little. O' course, the lessons help a bit."

"Lessons?"

"On Mrs. Norris's pianoforte," he explained. "She offered Mrs. Fairfax the use of it to teach some of the girls in the village. She plays right pretty, you know. Why, she's even got Miss Susan Kittery to make somethin' that passes for music . . ." Beals waggled his head. "Miss Susan's a winning little thing. No talent, though. Mrs. F. earns every penny she gets."

Despite Mr. Beals's attempt at reassurance, St. John knew very well that the few shillings Sarah made giving music lessons would not have been enough to sustain her and the child, no matter how simply they lived.

And he did not need the baker to tell him how she had made up the difference.

"I don't know what happened twixt the two of you all those years ago, but it seems you got off to a bit of a rough start, lad." Beals paused to give the tea in his cup a vigorous stir, the delicate spoon dwarfed by his beefy thumb. "And even though you're not askin', I'm goin' to offer some free advice," he said, leaning toward him and lowering his voice. "If you aim to get Mrs. F. to come back to you, you'll want to woo her to win her."

"Woo my *wife*?"

"Aye. Think back to your courtin' days. Do summat that'll make her happy. God knows she ain't had awt o' that in years, 'sceptin' the wee 'un."

In one sense, Beals's advice was sound. If St. John had any hopes of getting into Sarah's home to look for evidence without her calling down the wrath of half of Haverhythe, he might be best served by trying to get into her good graces first, perhaps even to make it seem as if he hoped to reconcile. Staying until the festival would give him ample time to devise a plan of attack.

St. John unfolded himself from the chair and gave the baker a nod. "I'll take it under advisement."

But inwardly he was still thinking, *Woo her?* Pay court to the woman who had likely cuckolded him and stolen an irreplaceable family heirloom in the process? He settled his hat on his head and prepared to meet the glare of the noonday sun. From across the street, the glint of gilt lettering on glass caught his eye.

Gaffard's
"Fine Things from the Four Corners of the Globe"

And all at once it struck him. He did not think he could bring himself to do anything for Sarah. But perhaps something for her little girl . . . ?

Without further ado, he stepped across the narrow lane, boot heels ringing against the cobblestones, oblivious to the sight of Sarah ducking furtively into a doorway up the street.

Chapter 6

"Yoo-hoo, Mrs. Fairfax!"

Dressed in a morning gown of green striped poplin, Fanny Kittery stood in the doorway of her husband's apothecary shop like a brightly colored spider in the center of her web, awaiting her unwary prey.

Clarissa clutched her mother's skirts. Sarah paused without stepping closer. "I can't chat this morning, Mrs. Kittery. I'm meeting Mrs. Norris to finalize arrangements for the festival. You haven't forgotten your promise to sell some of your delightful soaps to help our cause?"

"So you plan to stay on until Michaelmas, then?" Mrs. Kittery pressed. "I had thought perhaps, with the sudden reappearance of *Mr.* Fairfax, you would be leaving Haverhythe."

So insistent had been her recollections of the past and her anxieties about the future, Sarah had not fully considered how she ought to respond in the present. How would a woman who had believed her husband dead react to his sudden reappearance? She dearly hoped that shock was an acceptable response, because she did not think she could manage joy.

Fortunately, Mrs. Kittery required no response at all. "I guess one never can tell what the merry widow will decide to do," she concluded with a sneer.

The merry widow. It was a slight Sarah had not heard spoken aloud in years.

How could it hurt worse now than it had then?

"My husband and I have much to discuss. In the meantime, however, I intend to go on as I have done."

"You'll find that a married woman is not so free, Mrs. Fairfax." She stressed the word *married* in such a way as to make clear her doubt that any such bond existed between Sarah and the stranger who had just arrived in Haverhythe.

Sarah inclined her head, feeling the shadow of the noose fall along her neck. "No woman is truly free, Mrs. Kittery. I'll wish you good morning."

She had curved a hand around Clarissa's narrow shoulders to lead her away up the street, when she heard steps on the cobblestones behind her. Turning, she saw St. John striding purposefully into Haverhythe's only general store. Desperate to escape another meeting, Sarah all but pushed Clarissa through the first opened doorway that presented itself.

"Now then, I told Ma you'd be along, Mrs. F. Surely I did." Emily Dawlish set aside her workbasket and fairly jumped from her chair by the window, setting her glossy black ringlets bouncing. "But Ma said she didn't think it likely and stepped down to Widow Thomas's for a bit. Won't she be shamefaced to have missed you! And you, too, Miss Clarissa!"

Sarah looked about herself, bewildered, to discover they had landed in the seamstress's shop.

"Why, Emily," Sarah began, uncertain how to explain their sudden arrival.

But Emily Dawlish needed no explanation. "I knew when I heard the news that you'd want outta that old black dress, first thing. I would, if it was me."

Emily was just a year or so younger than Sarah, but unlike Sarah, she kept no dark secrets. Nothing had happened to blight the girl's vivacity. She was all smiling pink cheeks and shining black-currant eyes. Sarah knew for a fact that she had turned the heads of half a dozen young fishermen, but so far, Emily seemed to favor none of them. Though the shop belonged to Emily's mother, all of Haverhythe knew the real artistry came from the daughter's hands, and Sarah suspected the young woman was loath to surrender what Fanny Kittery was pleased to call Emily's "dangerous independence."

Sarah curled her fingers in the fabric of her skirt, her shield for more than three years. "Why, no. I hadn't thought to—"

But Clarissa eagerly clapped her approval and Emily already had a tape in her hands. "Of course you want a change. I saw your man walk up-along this mornin'. He's a right handsome one!" As she went about the task of measuring and planning, Sarah stood as mute as a dressmaker's dummy. "He won't want to see you wearin' the weeds like he were dead 'n' gone."

Sarah looked down at the dress that had been the badge of her suffering, her entry ticket into the society of unfortunate women who lived on Haverhythe's fringes, women like "Mad Martha" Potts and Mrs. Thomas and Mrs. Dawlish.

The Merry Widow Fairfax.

"Gaffard's has some new fabric, just in. Will we go down-along and—?"

"No!" It would never do to look as if she had followed St. John there.

Startled, Emily drew her hands away. "Mrs. Fairfax?"

"I'm sorry, Emily. A new dress would be lovely. But I don't need it. I'm sure my husband would not want me to spend—"

"Bother that." Emily laughed. "A man always wants to see his woman look her best, no matter what he says. I know just what to do. You leave it to me, and we'll just see if you don't have a new dress in time for the festival. I think Ma even has a new bonnet in back. Mrs. Kittery turned up her nose at it—said it weren't good enough. But with some new trimmings and such, I think it'll suit."

"I couldn't possibly—"

But Sarah's protests fell on an empty room. Emily had already ducked into the workroom behind the shop and was rummaging around in search of the discarded bonnet. She returned with a dainty chip hat decorated with feathers that would have perched on Mrs. Kittery's head like a wounded bird.

"Oooh!" Clarissa exclaimed, reaching out a hand toward the hat.

Emily held it just out of her reach and looked at Sarah. "Don't you worry. This'll be Mrs. Kittery's present to the happy couple, like." She smiled broadly. "What she don't know won't hurt her, eh?"

Sarah glanced down at her dress again. The black crape was rusty with age and shiny with wear. How good it would feel to wear something fresh and pretty again! She had always enjoyed pretty things, even if her dull brown hair and rather colorless eyes kept her from being pretty herself.

"All right." She whispered her reluctant consent, knowing what trouble those little words could cause. Once Emily had finished her measurements, Sarah gathered up her daughter and stepped cautiously into the street again, peering in either direction for any sign of her husband before darting along the footpath to the vicarage.

By the time they reached the vicarage, her exhaustion had got the better of her, and no amount of blinking could sweep away the tears that reduced Abigail Norris's carefully tended roses to blurry splotches of color.

"H-have you h-heard?" she choked out when Abigail opened the door.

"Mama?" Clarissa asked, worry marring her childish features.

"Ah, Miss Clarissa," Abby said, holding out a hand toward the girl. "I was hoping you'd come along with your mama. Cook has some fresh apple tarts in the kitchen, and I was wondering who we might find to taste one and see if it was good."

Sarah gave a nod, equal parts consent and gratitude, and Clarissa followed eagerly.

When Abigail returned alone, she enveloped Sarah in a sisterly embrace. "There, there, dear. Yes, I've heard. I imagine there are few who haven't," she added with a somber shake of her dark head as she released her. Abby, who was Sarah's elder by only a few years, would never be mistaken for a gossiping matron. But having come to the village when she was just eighteen, on the occasion of her marriage, the vicar's wife had a vast deal of experience with the ways of Haverhythe and its fascination with strangers. "The steepness of the lane is no obstacle to telling tales, I'm afraid."

Sarah allowed herself to be led into the drawing room. "But it isn't a tale. Oh Abby, what shall I do?"

Slightly breathless, St. John arrived at the handsome stone vicarage just steps behind Sarah, who had not turned to look behind her, almost as if she feared the devil was on her heels. He paused inside the archway that sheltered the front door, inhaling the sweet scent of late summer roses and grateful for the breeze that stirred the air.

To either side of the doorway, latticed windows stood open to catch that same breeze, and gauzy curtains fluttered behind them, shielding the rooms' contents from his gaze. But voices could be heard quite clearly coming from the room to his left, which overlooked the footpath that meandered toward the church.

"Oh Abby, what shall I do?" Sarah's tremulous voice revealed all the emotions he had suspected her of hiding the night before.

"Your husband's miraculous return is not something to be celebrated, I take it." An unfamiliar voice, with an accent that did not match that of most of the citizens of Haverhythe: the vicar's wife, he presumed.

If Sarah replied to her question, she did not do so in words. "Mrs. Kittery said—"

"Ah," Mrs. Norris interrupted, her tone knowing. "It's not like you to let Fanny Kittery get under your skin, Sarah. Let me fetch you a cup of tea and we'll talk. Make yourself at home. Play if you like. That always makes you feel better."

He heard the sound of a door opening and closing, followed by the squeak of a hinge and the rustle of papers, then the air around him filled with sound. The pianoforte was obviously of good quality, producing notes as round and mellow as the season, but the person playing it—well, she was exceptional.

He closed his eyes to shut out everything but the music, an unfamiliar piece as complex and rich as typical drawing room fare was tedious and flat. He had not even known she played. Well, that was not entirely true. He had assumed she would. Every young lady played a little—sometimes a *very* little—if she expected to be considered suitably accomplished to catch a husband. But this was talent of a different order, the kind of skill that might grace a concert hall. How could it have escaped his notice before?

That was, in truth, rather an easy question to answer. He had spent his brief courtship of Sarah Pevensey determined to notice as little about her as possible, and therefore he knew almost nothing of her beyond her dowry.

He tried to imagine how she would look as she played, her long fingers dancing over the keys, her spine straight but leaning into the notes from time to time to give them their power. But what would be her expression? Were her eyes focused intently on a sheet of music, or did she play with eyes closed, calling up those strains from somewhere deep within? Was she somber, or did a smile of pleasure quirk the corner of her mouth? Was she cool and pale, or had that becoming flush begun to steal along her throat?

So intent was he on realizing his vision, he had lifted his hand to knock for admittance before he caught himself, and lowered it once again. He allowed himself another moment to listen furtively at the door, but the concert was cut short by the return of Mrs. Norris with the tea tray.

"Here we are. Now, come and tell me what's happened."

The matter-of-fact tone in which the vicar's wife addressed Sarah suggested she was gifted by such performances so often they had become commonplace. For her part, Sarah seemed unperturbed by the interruption. She stopped mid-run, and he listened to her rise and cross the room. "Bless you, Abby." Despite the passion of the music, she sounded calmer, more in control of herself.

Control. Self-control. St. John pushed himself away from the doorjamb. He certainly did not need to descend to eavesdropping at the vicarage to learn the information he required. Besides, he wanted no affecting story to blunt the force of his determination.

Mostly, though, he wanted nothing to drown out the sound of the music that still pulsed in his veins. He turned and started back the way he had come, grateful that the position of the window afforded the women no view of his departure.

Then a movement in the window to the right caught his eye. Golden-brown curls and bright eyes peeped through a gap in the curtain. Clarissa was watching him.

He froze. Would she cry out? Run and fetch her mother?

Instead, she grinned.

He pressed a finger to his lips, which curved in an answering smile. He did not think a child so young could be sworn to secrecy. But the pact might give him a moment to get away.

She giggled and pressed one finger to her own mouth in imitation. Finding it covered with the remnant of some sweet treat, she began to suck on it, and St. John did not hesitate to use her distraction to take his leave.

As he entered the street and was once again immersed in the sights and sounds and smells of Haverhythe, he wondered why on earth Sarah had chosen such a place to hide away. He did not believe her story about his stepmother's involvement, so how had she made her way here? More important, why had she stayed? She would almost certainly have been better able to disappear in London, where one could very nearly get away with anything under cover of anonymity. But in a fishing village of a few hundred souls, her arrival would have been remarked upon by all.

"You must be Mr. Fairfax."

The feminine voice startled St. John from his musings, and he looked about him to discover that he was halfway down the street once again, in front of the apothecary's shop.

"I'm Mrs. Kittery," the woman said as she made a little curtsy.

The people of Haverhythe did not seem to stand on ceremony when they wanted information. St. John tipped his hat. "Good morning, ma'am. Pleased to make your acquaintance."

"Mrs. Fairfax and Clarissa went by not half an hour ago," she said, her dark, close-set eyes taking in every detail of his appearance as if storing away the information for later.

"Yes," he agreed. "On their way to meet Mrs. Norris. I hoped to overtake them, but they had the start of me and I did not want to interrupt Mrs. Fairfax's visit."

"How—thoughtful," she purred. As with Mrs. Norris, something in Fanny Kittery's speech set her apart from the other village residents he had met, although the quality of Mrs. Kittery's voice was far less pleasant. "You know, we were given to understand you had died. Your miraculous appearance has nearly overset us all."

"None more than Mrs. Fairfax, I do assure you."

His admission seemed to please her. "I for one am glad you are here. Your wife's arrival in Haverhythe raised more than a few eyebrows, you should know. Her story was so—incredible. There were those who found it quite *impossible* to believe."

It was easy to see that Mrs. Kittery had been among them. And as her husband was likely the only medical man in the village, he had probably been among the first to learn that the supposed widow was expecting. The apothecary's wife looked to be the type who would be only too glad to pass along a private diagnosis to her neighbors.

Her obvious delight in spreading gossip ought to have made her an ally to his cause, but something about Fanny Kittery did not sit well with St. John. He schooled his face to impassivity. What did it matter, really, what the strangers in this village had said or done to the woman with whom he intended to sever all ties?

But now he could guess on whom Sarah had been practicing the firmly set jaw and cold eyes that had greeted him yesterday afternoon.

He suddenly recalled a detail from his earlier conversation with Beals. "Mrs. Fairfax gives your daughter lessons on the pianoforte, does she not?"

"Er, yes. Indeed she does." His knowledge seemed to startle her. "In fact, it was I who suggested the lessons as a means for Mrs. Fairfax to earn her keep, rather than relying on charity—it pained her to have to do so, I know," she added, the words only serving to underscore her contempt. "I came here a dozen years ago, Mr. Fairfax. From Plymouth, you see," she said, the name of her birthplace falling from her tongue as if it had been Paris. "So I have always felt it my duty to set the tone of life in Haverhythe somewhat higher."

Probably she hoped to see her daughter one day restored to the more refined circles from which she herself had come, circles in which musical accomplishments would be held in high regard. Despite the pleasure afforded by shunning someone like Sarah, how often did one come across a competent teacher of that particular skill in a fishing village on the northern coast of Devonshire?

But then, Sarah was rather more than competent.

"Then you were instrumental in helping Mrs. Fairfax achieve some measure of acceptance here."

The supposed compliment did not sit well with Mrs. Kittery. "Oh, I can't take credit, Mr. Fairfax. It's Mr. and Mrs. Norris who did that, along with Beals, the baker. And people seem to dote on the little girl, Clarissa. Of course, folks do say you oughtn't to blame a child for the parents' sins," she acknowledged reluctantly. "In any case, over the years, people have proved willing to forgive Mrs. Fairfax for any—irregularities that might have been hidden in her past."

Against Fanny Kittery's better judgment, it was clear to see.

"I'm sure you underestimate your influence, Mrs. Kittery. I'll bid you good day," he said with a nod and walked back toward the pub, reflecting on everything he'd learned that morning.

Had everyone else in this trusting little village been duped by a jewel thief and lightskirt?

He could not afford to be taken in himself.

Chapter 7

Although St. John had slept in some strange places, Mackey's Pub in Haverhythe did not seem fated to be among them. Sheer fatigue should have robbed him of the ability to keep his eyes open, but he found himself in his room, lying on his back, staring up at the smoke-stained ceiling. It wasn't the lumpy tick mattress or the damp sheets that kept sleep at bay. It wasn't even the sounds of Saturday night carousing that erupted at intervals from the taproom.

It was the memory of Clarissa's eyes.

He could still see them peeping over the stone window ledge, bright and merry and a remarkable shade of violet.

He could not say, even now, what color he had expected, what color he had *wanted* to see. Her mother's eyes, a gray that shifted and changed like a sky threatening storm? No, those eyes gave him trouble enough already.

Sutliffe blue? Well, that would have answered one question. But it would hardly have made his task easier. What was it Fanny Kittery had said? *You oughtn't to blame a child for the parents' sins.* If he could prove Sarah was a thief, it would rob a child—perhaps *his* child—of her mother. That was a loss he understood too well. Despite his determination to rid himself of the woman he had never wanted to wed, was he hard-hearted enough to inflict such pain on an innocent little girl?

If he were honest with himself, he had expected brown eyes. It would have been fitting, somehow, if they had been the same dark eyes that haunted his nightmares, eyes glassy and unseeing as they stared up from David Brice's pale face where it lay in the dewy green grass.

St. John shuddered at the memory and looked down, half-expecting to see in his trembling hands a sword dripping with another man's blood. Accepting that sleep was not going to come, and in some ways not sorry for it given the path his thoughts seemed intent on taking, he hoisted himself from the uncomfortable bed and dressed. The passageway was dark, but he made his way along it and down the stairs, following the noise of the taproom.

The smell of fish and sweat and ale was almost as much an assault on his senses as the light and the noise that burst upon him as he opened the door. The pub was crowded. A few women could even be seen among the tables tonight. The eldest Mackey boy was behind the bar, while his father danced grudging attendance on his patrons. Gerald Beals was seated in his regular spot, talking with a man St. John did not know.

Avoiding every eye, St. John crossed the room and walked out the door, forgoing both hat and greatcoat. The cobbled street of Haverhythe was cool and blessedly quiet in comparison to the raucous pub. The sea breeze lifted his hair, and he turned to watch the play of a waxing moon across the water.

Without conscious thought, he was drawn to the massive quay that curled out into the bay, sheltering a shoreline now littered with boats of all sizes. Climbing its wide, worn steps, he found the stone walkway along its top slick with spray where the heavier waves of the incoming tide crashed against the solid pier only to fall back impotently into the sea.

To his surprise, he was not alone, despite the lateness of the hour. A figure stood at the far end of the quay looking out to sea—a woman, her skirts whipped by the wind. His first thought was that it might be Mad Martha, come to commune with her dead husband's ghost. But this woman was taller, almost certainly younger. Some other fisherman's wife, then, waiting for a boat that had not come in. What must it be like to go on, day by day, worrying and wondering what the next tide would bring?

As if trying to shed just such fears, the woman arched her back and lifted her face to the moonlight, and with a sudden and unwelcome quickening of his pulse St. John recognized Sarah.

He hesitated. He did not think she had seen him. He might turn and walk away. Of course, walking away got him no closer to his goal. It answered no questions and solved no mysteries.

So far, however, his encounters with Sarah tended to raise more questions than they answered.

When he was perhaps three steps away, she turned to face him. He had thought the sound of the waves had masked his approach. But she did not look startled to see him, merely angry.

"Have you come to make more threats, then? Come to remind me once again that you have the power to ruin me—to set my friends against me—to rip my daughter away?" With her loose hair and her wide, searching eyes, she looked as wild as her surroundings.

He had regretted his parting whisper in the baker's shop almost as soon as it had passed his lips. If the tip of a blade had not forced Brice to confess, how likely was it that mere words would intimidate Sarah into revealing her own perfidy, or the whereabouts of the stolen gems?

In the hours since, he had given much thought to Beals's counsel to woo Sarah. If he wanted to be free of her in the end, he must do whatever it took to find that necklace, and the search would go more smoothly if he gained some measure of her trust. He would have to worm his way into her house, her bedchamber, even—if necessary—her bed.

Here, under the moonlight, seemed the proper place to take the first steps in that direction.

"Threats?" He shook his head sadly. "Ah, Sarah. You misunderstand me."

"Oh, I think not, my lord," she ground out with mock courtesy. "Why else would you be here?"

"In Haverhythe?"

"On the quay. At this time of night." She pulled her shawl more snugly about her shoulders. Although they stood in the most open and public place in the village, everything about her posture proclaimed that she felt he had violated her private sanctuary.

So he stepped closer still, until they were standing shoulder to shoulder. "I was merely looking for a place to clear my head."

"Mackey's can be a bit rowdy on a Saturday night." She sounded anything but sympathetic.

"Mm," he agreed absently. "And I have had trouble enough sleeping since I went to Antigua."

"Have you?" she scoffed.

"Yes."

She gasped as she twisted around to face him. "Do you—do you mean to say that you really have been in the West Indies? But I thought—that is, Mrs. Potts said you told her—" Sarah frowned and began again. "You told Mrs. Potts that you had been there, I know. But I assumed you did so because you knew that I had told everyone my husband had died abroad—that it was just part of the tale you had concocted to amuse Mr. Mackey and the rest."

St. John managed a wry smile. "Your husband very nearly did die—in an open field just outside London."

Sarah's brow wrinkled in confusion.

"I met Brice. Did you know?"

"No." Her eyes darted to his scar. "I cannot believe you would challenge a man over a slight to my reputation."

St. John cut his gaze away, studying the glossy reflection of the moon on the slick stones beneath their feet. In the intervening years, he had almost persuaded himself that he had not dueled for her honor, but rather for his own—such as it was. Denial had become second nature. But he could hardly deny the duel's importance to the woman he was meant to be wooing. "More than a slight, ma'am," he said at last. "And then, believing I had killed him, I fled."

"Captain Brice is dead?" she asked hesitantly.

He tried to analyze the tone of her question. Regret? Relief? "No," he answered finally. "He survived—was sent on a mission to France, in fact. He returned a hero."

Another pause. "But you have been in Antigua all this time? That is why you have come for me only now?"

Had she honestly thought that he had simply let her go? That if circumstances had not prevented him, he would have made no effort to find her? But the answer, apparently, was yes. She had tossed aside her marriage vows, created a new life for herself, imagined she was safely out of his reach—that much was clear to him.

He nodded.

"Three years. What did you do there?"

"This and that. Mostly I worked as a sort of clerk for a planter's agent."

"A clerk," she repeated, raising one skeptical eyebrow. "Your father's name could not secure you something better?"

"Perhaps," St. John acknowledged. "If I had given it."

He could not be sure it was not a trick of the moonlight, but he thought he saw her swallow a smile. "Such a dangerous voyage—and destination. I cannot think that Lord Estley took well to the notion of his son and heir putting himself in harm's way."

"He learned where I had gone when it was too late to stop me."

"But you must have had some communication with him."

"The exchange of letters is an unpredictable business across such a distance." That was only partly true. Letters *had* come—a few coaxing notes from his stepmother, one demanding missive from his father. But St. John had answered all of them with silence. "The separation gave me an opportunity to sort some things out," he admitted at last, although he had not intended to reveal anything so near the truth. "You understand, I think."

Sarah's eyes swept across his face before turning back toward the water. "I understand that I have not been the only one in hiding."

He looked down at her and followed the line of her gaze along the waves. He thought he understood, finally, the attraction the water held. "Can one see all the way across the bay to Bristol?"

"On a clear day, I fancy I can." She shrugged. "But no—not really."

"Your parents—"

She shook her head, cutting him off. "Lady Estley insisted I must sever all ties. I did not know she had claimed I was dead. But at least that means Mama and Papa have not worried over me the last three years," she said, a convincing tremor in her whispered voice. He had had no notion she was such an accomplished actress.

He nodded his head in silent agreement with her words. The report of her death would have given Sarah's parents some sense that the chain of events begun on the night of the nuptial ball had been brought to a close, no matter how terrible. That much he knew from experience. But what would their reaction be when they discovered the report had been a lie?

"Why did you not go to them anyway?" A mere promise to his stepmother could not have prevented her, after all.

"Because they would have expected me to return to you."

Having had the dubious pleasure of seeing her in another man's arms just days after their wedding, he ought to have been prepared for such a declaration of antipathy toward her husband. Yet the words buzzed in his ears like mosquitos seeking blood, proving he had not been fully ready to hear them. "Was I so abhorrent to you, then?" he managed to ask after a moment. "Or was it your punishment you feared to face?"

"I feared a kind of punishment, yes," she said, her words muffled by the moaning sea. "A lifetime spent without love."

Love?

Under ordinary circumstances, they might have had what passed for a successful marriage—at least among those of his class. After an heir was born, they would have been free to go their separate ways. He probably would have taken a mistress eventually. He might even have looked the other way if Sarah had chosen to take a lover.

But *love?* That had never been part of the bargain. And it never could be.

With a shiver, Sarah turned her back on the ocean and faced St. John, dashing droplets of moisture from her cheeks—sea spray, though it looked remarkably like tears. "That dream is an old one. What happens now?"

"Things cannot stay as they are."

Her shoulders rose and fell in a visible sigh. "I suppose not. But I have one request I hope you will honor."

"If I can."

She drew another deep breath, as if gathering her courage. "The festival on Michaelmas. I, along with many others, have worked for months to ensure its success. Let me see it through—without interference."

It was not the favor he had expected her to ask. He had not thought Sarah the sort to get caught up in village merrymaking. Still, Michaelmas was five days off, and if he were going to be forced to spend a week here, he could use that time to his advantage. He tilted his head in a half nod. "That seems a reasonable request," he said, proffering his hand to seal the agreement.

She regarded the gesture with open skepticism. "And what sort of promise do you demand of me in return?"

"Why, nothing, my lady." After a lengthy pause in which he felt certain she intended to refuse him, she put her hand in his, and he shook it. Despite their surprising strength, her fingers felt impossibly small in his palm. "For the moment."

Just then a rogue wave broke high against the quay, driving water over its surface and thoroughly wetting them both. As she belatedly attempted to jump out of its path, Sarah's feet slipped out from under her. She began to flail, but St. John pulled her to safety and set his other hand around her waist to steady her.

She glanced down at the churning foam and then up at him. "It would be a terrible fall."

Seizing the opportunity the forces of nature had provided him, St. John allowed himself to look, really look, at the woman he had so reluctantly married.

Sarah was not beautiful. At least, not in any conventional way. Her features were quite unremarkable—nothing striking, not even singular. But the moonlight leant her skin an ethereal glow. Her shadowed eyes were dark as pewter, and her hair hung loose, teased and tangled by the salty wind.

No, she was not beautiful—not any more than the steely waters of the North Atlantic crashing below them could be called beautiful. Mysterious, yes. Potentially treacherous.

But compelling, nonetheless.

Perhaps it would not prove such an uncongenial task to pretend to woo her, after all.

"You are most welcome, Sarah." Keeping one hand at the small of her back, he lifted the other to sweep the hair from her face, stroking his fingertips along her cheek as he did so. He realized he had never seen her hair unbound before. Even on their wedding night, she had worn it in a long, tight braid. If he had taken the time to undo that braid, to find out what she hid beneath its taut twists, how differently their lives might have turned out.

"It occurs to me that the good people of Haverhythe will begin to suspect something's amiss if we don't spend more time in one another's company, if we don't show one another a little—affection," he murmured, lowering his mouth to within an inch of hers. "After all, we have been separated for three long years."

Whatever warmth the words had held was quickly cooled by the steely look in Sarah's eyes. If David Brice had looked at him in such a way across the field of honor, he might have turned tail and run.

"The good people of Haverhythe are either still in the pub or have long since taken to their beds. I'm quite sure this little display will be lost on them." She glanced over her shoulder at the village, as if seeking confirmation of her claim. "In any event, I'm surprised you care for what they think."

"I don't." With the pressure of his palm, he tilted her face so she could not avoid his gaze. "But you do. Would you rather your friends cast our reunion as fairy tale or melodrama?"

"What they imagine will depend at least as much on whether you play the hero or the villain," she tossed back. "Good night, my lord." Slipping free of his embrace, she turned to walk back along the quay, her damp skirts clinging to her long, slender legs.

Chapter 8

"Your husband will take the child, of course."

Lost in thoughts of Abby Norris's headache, the crippling pain in Martha Potts's joints, and the grim change in the weather such maladies foretold, Sarah nearly stumbled at hearing the vicar speak her worst fears aloud. Mr. Norris paused in their journey up the nave of All Saints' and gestured toward the pew usually occupied by Sarah and Mrs. Potts, now taken up by a set of broad shoulders clad in dark blue superfine.

As if on cue, St. John turned and gave her a cryptic smile.

And to think she had imagined the Lord's Day would offer some reprieve.

"Ow, Mama!" Clarissa attempted to throw off Sarah's fingers where they had sunk sharply into her little arm.

Perhaps, Sarah prayed as they walked toward her husband, *Clarissa will refuse to go with a stranger.* But such a hope was dashed when St. John patted the polished wooden bench beside him and Clarissa slid happily into place. "Mama play," she explained, and St. John nodded.

"Yes, I know. I am saddened to hear that Mrs. Norris was taken ill, of course, but I look forward to hearing my wife's contribution to divine services this morning, Mr. Norris."

"Mrs. Fairfax is always willing to help," Mr. Norris praised, urging Sarah toward the chancel, where the organ was ensconced.

As Sarah seated herself at the persnickety old instrument, she glanced back toward the pew. Clarissa had climbed into St. John's lap and was amusing herself with the shining buttons of his waistcoat. He ran his hand over Clarissa's mop of golden-brown curls and looked up at Sarah, his expression unreadable.

She quickly turned to face the organ and focused her attention on the music, but throughout the service she could feel his eyes on her back, studying her with an attentiveness no hymn had ever called forth before. She remembered the burning penetration of his gaze the night before, the feel of his strong arms wrapped around her, the whisper of his breath across her lips as he closed in for a kiss.

Her pulse leapt at the memory and her fingers stumbled over the keys. *Fool, fool, fool.*

Whatever he wanted, it was not her. And whatever she needed, it was not him.

She dragged her wayward thoughts back to the service and played until the organ's hollow-sounding notes told her that the church was nearly empty.

When she dared to turn around at last, St. John and Clarissa were gone.

Hearing nothing but the echo of Mr. Norris's fateful promise in her ears, she hurried out of the church, oblivious to the greetings of her neighbors, struggling to find one little child in the crowd. Hampered at least as much by her own anxiety as by the blinding midday sun, she located her husband and daughter at last, standing with the Thomases a few yards down the footpath.

"Mama!" Clarissa cried, holding up a motley collection of wildflowers in one grubby fist while little Bertie Thomas scouted for similar treasure nearby.

St. John turned and then stepped back to make room as she hurried toward them.

"Lovely as always, Mrs. F.," Nan Thomas enthused. "Weren't it, Bert?"

Bert nodded. "T'aint the Christian thing to wish the megrims on Mrs. Norris, but 'tis a treat to hear you play, ma'am."

"Yes, indeed, Mrs. Fairfax. A treat," St. John echoed, evidently amused by the man's choice of words.

"Thank you. It is an honor to be able to assist Mr. Norris," Sarah replied as the vicar joined their little group.

"Mrs. Thomas, I believe you were just about to explain to me how you came to know my wife," St. John said after a moment.

Bert laughed. "Everybody knows everybody in Haverhythe, Lieutenant Fairfax."

Lieutenant Fairfax? Sarah narrowly avoided snorting.

"Mrs. Potts is me ma," Nan explained. "And Mrs. F. here saved her life—saved all of us, really."

"Oh?" One dark blond brow shot up.

"I rather think it was the other way around," Sarah insisted, pleading silently with Nan Thomas to speak of something, anything else.

But if Nan received the message, it mattered very little, because Bert was quick to take up the tale.

"You're too modest, Mrs. F. You see," the young fisherman said, turning to St. John, "I were bad hurt, couldn't work." He spread his beefy hands before him and studied them for a moment, as if reflecting on their betrayal. "And Nan here were, well . . ."

He paused and Nan passed one work-roughened palm over a belly that had begun to round once again.

"I understand," St. John interjected mildly, as if such details were an expected part of polite conversation. By contrast, Edmund Norris's face turned a rather remarkable shade of pink.

"I'd been takin' care o' Mrs. Potts, and my own ma, o' course. But times got tough. Real tough." Bert jerked his thumb toward Haverty Court. "His lordship's steward threatened to turn Mrs. Potts out of Primrose Cottage if she couldn't come up with the rent. She started walkin' the quay again, like she did after Nan's pa drowned."

"Then Mrs. F. come along and asked if Ma would take in a boarder," Nan chimed in. "If it weren't for her, I reckon Ma 'ud be at the bottom of the bay."

Sarah felt St. John turn and look at her. "Is that so?"

Sarah could hardly deny it. After facing the village's censure for weeks, scraping by on the few coins she had happened to have in her reticule when she left London, and beginning to suspect her own "interesting condition," Sarah had passed more than a few nights tempted to join Mad Martha there.

Instead, she had joined her at Primrose Cottage.

"Nonsense, Nan," Sarah demurred. "If your mother had been as desperate as that, my little mite could hardly have saved her. She was simply kind and generous enough to take me in."

"You're too modest, Mrs. Fairfax—especially considering what happened next."

"And what was that?" St. John asked, turning to the vicar.

"When she saw the Thomases' situation, and realized they were unfortunately far from alone in their troubles," he explained to St.

John with a melancholy shake of his head, "she took a notion to begin a sort of pension for the men and their families. The Fishermen's Relief Fund."

"Really, I think Mrs. Norris deserves—" Sarah tried to interject, but her words fell on deaf ears.

"She had the vicar take up a collection," said Nan.

That gentleman brushed aside his own contribution. "And she got the women of the village to set aside a bit here and there—old clothes or salted fish—for those who needed it."

"Why, she even badgered 'em up at Haverty Court," exclaimed Bert. "She's done all but steal to see that fund built up."

Sarah watched St. John's eyes widen at the mention of theft. "Really?" he exclaimed. "Well, Mrs. Fairfax has always been remarkably resourceful."

"And o' course, there's the festival," Nan added. "We mustn't forget that."

St. John looked at Sarah. "Ah, yes. The festival. With proceeds to go to the, er—"

"Fishermen's Relief Fund," Sarah supplied brusquely. "If it doesn't rain," she reminded them all, casting a chary glance at the cloudless blue sky. "Come, Clarissa. It's time to go. Are those flowers for Mrs. Potts?"

After the obligatory protests from the children and cheery well wishes from the adults, Sarah turned at last toward the cobbled street. Clutching a bedraggled bouquet of weeds, Clarissa wandered a few paces ahead.

"Why did you not tell me?" St. John asked, drawing Sarah's hand through his arm.

Sarah longed to pull away but instead nodded a greeting at the Mackey children as they passed. "Tell you what?"

"About Mrs. Potts—the Fishermen's Relief—the festival. Too modest, perhaps?" He smiled, but his eyes were chips of ice. "Am I now to suppose that you stole that necklace and then took my stepmother's money for a noble purpose, rather than a nefarious one? Did you fancy yourself some sort of Lady Robin Hood?"

"Lady Estley has told you that she sent me money, and I will not deny having received it. But I deny most vehemently that I demanded it, or expected it." Sarah spoke in a heated whisper, for she was all too aware of Haverhythe's love of gossip, and the street around them was crowded. "How could I? I have nothing she wants—nothing anyone wants."

"You will forgive me, ma'am, if I express some doubt on that point."

"It little matters to me what you believe," she lied. "In any case, I put her money to good use. I started the Fishermen's Relief Fund."

That revelation succeeded in startling him into silence, but only for a moment. "If you imagine your good works here are somehow penance for your crimes—"

"*Crimes*, my lord? Of what crimes do you accuse me?" she demanded.

"I think you know your crimes, my lady," he insisted softly, glancing toward Clarissa and then back at her. "You were caught in a compromising position with another man. At the same time, a priceless family heirloom disappeared. Then you decided to run, rather than stay and proclaim your innocence—"

"But I did."

His steps halted. "I beg your pardon?"

"I did proclaim my innocence. On the night I first stood accused. But you did not hear me, it seems. Or you did not believe me." She darted her gaze away. "What hope have I of anyone believing me now?"

"Precious little," he agreed, an edge of indecision in his voice. "You cannot deny the appearance of guilt."

She forced herself not to flinch beneath the sudden intensity of his regard. "Appearances may deceive, my lord."

He tipped his head as if considering her response. "Indeed they may, Mrs. Fairfax. Indeed they may."

But before he could say more, Clarissa grabbed his free hand. "Play donkey."

After Sarah slid her oft-mended glove from his elegantly tailored sleeve, he bent to scoop up Clarissa, hoisting her onto his shoulder. At the child's squealed demand, he trotted along the cobblestones like a donkey, calling greetings to half the town as they went, earning smiles from everyone they passed, and arriving at the bottom of the street hardly out of breath.

So he had decided to play the dashing hero before the eyes of the village, eh? Well, then, let him learn just what such a role required. She could ensure it would not be simple child's play.

Sarah caught up with them just on the threshold of Primrose Cottage and laid a staying hand on his arm. "Meet me tomorrow on the quay. Nine o'clock."

"All right," he agreed, his eyebrows creeping up his forehead again. "Another moonlight assignation?"

"Nine o'clock in the morning," she replied, curving her lips in a small smile. "Come ready to work, my lord."

Sarah arrived on the quay early the next day and greeted Mrs. Norris and the handful of people who had agreed to help them prepare for the festival on Michaelmas. Colin Mackey had sent his daughter and his eldest son. Mr. Gaffard was there, leaving Mrs. Gaffard to mind the shop. The Rostrum brothers—Clovis and Hubert, two bent-backed fishermen too old to go to sea—stood side by side; after three years, Sarah was still not sure which was which. These, with a scattering of younger children who were eager to help but really too young to do so, were the army she had collected.

St. John was nowhere to be seen.

Apparently even a miserable bed at the Blue Herring held more appeal of a morning than a day of hard and likely thankless work— the kind a hero undertook regardless. She had expected it to be more of a challenge to reveal his true colors to the town.

"Abby, my dear, are you better?" Sarah walked immediately to her friend's side and took her hand.

"Much," Abigail Norris replied, although her smile was still weak and her brown eyes heavy-lidded.

"Well," Sarah said, giving Abby's fingers a squeeze and glancing at the sky, "we'll just have to pray the storm blows over before Thursday."

"And what storm is that, dear?" Abby asked innocently.

Sarah considered all the storms bearing down on her and only wished she could say which posed the more immediate threat.

"Gather 'round, everyone," she called with a clap of her hands. "And thank you for agreeing to help. Mr. Norris has made sure every parish within twenty miles knows about our little festival, so we must prepare for visitors. The plan is to have stalls for the bazaar set up here along the top of the quay," she said, gesturing above her, "and here below, in the evening, there's to be a dance under the stars."

It was unconventional—and all likely to be ruined if rough weather came in off the sea. But the wide foot of the quay, where the ships' cargos were loaded onto sledges and taken up the road, was the largest open area in town, as there were no assembly rooms. "The children can begin by sweeping off the stones and setting everything to rights. And if the men—"

"Ho!" Gerald Beals's voice rang out over the cobblestones. Sarah turned to see him leading one of a pair of donkeys drawing a sledge laden with lumber from an old barn at Haverty Court that had been damaged in a storm. "Here's the wood for the stalls, Mrs. F."

As she raised a hand to shield her eyes from the sun, she realized that the second donkey was led by St. John. He was dressed for work, as she had instructed—or at least, as best a man of his rank could be. Over his crisp white linen and buckskin breeches, he had put on an apron of some heavy stuff, probably borrowed from Mr. Beals. The light breeze off the water rippled his shirt and revealed the breadth of his shoulders beneath it. Tossing the donkey's lead to one of the little boys, he pulled off a glove to run a hand over his bare head, pushing his golden hair behind his ears. Then he came toward her, all blue eyes and dazzling smile.

"Mrs. Norris," he cried, extending a hand to the vicar's wife. "On the mend, I hope?"

Abby positively simpered. "Why, yes, thank you, Lieutenant Fairfax."

"Sorry I'm late, ma'am," St. John said, turning his charm on her. "Beals asked for a hand."

"Of course." Sarah nodded, casting Mr. Beals what she hoped would pass for a smile. "Once you've unloaded the wood, you can help the Rostrum brothers and young Colin build the stalls. You do know how to hammer a nail, don't you?" she asked sweetly.

His smile shifted slightly, but it did not leave his face. "I think, Sarah," he murmured, low enough that only she could hear, "what I've learned in the last three years would amaze you."

Thankfully, one of the little boys chose just that moment to tug at her skirts. "Coming," she called, and within moments, she was surrounded by a flurry of activity, showing the children how to sweep the sand so that it didn't fly up in their faces and sending furtive glances toward the knot of men as they set about their task.

St. John did not wait for instruction but jumped into the fray and offered what the other men seemed to find valued suggestions; by the time the sun was high in the sky, the first stall was standing and St. John had emerged as the carpenters' leader.

At midday the crowd had almost doubled, as the women of the village finished their household chores and brought their children down to the quay to join in the work. Fanny Kittery stood off to one side under the meager shade of a dainty parasol, frowning down at a girl not much older than Clarissa who had just swept a pile of dried donkey dung past her feet.

Feeling her lips twitch in a smile, Sarah turned her head to avoid being seen, only to discover Emily Dawlish standing by her side, watching the men work.

"I just come down to say that your dress'll be done by Wednesday teatime," Emily declared, her eyes never leaving the men.

"Why, Emily, you must be working your fingers to the bone! Really, it wasn't necessary."

But Emily foreclosed her protest with a shake of her head. "'Tain't nothin', Mrs. F. And no charge, neither," she added, giving Sarah a nudge with her elbow.

"How—?"

Emily fixed her glittering eyes on Sarah's face. "Your man come by, wantin' a couple o' things done up quick. Said he forgot to pack a change o' linen."

Forgot? More likely he had not planned to stay long enough to require such a thing.

"I told him I'd hafta get the cloth at Gaffard's," Emily continued. "He didn't make no mind about that, so I just added the muslin for the dress onto his bill. I figure, what do men know about the cost o' such things?"

Heaven only knew Sarah didn't have a penny to spare for frivolities. She felt torn between an obligatory protest at such deceit and a peculiar gladness for the girl's cleverness. Before she could determine which to express first, Emily turned her gaze back to the working men and sighed.

"Lord, mum. Word's abroad you're givin' him the cold shoulder, but I don't rightly see how you can!"

There was no denying that St. John cut a fine figure. And Sarah could not suppress a little twinge of pride at the thought that it was highly unlikely any other lady of his acquaintance—Eliza Harrington included—had seen him looking so. Gone were the accoutrements of a gentleman, the lace-edged sleeves and tight-fitting coat. In their place was a sweat-dampened shirt of fine cambric that clung to the muscles of his back like a second skin. Sarah had never known physical labor to make a man so appealing. But then, Sarah knew of no laborers who had St. John's good looks to start.

Watching him work, she could almost forget that he intended to see her pay dearly for crimes she had not committed.

The arrival of Mrs. Potts bearing two large baskets of food rescued her thoughts from taking such a maudlin turn. Clarissa darted to and fro like a hummingbird. Workers young and old fell on the repast, and before long, Mr. Mackey showed up, rolling a small keg of ale before him.

"Thought ye might've worked up a thirst," he said in his gruffest voice.

Sarah very nearly hugged him.

While the small crowd ate and drank and talked, Sarah looked at all they had accomplished in a few short hours. The stones of the quay and the landing had been swept clean, and what had this morning been a pile of discarded lumber was now a series of neat stalls. Mrs. Gaffard had brought a bolt of striped fabric and was draping it festively across first one and then another before stepping back to inspect the effect. Farther along the quay, the Mackey girl had gathered the youngest children, Clarissa included, and was amusing them with stories and games to keep them from getting underfoot.

Surrounded by her successes, Sarah did not realize she was no longer alone until a shadow fell across her shoulder.

"Admiring your empire?" St. John's voice came from behind her.

"I'm pleased, yes," she acknowledged, moving slightly, but not enough to face him. "It's a good morning's work. Now, if the weather holds and people come, I will consider it a success."

"The Fishermen's Relief seems a worthy cause, and I wish it well." He paused. "I cannot help but wonder, though, how this burden came to rest on your shoulders."

She raised one quizzical brow. "*Burden*, my lord? I would not describe it so."

"But the family at Haverty Court—?"

"Landlords sometimes fail to do their duty by the villages in their trust," she answered, cutting him a sideways glance. The marquess had spoken fondly of Lynscombe, the Sutliffe family seat, but Sarah had never seen it. St. John could not bear being immured in Hampshire, Lady Estley had confided to her.

"Sometimes landlords lack the means to make the necessary improvements."

She knew quite well why St. John had married her, just as she knew she had not imagined the defensiveness in his voice. Chancing a look in his direction, she glimpsed the stubborn set of his jaw. He looked in that moment quite remarkably like his daughter, and she almost smiled at the resemblance.

But she caught herself.

"Spending money is not the only way to fulfill one's responsibilities, my lord. Sometimes a bit of genuine concern for the people involved will reveal other ways to help." She cast her eyes over the little community gathered around her. "In any case, there is no family at Haverty Court now. I met the old earl once, but his health is poor. He spends all his time in London, where he can be near his physicians. I wrote to him last year with the idea for this festival. Six months later, his secretary sent word that I could proceed with his blessing."

"He ought to be grateful," St. John replied, his eyes still on the children at play along the quay. "And his son does not—?"

"One hears rumors of sons who spare little thought for the people and places that will make up their true inheritance, more's the pity." How did the people of Lynscombe fare in comparison to those of Haverhythe? She doubted she would ever know.

She felt him shift his weight, as if her words had succeeded in making him uncomfortable. "One can hope such sons learn the error of their ways."

"Indeed, one can," she agreed. "But Lord Haverty has no son. No children at all, in fact. His nephew will inherit, when the time comes."

"And what sort of man is he?"

"I could not say."

They stood in silence for a long moment. The skin along her spine prickled, as the heat radiating from his body penetrated the fabric of her dress. But she would not step away and give him the satisfaction of knowing how his presence affected her.

"Beals tells me there's to be a dance Thursday evening," he said at last.

Sarah nodded.

"A wonderful idea. And where will it be held?"

"Right here, where we're standing. The musicians will sit over there," she added, indicating with a wave of her hand the broad steps that led up the quay. "I had thought of using the ballroom at Haverty Court, but alas, that was not to be."

"Better this way, I think." She could not keep from looking at him then, suspecting him of laughing at her idea. But his countenance was sincere. "The people of the village would not feel as comfortable there. You will want them to enjoy themselves after all their hard work."

"Of course," she agreed.

"I do believe, though, that it should be tried first."

"I beg your pardon?"

She felt his fingers slide slowly down her arm and grasp her hand as he came around in front of her and made a bow. "Your dance floor. It ought to be tested."

And before she could protest—before she could offer any reply at all—he had swept her into a rollicking country dance, whirling her across the cobblestones and in and out among her neighbors, who soon began clapping a fierce rhythm to accompany them.

Despite the rough surface and his heavy boots, St. John moved with confident grace and effortlessly drew her along with him. The ribbons of her bonnet streamed past her chin like dark, delirious butterflies, and her fingertips tingled where they rested in his strong, work-roughened hands—skin against skin, most unlike a proper ballroom. Every cliché she had ever heard about dancing seemed suddenly to have become a profound truth. She did feel lighter than air.

"I've just realized this site has another advantage."

"What's that?" she asked, already slightly breathless.

"I heard you play so beautifully yesterday." Sarah accepted the compliment with a slight nod, wondering where this was leading. "But this lovely spot requires more portable instruments, so you cannot be expected to provide the evening's accompaniment." He stepped back with a smile and she mirrored his movement. "You will dance instead. With me," he insisted, drawing her close once again.

Shaking her head, she ducked under his arm. "I cannot dance only with you."

"You expect the rules of the ballroom to be observed under the open sky?"

They were back to back now, so she could not see his eyes. She felt safe in a teasing reply. "I intend to be properly sociable. If you look closely, you'll find that my dance card is already half-full."

"We'll just see about that," he said as he spun her around and went down the dance again.

In truth, she had expected not to dance at all. She had expected to haunt the fringes with the widows and matrons, watching others enjoy themselves.

In this one small way, perhaps, St. John's arrival was a reprieve.

All around them, others took up the unheard melody. Mr. Gaffard bowed to Mrs. Potts, while Mr. Beals took Emily Dawlish's hand and led her in a breathless romp across the landing. The older children joined in with untaught glee, inventing steps to suit themselves. Scandalized, Mrs. Kittery allowed her parasol to droop to one side, her lips creased with disapproval.

Sarah tipped back her head and laughed.

St. John's eyes seemed to glow with what she could only describe as approval. "Can it be that we've never danced before, Sarah?"

Instantly, she was taken back to the night of their nuptial ball. The musicians on the dais tuning their instruments, about to begin. Lady Estley in a flurry because St. John, who was to open the dance with his new bride, was nowhere to be seen. Her own eager—and, as it turned out, foolish—offer to look for him.

She had found him, of course. With Eliza.

Sarah stumbled, and although St. John could have carried her through the gaffe with ease, she could not seem to make herself move. Their abrupt stop brought the impromptu dance to a ragged close. Nervous barks of laughter came from the men, and the women lifted self-conscious hands to smooth their hair. It was as if a cloud had suddenly covered the sun.

"Sarah?" St. John coaxed, tucking a finger under her chin to raise it.

But she would not face him. How could she have let down her guard, even for a moment?

Then the screech of what sounded like seabirds filled the air, and Sarah chanced a peek at the head of the quay. All the little children were standing or kneeling at the edge facing the village. She had taken one step forward to admonish them when she saw Georgina

Mackey pointing down and shrieking. And in that terrible moment, the earth simply stopped spinning and ground to a shuddering halt.

A child's form bobbed in the still water of the harbor. And the wind at last carried Georgina's cries to Sarah's ears.

"Clarissa! *Clarissa!*"

Chapter 9

Heedless of her inability to swim, Sarah charged into the water. St. John's strong hands pulled her back. He had paused only to tug off his boots and now raced past her into the shallows. She watched helplessly as he waded up to his waist and then dove forward, his powerful strokes gaining on Clarissa's distant form, now little more than a bundle of rags being swept out to sea with the retreating tide.

A cry went up from the crowd when he reached her, although Sarah could no longer see either man or child. Her mind had turned inward, fearing the worst. How much water had Clarissa taken in? Had she struck her head on one of the massive pilings that supported the quay deep beneath the water's surface? Could the fall itself have broken her neck? Sarah sank to her knees in the surf and began to pray.

Hampered by the weight of the child and her wet dress, and no doubt fatigued from his frantic race to reach her, St. John swam more slowly now. For long moments, it looked as if he would never be able to persuade the ocean to give up its prize. But after what seemed hours, and was probably only minutes, his body broke through the surface of the water like Poseidon stepping from the sea, and he began to walk toward them, carrying Clarissa facedown over one shoulder. The Rostrum brothers hustled to help him, and together, they laid their dripping burden on the sun-warmed sand of the shore. St. John raised her arms above her head, rolled her on her side and back again, pressed against her tiny chest a few times, and then laid his ear against her heart and listened.

Sarah somehow restrained herself through that long series of motions before shouldering him aside with strength that surprised even her and falling on her daughter. So pale and so cold. She pressed trembling fingers against Clarissa's blue lips. Anything to hear her plead for a story or a spoonful of jam again. How could she ever have denied such little requests? "Oh, 'Rissa, 'Rissa," she murmured, whispering words in some long-forgotten language known only to mothers, covering her child's still form with her body, as if to shield her from the pitiless gaze of the world. Somewhere nearby stood Mrs. Kittery, no doubt muttering beneath her breath that this was a blessing in disguise.

Sarah again felt hands pulling at her, and she clawed the sand, scrabbling to maintain her hold on her child.

"Sarah." St. John's voice. St. John's hands, drawing her relentlessly away. "Sarah!" Sharper, more demanding. A tooth-rattling shake of her shoulders. "Listen to me. She's breathing, Sarah. Give her room. Give her air."

And suddenly, she could hear it: a bubbling, burbling sort of breath that in another moment gave way to a sputtering cough, and then the child vomited a prodigious quantity of salt water, twice, and sank back onto the sand with a moan.

"Mama?" Clarissa's lips moved to form the word, although Sarah heard no sound over the pounding of her own heart.

"Yes, dear one. Mama's here. Right here."

Clarissa gave another horrible retch. Her eyelids fluttered but did not open.

"Better get Kittery," someone called. "And Reverend Norris," added another voice.

"No. Oh, please, no," Sarah pleaded, although she was not sure with whom. "I want to take her home."

The brawny forearms of Mr. Beals came into view as he bent to lift her, but then another shadow fell across the sand. "I'll do it," St. John pronounced. "Give her to me."

Primrose Cottage was just a stone's throw away, but from this end of the beach it meant climbing a steep set of rickety stairs. Sarah followed St. John as he hurried up them, apparently without effort—and without his boots, she realized, as his wet, stocking-clad legs rose above her. Half of Haverhythe was on their heels, but she was aware of only what lay ahead.

Although she had come the long way around, Mrs. Potts had the start of them and was there first, standing in the open doorway like some wrathful guardian angel, allowing only St. John, Sarah, and Clarissa to pass. "Make yourselves useful," she charged, waving off everyone who had followed. Dimly, Sarah remembered that Mrs. Potts knew well what it felt like to be under the watchful eye of the village when a loved one had been drawn into the arms of the sea.

Once inside the house, Sarah snatched at her daughter. "Is she— is she—?"

Clarissa gave another listless, waterlogged cough, and Sarah felt tears of relief spring to her eyes.

"She's fighting, Sarah," St. John said, impatience edging his voice. "But she's not out of the woods. Mrs. Potts, fetch some towels. Get her out of this dress, now," he ordered as he carried Clarissa into the sitting room and knelt to lay her on the floor by the hearth. Sarah sank beside her daughter and began fumbling with the buttons of Clarissa's dress, her fingers numb with shock.

As soon as the fireplace had flickered to life, St. John turned back to Sarah. "Have you any smelling salts?"

She raised bewildered eyes. "Any—? No, I don't think so," she said, shaking her head before suddenly remembering something from the life she had shut up and put away so long ago. "Wait!" She scrambled to her feet and raced up the stairs to her room, her wet hems slapping against the treads. Fishing the chain and key from her bodice, she opened her trunk, rummaged through its contents, and unearthed a long-forgotten reticule, and inside it, a small vial of hartshorn.

She hurried back to the sitting room and found St. John running practiced fingers down Clarissa's limbs. "I don't think any bones are broken, and I don't feel any lumps on her head. But she's bound to have some bruises after a fall like that. Now, let's see if we can't wake her up a bit more."

As soon as Sarah waved the smelling salts beneath her nose, Clarissa began to cough and sputter with renewed vigor. Her eyelids fluttered again, but this time they forced their way open a bit and her bloodshot eyes latched first onto St. John.

"'Rissa splash," she managed to croak before her eyes drooped closed again.

Out of the corner of her eye, Sarah saw Mrs. Potts sink into the rocking chair, heedless of the pile of linen that fell from her arms to the floor. "Thank the Lord," the woman breathed.

"Dry her off, gently," St. John instructed, standing. "Then wrap her up well and I'll carry her to bed. Kittery should be on his way."

Sarah looked up at him. Had it really been just three days since she had first seen him standing there, dripping onto her hearth, and wished him at the devil?

"Thank you," she whispered. But the words were not enough. They never could be. "Thank you."

When the apothecary arrived, St. John stepped from Clarissa's cramped room under the eaves and onto the narrow landing, thankful once again to be standing upright. He had wanted to hear the other man's verdict, for he knew that despite the child's improving appearance, she might still have sustained significant and as yet unseen injuries from such a fall. But he also knew that compared to the comfort supplied by Sarah and Mrs. Potts, his own presence was quite inconsequential.

After a moment, the door opened again and Mrs. Potts joined him, relief easing the creases of her face. "He says she's not bad hurt. It's a miracle."

He expelled the breath he had not known he was holding. "Yes. Yes, it is."

The words seemed to draw her full attention to him for the first time. "Mercy, Lieutenant Fairfax," she gasped, using the rank he seemed recently to have acquired, a detail no doubt added to his tale by some well-meaning member of the village who had once heard Mrs. Fairfax's dead husband described as an officer. "You'll catch your death."

He doubted that. With the addition of a roaring fire to the warm autumn day, the small house was almost stifling. But he was beginning to be cognizant of certain discomforts.

"I'll fetch the towels," she insisted and shuffled down the steps.

In a moment she was back and thrust into his arms the pile of linen that had lain discarded in a heap by the hearth, still damp from Clarissa's hair and skin. "Here," she said, opening the other door on the landing and gesturing him inside. "You take off them wet things, and I'll see if there ain't somethin' o' my man's left that'll serve while yours dry."

He found himself in another slant-ceilinged room, not much larger than the other and even more crowded by the presence of a bed, a washstand, a small table, and a trunk, the contents of which were spilling onto the floor. Everything else was neat as a pin.

It could only be Sarah's room.

Stripping gratefully out of his sodden clothes, he hesitated for a moment over his drawers before adding them to the pile. He rubbed himself briskly head to toe with the rough towels before choosing the largest of them to wrap around his waist and looking about the room for a comb. Seeing nothing on the washstand, he turned to the table beside the bed, whose square top held just a lamp and two small volumes: a *Book of Common Prayer* and another, thinner book with tooled green leather bindings.

He picked up the latter and thumbed through it absently. It was a miscellany, not old but obviously well-loved, and since he had seen no other book in the house, he could imagine it received more than its share of attention. A handful of extracts, some poems, an engraving or two—nothing especially fine, but an expensive book, nonetheless. On the flyleaf someone had written "*For my dearest love*" and signed the inscription with the initials *E.N.*

E.N.? An unwelcome prickle of jealousy traveled along his spine before he realized that the book likely belonged to Sarah's friend, Mrs. Norris.

Sarah had been forced to borrow even the most innocent of pleasures, it seemed.

"Oh!"

He let the cover of the book fall back into its place and turned to see Sarah standing in the doorway. Her eyes darted about the room as if looking for a safe place to rest, and the rosiness that stained her cheeks was creeping toward her hairline.

"My apologies," he said. "I was—"

"I do beg your pardon, my lord," she spoke over him, ducking her head.

"What did Mr. Kittery say?" he asked, trying—as much as was possible for an almost-naked man standing in the bedchamber of his estranged wife—to restore some semblance of normalcy to the situation.

"He believes she will make a full recovery. Her breathing is much stronger, and she's resting comfortably now. But," she said, busying herself with straightening a towel on the washstand, "he said she'll be sore all over, so he gave me some liniment to apply night and morning."

He might have guessed as much. Even now, its sharp scent on her hands overpowered the soft floral fragrance he had come over the last few days to associate with Sarah.

"She's likely to have some bruising, too. But even if she's uncomfortable, do not give her laudanum. It slows the breathing, and her lungs need to work, to expel the water they took in."

"All right," Sarah agreed in a small voice. "Let me thank you again for saving her," she said after another awkward moment had passed, chancing a glance in his direction before dropping her eyes to the floor at her feet.

"I believe I did what any man—any human being—would have done, who was able."

"But how many would be able? Where did you learn to swim like that?"

"Lynscombe is surrounded by water. It backs up to the Channel, and in the park, there is a wonderful lake, deep and still." St. John smiled at the memory. "You shall—" Abruptly, he stopped himself. Had he just been about to speak as if she would see his childhood home someday?

It did not seem to matter if he had been so rash, for Sarah still looked as if she were not really listening. Her eyes had fallen on the trunk and its disheveled contents. Abruptly, she dropped to her knees, tucked the scattered items back inside it, and closed the lid, twisting the small key in its lock. Then she stood again, rubbing the key between her fingers like a sort of talisman.

Almost as if she had something to hide.

It was beyond churlish to press her now. But he knew he would regret it if he hesitated. She might remove whatever it was the trunk held that she so obviously did not want him to see, and he would always wonder whether he had missed the chance to recover some piece of the evidence he had come all this way to find, the evidence that would set him free from his father's mistakes at last.

What could he possibly have to lose?

Taking a step closer to her, St. John reached out and covered her hands with his own. The fragile gold chain on which she wore the key dangled between their clasped hands. "Tell me, Sarah—what secrets are you guarding with that little key?"

At last, she looked up and met his eyes. "No secrets. Just—"

The door swung inward, admitting Mrs. Potts, who carried an armful of well-worn clothes. "Best I could find," she announced, moving to deposit them on the bed. "Young Colin brought your boots up from the quay. They're standin' inside the front door."

St. John and Sarah sprang apart, and Mrs. Potts started, as if she had not realized Sarah was in the room. "Ooh, beggin' your pardon, mum. I'll just check on the wee one, shall I?" she asked even as she was backing out the door.

Sarah whirled, about to follow hard on her heels, then hesitated. "Here," she said to him, stretching out the hand that held the key. "I have nothing to hide."

He raised a hand to take it from her, and key and chain spilled from her fingers onto his open palm. After a searching look, Sarah turned and walked out the door, closing it behind her without saying a word.

Reluctantly, he closed his fingers around the key, feeling the metal warmed by her hand.

Perhaps he had something to lose, after all.

He busied himself with dressing first, a part of him hoping that she would return and demand the key back before he had a chance to open the trunk. But no such reprieve was granted him. Clad in the shirt and breeches of the late Mr. Potts—a man half a head shorter and a stone or two heavier, judging by the fit of the clothes—St. John dropped to one knee in front of the trunk, inserted the key in the lock, and opened it.

At first glance it contained nothing but a scant few items of clothing—a nightgown, a spare shift, and two vaguely familiar items far too fine for Haverhythe: a blue-green gown, and a heavy silk shawl woven with a pattern of peacock feathers. Surely Sarah had not fled London with so little to her name. What had become of the rest of her things? And why had these particular items been spared?

Digging deeper, he found a beaded reticule, now empty, which had no doubt contained the vial of smelling salts she had gone to fetch and was the reason for the trunk being open and in disarray when he had entered the room.

At the very bottom lay a thin bundle of letters tied together with ribbon. His hand hovered over them for a moment. She had told him she had cut herself off from family, so who had been writing to her? Were they love letters from Brice?

He slid one from the bundle and unfolded it just far enough to read the salutation. But what he saw defied his every expectation.

Enclosed find £5, per our understanding. A.S.

Amelia Sutliffe. His stepmother's hand. He turned the note over and looked at the direction: "*S.P.*," to be claimed at the post office in Upper Haverhythe, several miles away. His father had even franked it—ignorant of its contents, St. John did not doubt.

He thumbed through them all, glancing at the amounts. A few pounds here, a few more there. Once as much as twenty, in a note whose date suggested it had been sent shortly after Sarah's supposed death. And then he counted them. Seven such notes. His stepmother had been a poor correspondent.

And that was it. All the trunk contained. No sapphire necklace. No pile of banknotes. No clandestine correspondence between his wife and her lover.

Just a handful of grudging gift notes that totaled a mere fraction of the sum recorded on the memorandum he had found in his stepmother's escritoire. Although he could think of no reason for the discrepancy, he was beginning to suspect which was true and which false.

If extortion had been Sarah's game, she had played it very poorly.

He supposed he ought to feel disappointment, but what he felt foremost was disgust—with his stepmother, certainly, but mostly with himself. He began to replace the items in the trunk when he spied something small and dark lying on the bottom. A miniature case, he realized when he brought it into the open. Hesitantly, he flicked open the catch.

His own face looked up at him, unscarred and considerably younger, but full of self-assurance and pride. Good God, he hoped what he had seen in the years since it was painted had wiped at least some of that supercilious smirk off his face.

He recognized the picture as one that had been commissioned years ago; how it had come into Sarah's possession he could only guess. He supposed his stepmother had given it to her as some sentimental gesture of womanly affection, a feeling he had had every reason to believe Sarah did not share.

But even if she had had it thrust upon her, obviously it had not been sitting untouched at the bottom of her trunk for three years. The leather case was worn in places, the clasp loose with repeated opening and closing.

Restoring the contents of the trunk as neatly as he could, he closed the lid, left the key in the latch, and then made his way out of the house as quietly as a creaking staircase and squeaking hinges would allow. It was just dusk, but the strand and the streets of Haverhythe were deserted as he made his way back to the Blue Herring.

As he walked he tried to imagine his stepmother lavishing such attention on a picture, but it seemed unlikely, when she could have looked at the original almost any time she desired.

But he had no difficulty picturing Sarah's slender hands gripping the small circle of leather as tightly as they had held the key. What he couldn't understand was why.

What had she been thinking as she had done so?

Chapter 10

Sarah leaned back into the pillow, the silken sheets cool against her bare skin. A pair of candles on the bedside table cast a flickering light across St. John's broad, bronzed shoulders. As he loomed above her, his eyes, heavy-lidded with desire, met her own.

"There will be a little pain at first, my darling," he murmured, his lips brushing against her ear as the weight of one muscled thigh pressed between her legs, urging her to open to him. "But it will give way to pleasure."

He snagged both her wrists in one of his hands and drew her arms over her head, rendering her helpless to resist the torture of languorous kisses that spread their heat ever further down her body. As he moved against her, her heart began to race. Soon her breath was coming in sharp little pants and she began to feel slightly light-headed.

Suddenly, she could not breathe at all. Breaking from St. John's seductive gaze, she glanced down and saw the heavy collar of sapphires at her neck. St. John's long, tanned fingers were tangled in the necklace, drawing it tighter and tighter against her throat. Bright beads of blood appeared as the gold filigree pierced her pale skin.

She was choking, sputtering, struggling fruitlessly against him as he strangled her, an unholy gleam in his pale eyes . . .

"Mama!"

Sarah jerked herself awake. Clarissa stirred fretfully in her narrow bed and then gave a feeble cough and rasped out, "Hungry."

Rising stiffly from her chair, Sarah bent over her daughter and swept her hand across the child's brow, finding it considerably cooler than her own. "Of course, dear one. I shan't be a moment."

Hunger was a good sign, she told herself as she gathered up the woolen shawl that lay puddled on the floor. The candle had long since guttered, but she could make her way across the room by the gray light that crept in through the rain-spattered window. Nearly dawn.

She opened the door only to find Mrs. Potts on the other side of it, bearing a tray.

"Your timing is impeccable." Sarah smiled. "Clarissa is awake, and she says she's hungry."

"Lord bless us, of course she is, poor thing!" Mrs. Potts declared, sweeping into the room and depositing the tray beside Clarissa's bed. "Here's broth, and a bit of bread and milk, and even a spoonful of yesterday's pudding to tempt you," she cooed as she perched beside the child. "And tea for you, mum," she added, without taking her eyes from her charge.

Sarah rolled her head, trying to ease the kink in her neck caused by falling asleep in the old rocking chair. "Tha-a-ank you," she said, ineffectually stifling a yawn.

"Why don't you go and have a lie-down? I'll sit with the wee one for a spell."

She glanced at Clarissa, who was happily eating spoonful after spoonful of bread and milk, just as fast as Mrs. Potts could offer it. It seemed impossible to believe that just a few hours past, the girl had been hauled from the water, near death. But Mr. Kittery had assured her that children often made quick recoveries, even from the most horrific accidents. Even so, Sarah did not think she could drag herself away from the child's bedside.

After a few moments of standing uselessly in the doorway, however, she found herself accepting Mrs. Potts's offer, stumbling gratefully across the landing to her own bedchamber, and collapsing in a heap across the bed.

It was then that the fragments of her dream, swept hastily away by Clarissa's cry, returned to her in full force.

Her first feeling was guilt—guilt that any part of her, even the deepest recesses of her mind, had been focused on anything but her daughter's well-being. She should not have allowed herself to fall asleep, let alone to dream.

But since she had, she supposed she should be grateful that the twists and turns of her fevered brain had not forced her mind to see what her eyes had missed: Clarissa falling headlong off the quay, Clarissa struggling fruitlessly against the sucking tide, Clarissa being pulled beneath the surface of the sea.

And as for what she *had* dreamt?

The nightmarish ending was the easiest to make sense of. Although St. John was hardly the man to take justice into his own hands in quite such a dramatic fashion, she would do well to remember that he meant to see her pay a steep price for what had been lost—his honor, as much as that necklace.

Truth be told, it was the rest of the dream that troubled her.

Sarah shifted onto her side and caught a glimpse of the trunk, closed and locked at the foot of her bed. The events of the day before had forced her to acknowledge certain feelings, emotions from her past she thought she had shut up as tightly as the items in that trunk.

She had never seen a man's bare chest before, not even her husband's. In that long-ago handful of nights after their marriage, when St. John had come to perform his husbandly duty, he had always worn a nightshirt and had respectfully waited to enter her bedchamber until the candles had been doused. She had never imagined that a real man's body could vie with a marble sculpture of some Grecian god.

Remembering how St. John claimed he had spent his time in the West Indies, Sarah called to mind every whey-faced, stoop-shouldered clerk in her father's employ. Whatever they hid beneath their frayed frock coats and ink-stained cuffs, she did not think it could be *that*.

Although she was exhausted, Sarah hoisted herself from the bed and went to the washstand to splash her face with water. If she allowed herself to sleep again, she clearly could not trust the direction of her dreams. On the landing, she paused to peek silently into her daughter's room. Both Clarissa and Mrs. Potts had drifted off. Smiling to herself, Sarah crept downstairs and retreated into the kitchen, where she could neither see nor hear the rain that threatened to wash away months of planning and work.

But no matter the task she took up, the memory of her dream kept intruding. And nothing she did could ease her suspicion that there was reality at its core: She was vulnerable, and her womanly weaknesses only made her more so.

St. John was a danger to her—and some small part of her wanted to throw itself in harm's way.

"Is that you, Mrs. Potts?" Sarah called, hearing the front door open and feeling the gust of damp air that whispered down the passageway and into the kitchen. "Clarissa and I are just sitting down to tea."

"Oh, aye, mum, 'tis I. I woulda come in the back, but there's someone here wants to see Miss Clarissa."

Sarah didn't have to guess who the guest might be. She had seen Mrs. Potts depart half an hour past with a bundle tucked under one arm—St. John's clothes, she'd assumed—and make her way against a drizzling rain.

And he had come back with her. Of course he deserved to see how Clarissa had improved in a day. He had saved the child's life, after all. But Sarah had begun to fear she was never again to have a moment's peace. St. John had insinuated himself into the life of the village, invaded her dreams—did he have to fill Primrose Cottage with his voice and his scent and his overwhelming maleness, too?

"Who, Mama?" Clarissa demanded. Her voice was hoarse from coughing and her eyes were smudged with shadow; one night's restless sleep had not quite erased the fatigue of the previous day's adventure. And hidden by her dress were wide bruises across her chest and belly where she had struck the water, and smaller round ones that ringed her arms where St. John had grabbed her and pulled her to safety.

But those discomforts had only slightly diminished her energy. Clarissa slid from her chair and hurried to the kitchen door. "Mr. Sijin, Mama?"

Sarah masked a grimace with a smile and rose to her feet. "I don't know. Let's go and see, shall we?"

"Sijin! Sijin!" Clarissa clamored, barreling into the sitting room, where St. John stood before the fireplace, much as he had been standing when Sarah had first seen him following his arrival in the village. Now, however, there was a fire crackling in the hearth and Clarissa's few playthings were scattered before it. Sarah's black knit shawl was draped over the rocking chair and her workbasket was open beside it. Framed by the doorway, it looked to be a cozy domestic scene.

She wondered how and when—or if—she would be able to tell

her daughter that the man for whose attention she vied was her father. How would St. John react to hear Sarah correct Clarissa, to hear her say, "Call him 'Papa,' dear one?"

Worse, what if he decided to take matters into his own hands, to reveal his identity to the child and strip away the last bit of power Sarah held? She had no doubt that the man who had already charmed half of Haverhythe would easily win Clarissa's affection if he set out to do so.

St. John knelt as he had the first night and met the child eye to eye. "And how are you today, Miss Clarissa?" His wide smile revealed a row of perfect white teeth, but his pale eyes darted nervously over Clarissa's face and limbs, and then past the child to lock questioningly on Sarah.

"We're all well, thank you," Sarah answered, stepping into the room. "Clarissa has slept well and eaten well and is not to be persuaded away from her toys."

"I should hope not!" he said, rising to his feet. "For here is something new to play with, and I would be utterly downcast if Miss Clarissa should deem my gifts unworthy." He bowed elegantly while proffering two wrapped packages, and Clarissa giggled at his mock ceremony even as she reached out both hands to take the presents, one in each chubby fist.

As he helped her first with the ribbon and then with the paper, Clarissa eagerly pressed him. "What is it? What is it?" Turning to Sarah, she repeated the question.

"I can't guess, 'Rissa. Show me!"

The wrappings fell away to reveal a soft doll with frizzled yellow yarn for hair and a painted-on smile. Sarah had seen it many times in Gaffard's but had never been able to justify the expense. Now her heart felt ready to burst—or perhaps break—as she listened to Clarissa squeal and watched her hug the doll, then thrust it back into St. John's hands, shouting, "See! See!"

"I do see," he said, admiring the doll with an enthusiasm that did not seem feigned. "And what a charming dress. She looks like you— only not half so pretty," he maintained, returning it to Clarissa with a smile. "Now, what do you suppose is in the other package?"

"What?" Clarissa asked, eyes wide.

Again he helped her with the wrappings and shared her surprise at the discovery of a beautiful little book filled with brightly colored pictures of animals from around the world. Sarah's breath caught when she imagined the cost of such a thing and how quickly it might be ruined by a child's careless hands.

"May I see?" Sarah asked, and Clarissa reluctantly turned and laid it on her mother's palm. "How lovely! But I worry it will be . . . Perhaps it should be saved for another day."

St. John stood and lifted the book unceremoniously from her grasp, returning it to Clarissa. Sarah frowned at him, but a slight shake of his head was St. John's only reply. "I'd say that today is a perfect day—rainy days are always best for stories, don't you think, Miss Clarissa? Now, let me see." And he set about arranging her blanket on the floor and propping himself on one arm alongside it, his long, booted legs stretching almost into the center of the room. "Come, sit beside me and bring Dolly with you. She will want to look, too."

Clarissa obediently sat down and leaned against his chest, tucking the doll between them as St. John opened the book. "Do you suppose your mama would be so kind as to fetch a storyteller a cup of tea—for storytellers should be rewarded for their efforts, don't you think?" Clarissa nodded and giggled again.

St. John lifted his eyes over Clarissa's curls to send a glance in Sarah's direction, and she felt suddenly as if she had never seen this man before. Certainly she had never seen his countenance so open, his eyes so gentle, his smile so genuine—and all so different from the man who had haunted her dreams. What was happening here?

Sarah snagged her lower lip between her teeth and gave a nervous nod. "Of course. I won't be a moment."

"Now," he began, turning back to Clarissa as if sharing a great secret, "I'll tell you all about a friend of mine who lives in a very special place—the place where we get the sugar for our tea and cakes and puddings. Can you guess where that is?"

"Gaffard's!" Clarissa shouted.

Wisely, St. John did not laugh. "An amazingly good guess, my dear, but it's someplace more exciting even than that. Sugarcane is grown on islands far away, in the Caribbean Sea, where it's hot and sunny every day. But that's all right, because my friend likes it that way. He's a monkey."

"You know a monkey?" Clarissa asked, eyes wide with disbelief.

"Indeed, I do, and his name is Jasper. Now, Jasper is a friendly little fellow. He'd love to share your bread and jam." When Clarissa looked alarmed, he added, "Why, he'd no more hurt you than would the donkeys here in Haverhythe."

"Donkeys bite," Clarissa informed him solemnly.

"Do they? Then I shall have to be on my guard! But Jasper would never bite you, no matter what sort of tasty treat you had in your hands. He's far too clever. Do you know what he'd do instead?"

Clarissa shook her head, totally enthralled.

He pointed to the illustration. "He'd perch himself on your shoulder and wrap his tail around you here," he said, curling his free hand around her waist, "tap you on the other shoulder, and then reach around this way with his little hand and snatch it right from your fingers!"

Clarissa dissolved in a fit of giggles as St. John tickled her—but gently, as if he knew the bruises the fall had inflicted.

Sarah took a resolute step in the direction of the kitchen. St. John had proved he could be trusted with her daughter's life.

That certainly did not mean it was safe to trust him with her own heart.

Chapter 11

He had nearly run out of adventures for Jasper, so when Sarah returned with his tea, he stood gratefully and strode toward her, leaving Clarissa absorbed with the book's rich illustrations.

Lifting the cup from her hands, he took a sip of the sweet, hot drink. "Mmm. Thank you."

Sarah nodded absently, still watching Clarissa on the floor. "Have you spent much time with children, my lord?"

"A little," he said, recalling the eager, innocent black faces that had surrounded him on his every visit to the slaves' quarters on Harper's Hill Plantation.

"You are amazingly good with her."

St. John rested the cup in its saucer. "It is not difficult to like a child, Sarah."

"Your child?"

He could not miss the note of hope in her voice, although she was unable—or unwilling—to meet his eyes.

Dear God, but he wanted to believe that this child was his. The intensity of his longing surprised him. Years of practiced indifference had built a shell of ice around his heart. How could one little girl have melted it so easily?

Clarissa might be his daughter, of course. That could not be denied. Nothing about what had happened three years ago seemed clear to him anymore. Certainly he could no longer trust his stepmother's version of events—she who had been encouraging him to marry Eliza Harrington, all the while knowing his wife still lived!

But his stepmother's lies did not necessarily make Sarah honest.

"Anyone's child," he murmured at last, lifting the cup to his lips again.

Mrs. Potts bustled past them toward the fireplace, a welcome interruption. "Now's the time for wee ones to be in bed," she announced to Clarissa. "Come along."

"Mama!" Clarissa protested, clutching the book to her chest.

But Sarah shook her head and pried the treasure from her grasp. "Mrs. Potts is right. Come, give me a kiss. And say thank you and good night to—to our friend."

He had half-expected her to say "your papa." Would he have been sorry if she had?

"Good night, Miss Clarissa. And good night, Dolly," he added, touching their pink cheeks in turn.

"You shouldn't have," Sarah said again when their footsteps had retreated on the stairs. She began to gather up Clarissa's playthings and restore them to their basket on the hearth, pausing to run her fingertips across the cover of the picture book. "Such lavish gifts," she said with a shake of her head. "How could you—?"

The catch in her throat undermined the accusation in her words. When he laid one hand on her shoulder, she reluctantly turned to face him. One teardrop slid down her cheek, and she blinked furiously to keep others from following it.

"Sarah," he murmured reprovingly. Cupping her cheek in his palm, he brushed the pad of his thumb along her cheekbone, whisking away the wetness there. Dark, spiky lashes fanned across her pale skin as her eyes dropped closed. Threading his fingertips into her hair, he tilted her face and lowered his mouth to hers, brushing her lips with his own, feeling her softness and heat.

Two nights past, he had been determined to seduce her, mislead her, persuade her to bare her very soul to him. He had held her in his arms and contemplated the sort of controlled, calculating kiss that would make her confess all her crimes.

One night was as good as another.

But this was not that kiss.

With one hand at her back, he pulled her closer, exploring her deeply, tenderly, slowly, before dragging his mouth across hers and along her cheek, tasting the salt of her dried tears, trying to capture the scent of her hair and her skin, that delicate note that drew him like no rich perfume ever had.

"I did not think my buying the child a few trinkets would distress you," he whispered against her scalp. It was not a lie, exactly, although, of course, his motives when he had first purchased the presents had been far from pure. He certainly *had* intended to provoke an emotional reaction in her.

He just had not expected to feel anything in response.

"Hardly trinkets, my lord," she insisted, pulling free of his embrace and dashing away the remains of her tears with the back of one hand. "And hardly necessary. Her life was gift enough—especially when you might have let me drown trying to rescue her and solved all your problems thereby."

And then, on a choked sob, she ran from the room.

Almost before the scuffle of her steps had faded from the room, he heard the back door of the cottage slam. Without thinking, he followed her. Then, two steps into the cramped, windowless kitchen, he ran into the sharp corner of a deal table pushed up against a wall.

With a muttered oath, he groped his way into one of the high-backed wooden chairs that surrounded the table on three sides, rubbing the heel of his hand against his bruised thigh, welcoming the pain that brought him to his senses. What the hell was he doing, running after her? He should be running in the opposite direction—away from temptation, away from emotions he had no business feeling.

Behind him, the door swung open once more, narrowly missing his chair, and Mrs. Potts shuffled into the room, carrying the stub of a candle in a shallow dish. He made as if to rise, but she motioned him back down. "Sit," she ordered. Despite the breach of etiquette involved, St. John did as he'd been bid. Beneath the shadow of her cap, the widow's dark eyes appraised him sharply. "I've got summat for you."

Taking the meager light with her, she disappeared through a doorway just beyond the table, its lintel angled sharply where it ran beneath the staircase—a storage room pressed into service as a private chamber, he realized with a start. Why had the woman given up her cottage's only two bedrooms to Sarah and her daughter?

In another moment, she reemerged holding the candle, a bottle, and two mismatched tumblers, all of which she thumped onto the table without ceremony before taking a seat herself. St. John watched as the widow poured a dram into each of the glasses and pushed one in his direction.

What sort of salacious brew was she offering? Whatever it was, he could hardly refuse. "To your very good health, Mrs. Potts," he murmured, raising the glass to his lips.

With a sound halfway between a snort and a snicker, Mrs. Potts drained her own glass and returned it to the table. Somewhat hesitantly, St. John followed suit. But contrary to his expectations, the liquor that rolled across his tongue was smooth and mellow, of the sort his father would have welcomed into the cellars at Sutliffe House.

How on earth had Mad Martha Potts come into possession of a bottle of fine French cognac?

"Smugglers," she said, as if she had read his mind. "One day, my man come upon their hideout. No one about, so he pinches a bottle and brings it back to show me. A fortune, says he, just lying there for the takin'. So that night, he goes out again, plannin' to fetch back what he can. But his little skiff weren't built for booty the likes o' that. He was ridin' low in the water when the storm come up. Mighta saved himself if he'd tossed the lot into the sea. But he couldn't bear to see it slip away, I guess."

St. John remembered hearing that Mrs. Potts had watched her husband's boat go under. But why was she telling him this now? "I'm sorry, ma'am. Knowing it was such a senseless tragedy must make your loss even greater."

He watched as she squeezed the cork into the carefully husbanded brandy bottle. Few people of his acquaintance could have watched a loved one drown and not drained it on the spot. "My man never tasted a drop o' what he worked so hard to get," she mused, tilting the bottle in the candlelight to study its amber glow. "If he coulda been satisfied with what he had in front o' himself, he'd a had no call to go after the rest."

For a long moment, she said nothing else. Her eyes were fixed on the bottle, lost in her memories. The widow's story confirmed his suspicion that this part of the coast was no stranger to trade in illicit goods, an excellent place to be rid of famous gems that would have proved difficult to fence in town—at least, without the necessary connections. His own eyes wandered over the items that made up the room's scant remaining furniture: a battered washtub, a three-legged stool, and a cupboard with peeling green paint.

It seemed hard to imagine Sarah had succeeded.

If he could have looked at her life in Haverhythe and seen only emptiness—the separation from her family, the run-down cottage, the sparse contents of her trunk—he would have said simply that her plan had failed. But in truth, her life here was full. The Fishermen's Relief Fund. The festival. The respect and concern of the people of the village, everyone from the baker to the vicar. The sturdy affection of a woman like Martha Potts, who had cause to trust no one.

And, of course, a happy, healthy child.

Perhaps Sarah had succeeded, after all. And perhaps her successes had nothing to do with a dark-haired rogue or a missing sapphire necklace, and everything to do with the true character of a woman he had sworn he could never love.

Wishing he had not already drained his glass, St. John scraped his chair across the floor and stood.

"And I don't know why Mrs. Fairfax seen fit to up and leave you," Mrs. Potts continued, roused by his movement. "All I know is that she—unlike John Potts, God rest his soul—was smart enough to cut loose of something that was pullin' her under."

He met Mrs. Potts's steady gaze. He understood, finally, what the old woman meant to suggest with these cryptic phrases. She was implying that *he* bore the responsibility for Sarah's decision to run away. If he could have brought himself to care for the woman his father had demanded he marry, "been satisfied with what he had in front o' himself," Sarah would have had no cause to "cut loose."

The widow's accusation meshed quite nicely with Sarah's words on the quay about her determination to stay in Haverhythe, rather than going to Bristol and risk being forced to return to him.

And all of it fit with his growing doubt about what had really happened the night of the nuptial ball.

"I believe we understand one another," he said.

"I hope so, young man." The widow, too, rose to her feet and jerked her chin sharply in the direction of the kitchen door. "Follow the path up the hill and you'll find her."

St. John reached the door in two steps, but hesitated when his hand touched the latch. What did he mean to do with Sarah when he caught up with her?

As the widow retreated into her room beneath the stairs, cradling the brandy bottle along one arm, she looked back over her shoulder. "Like to be rough waters tonight. Take care, young man."

He nodded. "Thank you, ma'am. I intend to."

* * *

It was not difficult to see where Sarah had gone, despite the growing dusk.

The rain had stopped, but raindrops still clung to every branch and blade of grass—all but those that had been brushed by her skirts in passing. He found her at the crest of the hill, where the path ended at a ramshackle stone cottage. The door—wide, rough-hewn planks held together by rusted nails—stood open, and he could see into the single room, where Sarah stood at an unglazed window looking down on the sea, her fingers working the fringe of the shawl wrapped tightly around her shoulders.

St. John stopped on the threshold. "Am I intruding?"

"There are no hiding places in Haverhythe," she murmured, turning luminous eyes on him.

She motioned for him to enter, and he ducked through the low doorway, glancing about at the abandoned cottage. The room was surprisingly dry; the thatched roof might have been the last solid part of the place, however. Whatever furnishings there had once been were gone. All that remained was a low shelf built into the wall, which might have served the place of table, chair, or even bed, and the stone ring of a fire pit long cold. His eyes followed the smudge of smoke up the wall to the window opening that had been its only escape.

Sarah was watching him.

"What is this place?"

She shrugged. "No one seems to remember. A watch post of some sort, I suppose." She gestured out to the sea. "Even on a gray day, the view is quite spectacular."

He stepped beside her and looked down on the village, the quay, and the fishing boats drawing into the harbor, mere specks of light against the darkening water. The familiar peace of the spot called to something deep within him, something he believed had been destroyed long years ago.

"Whatever you think of me, I am not a monster, Sarah," he said at last. "To suggest that I would endanger a child for my own selfish ends, would stand aside and do nothing, while—"

He stopped, unable even to utter such a flawed defense. After all, had he not been guilty of precisely that crime once before: failing to act while a child's life hung in the balance?

"Forgive me." She broke into his thoughts before he could give them voice. "I spoke in haste. I am ... overwhelmed. Please do not think me anything but grateful to you for saving her life. I am glad you were here," she insisted, sounding as if she were trying to convince herself. "You even knew how to revive her."

"I did not know for certain," he admitted. "I had only seen it done. But what I saw was not something I was likely to forget ..." He hesitated, pushing back against the memories that threatened to break free of the shackles in which he had long contained them. A wrinkle of curiosity sketched across her brow, but he shook his head. "It is not a story fit for a lady's ears."

Sarah's eyes darted away. "You forget, perhaps, that I'm no lady."

He tipped his head to the side, considering. He had once said as much to his father, certain Sarah could never be a proper wife for him. But Haverhythe had shown him that, lady or not, she was a strong woman, strong enough to hear what he suddenly found he needed to say.

"It happened early one morning shortly after I had arrived in Antigua." The words rushed past his lips, eager to taste freedom at last. "I was walking near the docks on my way to my rooms when I heard an uproar and turned to see what was happening. A slave woman was climbing onto the deck railing of a slaver bound for Barbados."

She faced him again, eyes wide with disbelief. "Climbing *onto* a slave ship? Why on earth would she do such a thing?"

"Her child was aboard the ship," he answered quietly, another part of him loath to share this nightmare with someone else, knowing the stain it would leave on Sarah's memory would not clear his own soul. "I learned later that her master, the child's father, was selling the boy away—at his wife's insistence. While a crowd gathered to watch, the woman managed to get on board the vessel, find the child, and—and cast him into the harbor."

Sarah's arm slackened in his grasp.

"There are countless ways for an idle young man to waste time in the islands, and most of the crew of that ship had spent the night in the pub, as I had. They were caught off guard. The men scrambled to get into the water—"

"To rescue the child?" she asked hopefully.

He debated whether to allow her cherish such an illusion. "Yes," he admitted at last. "Just as they might have attempted to retrieve any other bit of valuable cargo that had happened to fall overboard."

Although she tried to suppress it, he could feel the shiver that passed through her frame.

"And then, before my eyes, the woman jumped in herself. To no one's surprise, she made no further effort to swim, to save herself or the child. But the crew managed to fish them out and attempted to revive them."

"And?" Sarah prompted when he paused. He knew she was thinking of Clarissa.

"They were . . . unsuccessful. The crowd broke up and went their separate ways, almost as if nothing had happened."

She hesitated. "And you?"

"I went back to the pub and—and tried to wash away the memory," he concluded with a shake of his head.

Perhaps she was right. Perhaps he *was* an unfeeling monster. And perhaps that ugly truth was not to be regretted—after all, *feeling* caused nothing but trouble and pain.

"And did you succeed?" she asked.

"No." The word passed his lips reluctantly. "Try as I might, I never could." He dropped his hand and turned away, unwilling to hold Sarah's steady gaze.

"It would be worse if you had," she insisted.

"But I might have *done* something."

"You did." She brushed his sleeve with her fingertips and then pulled back again. "You let that woman choose her fate. And then you saved Clarissa with what you learned that day. Let those things wipe away a bit of your guilt."

"Can guilt ever really be expunged?"

God knew, he had tried. That very day, he had sought out the young Scottish physician with whom he had crossed the Atlantic. Shortly after St. John had boarded the ship bound for Antigua, Murray had offered to stitch up the gash on his face, never asking any questions, and the two men had become friends of a sort. When St. John told him what he had witnessed in the harbor, Murray had introduced him to his employer, Edward Cary, a sugar planter's agent with an unusual reputation for compassion in a cruel place. Under Cary's watchful eye, St. John had served for more than two years, laboring, learning, longing to repay a debt he had never intended to incur.

Her lips quirked in a wry smile. "Once a thief, always a thief?"

After a moment's hesitation, he nodded in agreement. "Something like that."

"Yes, I believe guilt can be wiped away." Her gaze traveled toward the window and the dark water beyond. "If you are truly penitent."

After a long moment, she spoke again. "I saw one once, you know." She darted a glance toward him, but she did not quite meet his eyes. "A slave ship. In the docks near Papa's office. It was dreadful."

He wondered how much she knew about her father's business endeavors. When seemingly every ship in Antigua's harbors had had some Bristol connection, St. John had been forced to confront the likely source of his wife's dowry—the sale, if not of human flesh, then certainly of the goods slave labor produced.

Three years in Antigua had forced him to consider how much of his own life—and the lives of almost everyone he knew—had been made possible by the inhuman toil and suffering of others. It had been a most uncomfortable reckoning.

"Papa denied having any hand in the trade himself," she whispered, more to herself than him. "I suppose I was naïve to have believed him."

"Not naïve," he said. "Innocent."

Somewhere beyond, a branch snapped, underscoring his words like the *crack* of a judge's gavel. Sarah's outward flinch echoed his own inner reaction.

Sarah . . . innocent? What a preposterous thing to have said! Wasn't it?

He had come to Devonshire seeking proof of her guilt, intending to force his father to see the error of his ways, hoping for a chance to reclaim his freedom, his life. But what if he never found that proof? What if he were beginning to suspect it had never existed?

Worse, what if he were no longer certain he wanted to find it, even if it had?

For a long moment, neither of them spoke. Night air was creeping along the ground and up the cottage's stone walls. "It's getting late. I should see you home." He pushed away from the window and stepped to the center of the small room, inches away from where she stood, but not quite touching her. Although his eyes were growing accustomed to the gloom, soon it would be too dark to see, too dark to look into the depths of Sarah's eyes and read what was written there.

Perhaps that would be for the best. He did not know whether he could bear to see her suspicion or her disdain. And given their history, it seemed unlikely to be anything more welcoming.

Still, he could not keep from speaking. "Before we go back, though, there's one piece of business we left unfinished."

He could swear she was holding her breath. Did that kiss haunt her the way it haunted him?

He had kissed her before, of course. Surely he had. It was simply not possible that his lips had not touched hers at some point during their brief courtship or after their marriage. After all, they had made—

No. He scrupled to claim, even in the privacy of his thoughts, that they had made love. He had seen to it that their marriage was consummated, as duty required. If Sarah's long legs and soft skin had tempted him to linger over the act, he had *not* given in to temptation. And when his father had made it amply clear to him that duty also required he beget an heir, he had gone to Sarah each night and planted his seed, as perfunctorily as possible, feeling almost as if his father had been standing beside the bed, arms folded, watching to see that the deed was done.

The intimacy, the tenderness, of a kiss had not been required.

The last of the daylight shimmered through her thick brown hair, which was knotted with uncharacteristic looseness at the nape of her neck. One tendril had pulled free of its pins entirely, and when she tipped her head in an unspoken question, the soft curl shone invitingly. He reached out and lifted it with his fingertips, his knuckles grazing the turn of her throat.

Days ago he had decided to play at wooing his wife.

When had he ceased acting?

"Oh," she gasped, backing away toward the window, jerking the lock of hair from his grasp.

He dropped his hand to his side. "My apologies. I did not mean to startle you."

"It's all right. Foolishness, really." Trembling fingers traveled absently along her collarbone, and she shivered. "It's just that you reminded me of—of a dream I had."

Nearby, a cricket chirped, and from somewhere farther beyond, he heard the trill of a nightingale. He hesitated. But there was no mistaking the look in her smoky, heavy-lidded eyes. Sensual awareness rippled through his chest and settled in his loins. "A dream." He reached up to twist the wayward curl around his finger again. "About me?"

Her chin dipped ever so slightly, the movement almost lost against the twilit landscape framed by the window behind her. A whisper passed her lips as her eyelids fell.

"Yes."

Chapter 12

The night air whisked the word away. Behind closed eyes, Sarah waited, wondering if he would accept her forward—and undoubtedly foolish—invitation.

She had built a life in Haverhythe. She had friends. She had her child. She had purpose. But none of those things entirely quieted the longing deep inside her, the longing for something she could not quite name.

"Dreams have their pleasures," he murmured, leaning closer, his breath warm at her ear. "But none to rival flesh and blood."

Then his mouth found hers, his lips firm and demanding, almost as if there were something of which he hoped to persuade her—or himself. Gone was any pretense of gentleness or uncertainty. He touched her nowhere other than her lips and that loose lock of hair, and when she tried to back away, to retain some measure of control over her actions, if not her heart, the curl he had wrapped around his finger grew taut, drawing her back to him. Her scalp prickled, not with pain, but with the awareness that she was bound to him.

And for the moment, at least, she wished to be nowhere else.

Was it wrong to want him?

Unwise, certainly.

But in this moment, he was a mistake she was willing to make.

He traced the curve of her upper lip with a string of kisses, then nibbled and nipped his way along the lower, drawing its plumpness into his mouth and suckling when she gave a soft gasp of surprise. As if it were the opening he had long awaited, he slipped his tongue between her parted lips, teasing and tickling the soft flesh before setting up a steady rhythm of thrusting, drawing his tongue along the roof of her mouth, evoking another, far more intimate act of penetration.

In that moment Sarah realized that although she was a wife and mother, she was totally, utterly ignorant of what happened—of what *could* happen—between a man and a woman. The kiss they had shared in Primrose Cottage had been the comforting glow of a flickering candle. This was wildfire, licking through the undergrowth, devouring everything in its path.

And with a groan, she kissed him back, matching the slick strokes of his tongue, exploring the corner of his mobile mouth, the sharp edge of his white teeth—tentatively at first, and then with relish—parrying with thrusts of her own, and swallowing the answering groan of pleasure they elicited. St. John lifted his other hand to frame her face, stilling her to his kiss, as if determined to maintain a rein on their passion.

But Sarah, equally determined, slipped the tether, raising her own hands to slide beneath his coats and skate along his shirtfront, feeling the sharp angle of his ribs, the muscled wall of his chest, and the pounding rhythm of his heart.

"Sarah," he whispered, dragging his mouth away from hers and across her cheek. The scrape of his beard was a pleasant burn, and the heat of his breath in her ear was full of promise. She felt the rise and fall of his chest as he inhaled deeply, the ticklish flutter through her hair as he exhaled.

"Your scent, Sarah—I have to know what it is. You've been driving me mad with it for nearly a week."

She might have laughed if she could have spared the breath.

"Bluebells," she answered. "Or rather, soap infused with bluebells. Mrs. Kittery makes it."

She felt his shoulders stiffen, felt his fingers tighten along her scalp, as if her explanation were somehow displeasing. Surely he could not disapprove of such a small indulgence?

Then he drew in another hungry breath and nuzzled beneath her ear. "Then I shall have to give her my compliments."

Sarah meant to offer some mischievous reply. But before she could form the words, St. John's mouth left her ear and began to trace a searing path down her throat, stopping at the edge of her high-necked gown to nip a bit of flesh between his teeth and then soothe the lover's bite with the tip of his tongue.

His hands, meanwhile, journeyed along her shoulders and down her back before coming to rest on her buttocks and pulled her hard against him. His mouth covered hers in another urgent kiss as his fingers fisted in her skirt and inched it higher. She could feel the heat and weight of his erection where it pressed into her belly. Twisting in his embrace, she turned to face the window. This, surely, was the moment to pull away, to give them both time to come to their senses.

Then again, perhaps that moment had already passed.

Although she did not speak, he seemed to sense her uncertainty. "Let me, Sarah," he urged. "Let me watch the play of moonlight across your skin. Let me touch you. Taste you." He nipped impatiently at her earlobe. "Let me give you the pleasure I so stubbornly denied you—denied us both—years ago."

Sarah thought back to the nights following their wedding and released a shivery breath. "There's more?"

A low, knowing laugh. "Much more."

His right arm encircled her body, drawing her against him, and his hand cupped her left breast. As his thumb stroked across her nipple, which peaked instantly at his touch, the other hand came around and began to unpin her bodice.

In a moment the dress gaped open to her waist and nothing stood between Sarah and the night air but a shift worn thin with age. She chanced a glance at his hand, which continued to stroke and fondle her breast, and she could see the dark shadow of her areola beneath the clinging fabric.

She had not imagined that simple touches—some tender, some firm—could produce such an effect. Her breathing grew shallow, and she was conscious of a slow ache building between her thighs. She fought to keep from thrusting out her chest, from urging herself shamelessly against his artful caress.

At least such tortures could not last long. A moment more, perhaps, and he would do what was necessary to bring things to their swift and inevitable conclusion.

She would always have the memory of his touch, the heat of his palms, the pleasing roughness of his fingertips against the soft fabric of her shift and the softer flesh beneath.

But in a moment, surely, she would be back on familiar ground.

As he turned her slowly to face him, however, her attempts at reassurance skittered away like droplets of water on a hot skillet. His mouth claimed hers in another searching kiss, and she opened to him eagerly, unable to hold back a gasp as he squeezed her nipple between his fingertip and thumb, sending a pulse of electricity through every fiber of her being.

When his mouth at long last left hers, he blazed a trail of kisses down her throat, over her collarbone, and into the valley between her breasts. Pausing only to untie her shift, he snagged one hardened bud between his lips and suckled her, alternating once again between gentle teasing and heated urgency. His tongue traced the puckered edges of her areola, then snaked along the outer curve of her breast, laving it with luscious strokes before turning to the other and beginning the delicious torture anew.

Uncertain what to do with her hands, Sarah curled them around the stone window ledge to steady herself; after a while, St. John found them there, gently coaxed them free, and lifted her arms to encircle his waist.

He backed into the room, drawing her with him in a dance unlike any that had ever graced a ballroom. Her dress hung loose, and impatiently he brushed it over her shoulders. As Sarah followed where he led, the dress slid down her body and over her hips until it pooled around her ankles and she could simply step through it and into his arms, naked but for her shift, stockings, and shoes.

St. John released her only long enough to shuck off his greatcoat. "Cold?"

At the shake of her head, he turned and spread his coat on the ledge behind him and then scooped her up like the princess in some very naughty fairy tale and laid her atop it.

The coat formed a meager barrier against the damp, chilly stone, but Sarah was oblivious to discomfort. St. John knelt before her and removed her shoes. Then, trailing his fingers along her calves and over her knees, he untied each garter and rolled each dark stocking down her leg and over her foot.

She tipped her head back and closed her eyes as his hands closed around her foot and began to massage it, his knowing touch easing away the inevitable aches caused by scrambling up the bluff. When he'd done the same to the other foot, his fingertips slipped gently along her calf, tracing the contour of lean muscles developed by many such climbs.

"You have such lovely legs, Sarah. Like polished marble. But," he murmured, sliding his hands up her legs until he reached the hem of her shift, "no sculptor could hope to reproduce these curves."

As her last remaining garment edged higher, baring her knees, panic and passion flared and mingled in Sarah's chest. She could not possibly let him continue—not because she did not want him to touch her, but because she did. She had survived all these years, missing something she had never really known.

How could she expect to go on surviving once she knew?

The pad of one thumb swept across her thigh, while his other hand stayed at her knee, gently coaxing her legs apart, as if he sensed her hesitation but had no intention of allowing her to deny her own pleasure.

"Sarah?" Although the room was almost dark, she could still see the question in his eyes.

Daring to touch him, she speared her fingers into his hair and drew his head toward hers for another kiss and a wordless plea that he would leave at least a piece of her heart intact after this night.

Less demanding but no less hungry, the kiss, too, urged her to relent. She felt his hands slip beneath her shift, between her legs, ascending slowly until the tips of his fingers brushed the dark triangle of hair at the joining of her thighs.

And she opened to him, fearing and welcoming the madness that would follow.

As he stroked into her secret recesses, she felt unfamiliar wetness there, an ache that built and built. When she gasped into his mouth, he rewarded her with a firmer touch. His thumb nestled against the place that was the center of her pleasure and circled, slowly, until her hips were rising from the cold stone, lifting to meet his hand, begging for something, anything, everything.

Just when she was sure she could stand it no longer, St. John broke their kiss and lowered his head to her lap. His lips brushed the delicate skin of her inner thigh and she felt him inhale.

"Mmmm . . . bluebells."

The tone was playful. So were his fingers. And his lips, which were nibbling up her leg to join them. Surely he did not mean to kiss her—

When his tongue touched the place where his thumb had been, she jerked back in surprise, nearly sliding off the makeshift bed, scraping one shoulder blade against the rough, damp stone.

One strong arm snaked around her hip, steadying her, holding her captive to a kiss more intimate than she could have imagined. But recognizing her uncertainty, his tongue gentled, moving to explore, to tease, to taste—just as he had promised.

At first it was more than she could bear. And then, as the torment built, it was not enough. She found herself curling her fingers in his hair and shamelessly urging him higher, back to the spot where he had begun. As his tongue stroked and then his lips suckled that secret spot, Sarah felt every muscle in her body contract, straining toward something, climbing to a place where the air was clear and thin. When at last she reached the summit of that uncharted mountain, the peak burst upon her like a sudden summer storm—a lightning strike, sharp and bright, followed by peals of thunder, echoing for miles.

She came back to earth after what seemed an eternity in that heady ether and found herself on his lap, wrapped in his arms, shivering although she was not cold. To her shock, she realized that he was still fully clothed. Surely he meant to take his pleasure in return?

Her fingers slipped beneath his coat, intending to push it over his shoulders, but he reached up his hands to stay her. When she parted her lips to ask why, he laid one finger against them and looked past her, listening.

Once the *thump* of her own heartbeat began to fade from her ears, it was replaced by the sound of someone climbing the mud-slick path. A feeble patch of light bobbed across the ground in time with the careful footsteps.

"Mrs. Fairfax?" called a voice.

Sarah squeaked and jumped off St. John's lap. With guilty fingers, she scrabbled about on the dirt floor for her dress, jerked it over her head, and then fumbled to secure it, the pins having scattered. Wordlessly, St. John rose and wrapped his greatcoat around her, shielding her from the intruder's gaze.

"Mr. Norris," she exclaimed. "Whatever brings you out on a night like this?"

"Mrs. Potts told me where to find you, Mrs. Fairfax. I've news you must hear," he said, starting a bit when St. John emerged into the circle of light cast by the lantern. "Oh, Lieutenant, I didn't see you there. Very glad you're here, though. These are bad tidings, indeed, and I hate to have to deliver them."

"What is it, sir?" Sarah demanded.

"The old earl is dead," Mr. Norris replied, looking from one face to another for some sign of reaction, oblivious to what he had interrupted.

St. John curved his arm around Sarah's shoulders and shook his head. "A sad day for Haverhythe, I'm sure. But from what my wife has told me, not entirely unexpected."

"No, no," the vicar acknowledged with an impatient wave of his hand. "In fact, he's apparently been gone some weeks already. His nephew, Mr. Harold Bessmer, has been invested with the title, and the new Lord and Lady Haverty are expected at the court tonight. But in advance of their arrival, his lordship sent this—"

Mr. Norris thrust a damp letter forward, and Sarah pulled one trembling hand from the depths of the coat to take it from him. With St. John looking over her shoulder, she read:

By order of the seventh Earl of Haverty and out of respect for the dead, the celebration planned for Michaelmas is hereby cancelled.

Chapter 13

Listening to the droplets of rain as they rolled from the brim of his hat and pattered onto the flagstone floor, St. John found it nigh impossible to believe that the weather would improve in time, even if permission to hold the festival could be restored. He had come on a fool's errand, then.

Fitting, perhaps, for unless he had changed markedly in the years since St. John had seen him last, Harold Bessmer was a fool.

The footman who had opened the door had gone to fetch the butler, leaving St. John dripping where he stood, in the cold, dark, medieval hall of Haverty Court. Two massive fireplaces bracketed the room, but a fire had been lit in neither; the rugs were up and the tapestries down. On occasion, a servant scurried across the far end of the hall without glancing his way, as often out of livery as in it. He settled in for a long wait and allowed his mind to wander.

The earthy smell of dampness leached from the stone walls surrounding him. He had never found it a particularly erotic scent, until last night. With a shudder that had nothing to do with the chill in the air, he drew his greatcoat more tightly against him, but as he did, he could swear her scent rose from it—the sweetness of bluebells, overlaid now with a more sensual musk. Smell her, after so many hours had passed? Aye, and hear her, feel her, taste her, too.

He shifted awkwardly, adjusting himself. He was tempted to blame today's lingering frustration on the vicar's untimely arrival with a dose of chilly reality, preventing him from finishing what he had started.

Except that he had never intended to go so far. In the nights after their wedding, he had spilled his seed inside her body, but had otherwise ruthlessly held himself in check, as if he had known, instinctively, that to give anything more of himself to this woman would be to give her everything.

Last night, he had not meant to do even that much, imagining, he supposed, that by keeping his breeches buttoned, he had kept the most important part of himself secure. He had focused on Sarah's pleasure quite deliberately, imagining somehow that such an act would be less intimate.

It hadn't worked quite as well as he had imagined it would.

In giving her pleasure, he had got a great deal of his own. In baring her body to his gaze and his touch, he had also bared a part of himself to her, a part he had never meant to expose. Now he found himself plagued by a feeling that was equal parts unwelcome and unexpected.

Desire for the woman his father had coerced him into marrying.

Desire for a wife who had dishonored him.

Or had she?

Her reaction to his touch in the watchman's hut had been all innocence—the innocence of a virgin bride on her wedding night. If she had indulged in a dalliance since their marriage, it had been a brief and—dare he say—unsatisfying one, long ago.

To his shock, the jealousy he had once felt at the thought of another man's knowledge of her body now paled in comparison to the jealousy he felt at the possibility she might have shared something deeper with Brice. Something she had kept hidden from her husband three years ago, although he had caught tantalizing glimpses of it over the past few days.

Her soul, perhaps.

"Fairfax!" St. John's musings scattered when the newly ennobled Earl of Haverty himself strode across the floor with hand outstretched.

The years had not changed Harold Bessmer. Of course, since he had had at seventeen the thinning hair, fleshy jowls, and sagging paunch of a man of middle age, this was not saying a great deal.

Clasping his hands behind his back, St. John jerked his chin in a polite but aloof bow. He could not very well despise Bessmer for having done what he himself had done—along with almost every other young man of his acquaintance: living well and gambling recklessly on the mere promise of an inheritance. Having been a few years behind him at Eton, however, St. John knew of several other very good reasons to despise him.

Haverty was not the sort of man of whom he wanted to ask a favor, but as he had come to do just that, he would have to do his best to swallow his disdain.

"Good God!" Haverty boomed, turning the spurned offer of a handshake into an awkward invitation to precede him down a corridor off the central hall. "How long has it been?"

"More than three years," St. John replied as they negotiated a maze of twists and turns that led at last to a wood-paneled study. "I've been abroad."

"Well, and what brings you here?"

An excellent question. He had told himself that it was in his own best interest for the festival to go on tomorrow. Otherwise, Sarah might hold him to his promise, insist on staying longer.

But he was beginning to fear that the truth was somewhat more complicated—as truths are wont to be.

"I had . . . family business in the area." St. John bowed to Lady Haverty, who rose from her place near the hearth, where a meager fire did little to heat or light the room.

"Business. Figured as much—not a place to tempt a man like you, eh? You remember Fairfax, m'dear," he said, turning to his wife.

"Of course. How pleasant to see you again, Lord Fairfax." The countess curtsied with a mild smile. "I saw Lady Estley in town just as we were leaving," she added. "And the lovely Miss Harrington was with her. It always struck me as a shame you did not marry Miss Harrington, you seemed so perfectly suited."

St. John greeted the notion with an absent nod. Eliza knew, and at one time had claimed to share, his reservations about his stepmother. Now, however, it seemed the two had grown quite inseparable. Had something happened to inspire a change in Eliza's feelings? Or was she merely acting the part of a good friend, attempting to keep his stepmother's more extravagant tendencies in check?

"Of course, I understand that your late wife, God rest her soul, was a great heiress—even if the fortune was made in trade," Lady Haverty continued. She spoke with the air of one whose own fortune had been amassed in a far more suitable manner, even if it were far less substantial. "But perhaps, now that you've been given a second chance . . ." She cut him a sly glance, as if embarrassed by the forwardness of her own suggestion.

St. John could make no reply. He had been given a second chance, all right, just not quite in the way the countess imagined.

"Where are you staying, Fairfax?" Haverty interjected, clearly bored by the direction the conversation had taken.

"The Blue Herring. The rooms are"—he hesitated before deciding upon the most generous adjective he could safely apply—"dry. Mostly."

Lady Haverty gave a theatrical shudder. "Oh dear. If only we'd known. I do wish we could offer you better hospitality, but things here are in *such* disarray. This drafty old pile . . ." she said, her eyes wandering about the room. "Really, had we realized the house was in such a state of disrepair."

"I've half a mind to tear it down and start fresh," proclaimed the earl. Whatever the years had given Harold Bessmer, good sense did not seem to be among the accretions. "Something in the modern style," he added, "rather like you've done at Lynscombe, what?"

Simpering, Lady Haverty gave an eager nod of assent.

"My father would no doubt be honored to hear you express such approval," St. John replied with the slightest of bows. After almost a lifetime spent away from his family home, Lynscombe was little more than a hazy memory to him. He wondered sometimes why he had given in to his father's demand that he wed a fortune to save it. "But as the improvements of this century were made necessary by a fire in the last, I cannot recommend such extreme measures."

His hosts laughed rather uncertainly, and after a glance at her husband, Lady Haverty seated herself again, freeing the gentlemen to follow.

After a moment's uncomfortable silence, Lady Haverty asked, "How long do you mean to stay?"

St. John shrugged, feigning a sort of casual indifference to his surroundings. "Oh, not long. A few more days should see matters to a close." He had been diverted from the purpose of his visit long enough. With a glance toward the narrow, leaded panes of a rain-spattered window, he added, "I thought I might pass a bit of time at this festival the village is abuzz about."

Haverty cleared his throat and gave a shake of his head. "Sorry, old chap. Had to put a stop to it. It had a very bad look. Dancing on m'uncle's grave and all that," he said, patting his black armband—the only sign St. John had seen that this was a household in mourning.

It was difficult to claim to be sorry for the man's loss, when Haverty's every action proclaimed his satisfaction with all he had gained thereby. Nevertheless, St. John put on a somber face. "Oh, certainly, certainly. My condolences. Still," he added after a moment's pause, allowing a quick frown to dart across his brow, "it's unfortunate. I'm sure a great deal of effort was put into the planning."

"Effort?" Haverty grumbled. "Extortion, more like." St. John narrowly avoided wincing at hearing an allegation that seemed too often associated with Sarah. "Why, my uncle—"

"What is that horrible woman's name, Haverty?" clucked her ladyship. "For shame, hounding someone as old and ill as *dear* uncle, implying he didn't do all he could for the people of this village."

"I believe Mrs. Norris is one of the principal organizers of the event," St. John supplied, hoping to lead Lady Haverty off Sarah's trail.

"Norris?"

"The vicar's wife."

"Ah yes, the vicar. Rather prosy sort for my taste," Haverty huffed. "Glad I won't have to hear his sermons more than twice a year."

So the new earl meant to tear down the ancient edifice of Haverty Court, erect some modern monstrosity in its place, and then leave the running of it to his steward? There was nothing so very unusual in all that. It was what his own father had done, after all. Still, St. John began to think that Sarah's words about landlords who failed to do their duty might prove prescient where Harold Bessmer was concerned.

But he also knew that her finger had not really—or at least, not only—been pointed at the Earl of Haverty.

"*Norris,*" Haverty murmured to himself. "No, that's not the name." He rose and went to his desk, rummaging through the papers strewn across its broad mahogany top. "Ah, here's the letter," he exclaimed, squinting at the writing. "Fetch my spectacles, won't you, m'dear?"

Lady Haverty rose. "I'll ring for a footman."

"Michaelmas will have come and gone before the servants of this house would answer a bell."

"Yes, dear," the countess acknowledged with a defeated sigh. "I won't be a moment."

The two men stood in awkward silence, waiting for the arrival of Haverty's spectacles. "Has it really been three years, Fairfax?" the earl asked after several minutes had passed.

"Rather more, actually."

"You're brown as a berry, I'll say that! But you said you've been abroad—you must've left right after, er . . ." A tap at the door signaled the arrival of a footman. Haverty took his spectacles from the man's hand, curled the wire rims around his ears, and picked up the letter to peruse it once again.

"Fairfax!" He looked up at St. John, then back at the letter. St. John took some comfort from the fact that the Harold Bessmer he had known had struggled quite literally to put two and two together. It simply was not possible that he could deduce the truth. "That's an odd coincidence, eh?" Haverty continued after a moment. "Sarah Fairfax. Vicar says she's not even a local."

"All the more remarkable, then, that she should show such concern for the people of your village," St. John replied, mustering an expression somewhere between surprise and bemusement.

He did not share Sarah's faith in the power of penitence, but he could not deny that the people of Haverhythe needed help. And he did not think the man standing before him was likely to offer it. So, despite his reluctance, he would ask the favor he had come to ask. For the sake of the village.

"I understand your reluctance under the circumstances, but the people here would doubtless think well of the new lord for allowing the festival to be held tomorrow as planned, Haverty. It's all to the good of the local fishermen. And there can be no question that times here are hard."

"Aye, they're that. Gamekeeper says half my pheasants have been lost to poachers." Haverty appeared to weigh St. John's suggestion. "By jove, you're right. If this Fairfax woman is so eager to do the dirty work, why not let her?" He began to rummage about for pen and paper. The footman turned to leave, but Haverty waved a hand. "Stay a moment. I have a message for you to carry into the village."

The footman inclined his head and took up a position near the door.

"*Mrs. Fairfax*," Haverty muttered, turning his attention to the letter and scrawling as he spoke. "*Having considered matters further, I . . .*" The earl tapped his lip with the feather of his pen. "A young widow, Norris says. I wonder if she's a comely sort? Maybe she'd fancy expressing her thanks to me in person."

St. John could not keep his jaw from clenching. "I could not say, Haverty."

Another pause as the earl wrote, his lips moving soundlessly as his quill scratched out the words. He signed with a flourish and tossed the pen aside, spattering various papers with ink, but by some small miracle missing the letter he had just finished. "I didn't like to say so in front of Lady Haverty, but as I recall, you were in a spot of trouble before you left, Fairfax."

St. John cut a speaking glance toward the footman but made no other reply.

"Some family heirloom stolen by your bride, as I remember it. Didn't you call a man out?"

"Yes," St. John reluctantly confessed. He had hoped that the old scandal had been erased by Sarah's supposed death, or at least replaced by something new over the years. What a timely reminder that even on the wild coast of Devon, seemingly out of Society's reach, he still was not free of the past. Under the right circumstances, sins might be forgiven. But forgotten? That was another matter entirely.

In a little less than a week, he had grown surprisingly comfortable with the role of Lieutenant Fairfax. It had felt right, somehow, to work with his hands building stalls for a charity bazaar, to trade barbs with the village baker. To sit beside the fire in a simple cottage and tell stories to the golden-haired child curled against his side.

But he would do well to remember he was supposed to be playing a part. Amateur theatricals staged for an unwitting audience.

"Risky business, duels." Haverty sanded his letter, folded it, sealed it, and held it out to the footman, who stepped forward, expressionless, to take it. But the earl did not immediately relinquish the missive. "Yes, you're lucky to be here—and luckier still that the thieving strumpet drowned. I mean, fancy having to give your name to another bloke's get, eh?"

A vision of Clarissa's golden-brown curls and violet eyes rose before St. John, and the annoyance in his gut twisted and coiled into something stronger, something very like fear.

In daring to think of the future, he had neglected to consider the Havertys of the world and the damage they could do. It did not matter whether he forgave his wife, or even whether he'd begun to believe there was nothing to forgive. Society had not forgotten Sarah's disastrous debut performance. And Clarissa would be the one to suffer for it.

"Much obliged, Bessmer." With a stern frown he snatched the letter from Haverty's plump fingers and slapped it into the footman's hand as he strode past him and out the door.

By opening himself to Sarah and her daughter, he was opening himself to heartache.

And that was a pain he meant never to feel again.

"I finished it. Wednesday teatime, just like I promised, Mrs. F.," a beaming Emily Dawlish announced as she stood on the front step of Primrose Cottage, extending a paper-wrapped parcel. At Sarah's puzzled look, she added, "The new dress." And winked.

Sarah stepped back to let her in. "I hope it's nothing too fancy, Emily. I don't think it would suit, under the circumstances."

"And which circumstances would that be, then? Your husband's bein' alive—and as beautiful as one of God's angels—and a lieutenant?" she asked as she unwrapped the dress and held it out for Sarah's inspection.

Sarah reached out to touch the blue-sprigged muslin, but her fingertips hesitated in midair. It looked so delicate, so elegant. And the flowers. Sarah had thought never to wear blue again, although it had always been her favorite color.

"Don't you like it?" Emily sounded hurt.

"Oh, Emily." Sarah shook her head. "It's beautiful."

"Mrs. Gaffard had a new *Lady's Magazine* in—said this is all the rage now. I copied the style as best I could from the pictures. Seems awful plain to me," she confessed, frowning slightly, "but I thought you might like it."

"It's perfect." Sarah studied the dress's unfamiliar lines, the higher waist and softly gathered neckline. "What does one wear—underneath?"

"Not much and that's a fact. I made a petticoat to go along with it—bit of extra cambric from one of Lieutenant Fairfax's shirts, don't you know," she added with a sly smile, indicating a silky garment trimmed with wide sapphire ribbon that must have cost a pretty penny. Sarah hoped that St. John was particularly unobservant when it came to paying his bills.

"This dress means more than you can imagine," she said, taking the mound of fabric in her arms.

"Oh, *pshaw*, Mrs. F. It's just a trifle," Emily insisted. "Not more'n you deserve, and that's a fact—you, who's always thinkin' o' somebody else."

"Yes, well. I wanted to do what I could to give back." Sarah's gaze wandered out the window to the sky, which had been filled with leaden clouds all afternoon, although the rain had diminished. To her surprise, the sand and water glowed with the pinkish-red light of a setting sun. "Would you look at that?" she marveled.

Emily darted a glance toward the window. "Oh, aye. Tomorrow'll be fine. No cause for worry there."

Sarah swallowed against the lump in her throat and then picked up the note lying on the table beside her, running her finger along the crease and pausing to finger the Haverty seal, pressed deep into the disc of red wax. "I suppose you heard that the new Lord Haverty intended to call off the festival?"

She still did not know what had happened to change his mind. Perhaps Mr. Norris had talked further with him. Surely Abby must have been as distraught as she at the idea that their efforts to help had been so abruptly forestalled.

"Oh, aye. And that Lieutenant Fairfax went to him and asked him to have it on again. That's been all around Haverhythe twice, you can be sure."

"Lieutenant Fairfax?" Suddenly nervous, Sarah clutched the note to her chest. His generosity seemed out of character—at least where she was concerned.

"So they say, mum."

"Why would he have done such a thing?"

"Ain't it obvious, Mrs. F.?"

She had tried all afternoon to restrain a mind, a heart, and a few other parts quite enthusiastically determined to relive the memory of the pressure of his fingertips tangled in her hair, the heat of his palm against her breast, the brush of his lips against her flesh. She had tried to forget—and had failed utterly.

Desperate to avoid Emily's knowing smile, Sarah darted her eyes away. Unluckily, her gaze fell on the book he had given Clarissa, and she recalled first the charming story he had told their daughter, and then the terrible story he had told her later. His time in the West Indies had certainly changed him. In many ways, he was not the man he had been when he left.

But had he changed in the ways that mattered?

He had gone to the earl and persuaded him to allow the festival to continue. One nobleman to another. She wished she could believe that either of them really understand what the festival meant to this village. As a wealthy young woman in a thriving port town, she had been largely unaware of the hardships plaguing rural Britain. Now, however, she knew firsthand how people suffered, and how indifferent the landed aristocrats seemed to be to their plight.

Things cannot stay as they are, he had vowed.

Did the unexpected kindness St. John had shown toward the people of Haverhythe foretell a changed heart regarding his own responsibilities as the future Marquess of Estley?

Did last night's embrace mean his feelings toward her had begun to change, too?

Or were those things, even his time in Antigua, just paltry gestures of penance, while the larger problem at their root remained untouched?

Chapter 14

"Mama!" Clarissa looked up from her bowl, as much porridge on her face as on her spoon. "Pretty dress."

Sarah smoothed her palm down the sprigged muslin as if to reassure herself it was still there. The fabric draped over her limbs with unaccustomed softness. She felt rather naked out of mourning—although admittedly, not as naked as she had felt in the watchman's hut. And she had never really been a widow, of course, even with the black dress. Now all of Haverhythe knew it.

Today, they—and she—would discover who she was without it.

Mrs. Potts cast an appraising eye over her. "You do look fine. But where in God's creation did you get that hat, if you don' mind me askin'?"

Wishing she could have seen a bit more of herself in the small square looking glass over her washstand, Sarah reached up a hand and gave a little smirk of satisfaction as her fingers brushed the new flowered trim of the tiny chip bonnet. "Oh, that's Emily's doing. But I promised I wouldn't tell her secret."

"Looks like the kinda thing Fanny Kittery would sport—only on you it looks all right," she added. It was perhaps the closest Martha Potts had ever come to giving a compliment. "'Tain't very practical, though."

Sarah's smirk widened into a genuine grin. "I know. Isn't it wonderful?"

In a bid to recapture her mother's attention, Clarissa chose that moment to proclaim that she was not hungry and pushed her bowl away.

With a practiced hand, Mrs. Potts caught the half-full vessel before it clattered to the floor. "Wee ones who don't eat their breakfast shouldn't expect to go to the festival," she reprimanded, taking a cloth to the girl's face.

"Mama!" protested Clarissa.

Sarah shook her head. "Mrs. Potts is right, dear one. Although," she added, eyeing the tea and toast askance, "I don't feel terribly hungry myself."

"Nerves, mum," Mrs. Potts said, guiding Sarah to her recently vacated chair. "That's all. But you couldn't ask for a nicer morning. It'll all turn right th' end."

Sarah choked down a few bites, then drained her teacup. Mrs. Potts was right. Especially about the nerves. Still, she could not help but wonder what it would be like to see St. John today. Her forgiving heart wanted to believe he had avoided her the day before because he felt too much. But she ought to know by now that it was far more likely he felt too little.

Standing, she leaned across the table to kiss her daughter's forehead. "I'd best be off, Mrs. Potts."

"All right. I'll bring Clarissa down in an hour or so."

Sarah stepped out into the crisp, clear late-September morning and walked down the narrow lane that ran in front of the row of cottages overhanging the strand. In the miscellany she had borrowed from Abby, she had read several descriptions of out-of-the-way spots travelers deemed picturesque and charming. It had been one of the things that had given her the idea for the festival. This morning, she tried to imagine she was seeing it all for the first time—the colorful boats and wattle-and-daub houses and gray-green water. A rough pen-and-ink sketch touched in places by an artist's brush. Would the festival visitors see Haverhythe as she had come to see it? Or would their hearts remain untouched?

How badly she wanted to believe that a week in Haverhythe had forced St. John to realize she was not the kind of woman he had once imagined her to be. *Innocent*, he had called her. How badly she wanted to believe he had meant it in all the ways that mattered.

Surely, if he felt nothing at all for her, he would never have bought those gifts for Clarissa, would never have gone to the earl, would never have . . .

As she felt a girlish blush heat her cheeks, she gave herself a determined little shake. Hadn't she seen enough of life to abandon that old dream of a fairy-tale romance?

She had never stopped loving him, and she did not think she ever would. But that did not mean she needed to wander around with her head in the clouds and her eyes half-open.

He had broken her heart once, and she had run from the pain and humiliation, found a place to lick her wounds, and managed—somehow—to piece herself back together. Perhaps he had changed. Time would tell. But if she allowed him to break her heart again, the damage would be severe, for she would have lost not only her husband, but also her child.

As for allowing him to make love to her? Well, it was done, and she did not regret it now.

There would be ample opportunity for regret later, whenever she was alone and the memories of his touch refused to be contained.

The first person she spotted on the foot of the quay was Mr. Norris, looking a trifle bewildered as he watched several of the village shopkeepers set out their wares on the newly made stalls. A handful of strangers already walked among them.

"Is Mrs. Norris here?" Sarah asked, coming to stand beside him.

As if surprised to see her, Mr. Norris turned and shook her hand. "Why, Mrs. Fairfax! No, Abigail's feeling a trifle under the weather this morning."

Sarah frowned. "Again? Not another headache, I hope."

"Well, er—no. That is . . ."

Sarah had never known the vicar to be at a loss for words. Impatiently, she waited as he watched a young couple stroll past them and up the quay. The bright morning light picked out the silver hairs at his temples. He was a good deal older than his wife, nearly old enough to be Sarah's father, but Sarah had never doubted for a moment that the Norrises were deeply in love. She did not know what to make of his behavior. Was Abby seriously ill?

"It would seem that, um . . ." He pulled out a handkerchief and dabbed his forehead, although the morning air was cool. "It would seem that there's going to be a baby."

"Oh!" It was all she could do to keep from throwing her arms around the staid vicar and planting a congratulatory kiss on his cheek. To Sarah alone had Abby confessed her fear that such an event might never come to pass. "Abby must be beside herself. I have to go to her this instant."

"No, no." He held up a staying hand. "I don't think I'm meant to have told anyone yet. But as you are her friend . . ."

"And yours too, I hope."

"Oh, indeed. It's just that I felt you deserved an explanation for Abby's absence and, well"—he paused to give a sheepish grin—"I'm not very good at telling fibs."

Sarah smiled. "An occupational hazard, no doubt. But is Abby truly all right? Mr. Kittery has seen her—she is healthy?"

"Yes, yes. All is well. I suspect she'll come down-along a bit later. Mornings are—"

"Difficult," Sarah supplied with a nod, remembering all too well the queasiness and fatigue. "And when can we expect the happy event?"

"A bit before Easter, I'm told. A proper season for such a blessing."

"None better."

Just then, Mr. Gaffard motioned her over to the stalls. Turning toward Mr. Norris, she urged him to go home. "You should be with her. Come back later today, when she's feeling better."

He gave another nervous smile, nodded, and excused himself. Only as she made her way to Mr. Gaffard's side did she realize she had no idea where she would be when baby Norris made his—or her—appearance in the world. St. John's promise on the quay had secured her place until the festival. But what happened after today?

"Good morning, Mrs. Fairfax. And don't you look as lovely as the day in that new dress? Why, I hardly recognized you," Mr. Gaffard said with an old-fashioned bow. "So that's what Miss Emily was up to."

In the same playful spirit, Sarah bobbed a quick curtsy. "Why, thank you, Mr. Gaffard. Isn't it wonderful to see the sun again?"

As the merchant drew her attention to the position of one of the stalls, Sarah turned her back to the water. She did not see Fanny Kittery arrive, nor Mr. Beals and Mrs. Dawlish, each with items to sell.

Nor had they seen her, it seemed—or if they had, like Mr. Gaffard, they had not recognized her. They were standing to her left just a few feet away when Mrs. Kittery's voice reached Sarah's ear.

"That's right—a *thief*. I told everyone in Haverhythe there was something suspicious about Sarah Fairfax the moment she stepped foot in this village. Perhaps next time, people will listen."

"It just don' seem possible," insisted Mrs. Dawlish as she began arranging a selection of handkerchiefs and embroidered needle cases. "Why, look at all she's done here!"

"*Humph*," snorted Mrs. Kittery. "I'll wager that if folks got their hands on the record of donations made to the Fishermen's Relief, they'd find more than a few irregularities. Once a thief, always a thief." Stacks of paper-wrapped cubes of soap rose beneath her hands. "I'm just glad I never trusted her with any of *my* money for this little scheme of hers."

"Yet you're here today . . ." Mr. Beals's deep voice cut through the noise of the growing crowd, although he had spoken the words under his breath.

"Yes, well, I promised Mrs. Norris—and it's to her I intend to make my contribution."

"Still, it don' seem possible," Mrs. Dawlish said again. "I'd like to know who'd say such a thing."

A pregnant pause to whet the listeners' appetite. Sarah's skin prickled.

"Lieutenant Fairfax."

"No!"

Sarah jumped, fearful that the exclamation had escaped her own lips. But Mr. Gaffard droned on as if nothing was amiss.

"God's truth." Mrs. Kittery's nasal tones cut through the pounding in Sarah's head. "This festival wasn't the only topic of conversation when he paid that call up at the court. Lord Haverty and Lieutenant Fairfax had some prior acquaintance, you see, and his lordship mentioned the lieutenant's wife, who stole some valuables . . . and ran off with another man!" She waited, allowing the full import of her words to sink in. "Everyone, even Lord Haverty, believes she died. But we know better, don't we? That's how Sarah Fairfax came to Haverhythe, and why Lieutenant Fairfax tracked her here." Her audience's faces must have expressed some doubt, for Fanny Kittery's voice rose when she continued. "It's true, I say. Lady Haverty's maid came into the shop after a tonic for her mistress, and she had it from a footman who overheard the whole thing."

"Perhaps his lordship needs to keep a sharper eye on his servants," rumbled Mr. Beals.

"Oh, posh. Why shouldn't it come out that we've a viper in our midst?"

"We've that, right enough."

Sarah heard Mr. Beals's heavy step as he strode away, and the women's voices were lost amid the rising chatter surrounding them.

"But if we moved it over here—" Mr. Gaffard was saying.

"I'm sure you know best," Sarah interrupted. "Will you excuse me?"

Startled, Mr. Gaffard blinked at her. "Of course."

Sarah bowed her head and ducked between the two nearest stalls. She knew there was nowhere to run, but run she must, for she was dreadfully afraid she was about to be sick.

Although he'd been looking for over an hour, St. John had still seen no sign of Sarah when he came upon a weary-looking Mrs. Potts being dragged along the foot of the quay by Clarissa.

"Good morning," he said with a tip of his hat. "Is Mrs. Fairfax not with you?"

"Nay. I've been lookin' for her meself. 'Course, she'll be tough to spot in all this." The woman glanced about her uncertainly.

"Indeed." St. John wondered if Haverhythe had ever seen so many strangers. "She and Mrs. Norris must be pleased with their triumph. What a crowd!"

"I figured the rain would keep folks away."

"The roads are still good—or so I've heard." The crowd at the pub—locals gathering to pay their rent to Haverty's steward and visitors clamoring for a pint or a bed—had nearly overset poor Colin Mackey. St. John had thought it wise to leave before the man asked him to share his room with another guest or two. "The storm settled right along the coast, it seems, and didn't reach far inland."

"Clarissa!" Mrs. Potts admonished. "Stop a-tuggin' on my arm." Clarissa relented for a moment, but the sights and sounds of the festival proved too strong a lure. "Can't you see I'm talking to your—to the lieutenant?" Mrs. Potts caught herself, but her lips pursed in a frown of disapproval at this continued deception.

St. John laid his palm on the top of Clarissa's head, and the girl stopped moving long enough to look up and smile.

He still did not know what he meant to do on the morrow.

Oh, it was easy enough to vow to be ruthless when confronting Haverty's sneer of contempt. More difficult when he looked into Clarissa's dancing violet eyes. Nigh impossible when he recalled the silk-soft skin of Sarah's thighs.

"I want Mama," the child announced.

"I know, poppet," replied Mrs. Potts, her tone gentler. "Mrs. Fairfax left bright and early," she explained to St. John. "I told her I'd bring the wee one along after a bit, but . . ."

"I imagine she and Mrs. Norris are off somewhere, for I haven't seen either of them. Some crisis to be averted, perhaps."

Mrs. Potts looked into the sea of unfamiliar faces. "Mebee."

But St. John had the distinct feeling that Mrs. Potts suspected an entirely different reason lay behind Sarah's absence.

He wished to God he had never come to Haverhythe. If he had just misinterpreted his stepmother's note—or pretended to—he might still be ignorant of Mad Martha, little Miss Clarissa, and the Fishermen's Relief Fund.

But he had read the note. He had come to Haverhythe. He had found his wife.

His allegedly duplicitous, surprisingly determined, undeniably desirable wife.

Damn.

"May I take Clarissa and help her look for her mother?" he offered, wondering just what the widow gathered—or knew—about the state of affairs between him and Sarah. "That way, you can walk along the quay and enjoy the sights."

Although he had expected her to reject his suggestion, Mrs. Potts gratefully set Clarissa's sweaty palm in his. "Aye. Keep a good grip on 'er. She's quick."

Hardly had St. John time to laugh at her admonition when Clarissa jerked his arm with surprising strength, and they were off through the crowds. He soon understood the reason for Mrs. Potts's fatigue. The girl could dart easily where an adult could not pass, and in a blink, she had slipped from his hand and was lost to sight.

His height and bearing proved a distinct advantage over Mrs. Potts's efforts to keep Clarissa in check, however. Knots of people parted to let him pass, and he could see far enough into the crowd that her course was not difficult to track.

He found her in front of Mr. Beals's stall, eyeing a bun dotted with currants.

"You and your ma," Beals marveled, wrapping the treat in paper and handing it to her with a smile. "My best customers. Speaking of—"

"Say 'thank you,' Clarissa." St. John stepped up behind her and laid a hand on her shoulder, looking down with what he hoped was a stern frown at a face already covered in sticky crumbs.

"Why, good morning, Lieutenant. I was just saying that I hadn't yet seen Mrs. Fairfax today."

"We're on a quest, Mr. Beals—if she can be found in this mass of humanity, we mean to do it."

Clarissa giggled and tugged on Mr. Beals's apron. "Meg 'n' Thomas?"

"What's that, child? Bright Meg? Why, she's just fine—I'll tell her you asked after her."

"An' Thomas?"

Beals sent St. John a puzzled glance.

"The gray kitten," he supplied.

"Ah, of course. Why, he's growin' bigger every day. Won't be long before you can take him home with you."

Clarissa beamed. "Thank you."

While he rather thought Clarissa was thanking the baker for the kitten and not the bun as she had been prompted, St. John opted not to press the matter. Instead, he scooped her up and settled her on his shoulder. Perhaps a better view of the crowds would make her less tempted to escape.

"You're welcome, little miss," chuckled Beals. "Though I can't say as I think Mrs. Potts'll take kindly to a kitten scamperin' around underfoot," he added with a confidential wink.

St. John managed a wry smile, although the baker's words raised an uncomfortable question in his mind.

What sort of future did he imagine for this child who might be his?

He could go back and tell his stepmother he had been unable to find Sarah or the Sutliffe sapphires. Immerse himself in London life—alone, for even if he pretended to accept the story of Sarah's death, he could never marry another, knowing what he knew. Leave his wife and her daughter in Haverhythe, in Primrose Cottage, in peace, as she had once asked.

He wanted to believe his own peace would also be served by such an arrangement.

But he was beginning to wonder if it might not be destroyed.

Or, he could take his wife back and claim the child as his. But without proof of Sarah's innocence, they would still have to contend with the wagging tongues of Mayfair. Whatever he did or said, there would always be questions, always be doubts.

Suddenly, he caught a whiff of Sarah's scent on the air, slipping through the festival odors of food and ale and bodies. He turned sharply, a bloodhound on the trail of its quarry, and saw Mrs. Kittery standing nearby, unwrapping a pretty bar of soap to show to passersby.

Tightening his arm around Clarissa's knees, he strode toward Mrs. Kittery, who greeted him with a smug smile.

"Why, Lieutenant, good day to you." She acknowledged Clarissa with considerably less enthusiasm. "How generous you are with the child, sir. I do hope Mrs. Fairfax fully appreciates how fortunate she is. Few gentlemen would be willing to overlook certain—indiscretions." One brow rose, and she gave a telling nod in Clarissa's direction.

Although the woman had given voice to those dark suspicions in his hearing before, he had the distinct impression when she spoke now that something had changed. Or perhaps it was that he had at last come to understand the corrosive power of gossip where a small child was concerned. Glad for perhaps the first time in his life of the resemblance he shared with his father, St. John leveled his iciest glare on the woman.

The look set Fanny Kittery back on her heels, just as it had done to him countless times when he was a boy.

"I have not the pleasure of understanding you, ma'am," he said stiffly.

But Mrs. Kittery, it seemed, perfectly understood him. She blanched. "I—er—that is, I was only thinking that there are those gentlemen who can't abide to be around the little ones, more's the pity."

As if seeking some meager security against his wrath, she stepped around to the back of the stall and made a project of neatening the little pyramids of soap. St. John's eyes fell on the stack nearest him, the one from which wafted the maddening scent of bluebells.

He fished in his coat pocket for a coin and snapped one golden guinea against the board he himself might have hammered into place just days ago. "I'll take the lot, Mrs. Kittery."

"I—I beg your pardon?" she stammered.

"Every bar of the bluebell soap, if you please."

He had no notion what he would do with it all. Pitch it off the quay, perhaps. He only knew he could not bear the thought of the scent on some other woman's skin.

Even less did he want to contemplate the thought of another man smelling it on Sarah's.

Clarissa squirmed and leaned forward, stretching out one chubby hand for the shining coin and knocking his hat askew. To placate her, he reached back into his pocket for another and gave it to her. Clarissa chortled, turning the gold disc into the sun and watching it sparkle.

Mrs. Kittery's eager eyes followed the money.

"Have you any more of this soap at the shop?" he demanded.

"Why, I don't recall," she replied coyly.

"For that price, I believe I have a right to expect every bar, ma'am. *Every* bar. And," he added, thrusting his hand once more into his pocket, "I'll thank you never to make it again."

"But it's a favorite of so many of my customers—" she protested.

He laid a £10 note onto the makeshift counter. Fanny Kittery's eyes goggled. "I think this should more than repay your losses." As she reached greedily for the banknote, St. John pinned it in place with one long finger. "Just one more thing. After this, you will have no further need to speak to—or of—Mrs. Fairfax and her daughter again. Do we have an understanding, Mrs. Kittery?"

Her cheeks heated. "Of course, Lieutenant."

"Very good." He snatched up one of the bars and handed it to Clarissa, exchanging it for her other prize just before the coin made its way into her mouth.

Clarissa took the soap and gave it a noisy sniff. "Mmmm."

St. John choked back a sound somewhere between a laugh and a groan. "Mmmm, indeed. Now," he said, straightening his hat, "let's go find her."

Chapter 15

Dusk had settled over Haverhythe and the crowds had thinned considerably by the time he found her. She was standing to the side of the improvised open-air ballroom, in earnest conversation with Mrs. Norris, who was seated in a chair while Mr. Norris hovered nearby.

And St. John realized with a start that he might have glimpsed Sarah a half-dozen times that day and never recognized her.

It could have been the new dress. Or the fashionable little hat perched jauntily atop a pile of loose curls. Perhaps even the air with which she carried herself. Whatever it was, she seemed transformed. It would not be difficult to imagine her in a London ballroom, surrounded by her peers.

Gerald Beals approached her, bowed his head, and held out his hand. To St. John's surprise, Sarah smiled and took it, stepping onto the dance floor without hesitation. Tamping down a prickle of possessiveness, St. John scanned the other faces around him, searching for a partner of his own. But there were very few ladies of his acquaintance nearby. Mrs. Potts had long since taken Clarissa home. Clearly Mrs. Norris did not mean to dance. That left Mrs. Kittery and the ungainly Georgina Mackey.

St. John stepped across to the publican's daughter and bowed. "Will you favor me in the dance, Miss Mackey?"

Georgina blushed to the roots of her ginger hair. "I didn't think you or Mrs. F. would like to speak to me again, and that's a fact."

"If you are referring to the unfortunate incident on the quay, surely you don't believe we blame you?" He extended his hand, palm upward, and Georgina reluctantly laid her hand in his.

Her dancing was better than he'd hoped, if not exactly the sort to inspire poetry. When the figure brought them together again, she gave a nervous giggle.

"It's awful kind of you, Lieutenant. My pa was right angry when he saw what happened with Clarissa. He licked me good, don't you know."

They stepped apart again, and in the interval, St. John realized what his partner had said.

"You don't mean to say your father struck you, Miss Mackey?" he asked when she took his hand again.

"Oh, aye." She shrugged. "No more'n I deserved, I suppose."

"Clarissa's fall was an accident," St. John ground out, nearly forgetting the steps. He had thought that three years in the West Indies had inured him to violence. He had been wrong.

"Still 'n' all, I shouldn'ta had the little ones out on the quay," she said with a shake of her head. "Anyway, I'd as lief it be Pa as Henry."

"Is Henry one of your brothers?"

"Naw. He's my intended. But I know no man wants a woman who don't know how t' mind the flock."

As luck would have it, the intricate steps of the dance brought Sarah into his path at just that moment, and his scowl fell fully upon her. There was hardly time for a nod of acknowledgment before they were drawn apart again and Georgina Mackey's hand was back on his arm.

He considered briefly the efficacy of giving Colin Mackey a taste of his own medicine.

But he knew it would do little good. Doubtless few in the village would understand—to say nothing of share in—his wrath. Even Georgina seemed oblivious to the wrong that had been done to her. In her world, such correction was a father's prerogative and, afterward, a husband's.

And it was in this world that darling little Clarissa was being raised.

What kind of treatment could she expect to receive at its hands? He thought of Mrs. Kittery's glower of contempt. What kind of treatment had she already endured?

Well, no longer. Not if he had anything to say about it—and by God he did, whether he was her father or not. Whatever snubs she might endure from polite society could not be worse than the suspicions that dogged the child in this narrow-minded little fishing village.

When the dance was ended, he returned Georgina to her mother's side. Mrs. Mackey, a washed out–looking woman long past her youth, thanked him twice for his goodness. In his haste to extricate himself from the burden of her gratitude, St. John backed into Mr. Gaffard.

"Evening, Lieutenant. Have you been enjoying the festival?"

"It's had its moments," he said, thinking of his small triumph over Fanny Kittery.

"I'm glad to hear it," Gaffard said, nodding. "I almost didn't ask, given the rumors . . ."

"Rumors?"

He cut a glance at St. John's scar. "I'm not certain I should say anything more. I know how you military men like to settle your differences," he said. But when St. John scowled, he cleared his throat. "Mrs. Kittery would have it that you didn't go to his lordship about the festival at all, but rather because he's the magistrate. That you accused Mrs. Fairfax of theft, and . . . something worse."

The features of Sarah's dancing partner swam before St. John's eyes, to be replaced by those of David Brice.

"A lot of nonsense, I'd say," Gaffard continued. "There *were* questions about her, o' course, when she first came to Haverhythe, but I feel certain Mrs. F. would never have done something that wasn't proper."

Not the Mrs. Fairfax they knew, at any rate.

But what if there had only ever been one?

"You'll excuse me, Gaffard." St. John was already moving away from the nervous shopkeeper. He knew what had to be done.

"I say, Lieutenant," Gaffard called after him. "I didn't spread that gossip one step further than it had already gone."

But St. John had stopped listening. Like a bullet released from a pistol, he shot across the dance floor in four long strides. "Mrs. Norris. Norris. Beals. Ma'am," he said, with a curt bow to each of them and eyes only for his wife.

Sarah blushed. "Lo-Lieutenant Fairfax."

She had very nearly called him "Lord Fairfax." And at the moment, he would have welcomed the misstep. He was heartily tired of playacting.

"It is my dance, I believe, Mrs. Fairfax. If you will excuse us," he said to the others.

"Oh, of course," said Mrs. Norris, papering over the awkwardness with good cheer.

Sarah laid her fingertips on his arm. She would not meet his eye.

As the musicians took up their instruments, St. John glanced at the other couples gathering on either side of them and stopped short. "On second thought, Mrs. Fairfax, I believe I'd prefer a walk."

The sounds of the festival followed them up the cobblestoned street and had only just begun to fade when noise and light burst from the Blue Herring, where those who chose not to dance had gathered. Farther along, the street was quiet and dark. Here and there, Sarah saw a candle flickering in a cottage window, but they met no one. She released the arm she had taken only for propriety's sake and clasped her hands behind her back.

The sense of lightness and freedom with which she had greeted the day was gone. For a foolish moment, she had trusted St. John, and he had rewarded that fledgling trust by going to Haverty Court and exposing her as a thief and a whore. With Fanny Kittery on the case, how long before all the missing pieces of the puzzle that had been her identity fell into place? The life she had so carefully built here was about to be torn down.

To unsuspecting eyes, she had spent the evening joking with Mr. Gaffard, fussing over Mrs. Norris, and dancing with Mr. Beals, but beneath that calm façade, her mind had been whirling, searching for a way to escape, a place where she could take Clarissa and start over. She glanced up thankfully at the nearly full moon. By its light Bert Thomas could safely take them across the bay tonight, after the merrymaking had subsided. She had hated to behave as if he owed her some recompense for the assistance she had given his family, but she had nothing of value left to offer him in exchange for making the trip.

She did not even know whether her parents would take her in.

At last, St. John spoke. "You must be pleased by the success of the festival."

The festival? Digging the nails of one hand into the palm of the other, she mustered a civil reply. "I am pleased that so many in need will be helped, yes."

"And did you enjoy yourself?" he asked.

Sarah shook her head. "My enjoyment is entirely beside the point."

"That is not an answer to my question, Sarah."

The slight edge to his voice spurred her annoyance. "Very well, then. No," she snapped. "I did not enjoy myself."

"I am sorry to hear it," he replied. "Everyone else seemed to find it great fun."

They walked a few further steps in silence and paused when they reached the archway that led to the alley behind the long row of seaside cottages.

"How could you?" she cried. "You promised not to interfere. How could you go to the earl?"

"How could I—" He shook his head, as if trying to clear it of the echo of her outburst. "I went for the people of Haverhythe. I went to save your festival, Sarah," he said, his voice soft, as if he did not quite believe the explanation himself. "I went . . . for you."

For me? She could no longer imagine he had intended it as a kindness, but even if he had, it little mattered. The results would be cruel nonetheless. "Did you not realize that by revealing yourself, you would expose me?"

"Harold Bessmer and I were at school together. I had considered that a sort of advantage. I imagined I could . . . persuade him to do the right thing." He paused. "The *Widow* Fairfax was a perfect stranger to him—still is, I don't doubt. But unfortunately, he remembered all too well what *Lady* Fairfax, my wife, did three years ago."

She resumed walking, as if she could escape the simple logic of his explanation. "Well, now Mrs. Kittery knows, and soon the whole village will have heard what I am believed to have done. By tomorrow morning there will be nothing for me in Haverhythe but cold faces and cutting words." She meant never again to suffer that fate—and never to subject her daughter to it, either.

"I know." His long fingers curled around her elbow, slowing her agitated steps. "Gaffard told me what he had heard, and I guessed what must have happened. Please believe that was never my intent. I'm sorry."

She froze upon hearing the unexpected apology. "What happens now?"

She had asked the same question once before—would he give the same answer?

"I have been thinking all day about the best thing to do. I had almost determined to leave you here—to leave you in 'peace', as you asked." Despite herself, Sarah gasped. Was that still what she wanted? "But even before I knew what Mrs. Kittery had done," he continued, tucking her arm in his and walking as he spoke, "I had come to the conclusion that Haverhythe is no place for Clarissa." He paused, but she could not determine if uncertainty or reluctance halted his speech. "Nor for you, it seems. I thought, perhaps, you might be more comfortable in Hampshire . . . ?"

"At Lynscombe?" she whispered. They were nearly to the back door of Primrose Cottage.

His chin lifted in a cautious nod.

She very nearly forgot to breathe. Was he really offering to take her and Clarissa to his family home? To accept his child?

What would be her own role in this new arrangement?

"And," she began, unsure how to ask what she wanted to know. "Would I . . . that is, would we . . ."

He opened his mouth to speak, as if he anticipated her question. But before the words could pass his lips, he stumbled in the near-darkness of the alley. With the toe of his boot, he pushed some large, heavy object into the open so that it could be identified.

The brass banding of her traveling trunk gleamed in the starlight. St. John let out his breath in a low whistle. "Well, well, what have we here? I guess Harold Bessmer isn't the biggest fool in Haverhythe after all." He turned to face her, and in the moonlight, his eyes were as pale as seaglass. "Were you expecting my offer, ma'am, or has someone else made you a better one?" When she did not answer, he shoved the trunk against the wall with a muttered oath and moved closer to her still. "Tell me, Sarah, is there somewhere else you'd rather be?"

Fear licked along her spine. "I did not mean—I was angry and frightened, and I—"

"And you were going to run away, just as you did before," he finished. She could feel the heat of his body through the thin muslin of her gown. "Do you know, for the briefest of moments, I imagined I had caught a glimpse of the woman you really were—generous, creative, loyal. I actually feared I had misjudged you," he confessed with a wry shake of his head. "But now I remember why I was so reluctant to believe in you." Tossing up a hand, he brushed her aside.

"Well, go then. Do as you please, Sarah." He began to make his way back down the alley.

She would survive this. She had survived starting over once before, although she did not think she could have, had it not been for her daughter.

Then he spoke the words that she had dreaded hearing from the start.

"But Clarissa comes with me."

The tongue of fear became teeth. Raw, ragged pain tore through Sarah's heart, like nothing she had ever felt before. She scurried to catch up to him, stretching out a hand to claw at his coat sleeve. "No!" she pleaded. "You can't take her away from me."

His steps faltered only slightly. "I can, and I will."

He was right, of course—or at least, within his rights. The law gave women no say in what happened to their children, especially not women who had been accused of crimes.

And keeping a nobleman from his child was the one crime of which Sarah was actually guilty.

"You claim she is mine," he said, looking down at her, his gaze pitiless. "Did you imagine that once I knew of her existence, I would allow her to grow up in Primrose Cottage, to live out her life in Haverhythe, never knowing the truth?"

No.

But a part of her had hoped.

Then again, was it right to condemn the daughter of a nobleman to a life of penury in some obscure fishing village? She had been determined to do whatever it took to keep her child, but that did not mean she had never wondered how it would feel someday to watch a beautiful young woman who might have been the toast of the *ton* instead marry Bertie Thomas or one of the Mackey boys and then walk the quay at night, dreaming of something better.

Sarah shook her head.

"What I propose will be best for her," St. John concluded, in a voice that did not invite challenge.

"How can it be best for her to be separated from her mother?" She was teetering on the brink of hysteria, but she managed somehow to keep herself from screeching, knowing that her neighbors could hear every word.

She could have sworn that he flinched at her words, but when he replied, his voice was as cool as it had ever been. "Your actions have decided the matter," he said.

He had kept his promise to her about the festival. He had asked for nothing in return.

But now the day of reckoning had come.

Curling her fingers against his arm, she recalled Fanny Kittery's bitter accusations. Despite her new dress, she felt dirty and tattered. There was no use fighting with him any longer. She could not stay in Haverhythe. She could not surrender her daughter. What choice did she have?

"Please," she whispered. "Take me with you."

Chapter 16

"I can't believe it, Mrs. F. I never thought I'd see the day that I'd finally get a look at what's beyond Haverhythe—and in Lord Haverty's coach and four at that, with Lieutenant Fairfax for an outrider." Emily Dawlish turned shining eyes away from the window only long enough to smile at Sarah, and then turned right around again.

"I don't wish to seem unwelcoming, Emily," Sarah began. And, indeed, she was very glad of the company and the help on this awful journey. "But how is it that Lieutenant Fairfax came to ask you to join us?"

Emily pulled herself from the lure of the passing landscape at last, and her place at the window was quickly taken by Clarissa. "Well, last night, after the festival, I come across the lieutenant walkin' up-along. He seemed out o' sorts. Angry. A cold kind of anger—gave me a chill just to look at him, you know?"

Sarah nodded. She was quite familiar with the expression.

"Still, he asked after me all the same, polite as always. Truth be told, I was in a right huff, too, and I guess I was so distracted I started natterin' away, told him that *some* folks think I'm too green to understand the way the world works, too young to know my own mind—my own heart."

"Who could have said such a thing to you, Emily?" Sarah's first guess was the girl's mother, whose resentment of her daughter's gifts was sometimes thinly veiled. But something about the flush high along Emily's cheekbones made Sarah think that this time the hard words had been someone else's, that some man had at last succeeded in turning the beautiful young seamstress's head—while his own remained unbowed. Poor Emily.

"Oh, don't you mind about that now, mum. I didn't really think Lieutenant Fairfax was listenin' to me rattle on, either. But then he stops me and says, 'Miss Dawlish'—not 'Miss Emily,' but 'Miss Dawlish,' right proper, like—'Miss Dawlish, you've given me an idea.' Well, I didn't see how that could be, but I says, 'Yes, sir?' And he tells me that somethin' important had happened, and he was leaving Haverhythe first thing to go on a long journey. On his way to ask his lordship for the use of the carriage, he were. But he'd been worryin' what to do with the wee one. 'If you, Miss Dawlish,' he says, 'was willing to come along, it would solve a problem, it would. The girl would like to have a familiar face by.'" Emily dipped her chin toward Clarissa. "'And it'd give you a chance to see a bit more o' the world, besides.'"

There was something almost amusing about hearing St. John's precise aristocratic voice filtered through Emily Dawlish.

But Sarah did not smile. "So here you are," she said. Had he hired Emily as nursemaid because he feared Sarah would not see out the trip to its end?

"Aye, here I am." Emily ran one cautious, curious hand over the plush carriage seat. "Then the lieutenant told me to get along home, and I began to think it were all a grand joke. But first thing this morning, afore the sun was even up, a footman from Haverty Court come a'knockin' on the door and told me to follow him! Carried my bag and everythin'!"

"Ah. How thoughtful."

"Did he come for your things, too, mum?" she asked, eyes bright and unsuspecting.

"No. Lieutenant Fairfax was, er, kind enough to carry my trunk himself," Sarah confessed, remembering the way he had hoisted the trunk to his shoulder in the alleyway last night and walked off toward the Blue Herring without a backward glance. She had taken it for the answer to her plea.

Suddenly exhausted, she leaned back against the squabs and closed her eyes, feeling as if she had made this journey once before—three years past, to be precise. Then, too, she had wondered and worried what lay at the end of the road.

What had made St. John relent and agree to bring her along? She supposed he meant to divorce her, as he had suggested on the night of his arrival. By removing her from Haverhythe, he ensured that the coming war would be waged in a theater of his own choosing, with friends and family arrayed for battle on his side.

A divorce would scar them both, but for her the scars would be permanent. She must resign herself to living out her life despised and despising. Perhaps alone. Certainly lonely.

And what of her child? Would he keep Clarissa with him, accept her as his own? Or would he shunt her aside, leave her with some caretaker—Emily Dawlish, perhaps?

She had allowed herself to imagine that the years had changed him. But this was the familiar coldness, the familiar heartlessness, she had come to expect from him. She could have persuaded herself that the intimacies they had shared in the watchman's hut were only another of her foolish dreams, if she had ever known enough to dream of such a thing.

Hours later, she felt the carriage slow as they approached an inn, and Clarissa squealed when St. John cantered into view on a dapple-gray gelding.

"Look, Mama! Sijin!"

"What's that?" Emily asked, peering over her shoulder.

"My husband," Sarah explained with a nod as he cantered past. She felt vaguely resentful of the fact that her attention had been drawn to his figure on horseback. "*St. John* is his given name."

Emily's eyes grew wide. "Why, I never heard the like, Miss Clarissa. Why don't you call him Pa?"

Clarissa turned and gave a questioning look. "Pa?"

It was beyond the child's understanding, of course. Some of her playfellows had fathers. Others did not. That was simply the way it was. Susan Kittery had once innocently asked after Clarissa's papa and been told by her mother, in both Clarissa and Sarah's hearing, that Mr. Fairfax—if, indeed, there had ever been such a person—had likely been a scoundrel. Sarah had said nothing to contradict her.

But she realized now that she could maintain her silence no longer. Emily deserved to know something of the history of the woman to whom she had connected herself. She deserved to know where she was headed.

And Clarissa deserved to know her father.

Sarah cleared her throat softly. "I believe, Emily, there are a few things I should tell you before we reach the inn."

* * *

When he opened the carriage door, he was caught full in the chest by a curly-haired cannonball weighing all of two stone, and he leaned backward in surprise.

But it was not until she spoke that he almost lost his balance.

"Papa!" Clarissa shouted, clutching his neck and babbling about his horse, the carriage horses, all the horses in the inn yard.

He ought to have expected it, he supposed. The child could hardly go on calling him by his Christian name. And there was a joy he had not anticipated in hearing Clarissa call him "Papa."

But the joy he felt was accompanied by a curious sort of pressure in his chest that was almost, but not quite, pain. Would taking her away from Haverhythe really protect either of them from heartache?

Miss Dawlish exited next, ducking her head and dipping into a curtsy so low she nearly toppled into the muck. "Yer honor," she mumbled.

So, his days as "Lieutenant Fairfax" were over. Well, he could not say he was sorry. It had been a foolish, dangerous game to play, and he was lucky to have escaped with only a few more scars than he'd started with.

Finally, Sarah passed through the carriage door, without touching his hand or meeting his eye.

"I've arranged for rooms for the night, and a meal of some sort," he told her. "But, as it won't be ready for another half an hour, I propose we take a walk into the village." He gestured them away from the bustle of the inn yard. "Clarissa must be tired of being cooped up."

"Oh, aye," Emily Dawlish eagerly agreed, taking Clarissa by the hand. "An' I'm dyin' to stretch my legs."

With obvious reluctance, Sarah took his offered arm and they set off toward the village green. "It was kind of you to suggest a stroll. It is always hard on children to be confined," she said after a moment, nodding toward Clarissa, who had gamboled ahead with Miss Dawlish and was now spinning circles on the green until she collapsed in a dizzy, laughing heap. "But you needn't walk with us, after riding all day," she added, releasing his arm.

She clearly intended it as a dismissal, but St. John walked on beside her nonetheless. After another stretch of silence, she spoke again, but it seemed she had decided to move beyond mere pleasantries. "How long is it since you were last at Lynscombe, my lord?"

"More than fifteen years," he replied without hesitation.

He could not see her expression, as her face was hidden from his gaze by the brim of her bonnet. But her surprise was evident in her voice. "So long as that? I wonder you wish to return now."

Truth be told, he did not. His feelings for Lynscombe were . . . well, he imagined they were not unlike the memories inspired by the items Sarah kept in that trunk of hers. Precious and painful all at once. He would rather keep them locked away entirely.

"I passed a happy childhood there, ma'am." *Or part of one.* "Clarissa will, I hope, do the same."

"And will I—?" He heard again the convincing catch in her voice, the same sound that had captured his ear that night on the quay. "Will I be permitted to share any of it with her?"

He stopped walking. "Is that your wish?"

"Oh, yes. It is." The slightest hesitation. "But will you—?"

"I shall return to London as soon as you both are settled at Lynscombe."

Although she was no longer touching him, he could feel the tension ebb from Sarah's body. "For how long, my lord?"

He answered her whisper with firmness. "Forever, ma'am. My family owns several houses. I see no particular need for us to share one. So, as we have been doing for the past three years, I shall live my life and you may live yours—in Hampshire, if it suits you. Lady Clarissa Sutliffe, however, will remain at Lynscombe until it is time for her to enter Society."

It was not the offer he had been on the verge of making just last night.

Twice now, fate had intervened and prevented him from making a rash mistake where Sarah was concerned. Three years past, just as he had begun to realize that she was not at all the sort of woman he had imagined his father would choose for him, had begun to feel some spark of interest in her, had begun to suspect—no, fear—that he could care for her, she had been found in the arms of another man and then disappeared in a cloud of scandal. And he had been glad of the reprieve.

The past week had shown him he was still not out of danger, however. There was something undeniably attractive to him about the woman he had discovered in Haverhythe—her extraordinary musical gift, her concern for the people of the village, her fierce love for her daughter. It suggested a deeply passionate nature of the sort he could never have imagined in the woman he had married. And for a moment, he had allowed himself to be drawn to that passion. Like a moth to the flame.

Fortunately, he had stumbled over her trunk in the alley behind Primrose Cottage before he could suggest that they try to make something of their marriage. She had been going to leave him without a word, disappear again, just as she had once before.

He ought to have been relieved by the discovery. While she might not be a thief, she still was not to be trusted. If he had allowed himself to grow closer to her or the child, he inevitably would have been hurt.

Yet he could not fairly describe what he felt now as *relief*.

He heard Sarah's lips part, heard her quick intake of breath. At first, though, no words came. Finally, she said, "You do not intend to petition for a divorce, then."

"Do you mean to present me with the requisite proof?" he asked coldly.

"You refer to the gems, I suppose," she said, glancing up at him at last.

"Or something else." Knowing her eyes were upon him, he allowed his gaze to travel across the darkening green and come to rest on the child.

Out of the corner of his eye, he saw her head bow. "No, my lord."

"Then it seems I have little choice. Ours will not be the first marriage lived separately, nor the last, I'll wager."

"I suppose not," she agreed, a note of something very like sorrow in her voice. "And you will not . . . wish for an heir?"

He stiffened. Everywhere, God help him. "If such a need becomes pressing, rest assured, my lady: You will be the first to know."

Emily Dawlish chose that moment to take Clarissa's hand and begin their ascent of the grassy slope. Seizing the opportunity, St. John gave a brusque bow. "I trust you will find the arrangements at the inn to your satisfaction. We leave again at first light," he said, as he turned and walked away.

Chapter 17

He had not anticipated having to face a welcoming party when they arrived at Lynscombe Manor. Heavy with exhaustion, he wanted nothing more than to disappear into his rooms until he had had a chance to take stock of his situation and his surroundings.

But that, it seemed, was not to be.

"Fairfax!" His stepmother's girlish voice rang out against the lofty ceiling and marble-tiled floors of the entry hall. "Really, my dear, it's taken an age for you to arrive."

He had written to tell her of his plan to go on to Hampshire from Devonshire, but he had no notion she would take it for an invitation to join him. "It was not at all necessary for you to come, ma'am," he replied as he handed his coat and hat to Jarrell, the butler. "I know how you feel about the country."

"But your father simply insisted."

St. John rocked back on his heels, his flight to the stairway arrested. "Father is here?"

"Oh yes." Her eager nod set the lace on her cap aflutter. "When I told him of your letter, he was determined to meet you here."

He did not want to be fussed at by his stepmother.

And he most assuredly did not want to speak to his father.

Before he could escape, however, his father came striding from the back of the house, sporting hunting boots and a long drab duster. "Here at last, are you, Fairfax?" When his pale eyes fell on Sarah and Clarissa, they betrayed no surprise. St. John wondered how much his stepmother had revealed—and how near it came to the truth.

"Welcome to Lynscombe, Lady Fairfax," he said, stepping toward her and stretching out his hands for hers. "And this must be . . ."

"Clarissa," Sarah supplied. Her lips were pressed into a tight line, as if to seal off words that demanded to be spoken, but really, what more could be said?

His father dropped to one knee to inspect the child, his eyes scanning the tiny face in the same desperate search for some familiar feature that St. John had already undertaken. Followed, no doubt, by the same disappointment.

But at the sight of Clarissa's curly locks and violet eyes, his father seemed to breathe a sigh of relief. "Welcome to you, too, my dear."

Clarissa made a shy curtsy while still clutching Emily Dawlish's hand.

"Jarrell," his stepmother ordered the butler, "have the child and her things taken to the nursery."

"Yes, milady," the white-haired retainer said with a bow. Apparently deciding that Sarah and Emily were among Clarissa's "things," Jarrell ushered them all toward the servants' stairs in the rear.

St. John opened his mouth to correct the error, but his stepmother prevented him. "I'm so glad you're here, Fairfax," she said, threading her arm through his. "You know I dread ennui above all things, and Estley has some silly notion of staying for weeks—"

"Thought it might be nice to shoot my own birds for a change," his father interjected.

"And he insisted I come, too. Really, what could be duller? But thankfully Miss Harrington offered to accompany me," she added, with a rather uncertain-looking smile.

"Eliza is here?"

"At Wyldewood," she explained. "But I'm sure she'll be here every chance she has."

He nodded. Lord Harrington's estate was only a few miles away.

When the departing footsteps of Sarah, Emily, and Clarissa had faded, his father cut short their conversation. "We need to talk. My study, Fairfax."

The old resistance to his father's control flared sharply in St. John's chest. But it was a conversation that could not be avoided. After a moment's hesitation, he followed his father down the corridor, although he certainly had not forgotten the way, despite the time that had elapsed.

The Marquess of Estley's study was a purely masculine preserve of heavy furniture and dark wainscot. A shaft of fading afternoon sunlight sliced through a crystal decanter on the desktop but had otherwise little success in piercing the gloom.

He associated the place most with the punishments he had sometimes had to face, when Jarrell could not cover up his misdeeds or his mother's indulgence could not prevail. Stepping over the threshold, he felt as if he were stepping back in time, as if Father's summons had the power to transform him into a lonely, powerless boy once again.

They stood with the desk between them while his father lit a lamp, the flame flaring up from below to cast shadows beneath his eyes that made him look suddenly older, sadder. To his shock, his father lifted the decanter and sloshed a measure of brandy into two glasses. He handed one to his son as he motioned him into a chair and then perched on the edge of his desk, raising his own glass in a sort of salute.

"Welcome home, Fairfax," he said and drank.

Coming from his father, the words bordered on effusive. But then Lynscombe was the only place where St. John had ever felt any sense of closeness to the man. Over the years, the distance between them had grown insurmountable—so wide that even the breadth of the Atlantic had mattered very little.

When he said nothing in reply, his father asked, "Well?"

St. John hesitated, contemplating how best to approach his father's question, wondering what traps lay hidden beneath its treacherous breadth. "I hardly know where to begin, sir," he said at last.

"At the beginning, if you please."

Although he was sorely tempted to begin with his father's insistence that he marry a fortune—or perhaps even further back, with his father's decision to marry a spendthrift, he thought better of it. "Your wife has, I hope, told you where I have been, and perhaps even why."

"The story about how she was blackmailed into helping Lady Fairfax escape to some fishing village in Devonshire, you mean? Yes, she did." He cleared his throat gruffly. "With some, ah, encouragement. And did you find the Sutliffe sapphires there?"

"No, Father," he confessed with a shake of his head, pushing away the unwelcome memory of Sarah's sad, searching eyes as she passed him the key to her nearly empty trunk. "I did not. In fact, I have begun to doubt they were ever in her possession."

"I can't say as I'm surprised," his father interjected. "I always suspected that soldier chap, myself. But Amelia would have it that Sarah was the guilty party." He paused to take another swallow of brandy. "Well, blackmail or no, what matters now is that you've found your wife, and the damage done by these little . . . adventures can be repaired."

St. John swirled the liquid in his glass but did not taste it. "I shall do my best. Despite the uncertainty surrounding Clarissa," he ventured, "I have determined to accept her as my own."

A momentary frown of surprise creased the space between his father's brows. "Uncertainty?"

"About her parentage. No man could feel certain after seeing what I had seen—what we all saw—that night." He shook his head, trying to dispel the memory of Sarah in another man's arms. "And you must agree that the decision to keep the child's birth a secret bodes ill for my wife's fidelity."

"My God," his father whispered, almost to himself. "Can it be that you don't remember? I forget that your dear mother must be little more than a shadow to you now."

His *dear* mother? The woman his father had replaced in a matter of months? St. John thumped his glass onto the corner of the desk. "I assure you *I* have not forgotten her."

His father rose and walked toward a tapestry that adorned the wall opposite the desk. "I did not mean you had forgotten *her*. But from what you've said, you cannot, I think, remember *this*," he explained, pushing aside the tapestry with a surprisingly unsteady hand.

Behind the curtain hung a small portrait he could not recall ever having seen. Although the occasion for the painting no doubt had been to celebrate the birth of the child, the heir, the new mother clearly had captivated the artist's attention. She was seated in the center, the hems of her gown puddled at her feet, her slender arms wrapped lovingly around her infant son.

Around him.

The image of his mother he carried in his heart and in his head had faded and blurred with the passing of time. In the years since her death, he had seen no other picture, had imagined them all destroyed by a man determined to erase her memory from his life.

Her smile was demure but her cheeks were rosy, the perfect complement to the riot of brownish-blond curls piled high on her head.

He could swear his mother's tinkling laugh and gentle touch flooded over him, along with a wave of guilt that anything about her could ever have been forgotten.

Especially, of course, the mischievous sparkle in her remarkable violet eyes.

Clarissa's eyes.

It was all the proof of her parentage Society would require. And as for his own need for certainty? Well, a part of him had known the truth all along. But if the revelation did not shock, it did not precisely bring comfort, either.

"That beautiful little girl of yours will have you wrapped around her finger soon enough," his father cautioned, an unaccustomed sentimentality warming his voice. "Love of a child makes a man do foolish things, my boy."

St. John bristled. "What would you know about loving a child, Father?" He felt little compunction at flinging those sharp words at last, and less satisfaction in seeing them hit their mark.

A stony silence followed, broken only when his father asked, "Why did you come here?"

"I might just as easily enquire what kept you away," St. John snapped back. "It seemed to me a suitable place to raise a—*my* child."

"You mean to stay, then."

"No. I cannot." Taking up his glass again, he traced the faceted edges with his fingertip. "My wife may be innocent of the particular crimes of which she was accused three years ago, but I find that we are still quite—incompatible. It will be best for all parties if we continue to live separately. Sarah will stay here with Clarissa. I shall return to town."

"Unthinkable," his father said, washing down the assertion with the remaining contents of his glass, sounding once more like the man St. John remembered.

"That is not for you to say."

"Tell me, Fairfax," he asked after a long silent moment, his pale eyes focused on the empty glass in his hand, "how much of the village did you see on your arrival?"

St. John started at the abrupt change of subject. "None at all. I came on horseback, through the western meadow."

"Well, in the morning, go for an early ride—around the estate, through the town." He lifted the decanter, gesturing with it. "Then tell me again how you intend to dispose of Lady Fairfax."

"What has she to do with this?" St. John demanded.

His father gave a bitter laugh. "Everything."

"May I have your assurance that my wife's dowry has not all been squandered?" The words squeezed their way past his clenched jaw.

The heavy crystal decanter met the polished desktop with a *thud*. "You, my dear boy, are about to reap what you sowed. In your arrogance—your *disobedience*—you left me to negotiate the marriage settlements. Pevensey was a shrewd bird. Wanted to make sure his daughter was well taken care of. Arranged to portion out her dowry over a period of years."

The sudden sweat on St. John's palms nearly caused the glass to slip from his grasp. "Does she know?"

"Pevensey refused to tell her. Seems she had some silly notion of a love match." He let out a breath and shook his head, as if in despair of such foolishness. "This was his way of letting her think she'd got what she wanted. A fortune, to be delivered on condition of her happiness."

"Happiness?" The tightness in St. John's chest grew to an ache. "And how was such a thing to be measured?"

"He seemed to believe it would be ensured if you lived under the same roof. I tried to persuade him that, in my experience, such an arrangement was rather more likely to have the opposite effect, but he would have his way. And since the world thought Lady Fairfax dead and gone—and her happiness in such a state being impossible to determine," his father added snidely, "not one penny has been received."

At last St. John took a gulp of brandy, which burned its way down his throat with none of the comforting warmth of Mad Martha's ill-gotten cognac.

"But now," his father continued, "all can be set right, my boy, if you keep your wife right by your side. Closer, in fact," he said, leaning toward his son. "For there's a bonus for an heir. Pevensey liked to imagine himself the grandfather of a future marquess."

St. John dropped his eyes to the floor, refusing to meet his father's gaze.

"I've already written to the man. He'll be eager to see his daughter again—why, he's probably on his way here now," his father spoke over his shoulder as he moved to leave the room. "Let's hope he brings his purse."

When the door latch clicked into place and he was at last alone, St. John allowed his whole body to sag, wishing he could trust his trembling hand to lift the glass to his lips again.

He did not know how long he sat in his father's study, only that the lamp was low and the room otherwise dark by the time he rose to his feet and left the half-empty glass on the desktop.

In the corridor, he found Jarrell. "Ah, there you are, my lord," the man said. "Lady Estley asked me to tell you that dinner will be served in the family parlor in half an hour. I've taken the liberty of having your things put in the rose room."

The marquess's suite? Why wasn't his father sleeping there, as he had when St. John was a boy?

"Thank you, Jarrell. And have some hot water sent up, please," he added with a frown at his travel-stained clothes.

"Of course, sir."

When he entered the bedchamber, he found a fire burning brightly in the hearth—a ridiculous extravagance surely ordered by his stepmother because he had complained once in her hearing that three years in the West Indies had thinned his blood. Peeling off his greatcoat, he tossed it onto the bed and then opened a window to cool the overheated room, pausing to look down on the gardens that filled the angle between the wings of the L-shaped house. Beyond that, where the sky grew hazy, lay the English Channel.

After his father had expelled him from Lynscombe—for so it had seemed at the time—St. John had spent remarkably little time wondering how it got on, imagining, in the way a boy will, that all would continue to be as it had always been. So long as his allowance had been timely, he had had no cause to consider its source.

Certainly his time in the West Indies, where nearly every plantation was owned by an absentee and left in the hands of an overseer, ought to have taught him to see things differently. The lives of the laborers, the care of the land—everything had depended on the character of that one man, and he had quickly learned how few men were worthy of such trust.

By tradition, a marquessate was a border land, entrusted by the Crown for defense against all invaders. But scarcity had nonetheless found a way to invade Lynscombe. And the Marquess of Estley, despite his oath, had done nothing to stop it.

Nothing, that is, but to make a deal with the devil—in the guise of Richard Pevensey.

St. John was, when all was said and done, still a prisoner to his father's poor choices.

When he turned away from the view, he saw that his coat had slid off the bed and onto the floor. As he bent to retrieve it, the contents of one pocket spilled out: a rock polished smooth by the tide and a misshapen lump of bluebell soap. Clarissa's prizes, acquired the day of the festival in Haverhythe.

He had forgotten how children accumulated treasures, had forgotten somewhere along the way how the love of a child could turn an insignificant object into something truly valuable.

Snatching them from the carpet, he weighed both items on his palm before placing the stone on his bedside table. Then, as his restless, pacing feet carried him out of his room, he tossed the remnants of Fanny Kittery's soap into the fire.

Without conscious thought, he found himself in the elegant sitting room that separated the suite's two bedchambers. Gold cut-velvet draperies framed a pair of tall windows overlooking the back gardens. A camel-backed settee and two chairs in the French style were arranged before a marble fireplace. Near one window was a piecrust table with a shining silver tea service atop it; by the other stood a splendid pianoforte. All was in spotless readiness for the mistress of the house.

Seeing no light beneath the door opposite, he steeled himself and entered the bedroom that had been his mother's.

It was a scene out of some lurid gothic tale. He drew in a sharp, quick breath, and the mustiness of disuse stung his nostrils. Ghostly holland covers still draped across every surface. No window had been opened to freshen the air. No fire had been lit to drive away the damp.

He felt unaccountably disappointed. But what—or whom—had he expected to find there?

Closing the door, he returned to his bedchamber. The soap crackled and hissed on the fire as its oils fed the flame. The warm air was now redolent of bluebells. Muttering under his breath, he disappeared into his dressing room.

"I beg your pardon, my lord?"

Jarrell looked up from pouring a ewer of steaming water into the washbasin. When St. John made no reply, the butler finished arranging items on the washstand and began to busy himself with unpacking a trunk of clothes that must have been brought down from London. "The household is a bit short on menservants just now, so I thought it would be best if I assisted you personally," Jarrell said.

Having been without a valet for so long, St. John considered that, too, a ridiculous extravagance.

"Jarrell," he said, flicking open his razor and shaving carefully over his scar, "where is Lady Fairfax?" Even here, her scent was heavy on the air.

"My lord?" Jarrell paused in his unpacking and raised quizzical white eyebrows.

"Lady Fairfax. My wife."

"My lord, I had no notion there *was* a Lady Fairfax."

"She arrived with me this afternoon." At Jarrell's blank look, he added, "The woman in black." Sarah had been dressed in mourning the day they had left Haverhythe, and the bright sprigged muslin had given no sign of reappearing.

The butler dropped his eyes to the carpet. Jarrell had known St. John too long to be obsequious. This was genuine embarrassment. "I put her upstairs, in the nursery. I took her for the governess."

"Ah." He would not be surprised if she was content to stay there. And perhaps he would be more content if she did.

"I'll have the situation rectified straightaway, my lord," said Jarrell, handing St. John a towel and moving toward the door.

"Jarrell, wait—"

The elderly butler had been at his post too many years to reveal anything like surprise. His face impassive, he stopped and stood, ready to receive the young master's orders.

Was it possible to love a place? Perhaps. If a man were capable of feeling love.

St. John had been away from Lynscombe for almost twenty years, unwillingly at first, it was true, but quite deliberately at the last. He had told himself time and time again that he cared nothing about it. Lynscombe was not yet his responsibility, and God willing, would not be for quite some time.

Still, he had married a fortune to save it—and he knew, deep within himself, in the place some fool might be tempted to call his heart, that it had not been the act of an indifferent man to do so.

Just as dueling David Brice had not been the act of an indifferent man.

He had been ready enough then to believe his wife a liar and a thief. It had been a very convenient brick in the wall he had been determined to erect between himself and the woman he had never wanted to marry. But the mortar had always been rather flimsy stuff, and a few days in Haverhythe had eroded it badly. Now, half an hour in Father's study had knocked what remained of it to the ground.

He could not very well suggest that the Viscountess Fairfax remain in the nursery permanently. Every excuse he had had for keeping her at arm's length was gone. But to bring Sarah to the rose suite, to know she was sleeping just a few feet away, when as many miles would not be enough to . . .

"My lord?" Jarrell prompted.

St. John shook off his ruminations. "It grows late, Jarrell. And she will wish to see our daughter properly settled. Tomorrow will be soon enough."

"Very good, sir."

If the butler found such an arrangement strange, he did not show it as he finished his task, helping St. John into a fresh shirt and then smoothing the shoulders of his coat over it. "May I say, my lord," he said when he at last turned to leave, "we are all very glad to have the family at home once more. Like old times, it is," he said with an expression of satisfaction on his face that bordered on a smile.

St. John gave a curt nod of acknowledgment.

Perhaps his father had exaggerated the desperation of the situation. He would, as suggested, take an early ride, inspect the estate for himself. Then, when he saw that things were really not so bad, he would be within his rights to return to London, as he had planned, and do whatever he must to forget everything, and everyone, he left behind.

Chapter 18

Sarah's pen hovered above the square of watercolor paper—not proper writing paper, but the only paper she had been able to find in a search of the three attic rooms that made up the nursery. Or at least, the only paper that had not been emblazoned with the Sutliffe coat of arms.

A drop of ink hung suspended from the quill's sharp tip, threatening to blot the effort of hours. She had been working on the letter—well, two letters—since before the first pink blush of dawn had provided sufficient light to write by.

The first, to Abigail Norris, had come more easily, but only because she had pretended to be writing to a perfect stranger. The gossip would have spread through Haverhythe by now, of course, but Sarah refused to allow herself to think about Abby's reaction when she learned the gossip was true.

She had labored over the second letter, but still had managed to produce only a few sentences. Casting her eyes over the words one final time, she at last admitted to herself she could think of nothing else to say—or no better way to say what had to be said. Across the middle of the page, she wrote, "*Your loving daughter, Sarah,*" and put the pen aside. Finding no sealing wax in the small desk where she sat, she pushed herself out of her chair, drew her ragged woolen shawl around her shoulders, and walked across what must once have been the governess's room to the windows overlooking the front of the house.

Her gaze traveled across a parterre garden and down a long sweep of lawn. The village, far below, was almost entirely obscured by a carefully placed planting of trees. But what she had seen of it yesterday afternoon was still vivid in her memory.

At first, only a few dilapidated fishermen's huts had marred the coastal scenery. Those were a common enough sight and might be easily explained away. But when they soon gave way to dusty streets, abandoned shop fronts, and unkempt houses, the only explanations she could find offered no comfort. She had understood her marriage was to make life better for someone, even if it had not been her.

Dull eyes had followed the carriage's progress through the village of Lynscombe, seemingly drawn more by the movement than by curiosity. Shuffling along the street, a young woman had struggled beneath the weight of the bundle of rags she was carrying—no, a child, Sarah had realized with no small amount of shock. The church, with a gaping hole in its slate-tiled roof, looked as if a strong storm off the Channel would topple it. In the yard of an inn called the Red Lion, according to a sign that had faded to a rather sickly shade of pink, aimless young men clustered. She wondered that they had not fallen prey to the wiles of some conscription officer luring them with the king's shilling.

During the whole of their journey through the village, she had been unable to pull herself away from the carriage window. Now, however, she turned from the memory with a shiver and walked across the corridor to the vacant playroom. Thanks to the light from another row of high, narrow windows, these facing the gardens at the back of the house, the space was bright. But oddly quiet. Clarissa was still asleep, exhausted by their travels, and Emily had risen not long ago and gone downstairs to fetch breakfast. When they had arrived, not a toy had been in sight, but Clarissa had moved with a child's unerring instinct to the wall of cupboards. In the blink of an eye, she had emptied them of the set of blocks, army of toy soldiers, and cricket ball and bat now littering the floor.

Sinking to her knees in the middle of the room, Sarah slowly began to restore order to the space, although she knew the gesture to be a futile stay against the forces of chaos that would awaken soon enough. Absently, she arranged the jumble of wooden soldiers into orderly ranks, wondering as she did so whether St. John had been the last child to play with them.

She wanted to despise him for his coldness. But a part of her could not help but pity the lonely child he must have been, growing up in this house that seemed a world apart from the one that surrounded it.

She had not seen him since their arrival, when her attention had at first been taken up entirely by Lynscombe Manor, that monument to generations of Sutliffe prosperity, its elegant, symmetrical façade of Portland stone a shimmering pearl against the earthy, autumnal landscape.

The disparity between the house and the village below had pierced her heart. The Marquess of Estley, it seemed, was no better than the Earl of Haverty.

Her thumb rubbed across one of the soldiers' painted faces, worn away by time and a child's affection.

It remained to be seen whether his son would be any different.

Once inside the house, she had expected St. John's father to thunder at him, at her. But when Lord Estley had at last broken the silence, Sarah realized her error. There would be no raised voices, ever. The marquess spoke with a quiet authority that was far more chilling.

No one who met the two men could fail to be struck by the resemblance between them. When she had first met St. John and his father, she had taken girlish pride in the knowledge that her handsome soon-to-be husband would only grow more handsome with age. But until yesterday, she had never before realized how much St. John hated the resemblance. Perhaps he always had—she did not know.

Something about the unaccustomed sag of St. John's shoulders in his father's presence had given her the sense that the battle he was about to engage had its roots far in the past, long before Sarah had entered his life.

What story had St. John's father been told about her long absence and sudden reemergence into their lives? And what had been his reaction to it? He had bid her and Clarissa welcome to Lynscombe, but she could not help but wonder whether the warm greeting would soon be retracted.

Lost in her thoughts, she almost did not hear the nursery door swing open behind her.

"Do you need help with the tray?" she called over one shoulder, thinking Emily had returned.

"I beg your pardon, ma'am." A strapping young footman blushed to the edges of his powdered wig and bowed. "I was sent to fetch down your trunk."

"My trunk?" Sarah echoed, her eyes darting to the other room, where it sat.

"Yes, ma'am."

"But who—why—?" She scrambled to it, but not before the footman had bent to hoist it to his shoulder.

"Just following Mr. Jarrell's orders," he answered her partially formed questions as he strode through the doorway to leave.

The butler might be a footman's highest authority. But *his* orders had come from someone higher yet—someone in the family—Lord Estley. Was she being sent away at the first possible opportunity, ripped unceremoniously from her daughter?

Tears stinging her eyes, she groped her way blindly out the door, emerging into the corridor just in time to see where the footman had gone. She raced after him, down one, perhaps two, sets of stairs, through a maze of corridors and doorways, into another part of the house entirely. When he disappeared around a corner, she followed, not looking where she was going. One shoulder struck a wall, nearly knocking her off her feet.

And then the wall reached out and stilled her, steadied her, and she knew it for her husband.

"Running away again, Sarah?"

Caught by his arm, pinned against his length, she felt the words as much as heard them, the way they rumbled in his chest and stirred the wisps of hair at her ear.

"No, I—*yes*," she insisted, trying to break free. "My trunk!"

His eyes followed the footman as he opened a door and passed through it. "You needn't concern yourself with your luggage, ma'am," he insisted, setting her back on her feet. "Your things are merely being moved to more comfortable accommodations. Rooms better suited to the Viscountess Fairfax."

"The Viscountess Fairfax?" she echoed uncertainly.

"You may have found ways to avoid the title in Haverhythe, Sarah," he said, casting a disparaging glance over her black dress, "but I assure you that in Lynscombe you must expect to hear it often. And to suit your behavior to its worth."

Sarah straightened her spine. "When, my lord, have I ever done otherwise?"

The flick of a crop against his palm made her flinch. He was dressed for riding, she realized when she finally allowed her eyes to focus on him. Correction, he had just returned from a ride. Mud speckled his boots, sweat dampened his hair. And the subtly exotic scent of his cologne was now tempered with heat and horse. He had risen early, ridden hard by the look of things, and was returning to his chambers to freshen up before breakfast.

His chambers. The Viscount Fairfax's chambers. Which must be very near to . . .

She glanced at the door through which the footman had vanished with her trunk.

Oh.

She could not hide her blush, but it did not seem to matter, for he was not looking at her. His pale eyes were locked on his hands. Yet she sensed, somehow, that his own thoughts were traveling the same ground as hers.

"Do you ride, ma'am?" he asked after an awkward moment.

"No, my lord. Papa called it a country pursuit."

Another snap of leather against flesh. "Very well, then. We shall walk." And without another word, he set off down the corridor, in the opposite direction from which Sarah had come.

With a tug on her shawl to pull it into place around her shoulders, she followed.

Avoiding her gaze, he set off around the corner of the house, marching through the frostbitten remains of what had once been a formal garden, and into unkempt wilderness. His eyes sought and found a once-familiar path, although it was now so overgrown as to be almost invisible. Behind him, he could hear the sounds of Sarah's stumbling footsteps and labored breaths. With a muttered oath, he slowed and offered her his arm.

Still, they did not speak.

After a few moments, they crested the small bluff overlooking the English Channel. Here, only a few scrub trees, those strong enough to withstand the salt air, dotted the landscape. He stood beside her, listening to the seabirds and studying the seemingly random pattern of waves as they built, next upon last, each erasing evidence of what had come before it, like cherished dreams swept away by haunting memories.

He did not know why he had invited her—perhaps *ordered* would be a better word—to walk with him. What he needed was a moment's peace, something time spent with Sarah was unlikely to offer. Something his morning ride had certainly not provided.

It had been a far cry from his recollection of the place. But he knew his boyhood memory could not be trusted. Perhaps in truth, Lynscombe had not changed in the slightest since he had seen it last. Perhaps it had always been run-down and neglected and in need of capital to shore it up.

Well, he had it in his power to change things now.

For better or worse.

Thirty thousand pounds would allow mortgages to be paid, repairs to be done, improvements to be made, and then some. He could save Lynscombe, if he agreed to resurrect his marriage. If he were willing to play along with Pevensey's scheme and tell his wife he could not bear to be separated from her after all.

But that way, he was quite sure, lay madness. If a few days together had weakened his resistance, what might a month do? Or a year?

Experience had taught him that not caring at all was far preferable to caring too much. And he did not want to care—about Lynscombe, Clarissa, any of it. Especially not Sarah.

He did not *want* to care, but it was growing more and more difficult to deny that he *did*.

When he dragged a shuddering breath through his nostrils, she darted a glance at him. "Whatever it is you have to tell me, my lord, it cannot be worse than your silence."

"Are you certain of that, my lady?" he shot back.

"No."

Her voice was so soft that if he had not been looking at her, he would not have known that she had spoken. He walked a few steps farther. "The path continues along this ridge and goes down to the water," he explained, indicating a well-worn trail cut from the limestone, which led down to a sheltered stretch of the strand. From the cliff's edge, they could watch the incoming tide carve out rivers and islands among the sand. A dark line along the chalky face of the bluff marked high water, when the little spit of beachhead would disappear entirely. "Once the favored haunt of a little boy who fancied himself a pirate."

Cautiously, she craned her neck to peer down to the beach and shivered. "It is difficult to imagine you playing here. Growing up here."

"It was the only home I knew until I was almost ten years old."

"When your mother died," she ventured, more certainty than question in her voice.

He wanted no one's pity. Certainly not Sarah's. "Yes. Father married the present Lady Estley soon afterward—too soon, some might say," he acknowledged, striving to sound matter-of-fact. "My stepmother preferred—prefers—London and Sutliffe House at all seasons. And my father has been content to indulge her. Once upon a time, I imagined . . ." He slashed at the heavy beard of a stalk of grass with his crop, scattering its seeds to the wind. "Clearly, he cares nothing for this place."

"Perhaps there is another explanation for his absence." She paused. "Forgive me for asking this, but did your mother die here?"

"She did." After so many years, the wound ought to have healed, but beneath Sarah's prodding it still felt achingly raw. "She fell down the nursery stairs after coming to the schoolroom to listen to my lessons one morning. Her neck was broken," he said, pushing out the words over the sound of Sarah's gasp of horror. "And—and the child she had been carrying was lost, too. I knew nothing of that at the time, of course."

"Your father's grief must have been terrible."

"Grief, ma'am?" he scoffed.

"Is it not possible that your father left because he could not bear to stay in the place where she had been?" she pressed. "Perhaps by leaving he hoped to escape his grief . . . and his guilt."

He recalled his father's trembling hand as it drew back the tapestry that reserved his late wife's youthful beauty for his eyes alone. Thought of his father's choice not to occupy the suite of rooms he had once shared with St. John's mother. Grief? Guilt? He thrust those memories aside. "You are determined to persist in this delusion that one's past can be outrun."

"No," she demurred. "Although certainly one may be tempted to try."

"A grieving man would have observed a decent period of mourning," he insisted, his voice rising in spite of himself. "A grieving man would not have married the first silly female who threw herself into his path, and then ordered his son to call her 'Mama.' "

"He might have," she countered gently. "Grief has been known to drive men to madness. I can well imagine a father hoping to allay a young child's anguish in just the way you describe—flawed though the means undoubtedly would be."

"I assure you, he disdains such weakness."

Come, come, Fairfax, you are nearly a man. And men do not cry.

"Yes, of course." She paused. "Most men do."

He wanted to ask what she meant by that remark, but he feared he already knew. Another heavy silence fell between them, masked by the sound of wind and waves. Turning his gaze back to the water, he said at last, "I could never have believed, when I was a boy here, that I would one day grow up to see a pirate in the flesh."

"In the West Indies." The words were mumbled, as if her lips had suddenly gone numb. Antigua and Lynscombe were now tangled together for him in ways he was not sure he could explain. But Sarah seemed to need no explanation. "It changed you, that place."

"Yes," he agreed reluctantly. "The place. And the people."

When he had first arrived at Harper's Hill, Edward Cary had looked him up and down with considerable doubt, his eyes lighting on the angry-looking wound that ran down St. John's cheek, still red from the fiery sear of Brice's blade where it had opened his flesh, the sting and tug of sheep's gut where Murray's needle had closed it again.

"Have you any skills we need here?"

"No," St. John had been forced to confess. *"But I—I do not require much in the way of wages. I simply need—"*

"Occupation?" Cary had supplied the word with a knowing look.

"Yes."

Much later, when St. John had announced his intention to return to England, Cary had studied his face a long moment, his eyes lingering over the thin, white scar, the most obvious outward sign of the man he had been nearly three years past. *"Whatever it was that sent you here, I'm glad of it,"* Cary had said. *"But whatever it is that calls you home now, remember what you've seen, what you know. Remember the difference one man can make."*

A movement at the corner of his gaze jerked him back to the present. Sarah was knotting her ungloved fingers in the fringe of her shawl. "In all those years serving as a—clerk," she said, laying skeptical emphasis on the word he had once used to describe his work there, "you must have learned a great deal about the management of people, of land, of money. Perhaps some of that could be put to use here." He could see that the tips of her fingers were turning blue where the threads of yarn cut into her flesh and prevented the flow of blood. "You are seven and twenty now," she pointed out hesitantly, as if she expected him to dispute the number. "Perhaps it is time to come to terms with what will one day be yours. Perhaps it is time to persuade your father you can do more—"

"More than what, Lady Fairfax?" he snapped. She spoke only the truth, after all. But he did not want to hear it. "More than bed an heiress?"

She jerked away from his words as if struck. Dislodged by her step, a handful of small stones skittered and scampered their way down to the beach. Instinctively, his long fingers met around her upper arm.

"Be careful, Sarah," he cried, dragging her hard against his chest, pulling her to safety—although he felt in considerably more danger himself with her in his arms. Their hearts thumped in unison, an uncomfortably intimate rhythm. "You might have—" His voice rough with fear, he could not bring himself to finish the sentence. Alarm flared in her eyes as they flicked from his hand to the rocks below.

With the salty wind tangling her hair, she reminded him of the way she had looked that night on the quay at Haverhythe, terror and passion warring in her aspect.

Once he released her arm, she scuttled away from the cliff's edge, back to the relative security of the footpath. Before he could speak, apologize, explain, she darted off in the direction of the house.

What exactly had he brought her out here to say?

If he had declared a change of heart where their marriage was concerned, would she have welcomed his declaration? Or even believed it? Three years past, he had made no secret of the fact he had not wanted this marriage. And she had tried to run away from it herself—more than once.

Which told the true story of her feelings about him: the trunk stashed in the lane, awaiting a chance at escape? Or the much-handled miniature hidden inside it?

With a shake of his head, he followed her, deliberately holding himself a few yards behind, swiping at the undergrowth with his riding crop as he passed.

He was beginning to know his own heart, but until he felt more certain of hers, it would be far wiser to hold his tongue.

When he reached the manor, Sarah was nowhere in sight. A smart gig stood on the drive. As its driver descended, the hems of a set of bronze skirts peeped into view, followed by the toe of a delicate ankle boot. The brim of a jaunty hat. And a cascade of fire-red curls.

"Eliza!" he called, stepping forward to offer his hand. "How good to see a friendly face." He was sorely in need of someone who would not fuss or scold or shatter his defenses.

"Ah, Fairfax." She smiled. "Just back from your morning ride?" she asked, as her emerald eyes flickered over him.

He glanced down at his disheveled kit, almost surprised to find himself still wearing it. Long, scraggly blades of grass clogged the fringed tip of his crop. "Something like that," he concurred, thrusting it behind his back.

"Lady Estley was most insistent I arrive first thing," she said as they approached the house. "She is planning a party this evening to celebrate your return. Supper and cards. With all the most important local personages," she added, an acerbic little smile curving her lips.

He laughed. "A small party, then. Well, you are welcome at Lynscombe, Eliza. Whatever the circumstances." At the bottom step, he paused. "Do you know?" He did not add the words "about my wife." He could see by her expression he did not need to.

"Lady Estley was kind enough to share the shocking discovery with me. Three years spent in hiding, doing God knows what with God knows whom, a child born in the interim . . ." She broke off with a theatrical shudder.

"Have a care, Eliza," he warned. Their friendship gave her a great deal of license, but she must understand how things stood now. "You are speaking of Lady Fairfax."

"*Lady Fairfax*," she echoed. "Never say you've come to care for that shopkeeper's daughter you married? After all she's done? Why, even before the first scandal broke, you swore to me you never could."

"Pevensey is hardly a—" he began. But his feeble protest was arrested by her searching green eyes.

As she studied his expression, her own shifted slightly. Before he could read it, however, she had recovered and something like a smile quirked her lips. "Apparently, I would have done well to remember that promises are like piecrust. Easily broken."

At the top of the steps, Jarrell opened the door as if on cue. "Good morning, sir. Ma'am," he said, bowing them through. "I put the other guests in the green receiving room."

"Guests?" The word echoed in the empty hall.

The butler inclined his head again. "Mr. and Mrs. Richard Pevensey arrived not half an hour past, my lord."

Chapter 19

S arah flew up the wide central staircase to the first floor. If her head had not already been reeling from the strange encounter on the cliff, certainly the butler's announcement would have sent her into a spin. She paused only long enough to allow a footman to open the set of double doors, then entered the large and impressive room behind them.

Before an imposing marble mantelpiece in the center of an elegant green and gold room stood a middle-aged couple in traveling clothes. They grasped hands and turned as one toward the sound of her entry.

The woman came forward first, her brown hair streaked with gray as it had not been three years back. "Sarah?" she whispered, one tentative hand extended toward her daughter.

"Oh, Mama." Sarah tangled their fingers together and pulled her mother down to the nearest sofa, fearful her legs would not support her.

With a soft sigh, Mama held their joined hands in her lap and patted Sarah's absently, her eyes searching her daughter's face as if trying to assure herself this was not some fevered vision.

In his characteristically energetic fashion, Papa paced, his movement stirring the draperies. "And where have you been hiding yourself all this time, my girl?" he scolded.

"I have been living in a fishing village on the northern coast of Devonshire."

"So close?" her mother whispered.

Sarah's eyes dropped closed, as if they still felt the strain of looking out over the water, searching for some glimpse of Bristol in the haze on the horizon. "So close." When she was more composed, she met her father's gaze once again. "I told the people there I was a widow," she explained, plucking at her skirt.

"On what did you live?" Her mother gasped.

"I gave lessons on the pianoforte to some of the children in the village," Sarah answered, lifting her chin as she spoke, refusing to be an object of pity. "It was not much, but I was very careful with what I earned. I boarded with the widow of a fisherman. I lived simply. I made do."

Papa paused. "That's all very well and good, my dear, but really . . . three years?" His voice was sharp with annoyance. "I don't see how you could allow your mama to worry so. You know the state of her health."

"I do," Sarah acknowledged. Mama's health had been a source of concern for as long as Sarah could remember, although no ailment had ever been specified. She thought even now that her mother did not look as bad as she might have—fatigued by the journey, of course, and older, but not exactly ill. "I'm sorry, Papa. I thought it would be best if I left—that it would spare you some of the pain, some of the scandal."

Papa looked skeptical. "Still, to let us go on believing you had died—?"

She felt a twinge of guilt but pushed it down. She had decided to go, yes. But she had also been driven to do it. "I am sorry that you were hurt, sorry that you worried needlessly for me. But perhaps if I had seen even a glimmer of that concern on the night of the nuptial ball, I would not have felt that I had to leave."

Mama withdrew her hand and Papa said reproachfully, "What could we have done?"

She was accustomed to thinking of her mother as easily cowed. After all, Papa was a big man—tall, barrel chested, with a voice to match, and despite his tailor's efforts to smooth those rough merchant-class edges, they insisted on wearing through. Mama rarely did anything to invite his wrath. Certainly Sarah had never thought of her father as weak.

Until now.

When she looked at him, Sarah could only see his misguided sense of his own inferiority to men like the Marquess of Estley. "You might have believed in me. You might have come to my defense," she replied quietly.

"We thought you dead," her father reminded her. Mama gave a quiet sob and raised a handkerchief—a black-bordered handkerchief,

Sarah noted with a pang—to one eye. Papa stepped to his wife's side and patted her shoulder as a sort of silent reprimand of his daughter.

"But before that?" Sarah plunged ahead, biting back her sympathy—sympathy no one seemed willing to extend to her. "Did you really think I had stolen the sapphires?"

"That old necklace? Of course not." Papa sounded astonished. "Who could think such a thing? But it seemed quite likely that you had been duped by the one who did steal it."

Mama nodded gravely. "The situation with the officer had a very bad look to it. Anyone might be forgiven for thinking that you—that you and he—had . . ." She blushed and looked away.

"How could you believe it of me?" Sarah whispered. Neither one answered. "Well, I had *not*," she asserted, on her dignity. "But it was perfectly clear to me that everyone believed I had. So I left."

Sarah waited. Surely there were more words to be said after so many years. But for a long, painfully silent interval, none seemed to come. At last Mama rose and wandered around the room, studying its features. "All that is in the past," she said at last with what could only be described as a sense of relief, as if some long-disrupted order had finally been restored. "You've returned now, Sarah. You are where I always imagined you would be—the mistress of a nobleman's estate. The Viscountess Fairfax."

"Yes, my dream come true," she agreed, fighting to keep the sardonic edge from her voice. "After a fashion."

"What do you mean, 'after a fashion'?" Papa demanded.

"Lord Fairfax intends shortly to return to London to live. Alone."

Mama recoiled. Papa frowned. "Nonsense."

"I assure you, he does."

"Having seen the state of things here, my dear, I daresay he has discovered he cannot afford to."

Sarah had no notion how much it would cost to maintain their separate households. "Surely the family will not have run through the whole of my dowry," she reminded them.

"Your dowry?" Papa's lips twitched in a half smile.

"Yes. Thirty thousand pounds ought to—"

"Why, yes, I daresay it would," he interrupted. "If, that is, Lord Fairfax had much more than the *promise* of those thirty thousand pounds."

"What do you mean, Papa?" Her pulse leapt. "Did not my husband receive my dowry when we wed?"

"He might have, if not for your mama's stroke of cleverness just as my solicitors were drafting the settlements."

Mama, who had strolled across the room to examine some piece of bric-a-brac on a corner shelf, smiled without looking up.

How many times had she begged her mother to intercede when her father had grown stubborn about his plan to secure a title for his daughter? Now it seemed that she'd been in favor of marrying Sarah off all along. "What did you do, Mama?"

Mama replaced the china *objet* and made her way back to Sarah. "I knew you were apprehensive about this marriage, my dear. So I did what I could to encourage the growth of your husband's affections—to ensure that you would not be shunted aside." Sarah frowned her incomprehension. "I simply suggested that the money might be given out over a number of years, rather than all at once—with the proviso that the payments continued only as long as you and your husband lived under the same roof."

No. Sarah mouthed the word, but no sound came from her lips.

"I ought to have been more specific, I suppose." Mama gestured toward the windows and the rural landscape beyond. "I certainly did not mean for you to be shut up in the middle of nowhere."

"Lord Fairfax knew of this . . . stipulation?" Sarah forced the words past suddenly dry lips. That would certainly explain why he had found it prudent to keep her from falling to her death.

Papa shrugged. "I cannot say what he knew when you married. He seemed in rather a hurry to sign. But Lord Estley assured me in his letter that his son would be made to understand the implications of the arrangement."

"I'm sure he realizes he cannot afford to separate from you now, dear, despite any—lapses in judgment on your part," her mother reassured her.

Until that moment, Sarah had not realized a part of her, deep inside, had still been dreaming—dreaming of a fairy-tale resolution to the dilemma she faced, one in which her husband recognized her worth and reaffirmed their bond.

Until that moment, she had not fully understood why wiser heads frequently counseled, "Be careful what you wish for."

Would the handful of days she had now spent with her husband count for anything, or must they first make up for the thousand or so spent apart? She had no notion of the formula to be used for such calculations.

Thankfully, a tap at the door prevented Sarah from having to form a response. "Come in," she called, wondering how much of her reunion with her parents had been heard through the door—and by whom.

Emily Dawlish entered the room and looked around uncertainly before locating Sarah on the sofa and offering a belated curtsy. "Mr. Jarrell come and said there were guests who'd be wantin' to see 'Rissa." Emily reached a hand behind her skirts and drew the girl forward.

Clarissa clutched Emily with one hand and twisted the other in her pinafore. "Mama?"

Sarah dropped to her knees and held open her arms. "I'm right here, dear one." Clarissa ran to her with a gleeful giggle. "And here are some people you don't know yet. This," she said, freeing one arm from Clarissa's embrace to gesture behind her, "is your grandmama. And this gentleman is your grandpapa."

She felt Clarissa's head tilt where it rested on her shoulder. Gathering her daughter in her arms, Sarah rose to her feet and turned back to face her parents. "Meet Lady Clarissa Sutliffe."

Clarissa twisted so that she could study the unfamiliar faces.

Mama reached out with trembling fingers to brush away a lock of Clarissa's golden-brown hair. "Oh, Sarah," she whispered.

"Well." Papa's chest swelled, his eyes only for his granddaughter. "Well," he said again.

Clarissa seemed to see an opportunity in his open admiration. "Bring present?" she asked, turning her wide violet eyes on him.

Sarah started to shake her head in admonishment, but Papa only chuckled. "What's that? A present for you, little one? I regret to say I did not think to—but that oversight shall be rectified first thing in the morning!"

A shy smile curled Clarissa's lips.

"I'll take her back to the nursery, shall I, mum?" Emily asked, stepping forward.

"Yes, please, Emily," Sarah agreed. "I'll be up as soon as we're finished here."

Papa's doting gaze followed Clarissa out the door. "A pity, though, that she was not a boy," he sighed when the door had latched behind them.

"Not at all," Mama insisted. "A girl is a blessing."

Sarah turned, something in her mother's tone rendering those words suspicious. "I do not disagree, Mama, but is there some reason in particular—?"

Her parents exchanged a glance. "I promised Estley another ten thousand on the birth of a son," her father explained, looking somewhat chagrined by his own conniving.

Sarah sagged onto the sofa, and her mother took up the spot beside her once again.

"Yes," Mama agreed, "and if Clarissa had been a boy, there might have been . . . questions. Now you've been given another chance, Sarah. He will want an heir." She leaned forward to brush her daughter's cheek with a cool, dry kiss and whispered, "Just take care not to conceive quite so quickly this time. Remember, dear, a gentleman never expects a lady to be eager for the marital bed. The longer he must wait for his son, the more time you have to secure him."

Sarah drew back from the unwelcome advice and began to pleat her skirts, trying to distract herself from the memory of St. John's touch. The heat of his body as it met hers.

The chill of the bed when he left it—left her—the moment the deed was done.

Recalling their exchange at the cliff's edge, she understood at last what he had been trying to tell her with those cutting words about bedding an heiress. Awakened to a sense of his obligations by his experiences in the West Indies, he had decided to return to Lynscombe, despite the pain returning obviously caused him. For the sake of his home and the people there, he would make the necessary sacrifices.

Starting with her.

A love match? She had indulged in a foolish fantasy years ago. She had been a child.

Now she had a child.

If she were free to act only for herself, as she had been three years ago, she could refuse to be his sacrificial lamb. But for Clarissa's sake, she would have to accept this marriage. And everything that came with it.

"Really, Sarah," her mother sighed with an affectionately disparaging shake of her head, reaching out to stay Sarah's nervous fingers. "Black does not suit you at all. When you send Fairfax the next payment, Richard, include a bit extra for your daughter's clothes. One hopes the village has a tolerable seamstress. But the fabrics must come from town, I think . . ."

What would Mama say if she knew what had become of the last set of fine gowns her father's money had purchased?

Sarah opened her mouth to protest, but her mother merely gripped her hands more firmly.

"Don't say no, dear. You've earned it."

Forcing her parted lips into something she hoped would pass for a smile, she bit back her reply.

Not yet. But I'm about to.

Chapter 20

Although Eliza had warned him of his stepmother's plan for an evening with the neighboring gentry, St. John had found it impossible to believe such an event would actually transpire until confronted by a roomful of guests.

When he entered the winter parlor—so called after a series of seasonal landscapes that filled the four walls, the largest of which depicted Lynscombe Manor at the bleakest time of year—his eyes quickly scanned the room, searching for familiar faces. His father and Lord Harrington made up half of one foursome. Eliza and his stepmother were cozied up together on the far side of the room, apart from the card players.

On the sofa against the wall, Sarah sat between her parents, the three of them forming a sturdier fortification against intruders than St. John had ever managed to construct. He wanted to go to her, but before he could persuade his feet to move in her direction, another face—this one framed by a tightly curled gray wig—inserted itself into his field of vision. "There you are, lad," the elderly man said. "How wonderful to see you home again."

"Dr. Quiller?" he said, summoning the name of the village rector from some far corner of his memory. "I did not think a soul would recognize me after so long away. How glad I am to find you still here."

Dr. Quiller laughed. "Still here? Where else would I go?" Abashed, St. John opened his mouth to attempt an explanation, but the older man shook his head. "Think nothing of it, my boy. But I was not so old when you first knew me as I must have seemed to you then. You remember Mrs. Quiller, I hope," he said, turning back to the table.

"Lord Fairfax," the rector's wife said with a warm smile.

"Squire Abernathy," Dr. Quiller said, gesturing to a portly gentleman who bowed his head. St. John recognized the name of the prosperous farmer who owned a rather desirable tract of land that divided Wyldewood from Lynscombe. "And my curate, Charles Pickard," he added, motioning toward the fourth seat. But it was empty, its occupant having seized the interruption as an opportunity to make his escape across the room.

St. John asked, "Will you meet my wife, sir?" Perhaps the presence of the clergyman would smooth his way.

"Your esteemed father was kind enough to make the introduction, lad. But I shall—"

"What's that?" Mrs. Quiller asked, cupping her ear.

"Lady Fairfax," explained the rector, more loudly.

"Oh, yes." She nodded eagerly. "Charming girl. We did not even realize you had taken a bride, Lord Fairfax," she exclaimed. "And some time ago, from the sound of it."

"One might have thought your marriage would be an occasion for the family to pay a visit to the village, my lord," opined Mr. Abernathy with a frown.

"I—" St. John began, searching for an excuse.

But Dr. Quiller saved him. "Allow me to walk with you and introduce my curate. If I did not know better, I would suspect Charley of trying to sweep your lovely bride off her feet," he teased, jostling St. John with his elbow.

He looked in the direction the rector had indicated with a wink and a nod. Mr. Pevensey had risen and given his place to the curate, who was speaking animatedly to Sarah. She was smiling and nodding eagerly at what he said, while her mother sat, ramrod-straight, disapproval in every line of her features.

"But Arthur, your hand?" his wife reminded, gesturing toward the abandoned card game.

He laughed good-naturedly. "I won't be a minute."

St. John nodded his head to the others at the table and gestured for Dr. Quiller to lead the way.

"Very glad we are to have the family here again. So much time, so much—but all that will change, now," Dr. Quiller said as they walked, brimming with confidence. Then he leaned closer and lowered his voice. "It has pained your father, I know, to come back over the years and see how things go on."

St. John nearly stumbled. "My father has been here? Not recently?"

"Oh, not so recently, I suppose." The rector looked thoughtful. "Call it six months, perhaps. He doesn't come often, nor stay too long. That's how I know the sight of the place gives him pain. But now all that will change," he repeated. "Eh, lad?"

They had reached the place where Sarah, Mrs. Pevensey, and the curate sat, sparing St. John from having to give an answer.

"Mr. Charles Pickard, my lord."

The dark-haired young man had risen as they approached and now bowed. "Lord Fairfax. A pleasure."

"Pickard. Mrs. Pevensey." St. John returned the bow and then offered another to his mother-in-law, who stood and curtsied without relaxing her posture one bit. "You have met Dr. Quiller, I understand," he said to Sarah, who had also got to her feet. "I suppose he told you he was once my tutor?" He did not know why he felt constantly compelled to revisit these childhood memories of Lynscombe in her presence.

"He did. What a pleasure it must be to see a former pupil all grown up," she said, smiling gently at the older man. "I recall my own teachers with such fondness, but I think they must often wonder if I ever managed to master the things they were so eager to teach."

"Such is the lot of a teacher, Lady Fairfax," Dr. Quiller replied with a knowing laugh. "But we have at least the consolation of knowing that there will ever be a next generation of pupils to care for."

"Speaking of . . ." Mr. Pickard began.

"Now, lad," Dr. Quiller admonished his curate, "there will be time enough for that later."

"Mr. Pickard was just telling me of his hope to establish a school in the village," Sarah explained.

"Nothing elaborate, my lord," Pickard assured him. "I do not cherish some foolish hope of making the sons and daughters of fishermen into scholars. Just reading and writing, arithmetic, some basic principles of domestic economy, perhaps."

"I suppose that sounds quite radical?" said Sarah, cutting St. John an uncertain glance.

Radical? Certainly many would call it so. But seeing the spark of enthusiasm in Sarah's eyes, he pushed his hesitation aside. "It seems to me quite a sensible plan, the sort responsible landowners might put into action in a great many villages throughout England."

"It would go better under the guiding hand of a lady," Pickard hinted.

"And sadly, Mrs. Quiller does not enjoy the health to undertake it," added the reverend.

St. John nodded his understanding. "Perhaps you can persuade Lady Fairfax to give her time to your cause."

"I would be honored to help, Mr. Pickard," she said with a side-long glance of suspicion toward St. John.

Although it scarcely seemed possible, Mrs. Pevensey stiffened further at her daughter's words and declared, "Lord Estley is unlikely to approve."

"I will speak with him," St. John said.

Immediately, he wished he could take the words back. How much ought he to offer, when he was not yet sure what Sarah would accept?

Satisfied, the curate allowed Dr. Quiller to usher him back to the card game, although St. John could have sworn the younger man muttered something under his breath about Mrs. Quiller being a sharp. Mrs. Pevensey unbent enough to join her husband in contemplating the springtime view of Lynscombe Manor on the nearest wall.

Left alone in the company of his wife, St. John was not certain what his next move ought to be. Jarrell had informed him that the Pevenseys had spent the better part of the day closeted with their daughter. No doubt Pevensey had told her, or reminded her, about the terms of her marriage settlement. If St. John said now that he meant to stay with her, she would assume he was doing it for the money. For the sake of Lynscombe. And she would not be entirely wrong.

Nor entirely right.

So instead he said nothing at all. Offering her his arm, they walked in silence together to greet the other guests and his father.

He could hardly believe what Dr. Quiller had said about the man's regular visits to Lynscombe. Before yesterday, he would have been more tempted to imagine the clergyman had lied than to believe his father capable of showing such attachment to the place.

But perhaps he had merely been guilty of attributing his own failings to another.

When they arrived at the second card table, the gentlemen stood for another round of introductions. "Mrs. Abernathy," said Lord Harrington, "and her eldest son, Philip." The young man blushed and made an awkward bow.

"Fairfax has been in the West Indies for quite some time, I understand," Mrs. Abernathy said as she gathered the cards to herself. "I did not know your family had dealings there. Did you travel with him, Lady Fairfax?"

"I did not."

The answer seemed to satisfy Mrs. Abernathy for the moment. "Can't say as I blame you. Have you been in London while he was gone, then?"

"I—I have been in the West Country," Sarah replied.

"With your parents." It was not a question, and no one in the little circle seemed inclined to correct Mrs. Abernathy's mistaken assumption.

"Well, your return has generated no little interest, Lady Fairfax," Lord Harrington assured her. "I'm sure we have you to thank for my daughter's sudden willingness to come down to the country. She is forever telling me that Wyldewood is dull as death."

"Oh, Papa," Eliza scolded with a laugh, rising from her seat and coming toward them. "You know Lady Estley was most insistent about me accompanying her."

St. John could not help but remember that his stepmother had described things the other way around.

"Really, what else could I do?" piped his stepmother insistently from the far corner. "I cannot bear to pass the day alone, and I knew I would be positively abandoned by my husband the moment we arrived."

"Perhaps Miss Harrington looks forward to the ball tomorrow night," suggested Squire Abernathy from the other table, tossing in his hand as he spoke. "I'm sure there's at least one young bachelor here who would be willing to go down the dance with her."

Interpreting his father's remark to apply to him, the spot-faced young Abernathy gave a squeak of alarm.

"A ball?" Eliza murmured. "How exciting!"

"Really more of a dance," the squire's wife amended as she plucked a card from her hand and laid it down. "In the assembly rooms above the Red Lion Inn. To celebrate the harvest, you know."

"The harvest dance," echoed St. John's father, looking thoughtful. "It was held here at the manor when I was a boy. Perhaps next year, it will be again," he suggested with a glance toward his son.

"*Here*, my lord?" his stepmother echoed in alarm. "Really, whom could one invite beyond the present company?"

"Surely, ma'am, our circle of acquaintance, even in the country, is somewhat larger?" his father suggested with one raised eyebrow.

"Of acquaintance, yes. But one must be careful with extending invitations to Lynscombe that imply a greater degree of intimacy with the family."

Mrs. Abernathy, who must have recognized her place on the fringe of his stepmother's vaunted circle, did not seem to know whether to nod or shake her head. Eliza's mouth quirked in an expression of amusement that was not quite a smile.

Dr. Quiller suggested a few families, but the names were met with pursed lips.

"Yes, yes. I am sure they are very fine people in their way," his stepmother acknowledged, "but I cannot imagine they would be comfortable in the ballroom here."

"A harvest ball should take place where all who had a hand in the harvest will feel welcome." Sarah spoke so quietly that at first no one seemed to realize from whence the words had come. All eyes came to rest on her. "But mightn't some members of the family attend the dance in the village?" she continued. "As a gesture of goodwill?"

Resounding silence met the suggestion. His stepmother's eyes were round with shock. Eliza swallowed a smirk before darting a glance of sympathetic incredulity toward him. The rest of the guests seemed to have developed a sudden interest in the fan of cards in front of them or the pattern of the Turkish carpet at their feet.

After a moment, his father said, "I am intrigued, Lady Fairfax. Go on."

"She spoke too hastily, my lord," Mr. Pevensey interjected, stepping forward. "She is remembering the frolics she used to have at the Christmas dances I hold for my clerks, that is all."

No, St. John wanted to say. He was certain Sarah was thinking of Haverhythe, the festival, his own words about the dance being held where all would enjoy it. He was less certain what to make of the connection, however. Was she also recalling their conversation about a landowner's obligations to his tenants? After what she had seen, she could no longer be naïve enough to imagine that an appearance at a village dance would make up for years of mistreatment.

Mrs. Pevensey hastily confirmed her husband's opinion. "Not the sort of entertainment to which your family is accustomed. Sarah must learn not to be so forward with her opinion," she said with a scolding frown for her daughter.

His father continued to regard Sarah with something like curiosity for a long, silent moment before saying, "I find it an excellent suggestion, Lady Fairfax. We shall all go," he proclaimed in that voice that brooked no opposition.

For a moment, everyone stood or sat in stunned silence.

Sarah pulled her hand free and smiled quietly to herself as she moved to examine the stark winter landscape that nearly filled one wall.

She knew the dance was a small thing, especially in comparison to a school. But they both represented necessary changes if things in Lynscombe were going to improve. The Sutliffe family might imagine her dowry was all that was needed to restore what had been lost through the neglect of generations. In her experience, however, it would require something more.

A bit of genuine concern for the people involved, as she had once told St. John.

In other words . . . *love*.

Still raw from the pain of leaving Haverhythe and its people, she did not know whether she was ready to open her heart again. In time, though, she could learn to love this place. Perhaps St. John would, too.

It was not exactly the love match of which she had once dreamed, a dream whose death she had spent most of the day mourning all over again.

But it was a life in which she could feel fulfilled—sometimes, perhaps, even happy.

In a world in which so many had so little, could she really ask for more?

And she would have a school! It had been her fondest wish to start one in Haverhythe, but a wish far beyond the limited means of *Mrs.* Fairfax. As *Lady* Fairfax, however, what could she not do? A marriage like hers might have its advantages, after all. She imagined little heads bowed over their lessons. Practical lessons, yes, of course. But she would make sure there was a space in the curriculum for music . . .

Behind her, snippets of conversation began to erupt around the room once again. The card games ended and the pairings broke up as all awaited the announcement of supper. Lord Estley, Lord Harrington, Squire Abernathy, and Dr. Quiller gathered at one end of the room to discuss the local sport; both St. John and her father stood near them, but neither joined that conversation nor started one of their own. Closer to the fire, poor, sweet Mr. Pickard's ear was being bent by young Philip Abernathy.

The ladies clustered near where she stood, at the opposite side of the room from the gentlemen. Pleading a headache brought on by the fatigue of travel, her mother decided to retire.

Lady Estley, who had not moved from her comfortable lair, drew Eliza down to her side on the horsehair sofa just wide enough for two.

"Sweet, dear?" the marchioness asked, proffering a tin of crystallized pineapple. "Fairfax brought them from Antigua," she added as Eliza chose. "They are delectable. I do wish he had brought me a little black page to serve them, though. I delight in those exotic touches."

Sarah bit her tongue as she spied Mrs. Quiller approaching her.

"I must say, my dear, I found your suggestion of having the family attend the harvest ball in the village most interesting," the rector's wife said in a low voice.

Or rather, in what she no doubt had intended as a low voice. But as Sarah had gradually realized over the course of the evening, Mrs. Quiller was quite hard of hearing, with the result that her attempted whisper carried easily to the other ladies.

Lady Estley drew in her breath in an audible gasp. "'Interesting'? I for one cannot imagine what could have inspired her to suggest that the chief family of this neighborhood would dance in the public rooms in the village."

"But you must admit, ma'am," Eliza said, "the balls in which Lady Fairfax is involved are always *interesting*." Seizing on the bewildered faces of Mrs. Abernathy and Mrs. Quiller, she dusted the sugar from her fingers and leaned forward as if to share a secret. Time had not dimmed the woman's flame-colored hair or the wicked sparkle in her eyes. "You see, at the last ball attended by Lady Fairfax, she was wearing the famed Sutliffe sapphires, and they simply . . . disappeared."

Mrs. Abernathy gasped. "Good gracious, Lady Fairfax! What happened to them?"

Turning her back on the picture, Sarah folded her hands behind her back so that no one could see her nervous fingers twisting in her skirts. "Unfortunately, ma'am, I do not know. Lady Estley seemed certain they were stolen."

Eliza sent Lady Estley a glance.

"Ten to one the clasp broke and you simply did not notice," Mrs. Quiller suggested with an encouraging nod, much to Lady Estley's amusement.

"Perhaps," Sarah acknowledged. "On that occasion, I was a trifle—"

"Disguised?" the marchioness supplied wryly.

Recalling the empty wineglass and her stumbling footsteps across the library floor, Sarah felt her face heat. "I was going to say *distressed*."

"Distressed?" scoffed her mother-in-law.

"You, who had just captured the *ton*'s most eligible bachelor? What on earth could have distressed you?" seconded Eliza.

The oft-relived memories pricked her consciousness with the sting of a needle: Eliza's whispered words in her husband's ear. Lord Estley's patent regret at the necessity of his son's having to marry so far beneath him. Lady Estley's assumption that Sarah had been too dull-witted to realize how she was disdained by everyone around her.

This time, however, Sarah pushed those memories aside. It was ridiculous to continue to fixate on things that had happened so long ago. Had nothing else of importance or interest occurred in the last three years?

That might be true for Eliza or Lady Estley, but thank God, Sarah could not say the same.

She had spent a great deal of the last few days contemplating how the passage of time had changed her husband. She had almost forgotten it had changed her, as well.

If she was really going to be *Lady* Fairfax again—with all the privileges, and all the sacrifices, the role entailed—she was going to need to bring a bit of *Mrs.* Fairfax's toughness to the part.

"Do you know, Miss Harrington," she declared with a shrug, "I simply cannot recall."

Eliza opened her mouth, but before her reply came, another voice interrupted.

"Lady Fairfax?"

Sarah turned and found the Marquess of Estley at her elbow, offering his escort to supper. With a lift of her chin and a smile for Eliza, she curtseyed and accepted his arm.

Chapter 21

Music was coming from the pianoforte in the sitting room adjacent to his bedchamber. A Mozart sonata. The piece suited the instrument's bright tone. It suited the player, too, with its precise rhythms and intricate patterns—staggering complexity in the guise of simplicity.

As the sound of Sarah's playing had done once before, it drew him to the door. For a long moment, he stood and listened before lifting his hand to the knob and entering the room.

Instantly, the music stopped. "My lord," she said as she pushed away from the instrument and rose, her quicksilver eyes darting over him. "I was not expecting you."

When the music began, he had been reading. Or, rather, thumbing idly through a stack of novels someone had left on the bedside. As soon as supper had ended, Sarah had left to look in on Clarissa. He had lingered—over port, over conversation, over any excuse he could find. Anything to keep him from the temptation of crossing the single room that now separated them and coming to her tonight.

Yet sleep had eluded them both, it seemed. Here he stood in his dressing gown and she clad only in a night rail, her feet bare, her unbound hair cascading over her shoulders.

Her chin lifted defiantly beneath his regard. "Though I might have guessed that an extra ten thousand pounds would recall you to your duty."

Duty. In the nights following their wedding, it had led him to her bed. What he felt now was not duty.

It was desire. A flame that had been kindled—*re*kindled—in an abandoned hut in Haverhythe. Despite his reputation for iciness, she had left him burning. And if he thought about that night for one second more, she would see exactly how much he still wanted her.

"No," he whispered, ruthlessly banking that fire, but still not daring to step closer. Nothing could happen between them until he felt certain it was also more than duty to her. "I came because of the music. Will you play once more?" he asked. "For me?"

At first he thought she meant to refuse. But after a moment she returned to the instrument and began an unfamiliar melody. He could not find the words to describe it—it was not beautiful, exactly. But forceful. Haunting. As changeful as the tides. All at once he realized that she was playing the music that had surrounded her in Primrose Cottage, the rhythms of the ocean just outside her door. And he knew it must be a piece of her own composition.

What other treasures did this woman contain? He longed for the key to unlock them all.

Everything he had been forced to imagine while eavesdropping on the Norris's doorstep, he could now observe firsthand: her bright eyes open but unseeing, never once glancing toward the keys, arched fingers that never stumbled, the graceful curve of her wrists and her neck, the soft flush of her cheek, the way her whole body became one with the music.

"You are an artist," he said when she paused.

Her hands collapsed onto the keys and sour notes echoed through the otherwise silent room. "*I* am the daughter of a Bristol merchant," she whispered, lifting her eyes at last to look at him. "Surely you had not forgotten, my lord. It mattered enough to you once."

"It did."

Dishonesty now would get him nowhere, and he could hardly deny the truth of her words. She had been chosen as his bride because of her father's money. And although he had complained bitterly about having to marry someone so far beneath him, a part of him had been grateful for the distance between them. He had imagined it would make it easier to hold himself apart. Not to want her. Not to care.

"It is not *all* that matters to me, however."

With a huff of humorless laughter, she trailed her fingers over the keys, sounding a few random notes. "No, of course not. There is also the matter of my being a jewel thief."

The words jarred him, pushing him forward. Even if he were afraid of what he felt, that was no excuse for acting a coward. He could not allow her to continue to take the blame for what had happened between them all those years ago.

"A successful jewel thief could have done better than that cheap black dress."

As the implication of his words settled over her, she stilled. "Surely you do not expect me to believe that something has persuaded you of my innocence?"

Hesitating only for a moment, he crossed the room to her side. "*You* persuaded me." When she would not meet his eye, he knelt on the floor beside the stool on which she sat. "And Primrose Cottage. Mrs. Potts and Mr. Beals. Susan Kittery's lessons on the pianoforte. A guilty woman would not have done all she could to better the lives of everyone around her." *Oh, if she would only look at him.* "To say nothing, of course, of Clarissa."

Her head jerked around and her eyes snapped to his. "What of Clarissa?"

"She looks very like my mother. I was reminded of that when I saw an old portrait here. But even before that moment," he hurried to assure her, "I knew she was mine." He lifted his hand beneath hers where it still lay against the keys, turning her slightly so he could lay her palm against his chest. "I felt it here."

Good God, how had she played so beautifully with fingers of ice?

"Forgive me, Sarah," he whispered, covering her hand with his. "Forgive me for believing the worst of you then. I was wrong."

"I ran—"

"I was the one who ran away," he spoke across her. "Not you. Whatever these last three years have been . . ."

Her fingers curled against the silk of his dressing gown, as if seeking warmth. "They were meant to be my punishment, I believe."

"Yes," he conceded with a wry smile. "I'm quite sure my stepmother never would have believed you if you had insisted that marriage to me was punishment enough." At her frown of incomprehension, he reminded her of her words. "That night on the quay. When I asked if you feared to face your punishment. You said that the thing you feared most was a life lived—"

"—without love. Yes, I did say that," she whispered, a note of wonder in her voice. "And you remembered."

"At any rate, I hope that life at Lynscombe will not be a punishment to you," he ventured. "You will have your daughter with you. And your music," he said, laying his other hand on the pianoforte case. "Whenever you wish it, without having to walk to the vicarage. Oh, and Pickard's school." He knew he had not imagined the light that flickered into her eyes with his reminder. "It is a scheme well-suited to your gifts—so well-suited, in fact, I regret not having been the one to think of it."

"Thank you," she replied warily. "But I do not wish to get my hopes up. My mother was right. Your father is unlikely to agree to it."

"He will," St. John declared, hoping he would not have to say anything more. But she only looked back at him expectantly, as if curious about the source of his confidence. "First thing tomorrow, I plan to meet with my father's steward and learn how things really stand. Have a look at the books, tour the estate, meet the farmers. And then, I will talk with my father." He hesitated. "I intend to ask him to give me the management of Lynscombe. My stepmother will wish to return to town before long, and I—well, it is time someone looked after this place."

Because Sarah was right. Despite the risk, he could not continue to hold himself apart from the people and places that mattered.

Her cool fingers slipped from his grasp. "So you mean to stay."

He liked to think that he was acting with his head, acting in the best interest of those whose lives would depend on him. But he could not claim to be acting *only* with his head. Other organs demanded to be involved in his decision-making of late.

Even, perhaps, his heart.

"Yes." The firmness in his voice surprised even him. "I will stay."

Turning her eyes downward, she picked out the notes of a melancholy-sounding chord. "I suppose the terms of our marriage settlement have left you little choice."

"Even in the most difficult circumstances, we still have choices, Sarah." Reaching for her with a hand he prayed would not tremble, he slid his fingers along her jaw, lifting her gaze to his. "I am making a choice." *A difficult one. A painful one. But the right one.* "The choice to come home."

Her eyes searched his for so long he felt scorched by the intensity of her scrutiny. Waiting for her to speak, he was instead shocked when she slid her hands up his chest, stretched onto her tiptoes, and kissed him.

In some remote part of his brain, he recalled his promise to himself. He ought to set her back on her feet and return to his room. He had said what he had come to say.

But God help him, he was not that strong.

He kissed her back.

She knew she had once again been forward. And quite possibly foolish. But if she had held his gaze just a moment longer, he might have kissed her. At least by kissing him first, she could tell herself afterward that this had happened because she wanted it.

And oh, how she wanted. Wanted to believe that he truly thought her innocent. Wanted to trust the look she had glimpsed in his eyes.

Wanted *him*.

Her hunger startled her, and really, what hope did she have of it being satisfied tonight—or ever? For the hunger she felt was not only physical.

Three years past, on her wedding night, she had known little more than her mother had told her, and Mama had said nothing of pleasure, of joy, of the way a man's touch could spin a moment of bliss into an eternity of peace and light. Sarah had gone to her marriage bed not knowing enough to be disappointed at her husband's coldness.

Now, however, she knew. Knew what he'd held back. Knew what she'd been denied.

After those wicked moments in the watchman's hut, she had wondered what it would be like to look back on that night, to remember his touch when it was gone from her. What could be worse than the memory of a pleasure that would be forever after denied to her? What could be worse than being forever alone?

But now she very much feared it might be worse to be together. To feel him inside her, and wonder whether he despised her.

To want him still, and despise herself.

Then St. John wrapped his arms around her, crowding out her doubts. In another moment, she had lost all track of where her kiss ended and his began. When she pressed against his heat, he groaned and lifted her higher. Only the tinkling protest of the pianoforte brought them momentarily to their senses.

With her arms wrapped around his neck and her legs clinging to his hips, he carried her into his bedchamber and sat her gently on the hearth rug before a crackling fire. Had he, too, felt the chill—of uncertainty, of anxiety—that seemed to have settled into her very bones? The welcome warmth of the fire eased her muscles, and she felt her spine bow in a pliant arc as he leaned his body over hers, bending her gently backward.

But that was not exactly what she wanted.

Settling her hands against his chest, she levered herself onto her knees without breaking the kiss. The new position gave her a certain advantage. Now she was as tall as he, perhaps even taller, and she could push back, lean her body against his, feel him bend, ever so slightly, to her will.

She did not want to be taken.

Tonight, she wanted to take.

Running her fingers over his broad shoulders, she pushed the dressing gown away, baring his chest. Far from resisting, St. John spread his hands on either side of her waist, one hand steadying her while the other cupped her breast. Her nipple stiffed at the insistent stroke of his broad thumb.

Sarah cast off every remaining shred of uncertainty and ran her hands across his skin, tracing the curve of his breastbone and threading through the dusting of hair there before sliding the pad of her thumb over the small, flat circle of his nipple, curious to know whether her touch could have a similar effect.

His slight gasp of surprise was all the confirmation she desired. Her hands slipped lower, feeling his muscles ripple beneath her touch. When her fingertips at last encountered the tie of his dressing gown, she stopped.

"Show me," she whispered, suddenly shy. "Show me how to touch you."

For answer, he groaned and lifted his hands to her face, tipping her mouth back to his for another searching kiss. "My God, Sarah," he breathed against her cheek, his voice a ragged whisper. "I wish you would not."

Stung by his rejection, Sarah withdrew her hands from his body and curled them in her lap.

Remember, dear, a gentleman never expects a lady to be eager for the marital bed.

Perhaps Mama had been right.

St. John's hands found hers, tangling with them, prying loose her fingers until he could stroke her palms with his thumbs. "Don't misunderstand me," he murmured against her ear. "I crave nothing so much as your touch." He drew one of her hands slowly toward him until it brushed the rigid length of his erection. Although the touch could hardly have surprised him, he shuddered and quickly lifted her hand away. "I've thought of little else since that night in the watchman's hut." She gasped as his tongue traced the shell of her ear. "Do you remember telling me that I would get no satisfaction in Haverhythe?" When he paused, she managed the slightest nod, and he continued in a voice that sent a shiver down her spine. "Tonight, I intend to have satisfaction, Sarah. And if you touch me now, I fear . . . well . . ."

She could not stifle the nervous laugh that rose to her lips as understanding dawned. "Oh."

Perhaps Mama had been wrong. About many things.

Tracing her jaw with his lips, he paused once again at her ear. "Let me touch you instead. Let me come inside you."

She felt she ought to blush at such words, but the heat that was spreading along her skin now had nothing to do with shame. Tugging her hands from his, she reached to unfasten her nightgown with trembling fingers.

"Let me," he murmured, plucking at the bow between her breasts and slipping the thin cambric over her shoulders. A sudden flare of heat and light swept over her when she was at last bare to his gaze, his eyes traveling leisurely over every inch of flesh his fingers had exposed.

As he spread his dressing gown over the hearth rug, she realized he intended to lie with her there before the fire. Ought she to allow such a wanton thing with a proper bed just a few feet away? The moment was too magical to disrupt.

Settling back onto the silk, she opened her arms to him, welcoming his weight and the feel of his skin against hers. Every sensation was new and sharp: the oddly pleasurable prickle of the wool rug beneath her back only slightly muted by his dressing gown, the hair of his chest that tickled and teased her aching breasts, the graze of slightly coarser hair against her inner thighs as he urged her legs apart with one of his own.

And all of it, all of it illuminated by the flickering light of the fire.

She watched, her fascination tinged with embarrassment, as his lips trailed over her collarbone and down to her breast, pausing to draw its peak between them and then suckling her firmly. A moan rose in her throat and her hips lifted, seemingly of their own volition, urging her mound against the hard muscle of his thigh.

Answering her wordless plea, St. John moved down her body, his lips following the edge of her rib cage, the curve of her waist, the rising slope of her belly. His tongue flickered into the indentation of her navel, a teasing promise of what was to come, and she gasped, wishing she had the courage to curl her fingers in his hair and coax his head lower still.

But that, it seemed, was not the particular pleasure he had in mind.

Leaning his weight on one arm, he slid the other along her side, forcing her hips back to the carpet and slipping his hand between their bodies, cupping her with his palm and pressing the heel of his hand against the ache his kisses had built.

"Is this what you need, Sarah? Or perhaps this?" One long finger ruffled her dark curls and slowly circled the opening to her body until she felt a rush of moisture and her hips began to rise again. "Ah, so many delights yet to learn," he whispered, watching his hand as he pleasured her.

In the fog of desire that had settled over her brain, she could not decide whether he imagined himself student or teacher. And then that circling finger slipped inside her, rendering her feeble question moot.

He was guiding her once more up that still-unfamiliar climb into madness. But the route he had chosen to take was so different that at first she did not recognize it. She was aware only of the pulse pounding between her thighs, the breath sawing in and out of her lungs, and the certainty that she was about to die.

And moments later, when St. John shifted his hand ever so slightly, she did.

His mouth swooped over hers, swallowing her cry of rapture, and before she had time to gather the scattered pieces of herself, he had kneeled between her spread thighs and entered her on one deep stroke, filling her.

As he slowly withdrew and prepared to thrust again, she instinctively canted her hips, meeting his powerful stroke. Once. Twice. "Oh, God, Sarah," he groaned, pinning her with his weight so that she could not move with him. A fine sheen of sweat formed across his brow as he strained to hold back the rushing tide. Then a frenzied volley of thrusts. His dressing gown slid across the carpet beneath them as he drove into her. She could hear his rough breath at her ear and the slick wetness of their coupling. And finally, she felt the remembered rush of heat at her core as his seed spilled into her.

He collapsed atop her with a self-deprecating laugh. "Shameful," he said when he had caught his breath. "Utterly shameful. But the next time will be better."

Next time?

But of course there would be a next time. He had announced his decision to stay in Lynscombe, and was that not what she had wanted, for him to assume responsibility for his inheritance, to show he had truly changed? And if they were to live together, a resumption of relations between them was inevitable; even without her father's terrible offer hanging over their heads, St. John would one day expect an heir.

Making love, people called it. She had let herself fly to him, holding nothing back. Not her body. Certainly not her heart.

It would be ridiculous to go on thinking of the joining of their bodies as a sacrifice or a punishment when it soon might give her another child—children, if the first was not a boy. And tonight, at least, it had also brought warmth. Intimacy. Pleasure.

Even if she could never have his heart, she could have this.

Only a fool would complain.

"Next time," he whispered as he rolled away and carried her with him, cradling her against his chest, "I will be all yours, to do with as you please."

"All mine?" Sarah nestled her cheek against his shoulder, hiding the tears that threatened to spill from her eyes. The temptation to hope was too strong. "Someday, I shall hold you to that promise."

When St. John awoke in his bed some hours later, he had no memory of how he had got there. The room was dark save the glow of the dying embers in the fireplace.

And something was tickling his thigh.

"Did I wake you?" Sarah asked, burrowing up from beneath the covers. "I'm sorry." Her expression was anything but contrite. "But you did say . . ."

He ran his hands over her shoulders, drawing her gently upward until he could capture her mouth with a searching kiss. "So I did." Then he lay back, closed his eyes, and allowed her to indulge her curiosity, grateful for this proof of her desire. "I'm in your hands."

Much to his surprise, she began by running her fingers through his hair and then tracing the contours of his face, along his brow, around his jaw, down his scar. When he tried to turn away from her scrutiny, she gave a *tsk* of displeasure. "It gives your face character," she insisted. "It reminds me of your bravery."

St. John smothered the scoffing laugh that rose to his lips.

"And your foolishness," she added, almost as if she had read his thoughts.

As she moved down his body, she stroked and then kissed everything within her reach, learning him in a way no other woman ever had.

Her passion was an unexpected gift. Not that he had seen no signs of it. It was there in her fierce devotion to her daughter, in the beautiful music that flowed from her fingertips, and even, he supposed, in the fury she had vented on him once or twice.

But he had never imagined that her explosiveness would extend to the bedchamber.

When her mouth reached his abdomen, her unbound hair once again tickled his groin. And then she paused. He felt her shift her weight and realized she was no longer touching him. Chancing a peek, he caught her studying his manhood with wonder-filled eyes as it grew and hardened beneath her gaze.

"Touch me," he breathed when he could stand it no longer, and then hastily added, "if you wish."

She reached out with tentative fingertips. In her uncertainty, she teased and tormented him—although he was sure she did not mean to—until he gave in to his own desperate need and showed her how to hold and stroke him. Closing his eyes again, he surrendered himself to the sensation of her touch.

And then he felt her lips on him *there*. The gentle kisses she was stringing along his hardened length were more sweet than sensual. Still, the feel of a woman's mouth on his cock had not been so frequent an experience that he had grown complacent about the sensation. Idly, he considered whether he ought to stop her. Surely a gentleman would not allow a lady to—

Then she took him into the wet heat of her mouth, and all thoughts of stopping her scattered on a deep groan.

Sarah looked up at him with anxious, uncertain eyes.

"Yes," he hissed in answer to her unspoken question. Twisting his fingers into her hair, he urged her back to her task in a most ungentlemanly fashion.

Fortunately, Sarah did not seem to mind.

What she lacked in technique she more than made up for with her enthusiasm, and in another moment, St. John was clawing the bedsheet in a desperate attempt to retain some measure of self-control. He had already tumbled her on the bloody hearth rug, for God's sake, demonstrating all the restraint of an untried schoolboy. And now this?

Nevertheless, it was almost all he could do to cup her shoulders and lift her mouth to his for a somewhat more conventional kiss.

"Was that—?" she asked hesitantly when they broke apart.

He laid one finger against her lips. "It was perfect. Too perfect."

Beneath his fingertip, her mouth curved into the most delicious pout. "But you said I might do as I pleased."

St. John could not argue with her logic. So he kissed her instead, reveling in her warm weight where she lay across his chest. He stroked his hand down the curve of her spine and over the swell of her buttocks. She was kneeling on the bed beside him, her bare bottom tipped upward so that she could return his kiss.

Dragging his mouth to her ear, he gave a whispered command. "Come on top of me," he urged as his fingertips dipped into the hollow at the top of her thighs.

Sarah shot him a skeptical, uncertain look, but she braced her hands against his shoulders and straddled his hips. "Like this?"

He shifted slightly, enough that the head of his cock nudged her damp curls.

Her eyes widened. "Oh."

Setting his hands on either side of her pelvis, he helped her slowly lower herself onto his shaft. "I think if you are to make your life in the country, Lady Fairfax, it is time you learned to ride," he teased when she was fully seated. "Are you ready to take the reins?"

She moved hesitantly at first, accustoming herself to the sensations produced by this new position. But in a matter of moments, her confidence grew. She built to a rhythm and her eyes began to look glazed.

He was determined to allow her to find her own pleasure, but that did not mean he could not offer a little assistance along the way. He lifted his head and caught one taut nipple between his lips; as he had expected, Sarah leaned forward to encourage him to suckle her more deeply and discovered, quite by happy accident, the difference a slight change in angle could make.

Sliding one hand over her hip and across her abdomen, he nestled his thumb over her clitoris and then bent his knees, deepening his penetration. But he waited until he was sure her climax was nearly upon her before lifting his hips to meet her downward thrust, filling her as she ground against him.

And she shattered, her whole body clenching around him as she cried out. He waited for the tension to ebb from her before gripping her hips and taking his final pleasure, muffling his own cry of surrender against her shoulder.

"So," he murmured at her ear a moment later, "how did you like your first lesson?"

Her answering laugh was distinctly short of breath. "You shall find me an eager pupil."

Suddenly, he realized why it was dangerous to allow a woman to filch the reins. He was going to have the devil's own time getting them back.

And he was going to enjoy every minute of the attempt.

Catching the bedcoverings in one hand, he drew them over their still-joined bodies. He searched his heart and his mind for some lingering traces of misgiving or doubt. But a new and more powerful emotion had swept them away.

He was falling in love with his wife.

And that, he was quite sure, was the most foolish—but perhaps also the bravest—thing he had ever done.

Chapter 22

"I do so regret being unable to attend the ball this evening," Sarah's mother said, plucking fretfully at the coverlet with long, slender fingers.

"Best not to tax yourself, Laura," insisted Papa. "You'll feel better for it in the morning."

"What a trial it is to have been cursed with such a delicate constitution."

From her position at the window overlooking the front of the house, Sarah spared only half an ear for their conversation. She was wondering how St. John's conversation with his father's steward had gone. And of course, the one with his father.

She was not sure when St. John had left her side that morning. Sunlight had been spilling across her pillow when she had awoken to the realization that she was alone in the big bed.

She had woken once before, when the light was still gray, to feel his body curled protectively around hers, like two spoons nested in a drawer. When she had snuggled closer, craving his warmth, she had also felt his arousal. Much to her surprise, he had loved her a third time, never speaking, just shifting her leg ever so slightly and entering her from behind. She had had no notion that such a thing was even possible.

He had promised it would get better. And he had been true to his word. This time, he had set a leisurely pace that allowed her to absorb every sensation—his shallow thrusts and gentle, searching fingers had brought her to climax twice before he had surrendered to his.

Heated by the memory, she leaned her forehead against the cool glass, hoping to hide her blush.

"Sarah!" Her mother fixed her with remarkably sharp eyes, for one supposedly so ill. "I hope you're feeling all right. Your color is high."

"Yes, Mama." What would her mother say if she knew how thoroughly her advice regarding the marital bed had been flouted? All day, Sarah had been conscious of a few unfamiliar—if not unpleasant—twinges. Her body still thrummed with unaccustomed sensations, while her mind tried to wrestle her heart's doubts into submission. "Everything is perfect."

"Well, you seem remarkably inattentive today. As I was saying, I hope no one will be offended by your wearing a day dress this evening. It seems ill-befitting the future Marchioness of Estley."

"Pray God, those duties will not be mine for years to come," Sarah said, glancing down at the blue-green silk she had kept packed away in her trunk all those years. She had never thought to have occasion to wear it again. "In any case," she continued, recalling the signs of abject poverty she had seen, the struggles the curate had described to her, "I cannot think lavish gowns will be expected in the country. The money required for them might better be spent assuaging real need."

"I daresay three years of back payment will go a long way toward improving that dumpy little village." Mama sighed, sounding as if she could not imagine a worse way for her daughter's dowry to be spent.

"Speaking of the village," Papa said, casting a glance toward his wife, who frowned and pursed her lips in disapproval, "when I went looking for a present for Clarissa this morning, I saw someone unexpected."

Sarah lifted her brows. "Oh, and who was that?"

"Captain Brice."

At the name, her pulse ratcheted upward, but its erratic beat said more of fear than the fascination others supposed she felt. "Are you certain?" she gasped.

"Perfectly," Papa replied. "I do not think I shall ever forget that face, for all that he looked a bit the worse for wear for his time among the French."

She could see from her parents' expressions that both were reliving the last time they had seen the handsome young officer. "What on earth would he be doing here, I wonder?" Mama asked with a pointed look, as if trying to divine something written on her daughter's face.

Sarah dropped her gaze to the floor and shook her head. "I have no notion, Mama. I have had no association with the man, and I would far rather hear nothing of him." Inwardly, she prayed her father was mistaken. And if he was not, perhaps the man's presence here was a mere coincidence.

But what business could a man like Captain Brice have in a place like Lynscombe?

"I should go," she said, turning from the window. "The carriage will be on the drive any minute, and I would not want to keep the others waiting."

"Certainly not," Mama agreed. "You will make our excuses to Lady Estley?"

"Of course."

"And tell Lord Estley who I saw?" her father prompted. When Sarah made no reply, he added, "You would not wish it to seem as if you were keeping a secret."

"No, Papa," she agreed reluctantly. If Captain Brice's presence was not disclosed, and something untoward happened, she knew where the weight of suspicion would fall. Her shoulders had only just begun to ease after carrying that burden for so long.

When she descended to the receiving room near the manor's grand entrance, no footman was in sight. She drew a steadying breath and opened the door herself.

Lady Estley and Eliza Harrington were seated together, as was their wont, while Lord Estley stood nearby. St. John had not yet arrived. Straightening her spine, she marched to Lady Estley and dropped a perfunctory curtsy. "Good afternoon, ma'am. I come bearing my parents' regrets. My mother has taken ill and feels unequal to accompanying us."

"Ill? Nothing serious, I hope," Lord Estley interjected, stepping closer. "Shall I call a physician?"

From what she had heard, Sarah would have been surprised to learn that the village boasted so much as an apothecary, but she offered what she hoped was a gracious smile and declined. "I don't believe that will be necessary, sir. It is just a bad cold, no doubt made worse by the strains of travel. I have just left her resting comfortably and in my father's care."

"A pity your father will miss the evening's entertainment," said Lady Estley, sounding ever so slightly jealous that someone else had found an excuse for doing so.

"An evening of rest and quiet will do them both good," she said. "Papa has spent the better part of the day in the nursery and must be exhausted himself."

"Ah, with Lady Clarissa." Lord Estley smiled. "So his journey into the village was successful, then?"

She opened her mouth to speak, to share the disturbing piece of information her father had imparted. Breath passed her lips, and then was snatched back. She nodded.

Turning from her father-in-law before he could read the uncertainty in her face, she saw Eliza Harrington approaching, wearing a smile that seemed to have been manufactured for the occasion. "I must say, Lady Fairfax, your charming frock is just the thing for a country dance."

Sarah smoothed her hand over her dress. It was no ball gown, to be sure—as her own mother had reminded her not a quarter of an hour past. And now several years out of fashion. But *frock*, indeed. Once upon a time, she had imagined it quite elegant. In a past life, it had been her favorite.

"Thank you," she replied, mustering her own false smile.

"But are you not worried about the night air?" Eliza asked. "Perhaps you should send for your pelisse."

Behind her, Lady Estley appeared startled by the suggestion. "It's as warm as midsummer today," she countered with unusual forcefulness, "and the assembly rooms are bound to be overheated. I'm sure she has no need of one."

"At this time of year especially, it may turn damp with very little notice," countered Eliza as St. John entered the room and came toward them.

"Perhaps Miss Harrington is right. You would not wish to take a chill when you step outside after an evening of vigorous dancing," her husband insisted in a voice that warmed her to her toes. "There's a shawl meant to go with that dress, is there not, Lady Fairfax?"

He had seen it, of course, and quite recently, too—folded in her trunk. She nodded.

"Shall I fetch it?"

Lady Estley fluttered bejeweled fingers in his direction. "Nonsense, Fairfax. Ring for a maid."

"Most of the servants have been given the night off. No doubt they are already on their way to the Red Lion. It will be faster if I go myself." He drew Sarah toward the door with him, and before he left on his errand, he lifted her hand to his lips and asked in a voice meant for only her ears, "I trust you had a pleasant morning?"

Heat sprang into Sarah's cheeks. "And night," she managed to quip.

"I am glad to hear it," St. John murmured, his voice rich with the promise of nights and mornings yet to come.

"And you?" she asked, meaning to enquire after his meetings.

But he sent a languid gaze down her body that set her heart racing. How could those cool eyes hold such heat? "*Pleasant* does not begin to describe it," he said softly, his mouth upturned in a rather wicked smile.

Sarah swore she could feel Eliza's eyes on her, but when she turned, Miss Harrington was gazing at a picture on the opposite side of the room. She and Lady Estley had broken up their tête-à-tête. In St. John's absence, the moments ticked by in silence. Lord Estley wandered to look out the garden doors; her mother-in-law shifted to a chair closer to the empty fireplace. Sarah twisted her fingers to keep herself from twisting her skirts.

When St. John returned, the shawl draped over one arm, he stood lingering at the threshold, as if reluctant to cross it. "Sarah?"

Although his voice was barely a whisper, she heard the question in it and went to him immediately. The warmth in his eyes had been replaced by something colder. Something very like anger. Hesitantly, she took the shawl from him. The fringe of the peacock feather patterned silk slithered away to reveal his outstretched palm.

Coiled upon it lay the Sutliffe sapphires.

With a cry, she brushed past him and out the door. Surely she could be forgiven for not wishing to hear again the all-too-familiar accusations. In any case, he made no move to stop her. As she left, she caught another glimpse of the unreadable emotion in his eyes.

What was he thinking? She could not bear to learn the answer.

In a quiet, private moment, he had claimed to believe her innocent. He had asked her forgiveness. And despite her determination not to live in some fairy-tale world, she had allowed herself to hope that his words might be the first steps on a journey toward something more.

But could his feelings stand up to family and friends who had always believed her capable of terrible things, even when there had been no proof? For now they had proof in spades.

It is foolhardy to run, her head reminded her flying feet. *It only makes you look guilty.*

No. The necklace had already done that.

The Sutliffe sapphires. Those blessed gems that she had once been so proud to don because she had seen them as a mark of her father-in-law's acceptance—believing, naïvely, that if she had won Lord Estley's approval, then her husband's could not be far behind.

"Pretty Mama," Clarissa exclaimed.

Sarah started to find herself in the nursery. How had she got here? Gathering the child from her place on the floor, she clutched her against her breast. Hot, silent tears dripped onto her golden-brown curls.

"What's happened?" Emily asked, hovering nearby.

Sarah shook her head. It was an excellent question—one for which she had no answer.

Where had the necklace come from after all this time? And how had it turned up in her things?

When Clarissa struggled against her smothering embrace, she put her down and allowed her to return to serving her doll on the delicate tea set her grandpapa had found in the village.

"I'm afraid I must ask you to promise to stay with her, Emily," Sarah said, turning to her friend with a fierce, breathless whisper. "Somehow."

"Of course, Mrs. F.," Emily replied, lapsing into the more familiar address. "Are you goin' someplace?"

A year from now, would the child remember Haverhythe? Would she even remember her mother?

Sarah rose from the floor and strode across the room, and then turned back to Emily. "No. I'm done with running from a crime I did not commit. I'll stay right here until they send me away." *Which will likely be soon*, she added silently. "Running is for the guilty."

Emily looked bewildered, but she nodded. "Good for you, mum."

Sarah drifted over to the window. She looked out at the bright sky over the Channel, then down at the darkening garden, where the light pouring from the room she had left just moments ago cast jagged shadows. A movement closer to the house caught her eye.

Eliza was strolling across the flagstone terrace. Alone.

She could still hear St. John's murmured words to Eliza Harrington on the night of the nuptial ball. *She can never have my heart. And you know why.*

Sarah had always known why. His heart had belonged to Eliza. But Eliza had wanted more than his heart. Was she at last going to get it?

Tonight, when Sarah had left St. John's side, Eliza had no doubt stood ready to slip into the vacant place. But she certainly hadn't stayed there for long.

Sarah's eyes followed Eliza as she made her way down the steps and hurried toward the garden, as best her dancing slippers would allow. Where on earth was the woman headed? She seemed always to be by when something bad happened to Sarah—it would not have surprised her one bit to see Eliza's gloating smile as the magistrate dragged her off.

Curiously, though, she hadn't stayed to witness it.

Perhaps, under the circumstances, the others had foresworn the dance and Eliza had determined to go on without them. No doubt the farmers and fishermen of Lynscombe had never seen anything quite like the pale green gown that complemented Eliza's fair skin and red hair like the patina on copper. Its daringly low neckline revealed an expanse of snowy bosom, but offered meager protection against the evening air. *She ought to have taken her own advice and sent for a shawl,* Sarah huffed to herself as she gathered up her own, still trailing on the floor, and pulled it more securely around her shoulders.

The shawl.

The necklace.

Eliza.

What at first seemed only jumbled notes began to form a chord in Sarah's mind. As she watched the woman turn onto the path that led to the Channel, she decided to follow her. "Emily," she announced, "I have to go out."

Emily's brow wrinkled. "But you said—"

"Yes, I know. I'll be back. It's just that I . . ." She shook her head. "I've no time to explain. Just . . ." She snatched a nearby scrap of thick watercolor paper from the low table where Clarissa took tea, and among the silly little sketches she had made to amuse Clarissa earlier in the day, she scratched out a few words with the stub of a pencil. "Just see that my father gets this, all right?"

Eyes wide, Emily took the folded note and nodded.

With a longing glance at her daughter, Sarah slipped from the nursery and down the back stairs. She did not yet know for certain what role Eliza Harrington had played in the reappearance—or disappearance—of the Sutliffe sapphires. But she meant to find out.

She did not intend to give up on the possibility of happiness. At least, not without a fight.

Chapter 23

Dimly, he heard his father's grunt of surprise, his stepmother's gasp. It was like some badly done parody of that long-ago night in the library at Sutliffe House.

With the added sound of Sarah's footsteps racing away.

"I always knew she was guilty," his stepmother insisted.

His father gave a reluctant nod. "It certainly looks that way now, Amelia."

Eliza stepped forward and laid her hand on his arm. "I'm sorry, Fairfax. I can see your disappointment. But it is better to know the truth."

The truth?

Yes, he had found out the truth, as surely as he had found the necklace in Sarah's trunk.

Had it been just last night he had imagined himself falling in love with his wife?

Well, the truth was, he had already fallen.

He was in love with his wife. He tested the emotion in his mind, like a man tests a frozen pond to see if it will bear his weight, fearful of what lies beneath. He had done what he had sworn never to do, because love led inevitably to loss.

In his hand he held the proof of her guilt, the gems he had gone all the way to Haverhythe to find. But he had discovered something far more important in that obscure little village.

Sometimes, the reward of loving someone was worth the risk.

Curling his fingers around the necklace, he hurled it across the room. It struck the mantel with a sharp *crack*, and a sparkling shower of blue and gold tinkled onto the hearthstone. His stepmother flinched as the pieces skittered across the floor.

"Fairfax!"

His father's angry bark split the momentary silence that had fallen over the room. St. John half-expected his next words to be, "My study!" But no matter. This time, wherever the conversation took place, he intended to stand his ground.

"I do not know where that necklace has been hiding," he said, slipping away from Eliza's touch. "But Sarah never stole it. She is, and always has been, innocent."

But why, oh why, had she run?

"Innocent?" his stepmother echoed, incredulous.

Eliza looked stung, but she recovered quickly. "This is really a family matter. I will—why, there is still a bit of daylight left, I see. One forgets how early farmers and fishermen dance and dine. I will take a turn or two about the terrace. I daresay a breath of fresh air would do me good."

She stepped quickly across the room to the French doors. When she opened one set, a brisk wind swept up the draperies, tangling them with her skirts. Without a backward glance, she stepped outside and closed the doors behind her.

"How could you do such a thing?" His father had gone to kneel on the hearth, his eyes locked on the pieces of the ruined necklace scattered across it.

"How could I—? Of course. That bloody necklace has always meant more to you than I do," St. John snapped.

"No," his father asserted with a shake of his head. But still he could not seem to tear his eyes away from the jewels.

"It's a mere *symbol*, Father," St. John said, stepping closer.

"Yes, of course it is." His father turned to face him at last, his face pale with shock and barely restrained fury. "A symbol of this family. And as such, I would think you would handle it with more care. In 1601, when a young London merchant helped to finance the first voyage of the East India Company, he was rewarded with these gems and the rank of Baron Lyn." St. John recognized the name as one of his father's lesser titles. "These gems represent the daring, the determination it took to raise this family above its origins, to raise us above—"

"People like the Pevenseys?" St. John finished snidely. For whatever the first Baron Lyn had accomplished in lifting himself above the masses, his descendants had managed to cast them down once again, and now the only thing that would save them was an infusion of cold, hard cash. Cash from a Bristol merchant's coffers. When his father had put those jewels around Sarah's neck, the family journey had come full circle.

His stepmother gave a self-satisfied little snort, but his father looked abashed.

"You saddled me with the burden of cleaning up your messes. Well, now I'm returning the favor," St. John said, jerking his chin disdainfully in the direction of the hearth. "Lynscombe is the bit of our history that matters to me, and Sarah can help me save it."

"Her father's money can help you, you mean."

"No," he insisted. "I mean my wife. And I won't allow an old piece of jewelry to dictate my future with her."

"Your mother hated it, too."

His father's voice had fallen to a mournful whisper—a sound so uncharacteristic St. John felt certain he must have misheard what the man had said. But the quiet words kept coming.

"I tried many times to persuade her to wear it. But she never would. She said it felt like death around her neck." His father's gaze had fallen back to the floor, but he was no longer looking at the broken necklace. Instead, his focus was somewhere much further in the past. "I thought perhaps if I—if I had the gems reset, something in a modern style, she would relent. She was otherwise always so eager to please."

Out of the corner of his eye, St. John saw his stepmother rise unsteadily from her chair. He was not surprised. She had always detested any mention of his mother.

"So, one day," his father continued, speaking mostly to himself, "I took it from the safe here and set out for London. I did not tell her where I was going. I was almost to the jeweler's when the messenger found me, told me she had had—an accident . . ."

The silence that fell was broken only by the scuff of his stepmother's slippers against the floor.

Your father's grief must have been terrible.

St. John tried to shake off the memory of Sarah's words. His father did not feel grief. Or guilt. His father was incapable of feeling. St. John had learned from the master.

Hadn't he?

"Father," he whispered, taking a step toward him, seeing for the first time a brokenhearted man who had loved his wife, the mother of his child.

Without Sarah, St. John might never have understood how much.

"If I had been closer," his father murmured, still studying the floor. "Been *here*, as I should have been, then perhaps . . ."

"It was no one's fault, Father," St. John insisted, laying a hand on his shoulder. "And there was nothing anyone could have done to save her."

When his words of consolation seemed to have no effect, he pulled a handkerchief from his pocket and crouched beside the fireplace, collecting the broken pieces of the necklace on the square of linen. "Forgive me, Father. I had no idea. I will, of course, see the necklace repaired."

No sooner had the promise passed his lips when he saw a large chip in one of the stones. His stomach clenched. Then, as he examined the wreckage scattered on the floor around him, he spied another broken piece, and still another, and finally shards of gemstone that were little more than blue dust.

He studied the ruined stones on his palm, nudging one of the pieces with his fingertip. Priceless sapphires reduced to powder? Almost as if they were made of—

"What is it?" His father leaned forward to examine what St. John held in his hand. "Why, those aren't the Sutliffe sapphires! That is nothing but a worthless bit of pinchbeck and paste." He whirled about. "Do you hear that, Amelia?"

His stepmother froze just a few steps from the door. "Paste?" she echoed, turning back to face them, her eyes wide. "How can that be? Why, that sneaking little thief must have had a copy made. She's probably been living well on the money from the sale of the original and now planned to worm her way into this family's good graces by passing that off as real."

"It looks that way," agreed his father reluctantly as he stood.

It might have sounded like a reasonable explanation, but it did not sit well with St. John. For one thing, he had seen Haverhythe.

"No."

His stepmother jumped when he spoke, jerking her hand from the doorknob as if the metal were hot.

"Where are you going, Amelia?" his father asked her.

"Why, I—I am really not needed here, and the air in this room is just stifling. I thought I would join Eliza."

"Eliza is on the terrace." St. John darted a glance toward the doors through which she had passed moments ago, but the curtains obscured his view.

She tittered. "Of course—how silly of me!" But she made no move in that direction.

He paused to consider. "When Father announced that Sarah would wear the Sutliffe sapphires at our nuptial ball, did you not have to fetch them for him?"

"I, er—I do not recall. So long ago . . ."

But his father's memory suffered no such impairment. "She did. I had always stored them in my private safe in years past, but eventually I allowed Amelia to keep them with the rest of her jewels. She had such a fondness for wearing them."

"I did," his stepmother agreed, straightening her spine in a show of dignity. "Unlike some, I was proud to do so. I understood their true value, all that they represent."

"Yes. I remember often seeing the gems around your neck," St. John acknowledged. "Still, is it not possible that something might have happened to the necklace before that night? Was it never out of your possession? Taken for repair, perhaps? If so, the switch might have been made long ago. Did you notice anything unusual about the necklace when she brought it to you that night, Father?"

He shook his head. "I did not. But I confess I did not study it carefully."

"You might not, even if you had," St. John insisted, weighing the wreckage on his palm. "This appears to have been a quality copy. I think it would have been quite difficult to tell." He paused to study his stepmother's rather nervous expression. "Would it not, ma'am?"

His father looked from one to the other. "Would someone be so kind as to explain just what is going on here?"

"Ask your wife," he said coldly, "if you trust her to be honest."

"Fairfax," gasped his stepmother, sounding hurt.

"Well, Amelia?" His father turned pale eyes toward his wife.

"I refuse to take all the blame for what happened," piped his stepmother, leaving her post by the door and coming toward them.

"Amelia, what are you talking about?"

"Really, Marcus, it was mostly your fault."

His father stiffened. "How so?"

"I understood the need for a quiet courtship, so I did not protest. You were still in mourning, after all, and with a young child to think of. How I longed for the whirl of parties and balls again, though. I imagined the figure I would cut as the Marchioness of Estley. The gowns, the gems." She sighed. For the first time it struck St. John that the childish vacancy in her eyes was not entirely put on. "I never dreamed that even after your mourning ended you would refuse me those simple pleasures, even permission to decorate my own home in my own taste," she continued with a shake of her head. "You were forever reminding me to be careful with money. And the parties to which we did go were so deadly dull. Until one night, someone—I don't remember who—suggested I might amuse myself in the card room."

"Did you—*gamble*?" his father rasped out.

She made a dismissive gesture with her hand. "I had to do something to drive away the boredom. And to supplement that rather pitiful allowance you gave me. And, it turns out, I was quite good at it," she explained with a nostalgic sort of sigh. "Too good for the sorts of games one comes across in the card room at a ball. Then one night, I was invited to a private party and the stakes were rather higher. I *played deep*, as the dandies say. Too deep, as it turned out. I did not think a gentleman would call in a lady's vowels. But there it was." She shrugged. "I needed money—and when I asked you, Marcus, you insisted there was no more to be had."

"Let me understand," his father said after a moment had passed. A dull, mottled flush had spread across his face. "You pawned the Sutliffe sapphires to pay a gaming debt?"

"But first I had that exquisite copy made," she noted, as if that excused what she had done. "Worthless it may be, but it cost a pretty penny I do assure you. And you were none the wiser."

"That explains why, when Sarah stole it, you were only too happy to help her disappear," her husband said. "It covered up what you had done."

"Sarah didn't steal it," St. John reminded him sharply. "So, what really happened that night?" he asked as he turned to his stepmother.

She rounded on him. "Between your wife and the officer? I'm

sure I don't know. Perhaps the clasp broke while they were . . . well, you know—and the thing got lost in the cushions of the chair."

Her words roused an old specter: the image of Sarah in David Brice's arms. But he found it was an image that no longer had the power to haunt him.

"Surely someone looked—"

"Oh yes." She nodded, cutting across him. "Someone looked."

"And someone found it, didn't they? Who?"

"Miss Harrington."

"Eliza?!"

"Yes, indeed. That very night. You had already gone after Brice," she explained. "Your father had shut himself away. She came and showed it to me. But when I tried to take it from her hand, she said that perhaps she should give it to my husband instead. That's when I realized she had discovered it was paste."

The pieces of the past fell into place with startling rapidity: the crumpled memorandum he had dislodged from his stepmother's desk; Sarah's supposed demands for money; the discrepancy between the amount on that paper and the notes in Sarah's trunk.

The fact that Eliza was never far from his stepmother's side.

"Eliza has been blackmailing you—threatening to reveal the truth about the necklace if you did not pay for her silence."

His stepmother nodded without meeting his eye.

The part of him that had clung with perhaps naïve desperation to the notion of Sarah's innocence offered surprisingly little resistance to the suggestion of Eliza's guilt.

The missing necklace had been in Eliza's possession all along. And now his oldest friend—or so he had always imagined—had put it in Sarah's trunk and then suggested someone fetch her shawl, intending it to be discovered.

He glanced toward the terrace, wondering why Eliza would have done such a terrible thing. He would find out. But first—

"You let me suffer—let *Sarah* suffer—all these years . . ."

"Suffer?" Shock propelled the word from his stepmother's mouth. "You never wanted to marry the girl anyway. You were well out of it. It did not matter that the necklace wasn't real," she insisted. "Or even that she hadn't stolen it. She was still a thief at heart, and I knew it. She wanted what ought never to have been hers. And if she had been truly innocent, she never would have been so willing to leave."

"Amelia, what have you done?" His father's voice was so soft that in another man, the tone might have been mistaken for gentleness.

"*I* am the one who suffered." She pouted, sinking back into her chair. "Thanks to her, my home was ransacked by Bow Street Runners. Your darling Fairfax risked his life in a duel and then went into exile. I kept my silence through it all. But, like Sarah, I grow weary of keeping secrets. If you had not made me promise to begin to keep better track of my expenditures, Marcus," she added with a bitter shake of her head, "your son would never have discovered where she went."

"But I did," St. John murmured. "I found her."

He folded the handkerchief around the broken bits of glass and passed the bundle to his father. "You will excuse me. I must go to her," he said as he strode across the room.

"St. John."

He paused, almost to the door.

He did not think he had ever heard his given name pass his father's lips—he had, after all, been "Fairfax" from the moment of his birth. No, that had been an intimacy reserved for his mother. Lately, oddly, for his daughter. And perhaps someday, if he were lucky, for his wife.

"I have made mistakes where you were concerned," his father acknowledged with a downward glance at St. John's stepmother. "But Sarah, I think, was never one of them."

St. John nodded. He understood, at last. He looked forward to the opportunity to build a different relationship with his father.

But first he had to stop his bride before she ran out of his life forever. He made it only a few steps beyond the threshold before he broke into a run himself.

When he did not find her at the pianoforte, as he had hoped, he knew where she must have gone. Pushing aside his trepidation, he followed her. As he had feared, ascending the steep steps to the nursery was like climbing into his past. Every step, every shadow was familiar to him. But this time he did not try to cast off those memories.

He let them pour over him, their healing power blending with the hurt. When he burst through the door moments later, his eyes fell first on Clarissa sitting on the floor with her doll, and his heart lurched. In his fear, he had never stopped to consider how wonderful it would feel to see a child—his child—playing in the place where he himself had played, long years ago.

But there was no sign of his wife.

"She's gone, then." He had wasted precious moments—years—because he had been afraid to face his feelings, afraid to face the truth.

Emily started and jerked to her feet, her needlework spilling from her lap and onto the floor. "Lawks, sir. What a fright you gave us. I thought you were Mrs. F."

Clarissa toddled over and tugged at his hand. "Play wi' me, Papa."

He ran a hand over her curls. "I can't now, little one. But I will. Did she say where she was going, Miss Dawlish? Did she say anything at all before she left?"

"I could see somethin' had happened to upset her. But she wouldn't say what. I asked if she was going to leave, and she swore she meant to stay." Emily shook her head. "Said runnin' was for guilty folk."

Deflated, he asked, "What happened to change her mind?"

"I dunno," Emily replied with a shrug. "She was pacing about and stopped at that window."

Lifting his daughter into his arms, he walked to the place Emily had indicated, and looked out, though he knew what he would see. The back garden, the cliffs, the Channel. The surest route of escape from Lynscombe—of whatever kind Sarah meant to effect.

"Did she take anything with her?"

"Why, no. She just—Mercy me, Lieutenant!" Emily shrieked, patting her breast and withdrawing a folded sheet of paper. "I forgot. She wrote this."

With a gentle hug, he put Clarissa back on the floor with her doll before snatching the note from Emily's grasp. She brought her candle closer, and his thumb smudged a childish sketch of a cat as he unfolded the paper and read:

Papa—
Whatever happens, I ask you to grant my husband the entirety of my dowry at once, for the sake of our daughter and the village of Lynscombe.

Her dowry. Of course. She believed that was the only part of her he needed.

His gaze returned to the note and he repeated the phrase, "*Whatever happens.*" He could not like the implication of those words. And then he saw that at the bottom of the page, in a shakier hand, she had added:

> *I believe Miss Harrington had a hand in the theft of that necklace, and I intend to prove it.*

Jerking his gaze back to the window, he scanned the terrace for any sign of Eliza. But she was nowhere to be seen. Then his eyes traveled the unkempt path that wound down to the sea.

"Thank you, Miss Dawlish," he said, folding the note and tucking it into his coat pocket. "I believe I know where to look."

He only hoped he was not too late.

Chapter 24

Away from the shelter of the house, the breeze grew stronger, its summer warmth replaced by autumn's chill. It whipped Sarah's hair free of its pins and sent it twisting and tangling about her face. She clutched her silk shawl tightly around her shoulders; every moment the wind threatened to snatch it free of her grasp and whirl it away.

Eliza did not glance behind her, but Sarah maintained a careful distance between them nonetheless. When Eliza paused to clutch a stitch in her side, Sarah stopped. When Eliza slipped out of sight on a turn of the path, Sarah sped up.

Soon the sea stretched before them, the Channel's gray water whipped into snowy froth by the wind. Scrubby sea grass snagged Sarah's stockings; even her sturdy shoes—for she owned no dancing slippers—were no match for the rough ground. But she pressed on, to the spot where St. John had revealed why he had left Lynscombe, and perhaps had first begun to realize why he needed at last to come home.

Eliza paused at the cliff's edge to scan the horizon, her red hair streaming behind her.

And then she jumped.

The wind ripped a scream from Sarah's throat before she realized that Eliza had merely dropped onto a ledge that formed part of the trail down to the strand. As she peered cautiously over the cliff, expecting to see Eliza's body on the rocks below, the other woman looked up at her from just a few feet away and laughed.

"Why, what a pleasant surprise, Lady Fairfax! Care to join me for a walk on the beach?"

Despite the dizzying and deadly prospect before her, Sarah swallowed her fear. She wanted answers to questions that had been haunting her for three long years. She followed Eliza down.

Although the path was neither so narrow nor so steep as it had appeared from above, she clung to the chalky face of the cliff, its roughness tearing at her gown and shredding her gloves.

Eliza moved with far less difficulty, as if the descent were familiar to her. Sarah watched how she moved along the trail and avoided the spots Eliza's feet had skirted. In a matter of moments, the other woman was standing on the sand, looking toward the water.

When Sarah at last traded the crumbling chalk for more solid ground, her breath was as ragged as her clothes. "What have you done, Miss Harrington?" she asked when she was at last able to speak.

"Done? Merely arranged matters so that things can be the way they always should have been."

"And how is that?"

Eliza's lips curled in a cruel sort of smile. "I think you know, Lady Fairfax. You overheard what I told your husband the night of your nuptial ball. I meant for you to overhear, after all," she admitted coolly. "He should have married me."

It was confession enough to make Sarah's heart jerk into her throat.

"Yes, I was always meant to be Lady Fairfax, and eventually, the Marchioness of Estley." Eliza began to stroll along the beach as she explained. Reluctantly, Sarah followed. "You see, my father and your husband's father are old friends and near neighbors. When I was born, Papa began to fantasize of one day joining the two families. I grew up believing my future was already settled."

They passed under a stone archway that had been carved by the power of the sea, then over a narrow strip of dry strand along the cliff, where an inlet cut in toward the shore. Beyond it lay a wider stretch of beach. In the distance, Sarah could see an abandoned skiff washed up on the shore. As they walked toward it, Eliza continued her story.

"I understand that you have a child, Lady Fairfax—a daughter." Sarah's heart thumped erratically in her chest, and she gave a chary glance over her shoulder, although the house was entirely out of sight and she knew she had left Clarissa safe in the nursery. "Can you imagine, if you chose her husband for her today, how she might feel about that man when she is a woman grown?"

Sarah gave an uncertain shake of her head. "I cannot."

"This man she had known from a child," Eliza pressed, "with whom she played on this very stretch of beach. This man around whom every plan for her future had been built. The first to kiss her, the first to—ah—" She seemed to catch herself with a wicked smirk and shook her head. "But that would be telling tales, would it not?"

Sarah blushed and looked away, trying not to imagine the intimacies this woman must have shared with her husband, feeling as if her heart were tearing in two. "She would love him, I hope."

Eliza nodded, then paused, as if considering the implications of Sarah's reply. "So, what do you suppose she might do when the man she loved was snatched away by another?"

Anything. Everything.

For the first time, Sarah began to question the wisdom of following the woman to such an isolated spot. She stooped and pretended to inspect her shoe, scrambling for an excuse to get away.

Obligingly, Eliza stopped and waited. "One morning, Papa came to me, grim-faced, and said that Lord Estley had found another bride for his son, one with fortunes more suited to the family's needs," she continued when Sarah at last stood. Despite the dull roar of the waves, Sarah could hear the edge in her voice. "Almost immediately Papa began to talk of a match with Mr. Abernathy instead. Philip Abernathy, whose idea of sparkling conversation is a debate over the best sort of apples to be put into a tart." Eliza turned and looked at her. "The future of which I had dreamed was to be unceremoniously ripped away."

"So you decided to fight for your dream." Sarah could not admire Eliza's actions. But she was beginning to understand them.

Eliza nodded. "I did, although I confess, at first I did not know how. When I called on Lady Estley, however, it came to me. It was clear she disdained the match as much as I, although heaven knows she was eager enough to have your money at her family's disposal. Her every word expressed scorn for you, your birth, your looks. 'Would you believe,' " Eliza said, in a passable imitation of Lady Estley's shrill voice, " ' "Estley imagines he can disguise those flaws by draping her in the family jewels?' "

Sarah felt her mouth drop open in a soft *"Oh!"* of understanding.

"Oh yes. I hoped that if I could find a way to make it seem as if you had stolen them, it would provide sufficient cause to put an end to your marriage. But the more I thought, the more I realized I would need assistance in carrying out my plan. A few nights later, I happened to be at Vauxhall when I overheard a group of young officers complaining about the high cost of purchasing a promotion—those who hadn't the funds were forced to risk their lives to advance. There was a great deal of bravado being spouted, of course. I rather suspect they had been drinking to excess," she confided in a broad whisper, as if there were someone nearby to overhear the allegation. "Captain Brice was among them. When he asked me to take a stroll along one of the alleys, I accepted. We . . . talked, and I suggested I might know of a way to help him to acquire the money he desired."

Without conscious thought, Sarah lifted her hand to her throat, as if feeling for the necklace.

"That's right," Eliza averred, a sardonic gleam in her eye. "We met twice more in secret to plan. I would provide a distraction, send you into his path. You already know how I managed to do just that," she added with a cutting smile. "He was to do whatever it took to comfort you. Most important, he was to get the necklace and hide it well. I stressed to him that it was essential to claim that the necklace was already missing when you joined him in the library—otherwise, suspicion might have fallen too easily on him."

Sarah struggled to absorb the implications of everything Eliza was saying. "But your plan still might have failed if we had not been found—found—"

"In a compromising position? That's right," she agreed. "I did not know whether an accusation of theft would be enough to get rid of you. That was why it was necessary to bring a man into my plan. I could not very well make it look as if you had cuckolded Fairfax without one." She laughed. "I do believe Captain Brice has a future on the stage once his military career is over. He played his part to perfection. And you, Lady Fairfax—well, you really must be more careful with wine. It can go to your head, you know," she cautioned, wide-eyed, with what almost passed for earnestness.

"You—you drugged me?" Her fuzziness, her confusion, her headache the next morning all suddenly made sense.

"Think of it as helping you to relax. And while you two, er, occupied yourselves in the library, I persuaded Fairfax to join me there for one last tryst. I had already arranged for footmen to deliver two messages simultaneously: one to your parents, informing them that Lord Estley wished to meet; and one to Lord and Lady Estley, saying that Fairfax needed to speak to them. *Et voilà!* The new bride in the library with the officer, for everyone to see," she announced, sweeping her hand before her as if displaying the tableau she described. "But, alas, without the family jewels."

"The necklace was in the library all along."

"Of course. After the room had emptied, I went back and retrieved it from the place he had hidden it. It was then that things began to get . . . interesting, shall we say. I left the ballroom to meet with a man in Covent Garden. Perhaps you know the sort of man I mean?"

Sarah nodded blankly, barely certain of what Eliza had asked. She was reliving that night, that awful night—the pitiless faces, her parents' shame. St. John's cold indifference. If he had been anticipating a tête-à-tête with Miss Harrington, then the scene in the library must have been doubly disappointing to him.

The horrible memory absorbed her to the point that she almost missed Eliza's next words.

"Imagine my surprise when he told me the Sutliffe sapphires were nothing but an exquisite forgery."

"Not . . . real?" she mumbled. But then, nothing else about the evening had been, either.

"Almost worthless. I was frantic. I had promised Captain Brice a good deal of money for his role, and now I had nothing with which to buy his silence. My perfect plan was collapsing around my ears." Eliza's green gaze drifted over the seascape. "Then I happened to remember Lady Estley's concern about your wearing the gems, and I began to wonder . . ."

"She knew the gems were false?"

"Indeed. As it turns out, she had had the copy made—after having pawned the original to cover her losses at the card table." In spite of herself, Sarah gasped at the revelation. "Of course, it took some doing to get the truth from her. But she was understandably reluctant to have her husband learn what had happened to his precious family heirloom. She paid me handsomely to keep her secret. Not once, but many times."

"You kept the false necklace," Sarah said, recalling the story St. John's stepmother had spun for him about being blackmailed over the jewels. So it had been true—only the name of the blackmailer had been changed.

"I'm no fool," Eliza huffed. "I also persuaded Lady Estley to send you away, knowing it would confirm your guilt. Then I learned that you had drowned in the attempt to escape—better yet!"

"She did not tell you I was alive?" Sarah noted, surprised. So the marchioness really *had* managed to keep the secret—a number of secrets, it seemed.

"No." The admission seemed to pain her. "But once I learned the truth, I realized I could not let the little matter of your survival get in the way of my success."

Eliza's matter-of-factness in speaking of another's death chilled Sarah's blood far more than the brisk wind coming off the Atlantic. She should have known the woman would never have revealed so much if she had had any intention of allowing her an opportunity to repeat it to another.

Fear thrummed through her body. In the moment, she could think of no better distraction than to keep Eliza talking.

"What of Captain Brice?"

Eliza waved a hand, as if the detail were trivial. "He was sent on a dangerous mission, from which he seemed unlikely to return. And as I had not yet paid him for his part in our little play, I had both the necklace and the money." As if they were close friends, she threaded her arm through Sarah's and resumed walking, pulling her along toward the little boat. Only when they at last reached it did Eliza release her arm.

The tide scrubbed the stern with an insistent rhythm. Sarah glanced inside the small vessel, looking for something, anything she could use to save herself. Could she wield one of the heavy oars and knock Eliza down?

"I had only to wait until Fairfax returned to me," Eliza continued as she leaned against the gunwale, blocking Sarah from reaching into the boat. Her eyes wandered up the beach, in the direction from which they had come, and she gave a self-satisfied smile. "And, look! Here he comes now."

Sarah turned to see St. John, clad only in his shirtsleeves, striding forcefully across the strand.

When he was close enough to hear her over the sound of the

water, Eliza called to him. "It would have been better, Fairfax, if you had not lost your temper and thrown that blasted necklace across the room. When I heard it hit the wall, I knew the forgery would be discovered."

"And it was," he said.

"So, how did you leave things at the house, my dear?" Eliza asked, pushing away from the boat. "Does your father now realize what his silly wife has done?"

"Yes."

"He should know Miss Harrington was involved, too," Sarah inserted, managing, somehow, to keep her own voice composed. "It was she who arranged the necklace's disappearance on the night of the ball. With Captain Brice."

The information did not seem to surprise him. Or if it did, his eyes still never left Eliza. "Why? Why would you do such a thing?"

Eliza looked pained, clearly hurt by his lack of understanding. "To rescue you, of course. To set you free."

"Free," he echoed.

"I did all of this so you would see your wife for what she is. A social climber. A schemer. A—"

"A thief?" he suggested.

Eliza smiled then and walked toward him, her hands outstretched. "Oh, you scoundrel. What a start you gave me. I might have guessed you didn't mean it when you proclaimed her innocence."

St. John stepped toward Eliza and took her hands in his, his pale eyes never leaving her face.

Sarah's heart lurched, pulled as it was in two very different directions. Had he really stood up for her, said he did not believe her guilty, despite the evidence? If so, then why hadn't he come to her side now?

According to Eliza, this was a place where the two of them had often played in their childhood. Now, in the fading light and against the shimmering sea, they looked for all the world like two lovers meeting on the beach. Standing in the place where they were born, born to be together. Looking deep into one another's eyes, holding hands . . .

Sarah's restless gaze traveled over the pair and then locked on the place where they touched.

St. John was not holding Eliza's hands. He was pinning her wrists.

And then he shook his head and she heard him ask, "Are you mad?"

As he looked into Eliza's eyes, St. John realized that the answer to his question very possibly was *yes*.

When he had seen them standing together on the beach, his first feeling had been relief. He was not too late—or at least, not quite. He had raced forward, despite the tide.

Now, however, he realized the full extent of the danger they were all in.

Was Sarah all right? He longed to look at her, reach for her, go to her, but he feared that to do so would draw down more of Eliza's vengeful wrath.

"You don't mean that. Come, my love," she urged, tipping her chin in the direction of the boat. "This is our chance."

Standing so close, he could not help but be struck by Eliza's beauty. But he could also see now that her beauty was surrounded by a hardness, like a thick layer of ice encasing a winter rose, destroying what it seemed to protect. Had he failed to notice it years ago? Or was this shell of more recent acquisition?

"I can certainly understand why you might be desperate to get away." Sarah took a step toward him as she spoke, but her eyes never left Eliza's face. "Now that Captain Brice has followed you to Lynscombe."

Beneath her wind-roughened cheeks Eliza turned deathly pale. "H-he is *here*?" A sort of wildness overspread her features and she jerked against his imprisoning hands.

"Yes," Sarah confirmed. "My father saw him this morning in the village."

In the village? St. John tightened his hold on Eliza. Why hadn't Sarah said something sooner? Because she had feared what he would do when he knew? He had told her he believed her innocent, but she was not yet ready to trust his word, it seemed, not yet ready to believe he had spoken the truth. Last night she had given in to her body's desires, and his own. But her heart, it seemed, was not yet his.

Well, then, he would find another way to win it.

"I could not imagine what had brought him here," Sarah was saying. "Until now. You said you promised him a great deal of money for his part in the theft of the necklace—more, I suppose, than Lady Estley has been able to supply."

"Yes," Eliza grudgingly admitted. "When he returned from France I explained how things stood and gave him what money I had. But, of course, it was not nearly what he expected. He's been hounding me ever since, threatening to expose me. But I did not think he would follow me from London."

"You placed the gems in Sarah's trunk," St. John said, "hoping to destroy his hold over you."

"I was more concerned about her hold over you," she said, her eyes darting between Sarah and him. "Why did you play the jealous husband all those years ago? Challenging a noted marksman to a duel. You might have been killed, and over a woman who could mean nothing to you! Did you know that I went to him, pleaded for him to choose swords, to give you a sporting chance?"

"How—considerate of you to intervene." Despite the cool air on his skin, the old scar burned with fresh heat. "And how kind of him to agree. I hope I shall have an opportunity to express my gratitude to him in person."

"There seems to have been a slight flaw in your plan, Miss Harrington," Sarah observed coolly, disrupting the vengeful train of his thoughts. "If both Lady Estley and Captain Brice knew you had the gems, and both are here now to confirm it, doesn't that make it rather clear that *you* are the guilty one, not I?"

"The only flaw in my plan is about to be rectified," Eliza snapped. "Let us go, Fairfax. Together. As we were meant to be. You needn't worry about her anymore." She tossed a disparaging glance over her shoulder at Sarah. "Leave her here and you'll soon be free of her forever."

As the water pushed closer, it was only too clear what she meant. Could Eliza—this woman he had known almost all his life—truly be so calculating, so cruel?

But he already knew that answer, too.

"I cannot."

"Of course you can," she insisted. "After all I've done for you, surely you do not mean to deny me."

"I belong here, Eliza. At Lynscombe."

Her grass-green gaze flickered over his face. "I suppose I can take some consolation at having been thrown over for that shabby village rather than your shabby wife." The small boat shuddered and lifted from the sand with the force of the rising tide. "Don't be a fool, Fairfax," she said, fright sharpening her voice as she struggled against his hold.

Sarah spoke then with quiet determination. "Let her go."

Reluctantly, St. John released her wrists.

Once free, Eliza scrambled into the little boat and took up the oars. "You *must* come with me, Fairfax. *Now*."

He shook his head.

Eliza's scowl traveled from him to Sarah and back again. "I see. You always were too sentimental about Lynscombe by half. Well, suit yourself." Her brittle laugh tinkled over him like droplets of frozen rain. "I wish you joy of your choice." And she pushed off with surprising strength, making her way against the tide.

At last he could reach out a hand for his wife.

She was standing little more than an arm's length away, her slender fingers pleating her skirts with the crisp, careful movements he had once imagined a show of calculated calm, and which he now recognized as a sign of her unease. As he stepped toward her, he felt his shoe fill with icy water.

Automatically, he looked down, although he knew what it meant. Waves had eaten into the beach, carving the hard-packed sand with ease and leaving pools and rivers in their wake. The sea drew back for a moment and then pressed forward again, swirling around their ankles, soaking the hem of Sarah's gown. The danger posed by Eliza had momentarily driven all thought of the encroaching tide from his mind.

He looked over his shoulder. He saw no sand.

Only water.

He had not realized they had walked so far. Even at the tide's lowest point, the sandy frontage was narrow, bordered on either end by outcroppings of rock that reached far into the Channel. Unless one approached by sea, the only way to reach the little spit of beach was by climbing down the cliff. The only way out was up. Where they were standing, however, the cliff was almost sheer. The nicely terraced trail they had descended was separated from them by water that in places was already waist-deep and rising.

He glanced behind him, but Eliza was nearly out of sight. Pushing away the horrible realization that she was willing to strand them there to save herself, he snagged Sarah's hand in his.

She understood their predicament. He could see that at first glance.

"I don't suppose you can swim?" he asked, forcing a sort of half smile to his lips as he slipped off his shoes, tossed them aside, and tried not to imagine his father having to identify them in the absence of their owner.

"Another country pursuit," she answered wryly with a shake of her head.

He recalled her willingness to charge into the water after her daughter. Her bravery. Her foolishness. He forced an answering smile to his lips. "In the spring," he promised, cupping her face in his hands and pressing his lips to hers, feeling their chill, tasting salt. "I'll teach you. When the weather is warm and the water is calm, there are few pleasures to equal it."

As he spoke, he tugged her shawl free from her grasp and felt his way to the end of the wide band of silk. "I'm sorry, Sarah," he said as he tore through its length, splitting it neatly into two narrower strips, knotting them tightly together, and then dipping the knot into the surf, wetting it so it would not give way.

She gasped but made no other protest, not even as he tied one end of the makeshift rope around her waist and began to lead her into deeper water, away from the rocks on which they might be dashed, gripping his end of the shawl so tightly that his fingers soon began to ache.

They made slow progress, their goal seeming to recede with every step, the water dragging them toward it before pulling them back, and rising with every passing moment.

By his estimation, the tide was nearly at its highest point. To reach the cliff now, they would have to cross the surf line, where the waves broke and roiled and whirled back into the sea. He doubted her ability to fight her way through it, hampered as she was by her skirts and her fears.

He could see only one solution.

Dropping the end of the shawl, he put both hands on her shoulders, water lapping his fingers where they gripped her. "Do you trust me?"

She hesitated. The sea inched higher.

"Yes," she whispered at last.

He mimed for her to draw a deep breath.

And then, feeling as if he were ripping his heart from his chest, he pushed her under the water.

Chapter 25

She burst up through the surface of the icy water, sputtering, choking, blind. Her arms and legs flailed wildly, straining for something solid and safe, when she realized suddenly that her feet could touch the ground. So could her hands, she discovered, as her benumbed fingers scrabbled against the rough chalk face of the cliff.

When she had gained a handhold and was certain she was upright, and alive, she dared to open her eyes and look around. She expected to find St. John beside her, still gripping the end of her shawl.

But its green length floated free, swept forward and backward with the movement of the water, like the fronds of some peculiarly elegant variety of seaweed.

Relaxing her grip on the rocks only slightly, she craned her neck to search for him in the water that still rushed behind her.

She spotted him at last, farther away than it seemed he ought to have been, but swimming mightily with the powerful strokes that had once saved Clarissa's life. No matter how hard he swam, however, he got no closer. Even as the tide rolled toward her, the water seemed to sweep him up and suck him back. Pushing her to safety had put him in danger. Why could he not make his way to her side?

All at once, Sarah remembered how Martha Potts had first described her husband's drowning. *"He swam for the shore, but his heart weren't in it. The sea wanted him for her own, I guess. Leastways, she kept dragging at him and dragging at him until he couldn't fight no more."* She recalled fishermen speaking in awed tones of the invisible current that held a man back, that would pull him under if he couldn't get free of it, teasing and torturing him the way a cat plays with a mouse it means at last to eat.

"St. John!" she screamed. "Swim away!" She let go of the rock with one hand and waved him off, certain he would think her mad. But it was the surest way to escape the treacherous crosscurrent in which he had been caught, or else he would drown just a few feet from shore.

Whether it was her frantic gestures or his own fatigue that did it, he relented slightly, and a wave carried him out of the current to a place where he could swim more freely. In a few more strokes, he was almost to her, but so drained by his exertion that she feared the next wash of the still-rising tide would sweep him away forever.

Letting go of the cliff face, she reached down to untie the knot at her waist, tugging and tearing at the salt-stiffened silk with frantic, fumbling fingers until it gave way. She wrapped one end around her wrist and let the other float free, stretching across the water to her husband.

With a last weak effort, St. John lunged toward it.

His fingertips caught and tangled in the fringe.

Wordless prayers streaming past her lips, Sarah began to pull him carefully to shore, until he, too, had solid ground beneath his feet. He collapsed beside her, his cheek pressed against the chalky cliff, one as pale as the other.

After a long moment, his eyelids fluttered and his blue eyes came to rest on her. "Sarah," he breathed.

"St. John." She could feel the tears streaming down her cheeks, mingling with the salt water that surrounded them. "Thank God."

He smiled weakly and closed his eyes again.

Clenching her jaw so her teeth would not chatter, she asked, "Can you climb?"

He nodded, and after he had caught his breath, they made the slow ascent. By the time they reached the top, the last of the day's light had slipped from the sky. The wind had died down, but the air had grown cooler, and they lay in the rough scrub, side by side, soaked and shivering.

Eventually St. John struggled to a sitting position. "Do you think you can make your way back to the house?"

She raised herself up and studied the path, at the end of which gleamed the distant lights of Lynscombe Manor. "I c-can t-t-try," she ground out from between chattering teeth. But none of her limbs seemed willing to honor that commitment.

"Shock," St. John said, reaching across the ground for the coat he had evidently discarded before making the descent and wrapping it around her shoulders. "Let's see if we can't get you warmed up first." With searching eyes he looked about them and then murmured, "I wonder," more to himself than her.

Burrowed into the blessedly dry fabric, Sarah watched as he got stiffly to his feet, walked back to the cliff's edge, and lowered himself onto the ledge. Curious, she half-crawled to a point at which she could see what he was doing. He had located a deep crevice in the cliff face and was pulling loose a few stones and the abandoned bird's nest that filled it. In another moment, he uncovered some smallish brown object, which he showed eagerly to her.

"I can't believe it was still there."

She looked at the little wooden box, with its rusted hinges and straps, and then up at St. John.

"A pirate's treasure chest," he explained. "And inside . . ."

He pried it open and revealed its contents, the sorts of things that would have made a boy's eyes gleam: a dull knife, sundry buttons that looked like coins, a tattered bit of vellum, and—a tinderbox.

Then he gathered dry brush and a few sticks, and in a matter of moments, a feeble spark had caught and the first tongues of fire began to lick along the wood.

With careful tending, sturdier flames began to light up the sky, driving away the twilight and making all around them appear even darker. She followed St. John's gaze over the water, in the direction Eliza's boat had taken.

"Why did you tell me to let her go?" he asked. "Do you not believe she ought to face the repercussions for her actions?"

"She already has," she said quietly. "She has lost the man she loves."

He shook his head in sharp denial. "Whatever Eliza felt, or feels, for me, I cannot call it love."

Sarah shrugged.

"If I did not know better," he said, tilting his head to the side, studying her expression, "I would think you pitied her."

"Is it so strange, then?"

His gaze wandered out to sea again. "No more strange, I suppose, than the pity I find I feel for my stepmother. I do not know if I can forgive her for what she did to you, but I realized tonight that her life has not been what she hoped it would be, either."

Sarah's ribs ached as she drew a deeper breath, gathering her courage. "I did not know until Eliza told me that you had been betrothed. I thought—"

"Betrothed?" he repeated, his shoulders suddenly stiff, as if the word were an accusation. "We were never betrothed, although certainly we all knew it to be her father's fondest wish." He paused, and his posture softened slightly, along with his voice. "But when we were younger, we were . . . very close. The connection between our families permitted certain—liberties, I suppose one might call them. We were more intimate than perhaps was wise."

She did not need to ask what he meant.

His fingers traveled the ground between them until they found hers, and against her better judgment, she let him take her hand. He turned her palm to the flickering firelight, studying the raw, red skin, pausing over a deep cut she had not even realized was there. With his other hand, he reached for his cravat, sliding the length of damp linen free of his collar and wrapping it gently but firmly around her injured hand.

She winced at the pressure, but the throbbing pain in her hand was nothing to the pain in her heart.

"The night of our nuptial ball, I heard you tell Eliza that your heart would never be mine," she whispered. His words had been burned into her brain. Even the years that had passed had done little to mute their echo. "Because it has always been hers?"

"No. It was never hers," he insisted. "What you heard that night, what she seems to have imagined I meant . . ." His voice drifted off, as if he were trying to remember some detail from another man's life. "I said you would never have my heart because I felt quite sure I hadn't a heart to give."

He glanced behind her toward the house and then back at the expanse of water and sky before them. "I was born here, Sarah. This was where I first knew love. And when my mother died, and I was forced to leave this place, I feared that my capacity to love left me." Finally, his pale eyes settled on her. "Eliza was right about one thing. When I saw you with Brice, I was jealous."

She could not help starting at this revelation. "Do not speak of him, please. I swear he never—we did not—"

"I know," he spoke across her. "I think a part of me always did. But nonetheless, I discovered something important that night. What I felt when I saw you in another man's arms showed me how wrong I had been. About you. About myself. And I was afraid of those feelings. I realized that could only mean I cared for you far more than I had intended. So I fought against them. Then, like a coward, I left."

She could hardly wrap her mind around what he was telling her, the lengths to which he had gone to cut himself off from his emotions. From his past.

From her.

The moon was rising, the horns of its crescent seeming to snag on the day's last delicate clouds. She watched as it freed itself from their clinging hold to cast its feeble light across the water.

"But now you've returned," she pointed out. "You feel a renewed sense of responsibility to this place, one my dowry can help you meet. And I am . . . I am glad of it, for the sake of the people here." She fingered the tattered edge of her skirt. "I have asked my father to give you the money from my dowry outright, whatever happens."

"Your note, you mean?" Reaching toward her again, he slipped one hand into the pocket of his coat where it lay across her thigh and withdrew a familiar scrap of paper. She gasped and snatched at it, but without ceremony, he tossed it into the fire. In the blink of an eye, the paper had curled into ash.

" 'Whatever happens'? You are my *wife*." He took her restless hand in his and with one fingertip, he touched the gold band she wore, turning it so it gleamed in the light. The urgency with which he spoke sent another shiver through her. "Lynscombe needs your father's money, I'll not deny it." A pause. "But *I* need *you*." He lifted searching eyes to her face. "I love you, Sarah."

"You . . . love me?"

"After last night, can you doubt it?"

She tugged anxiously against his hold, but he did not let her go. "One may . . . do such things, feel such things without love, I believe."

"Yes," he agreed. "One may. But last night, I did not. I wish I could deny that I ever had," he continued quietly, almost mournfully. "Young men tell themselves that love is a trivial thing. They imagine it some weak synonym for coquetry or lust or—"

"Desire," she supplied reluctantly. "Eliza is very beautiful."

"Yes," he agreed. "But not so beautiful as you are."

Sarah gave a snort of disbelief.

"Why do you deny it?" he challenged. "Hers is a beauty of externals. Your beauty, on the other hand, comes from a place deep within you—so deep that at first I could not see it. If I did not know better, I would accuse you of trying to hide it from me. But it does not matter—I see it now. And I do not intend to let it out of my sight again."

She could feel the heat rising to her cheeks and hoped the glow of the firelight disguised it. "Those are fine words, my lord, but—"

He laid one long finger across her lips to stop her. "Oh no, Sarah. Don't try to hide behind such formalities. You said my name once. Say it again."

How, as he had lain there gasping what she had feared might be his last breath, had he been able to spare the energy to notice that treacherous slip of her tongue?

"Very well," she muttered around his finger. "*St. John.* But—"

He shook his head. "Once more," he said, lifting his finger away to replace it with a gentle, searching kiss.

"St. John," she breathed when their lips parted.

She felt rather than saw his smile. "Better. Now . . . you were saying?"

What *had* she been saying? She gave an uncertain shake of her head.

"You are beautiful to me," he said again when she did not answer. "And I'll thank you not to argue with me about it."

From somewhere deep inside, Sarah dredged up the daring to reply, "Yes, my lord."

St. John raised one eyebrow and gave a slow, admonishing shake of his head. "Oh, Lady Fairfax. What am I going to do with you?"

To her mortification, something deep inside her quivered at the delicious darkness of his regard. But in another moment, a smile tugged at one corner of his mouth and dispelled his show of sternness.

That, she feared, was a weakness Clarissa would soon learn to exploit.

Some pang of emotion must have crossed her face at the thought of their daughter, for St. John's expression shifted again. "Oh, Sarah. I am sorrier than you can know that I have wasted so many years of our life together. Sorry that I ever doubted you. But if those mistakes taught me how much you mean to me, I cannot entirely regret having made them."

"Did you really throw the necklace and break it?" A rather embarrassed nod. "Why?"

"Not for the reasons you imagine," he said quickly. "I knew there must be a reason why it was in your trunk. I still believed you were innocent." His eyes dropped to their joined hands, almost as if he expected to see the jewels there. "But I also realized that it would not matter to me if you were guilty. I would love you just the same. I suppose that does not really explain why I did it . . ."

"Better than you can know," she assured him, remembering the curious mix of emotions she had felt as she threw his picture across the room on the night of his arrival in Haverhythe.

"Speaking of your trunk, there is something I have been meaning to ask you for some time." He paused as if awaiting permission for his question, so she tipped her head in the slightest of nods, granting it. "The miniature. It struck me as an object that had received a great deal of your attention. And I wondered, how did you come by it?"

Had he read the direction her thoughts had taken? She could almost feel the curve of the miniature case pressed into her palm, as it had been on that morning so long ago. "I stole it."

His grip on her unbound hand tightened. "Good God, Sarah. Why would you do such a thing?"

"I wanted something to remember you by," she whispered.

"Oh, Sarah . . ." Her words gave him hope. But as he watched her eyes filled with tears, the weight in his chest began to shift and sink like the contraband that had brought down John Potts's boat.

"When my father announced he had formed a match for me," she said, speaking across him, pulling back from his touch, "like you, I dreaded what was to come. Your title—or rather, your father's—was of no interest to me. I had no desire to mingle in the first circles of the *ton*. I wanted a different sort of life. But then I saw you. So very like the man in that portrait. So handsome. So charming."

"No," he denied soberly. "I think we both know I never behaved with charm toward you in those days."

"Perhaps not," she acknowledged. "But I did not let reality interfere with the personal fairy tale I had concocted, the one in which you realized I was worth more than my dowry. In which I captured your heart," she confessed in a whisper.

"You have," he insisted. Was there still the possibility that he had captured hers, as well?

"I knew you were but the prize my father's wealth had bought," she countered, shaking her head. "I knew I could never have won you on my own. I knew I was not really cut out to be the Viscountess Fairfax, despite my parents' dearest hopes and sincerest efforts to prepare me for the role."

"A strict governess, drawing masters, lessons on the pianoforte? No, those things were poor preparation indeed," he acknowledged as he watched her brows creep up her forehead. "The best thing you ever did to prove you were worthy to be Lady Fairfax was to run away."

A skeptical noise burst from her lips, but he held up one finger to stop her from speaking. "Let me finish. Because if you had never gone to Haverhythe, I would never have had to find you. I might never have realized you are capable of working miracles. *You* might never have realized you are capable of working miracles." Lifting his hand, he gently cupped her face. "You might have continued to believe yourself unworthy of dreaming your own dreams—and achieving them."

She closed her eyes against his gaze. "For all these years, whatever my heart chose to believe, my head told me you were not that fairy-tale hero. But I could never quite bring myself to let you go . . ."

"Don't," he breathed. "Surely you of all people would not deny me my happily-ever-after?"

"Life is not a fairy tale," she said as she opened her eyes and shook her head against his palm. "I know that now. The 'ever after' is not always happy. There will be times of sadness. And struggle."

"Yes," he agreed. Those were the very things he had feared most about opening his heart. Now, however, he understood they were not all. "But also, God willing, joy."

In the stillness that followed, he could hear her breath leave her body. "Tell me, Sarah. What did you see when you looked at that old miniature?"

She glanced again to the darkening sea. "The face of the man with whom I fell quite foolishly, quite hopelessly in love—from the very first moment I met him."

Somewhere behind his breastbone a spark of hope flickered to life.

"But, of course," she continued, "you are no longer the young man you were in that picture."

"No," he conceded. "I am not." He slipped his fingers into her damp hair, tilting her head toward him. "So tell me, what do you see when you look at me now?"

Warily, she met his gaze. Then she dashed at her eyes with the back of her clumsily bandaged hand, drew in a shuddering breath, and . . . smiled. Not one of those small, mysterious smiles that had begun to threaten his sanity. But a wobbly-lipped, genuine grin.

"I see the man I love," she said. "The man I've always loved. Even when I shouldn't have."

He lowered his lips to hers, tasting the trembling softness of her mouth. Raising his other hand to frame her face, he drew her closer and she came willingly, slipping into his embrace as if it were a well-worn garment.

After a time, he could feel that the fire beside them was dying down and the chill of the night air was pressing closer. "We should go home, Lady Fairfax," he said as he reluctantly shifted to rise and then helped her to her feet. "Everyone will wonder what has become of us—and I myself would rather avoid being discovered here by a search party, my little fugitive."

Sarah glanced behind her, and her lips lifted in a mischievous smile. "No, no more search parties. I promise never to go missing again, my lord."

"See that you don't," he ordered, trying to mold his face into a frown. "But just to be clear, you *are* a thief, you know. You've stolen my heart."

A delicate blush warmed her cheeks and far more than his heart. "That is only fair. You have had mine from the first."

He leaned toward her, setting his lips to an indentation at the corner of her mouth that was almost, but not quite, a dimple. "I did not deserve it then," he whispered against her cheek. "But I intend to spend a lifetime earning it."

"See that you do." She smiled, reluctantly drawing back from his lips to glance toward the house. "I suppose it can't have been much more than an hour, but it seems an eternity has passed since we left. Do you suppose the harvest ball has gone forward without us?"

"The ball?" He shook his head. "I think there never was a ball." Sarah's brow wrinkled in confusion and disappointment. "But I suspect the stomping and reeling and carousing at the Red Lion will go on for some time yet," he explained. "And that the people of

Lynscombe are enjoying themselves all the more for the absence of 't'grand folks up t'house.' "

She laughed, a wonderful, magical sound. St. John bowed and held out a hand for hers. "May I have this dance, ma'am?"

Sarah looked up at him, then down at her tattered dress.

"I regret to say that I am not suitably attired, my lord," she declined with a shake of her head.

"A pity. It was a lovely dress. How could I ever have forgotten it?" he asked, his eyes roving over her. "You were wearing it the first time I saw you."

He could picture her in it, standing in the morning room of her family's town house, accepting his grudging proposal of marriage with that small smile he would come to know so well, even as her fingers nervously worked the fringe of a heavy silk shawl drawn about her shoulders like a shield.

"And you kept it," he marveled. "All these years." She had held on to that piece of their past, and now he understood why. It made him eager to realize the future of which she had been dreaming on that day. "But I cannot help but wonder, what happened to the others?"

For a long moment, she did not answer.

"I had been in Haverhythe for a few weeks when I learned that 'Mad Martha' Potts hadn't the means to pay her rent," she said at last, her voice so quiet he had to strain to hear it over the moan of the outgoing tide. "Everyone in the village was certain she meant to throw herself off the quay one night. At first I did not see how I could help her—I had nothing of value. And then I realized . . ." She looked down at her dress and pleated the silk between two fingers of her injured hand. "Mrs. Dawlish bought them from me. She said she had a customer who would happily pay top price for the latest London fashions."

"Oh? And who was that?"

"Fanny Kittery."

"Ah, my Sarah," he whispered into her hair as he clasped her to his chest. "My clever, creative, generous Sarah."

When he released her, she frowned. "I suppose I'll have to go back to my black."

"Must you? I rather like you wearing nothing at all," he teased. She looked sidelong at him, half-scolding, half-intrigued. "What of the dress you wore to the festival in Haverhythe?"

"I left it behind, thinking perhaps that Mrs. Potts might need . . ." Her voice trailed away on a note of worry. "Besides, it was not a dress for travel, and my trunk was already packed, if you recall."

How could he ever forget?

"I'll tolerate those widow's weeds only as long as it takes for you to have something else made. First thing, send for Emily Dawlish." Sarah reached up to kiss him, pressing the length of her body against his. "Well, perhaps not *first* thing," he murmured around her lips. He did not think he would ever tire of kissing her, for each touch of their lips was at once new and familiar, comfortable and exhilarating. "Have her buy whatever she needs," he insisted when he at last lifted his head. "But be sure the shopkeeper knows—I always inspect my bill."

Sarah's pewter eyes flared at the reference to Emily's underhanded purchases at Gaffard's. "You knew?"

"I knew."

Fighting the temptation to sink down beside the glowing embers with her, he instead began to move, leading her in a dance at once unknown and yet so much a part of them that the steps seemed second nature—the bridal dance he should have claimed three years before.

Together they glided across the rough ground, moving to the elemental music of the waves.

Epilogue

December 24, 1796

Sarah watched as delicate flakes drifted down from the sky, twinkling merrily in the moonlight, coating the ground in a blanket of white, cheerfully indifferent to the Marquess of Estley's stern proclamation that it *never* snowed before Christmas.

He had retired an hour or more ago, and she had intended to follow his example. But still she sat, gazing out the window of the sitting room, drowsing beneath Clarissa's warm weight.

She thought of Mama and Papa in Bristol, bidding good night and happy Christmas to their friends and neighbors and Papa's clerks, Papa's eyes shining with satisfaction and Mama humming some dancing tune in spite of herself.

She thought of Lady Estley in London, where she had been since the autumn. Lord Estley had said little of her return to town, and St. John had said even less. She did not know whether it had been Lady Estley's choice to go or not. Presumably the marchioness had found some entertainment to while away the days—other than the amusement to be found in the card rooms, for her husband had put her on a strict allowance, locked away the valuables, and severed every line of cash or credit to which his wife had had access. Sarah could not claim to miss her.

But she thought most of St. John, who had promised to be home for Christmas Day. As she watched the snow fall, she could not help but wonder about the mysterious business that had taken him away. She worried, too, although she knew she shouldn't. Surely he had sense enough to stop for the night and was tucked away in some posting inn, safe and sound. He could not travel tomorrow, it was true, but they would be together again soon. One day, more or less, did not matter.

Christmas would be a quiet affair, however—just Lord Estley, Clarissa, and herself.

Not that any day with Clarissa in it was truly quiet. But in this moment of peace, as her daughter lay sleeping on her breast, breathing softly against her neck, it was easy to forgive her rambunctiousness, to hold her close and dream . . .

Sarah did not realize she had fallen asleep, but she awoke to the sound of a gentle voice in her ear.

"Happy Christmas, my love."

She opened her eyes, blinked twice, and smiled. St. John leaned over her, brushing his lips against Clarissa's curls.

"Jarrell told me where I'd find you," he whispered. He had obviously come straight to their apartments, for she could still see the snowflakes melting on his greatcoat. He held a small wrapped parcel under one arm, and his other hand was thrust deep in his pocket.

"I'm so glad you're home," Sarah said.

"You weren't worried?" he asked with a teasing tilt of his head.

"Perhaps a bit," she confessed.

Clarissa stirred but did not open her eyes. "Papa?"

"That's right, dear one."

She murmured some incoherent reply that sounded suspiciously like "Present?"

"As a matter of fact, I do have gifts for my darling girls," he said. Clarissa roused herself with a stretch. "But Mama shall have hers first." Reluctantly, Clarissa nodded her acquiescence and slid off Sarah's lap. St. John laid the parcel in her place. With deft fingers, Sarah untied the string, and the paper fell open to reveal a pretty wooden box.

"Why, it's soap," Sarah exclaimed when she lifted the lid. "Bluebell soap."

Clarissa leaned over the box and inhaled enthusiastically. "Mmmmm."

Sarah felt her eyes widen and, fighting a smile, glanced up at St. John. He gave a chagrinned sort of shrug, but the roguish twinkle in his eye could not be mistaken.

"My goodness, this will be enough to last a lifetime," Sarah insisted, taking refuge in the contents of the box as her face heated.

"I hope so, for it's likely to be the last of it. It seems that our dear Mrs. Kittery has, er, mislaid the recipe."

She raised her eyebrows. "Mrs. Kittery? You saw her in town?"

"No," he answered slowly. "I was not in town. I went to Haverhythe."

"Oh!" What on earth had called him there? And why hadn't he told her he was going? "How is . . . everyone?" she asked instead.

St. John smiled. "*Everyone* is well, I believe. Mrs. Potts condescended to shake my hand but could not be persuaded to stop calling me Lieutenant Fairfax. Mrs. Norris is—wait, I have a letter here somewhere." He finally pulled his other hand from his pocket and patted about the breast of his greatcoat.

"Mama?" Clarissa tugged impatiently at Sarah's sleeve.

Sarah's eyes followed her daughter's gaze to the coat pocket her father's hand had so recently vacated.

Something still moved within it.

"What dat is, Papa?" Clarissa asked hesitantly, pointing one dimpled finger at his coat.

"Hmm?" St. John replied absently, still making a great show of looking for the letter. "Oh, this?" He reached back into the pocket, pulled out a mewling ball of gray-striped fluff, and handed it to Clarissa.

"Thomas!"

After a few moments of stroking and admiring the kitten, Clarissa put it on the floor—much to Sarah's astonishment—and ran to hug St. John's knee. "Thank you, Papa," she cried, unprompted.

Sarah watched as St. John ran a hand over his daughter's head and smiled down at her, his own eyes curiously bright. "You're welcome, my pet."

Clarissa turned back to the kitten, which had discovered the string from the box of soap, and in another moment it was difficult to say who was enjoying their game more, as she raced squealing around the room, dragging the bit of twine behind her, and he scampered after, pausing to stalk and fluff and pounce whenever Clarissa hesitated.

"And here, my dear, is your letter," St. John said, suddenly able to locate the wayward missive with ease and offering it to Sarah with a flourish. "I'm sure it will tell you much more about the goings-on in Haverhythe than I ever could."

She very much doubted it. For one, Abigail Norris was no gossip.

And even if she were, the thing Sarah most wanted to know was the one thing Abby was least likely to reveal, the thing she had not mentioned in any previous letter that had come.

"How is she?" Sarah asked, running her finger over the impressions left by Abby's pen.

"Perfectly well, I believe," was St. John's calm reply.

"Truly?"

"Why, Lady Fairfax, surely you do not suggest that I would have been so ill-mannered as to have observed Mrs. Norris's delicate condition?" He shook his head in a mock scold, shrugged out of his greatcoat, and came to sit in the chair beside her. "Apart from a certain rosy glow in her complexion, and the fact that the vicar looks fit to burst—whether with pride or anxiety, I could not hazard a guess—it's all quite cleverly disguised by one of those fashionable new high-waisted gowns, or so Mrs. Dawlish assured me. You know I can hardly tell one dress from another, my dear," he added with a grin. "I heard almost no gossip at all about it—except for what I was told, confidentially you understand, by Mr. Gaffard, who got it from Mackey, who heard that Mr. Kittery suspects there might be twins on the way."

Sarah followed the long train of informants to the end and then gulped. *Twins?*

On the one hand, it seemed like a fitting blessing for a couple who had thought for so long that they would never have a child. "But is there not some risk?" she asked.

"Some," St. John acknowledged more soberly. "But you can be sure that Mr. Norris does not allow her to exert herself unduly, and she seems in the very bloom of health."

Did she imagine the wistful expression in his eyes?

"It's far too quiet in here," Sarah said, rising to her feet to cover her sudden nervousness. "Clarissa," she called, "you aren't hurting Thomas, are you?"

She found the two curled up in sleepy contentment on one of the chairs nearer the hearth. "No, Mama," Clarissa insisted. The kitten purred.

She felt St. John's eyes on her as she came back to her seat and arranged her skirts around her.

"What of Mr. Beals?" she asked after a moment's silence.

"Ah, poor Beals," St. John sighed with a shake of his head. "He's in sorry shape. Veritably struggling to get by, the sales of his currant cakes dropped off so precipitously after you left." Sarah pursed her lips to keep from smiling. "Although—it seems you were not his only customer," he added with a meaningful look. "He happened to ask, quite out of the way, if Miss Dawlish ever spoke of returning home."

In spite of herself, Sarah gasped and looked up. "Emily?"

He nodded. "Who may or may not at this moment be poring over a letter that Gerald Beals may or may not have tucked into my hand when I left, while muttering the closest thing to a prayer that I suspect has ever passed that crusty baker's lips."

And sure enough, when a few more minutes had passed, Emily came in, dark eyes shining, a certain bounce in her step, and one hand pressed to her breast as if clutching some bit of clandestine correspondence secreted there—or guarding the heart beneath it.

"Bed this instant, little miss. I won't hear another excuse," she proclaimed in a rare display of firmness when Clarissa began to protest. But when Clarissa held up the kitten, she softened visibly. "Oh, gracious me, what a precious little thing. And hasn't it the look of Bright Meg about it, milady?" she asked, looking to Sarah for confirmation.

Sarah nodded, not certain she could trust herself to speak.

"I had a bit of news from home, mum," Emily continued. "Someone paid up the rent on Primrose Cottage for the rest o' Mrs. P.'s life! Lord Haverty's agent let it slip one night in Mackey's. Why, just think! Who coulda done such a thing?"

Sarah twisted to look at her husband, who refused to meet her eye. "It's a mystery," she acknowledged, fighting a smile.

"Now, Clarissa," St. John admonished, scooping up the kitten and handing it to Emily. "If you do not want Thomas to spend his first night here in the kitchens with Mrs. Hayes, you must do as Miss Dawlish says."

Clarissa's lower lip trembled. "Yes, Papa."

At Emily's urging, Clarissa kissed her parents good night and then, with an enthusiasm that caused the kitten to squirm, took Thomas in her hands and led the way to the nursery.

"Emily Dawlish and Gerald Beals," Sarah murmured incredulously when the door had closed. "How could I have failed to see—?"

"I suspect either that they did not want anyone to see, or more likely, that there was nothing to see. Perhaps they realized the depth of their feelings only after they were apart."

Sarah could not disagree with him. After all, love sometimes blossomed under the unlikeliest of circumstances.

"Well, whatever the case, by the look on her face," he continued, "I fear we'll soon be in need of a new nursery maid."

Fighting a smile, Sarah nodded.

In the peaceful silence that followed, St. John slouched comfortably in the chair and closed his eyes. She could see the exhaustion etched on his face, and she knew that at least the last miles of his journey could not have been easy ones.

"Whatever made you go to Haverhythe?" she asked quietly, thinking he might have fallen asleep. "Rather a long trip for a kitten, some soap, and a letter, don't you think?"

His eyes opened and leveled their steady gaze on her. "I'd travel to the ends of the earth to make you happy, Sarah—and our daughter, too. Besides," he added, with a wry glance toward the soap, "I've always favored homemade gifts at Christmas."

"Oh," she breathed as her lips curved upward. "I'm glad to hear it, for I have—" She pressed her fingers to her lips and then let her hand drop back into her lap.

She had thought the gesture had gone unnoticed, but she saw then that St. John's eyes had followed the fall of her hand and watched it settle, quite without meaning to, on the curve of her belly.

"Sarah?" His pale eyes darted back to her face.

She gave a quick nod. "You must understand, I don't *know*," she cautioned. "It's too soon to be certain. But there are signs. I have hopes."

He was on his feet in an instant, sweeping her into his arms. "Oh, my love."

Tears started into Sarah's eyes. "You are pleased?" she found the courage to ask.

"More than pleased. Elated," he insisted. "I will confess that seeing Mrs. Norris made me cognizant of all I'd missed. And when I saw Norris, I was quite jealous of any man who was lucky enough to share in such joy."

She thought of the sickness and fatigue and pain and considered for a moment whether she ought to correct him, or at least warn him.

But then he was setting her on her feet again and cupping her face in his hands and kissing her, and the thought danced away like the snowflakes swirling outside the window. His lips skated across hers with heart-stopping tenderness.

And in that moment, all she knew was joy.

Historical Note

From the late seventeenth century until the early nineteenth, Great Britain's most valuable colonial possessions were a few small islands in the Caribbean Sea—places like Barbados, Jamaica, and Antigua—where sugarcane could be grown. In what would come to be known as the Triangular Trade, money and goods from Britain were used to purchase African slaves and ship them to plantations in the West Indies; the sugar produced by slave labor was sold at great profit in Britain, enabling the cycle to continue. Sugarcane's almost year-round growing season and intensive harvest demands, combined with the disease-ridden tropical environment, made sugar production especially brutal work. To maximize profits, slaves were given little in the way of clothing, food, or rest, and overseers enacted horrific punishments to extract labor and to quash resistance.

In the Runaway Desires series, characters confront this ugly reality, come to terms with their roles in it, and challenge it when they can. In this, as in so many ways, the heroes and heroines of romance are unfortunately far from typical. Most eighteenth-century Britons, far removed from the West Indies, were indifferent to slavery. Others regarded it as a positive good, both in economic terms and as a means of "civilizing" Africans, views reinforced by propaganda from the powerful West India Lobby, made up of planters, merchants, bankers, and Members of Parliament. An anti-slavery movement did not emerge until the closing decades of the century, when the tide slowly began to turn. In 1772, Chief Justice Lord Mansfield issued a ruling challenging the legality of slavery, widely interpreted to mean that any slave brought to Britain from the colonies was free on English soil. Following fierce debate in the 1790s, the slave trade was outlawed in the British Empire in 1807, and slavery itself was formally abolished in the British colonies in 1833, though many of the harsh conditions and attitudes persisted long after.

Keep reading for a sneak preview of
TO TEMPT AN HEIRESS
The next in Susanna Craig's
Runaway Desires series
Available December 2016
From Lyrical Books

Chapter 1

Near English Harbour, Antigua
October 1796

Captain Andrew Corrvan would never claim to have acted always on the right side of the law, but there were crimes even he would not stoop to commit.

Kidnapping was one of them.

This conversation ought to have been taking place in some dark, dockside alley, not in the sun-dappled sitting room of the little stone house occupied by the plantation manager at Harper's Hill. Andrew had never met the man before today, although he knew him by reputation. Throughout Antigua, Edward Cary was talked of by those who knew him, and by many more who didn't, as a fool. As best Andrew had been able to work out, he had earned the epithet for being sober, honest, and humane, a string of adjectives rarely, if ever, applied to overseers on West Indian sugar plantations.

As the afternoon's exchange suggested, however, even a paragon of virtue could be corrupted by a villainous place. Why else would Cary be attempting to arrange the abduction of a wealthy young woman?

"So, the talk of valuable cargo was just a ruse to lure me here?" Andrew asked.

"Not at all," Cary insisted with a shake of his head. "Between her father's private fortune, which she has already inherited, and Harper's Hill"—he swept his arm in a gesture that took in the plantation around them—"which she will inherit on her grandfather's death, Miss Holderin is worth in excess of one hundred thousand pounds."

Despite himself, Andrew let a low whistle escape between his teeth. The chit would be valuable cargo indeed. "And how do you benefit from sending her four thousand miles away?"

"I don't," Cary said, and behind that rough-voiced admission, and the mournful expression that accompanied it, lay a wealth of meaning. So the man had taken a fancy to his employer's granddaughter, had he? The more fool, he. "When Thomas Holderin was on his deathbed I gave him my solemn oath I would do all in my power to look after his daughter."

"And now you wish to be rid of the obligation."

"I *wish*—" he began heatedly. But apparently deciding his own wishes were beside the point, he changed course and said instead, "I believe she will be safer in England."

"Then book her passage on the next packet to London." Andrew thumped his battered tricorn against his palm, preparatory to placing it on his head and taking his leave. At his feet, his shaggy gray mongrel, Cal, rose and gave an eager wag of his tail, bored with all the talk and ready to be on his way.

"If I could, I would. I have tried many times to reason with her. But Miss Holderin is . . . reluctant to leave Antigua. She believes she is more than a match for the dangers the island presents." Cary turned toward the window. "She is wrong."

Andrew followed the other man's gaze. Fertile fields, lush forest, and just a glimpse of the turquoise waters of the Caribbean Sea where they touched a cerulean sky. It would have been difficult to imagine a less threatening landscape, but Andrew knew well that appearances could deceive. The dangers here were legion.

"Why me?" Andrew asked after a moment, folding his arms across his chest and fixing the other man with a hard stare. "Do you know the sort of man I am?"

Unexpectedly, Cary met Andrew's gaze with an adamant one of his own. "I do. You are said to be a ruthless, money-hungry blackguard."

Andrew tipped his chin in satisfied agreement. He had spent ten years cultivating that reputation.

"But of course, the sort of man you are *said* to be might not be entirely accurate, I suppose," Cary continued, steepling his fingers and tilting his head to the side. "Your crew tells a slightly different story, Captain."

Despite himself, Andrew shifted slightly. The movement might have gone unobserved if not for the dog, whose ears pricked up, as if awaiting some command.

One corner of Cary's mouth curled upward as he glanced at Cal. "Most of the sailors on your ship were admirably tight-lipped, rest assured," he said. "But then I happened to make the acquaintance of a fellow called Madcombe. New to your crew, I believe."

Andrew jerked his chin in affirmation. There was no denying Timmy Madcombe was a talker. He might have told Cary anything, and probably had.

"He seemed most grateful to find himself aboard a ship captained by what he called a 'r'al gent,' you will be pleased to know. 'Good grub, a fair share, an' no lashin's, neither,' " Cary added, mimicking Timmy's voice—right down to the occasional crack that gave the lie to the lad's claim of being fourteen. "If that proves true, such a style of shipboard management would make you rather unusual among your set." This time, Andrew was careful not to move, offering neither acknowledgment nor denial. Still, Cary seemed to read something in him. "Yes"—he nodded knowingly—"Madcombe's story, and the vehemence with which the rest of your crew attempted to keep him from telling it, made me wonder if you are quite as ruthless as you wish to seem."

"If you are willing to take the word of that green boy, you must be desperate, indeed," Andrew said, pushing back against Cary's probing.

"I am." Cary flicked his gaze up and down, taking in every detail of Andrew's appearance. "Desperate enough to hope that in some ways at least, you are as ruthless as you look—despite any assurances I may have received to the contrary. For it will take a ruthless man to succeed."

"I take it Miss Holderin's is not the only resistance I can expect to encounter if I take her away."

"Hers will be formidable," Cary warned. "Do not underestimate it. You may be required to use some rather creative measures to get her aboard your ship."

Creative measures? A sudden sweat prickled along Andrew's spine. Nothing about this situation sat well with him.

A welcome breath of wind stirred the draperies behind him, drawing cooler, sweetly scented air through the house, scattering some papers across the desk beside which Cary stood. "But I will confess, her opposition is not my primary concern," he continued. "As you might imagine, an heiress of Miss Holderin's magnitude receives a great deal of attention—unwelcome attention—from prospective suitors. And one of them is not content to accept her refusal."

"If she's turned the man down, what of it?" Andrew dismissed the supposed menace with a shrug. "He can't bloody well drag her down the aisle, bound and gagged."

"Can he not?" Cary asked. Absently, he neatened the stack of papers disordered by the breeze, weighting them with a green baize ledger, never raising his eyes from the desk. "I wish I shared your certainty about the matter. But we live on the very edge of what might be considered civilized society, Captain, and Lord Nathaniel Delamere has lived the sort of life that has put a great many influential men in his thrall. Men who would be willing to look the other way if some injustice were done. Planters. Merchants." At last he lifted his gaze. "Even a clergyman or two."

"There's something rather odd about your determination to go against Miss Holderin's express wishes in order to keep another man from doing the same," Andrew pointed out.

By the expression on Cary's face, Andrew guessed the irony had not been lost on him. "If she learns what I've done, she will never forgive the betrayal—I know that. But Delamere will stop at nothing to get his hands on Harper's Hill and Thomas Holderin's fortune. And once he has what he wants, what will become of her? She will not listen to reason. What ought I to do?"

The question hung on the air between them for a long moment.

"A desperate man. A dangerous voyage. And an heiress who doesn't want either one." Andrew ticked off each item on his fingertips. Perhaps it was her plantation manager from whom Miss Holderin most needed to be saved. "I thank you for the consideration, but I think I'll pass. Find another ship to do your dirty work, Cary."

"Would you have me trust her with just anyone? I have reason to believe you're a man of honor. Besides," he added frankly, "yours is the last private vessel in the harbor over which Delamere has no hold. You are my best hope, Captain Corrvan."

But Andrew had learned long ago not to be swayed by another's tale of woe. "London is not on the *Fair Colleen*'s route," he said, moving toward the door and motioning the dog to follow.

Before he could take more than a step or two, there was a knock at the door. "Put down that musty old ledger, Edward," a feminine voice rang out in the corridor. "Angel's Cove is beckoning. I can ask Mari to pack us a—oh!"

Startled by the intrusion, Cal charged toward the door, barking furiously. The woman dropped the book she had been carrying and let out an inhuman screech of alarm. Suddenly, the once-quiet sitting room was a flurry of activity: a flash of brown hair, more shrieks, and two snarling leaps into the air.

"Cal!" Andrew grasped the dog's collar.

Stepping past him, Cary shouted, "Stop that racket, you little devil."

More defiant screeches, another brown blur, and Andrew at last sorted out the source of both the noise and the confusion: a little monkey, who had been driven up the wall by Cal's unexpected greeting and now clung to the curtain rod, taunting the dog. Cal strained against his collar, trying to lunge at the unfamiliar animal, and Cary's brow was knit in a fierce frown.

On the floor sat the woman, perhaps two- or three-and-twenty, her heart-shaped face framed by red-gold curls that tumbled down her back in inviting disarray, barely contained by her broad-brimmed straw hat. She was emphatically *not* screeching. That had been the monkey.

No, the woman was laughing.

Once she had recovered her breath, she scrambled to her feet without waiting for an offer of assistance from either man and instead held out her hand to the monkey. "Come, Jasper. Mind your manners."

When Jasper refused with a mocking grin and a vigorous shake of his head, the woman shrugged and turned toward Andrew. "My apologies. He doesn't respond well to being startled. But you couldn't know that, could you?" she said in a hearty voice, ruffling the dog's shaggy gray ears once her hand had been sniffed and approved. "What a brave boy . . . Cal, did you call him?"

Then her fingers met Andrew's in the dog's rough fur, and with a gasp of surprise, she jerked her hand away. Had she felt it, too, the warning spark that had passed between them when they touched?

She glanced upward, and Andrew, who was still bent over the dog, found himself just inches from the most startling eyes he had ever seen. A swirling mixture of blue and green and gray for which there was no name.

He straightened abruptly and tugged the dog a respectable distance away. "Caliban, actually."

"Caliban?" she echoed, wiping her hands down the skirt of her brownish-green dress, which was already smudged with dusty handprints.

"After the half-man, half-beast in—"

"In *The Tempest*," she finished. Something that was not quite a smile lurked about her lips, and her blue-green eyes twinkled. "By Mr. Shakespeare."

"It seemed a fitting name for such a mongrel," Andrew said with a glance at the dog's feathery tail where it thumped against the floorboards. Since when was Cal's affection to be won with a pat on the head?

When he turned back to face the woman, he found his own appearance an object of similar scrutiny. "And you are?" she asked.

"Captain Andrew Corrvan." Cary inserted himself between them and completed the introductions. "Miss Tempest Holderin."

"Tempest?" Unable to keep the note of disbelief from creeping into his voice, Andrew still managed a bow. Although he had cast aside most other hallmarks of a gentleman's upbringing, too many years of training had made that particular gesture automatic.

Cary's explanation was predictably measured. "Her father was . . . unconventional."

"A lover of Shakespeare," Tempest Holderin corrected. Her eyes flashed, and at once he realized why their unusual hue looked so hauntingly familiar to him. They were eyes in which a man might easily drown, the precise shade of the sea before a storm.

Perhaps Thomas Holderin had known what he was about, after all.

"The two are hardly mutually exclusive," Andrew remarked, a part of him hoping she would rise to the challenge in his words. "No matter how much your father might have enjoyed the Bard, you cannot deny that the more conventional choice would have been for him to choose the name of a character from one of Shakespeare's plays, rather than naming you after the play itself."

"Perhaps he felt Caliban wouldn't suit," she shot back, lifting her pointed chin.

Andrew fought the temptation to smile. "I was referring, of course, to Miranda."

His familiarity with the play seemed to surprise her. " 'O brave new world, that has such people in 't!' " She quoted Miranda's famous line, the moment at which the sheltered heroine of *The Tempest* glimpses a handsome young man. But she spoke it with the sort of half sigh more befitting the character's world-weary father, Prospero. "No, Miranda would never have done. I assure you I am not so naïve as she. Particularly where men are concerned," she added, not quite under her breath.

"If you'll excuse us, Tempest." Cary seemed to find little amusement in the exchange. "Captain Corrvan and I have a matter of urgent business to discuss."

"Business? Excellent," she declared, standing firm. "I've been meaning to ask you about Dr. Murray's report on Regis's leg. And have you heard from Mr. Whelan? I know the harvest is almost upon us, but I won't have people put to work in the mill if there's danger of it collapsing."

"Murray called here this morning and pronounced Regis's wound almost healed," Cary told her. "No sign of infection. And I intend to follow up with Whelan tomorrow. You know I have no wish for anyone to come to harm."

"Of course not, Edward," she said, softening. "But you've been so dreadfully busy since Mr. Fairfax left us. Why, sometimes I think I ought to have forbidden him to leave."

"We are not all so susceptible to the stamp of your foot, my dear." Cary's lips were stretched in a forced smile. "Besides, although his head seemed sound enough, I always suspected Fairfax's heart—or a piece of it, anyway—lay in England."

Miss Holderin made no comment on Cary's sentimental twaddle, but her expression said all that was needed. "Why won't you let me help? I might speak to Mr. Whelan," she suggested, shifting the subject.

"You will do no such thing."

Andrew expected her to pout in response to Cary's flat refusal, but he was quickly disabused. Tempest Holderin looked quite accustomed to hearing such commands, if not accustomed to obeying them. A frown creased her brow, but Cary did not relent. Although far from immune to those eyes, it seemed he had at least learned to judge the difference between squall and hurricane. "It is not safe for a young woman to go about English Harbour unattended."

"You cannot expect me to sit idly by and—"

"Idly?" Cary looked her up and down. "Somehow, I doubt you have been idle. Is that chalk dust I see on your skirt?" At her somewhat abashed nod, he shook his head. "How many times have I told you—?"

"Not to teach them? It's only letters and numbers, Edward. What harm can it do?" she argued as she attempted to brush the evidence from her dress.

"In these days, with rumors of an uprising on everyone's lips? It would do a great deal of harm if you are caught—both to them and to you."

"Then I won't get caught." Failing in the attempt to improve the dress's appearance, she straightened and clicked her tongue to the little monkey. "Come, Jasper. It seems we're interrupting." Cautiously, the monkey made its way down the drapery and onto her shoulder. Cal strained against Andrew's hold and snapped at the air in one desperate, final attempt to catch his tiny tormentor.

"A pleasure to meet you, Caliban," she said with a smile for the dog. "And you, too, Captain."

"Wait."

With his free hand Andrew swept up the book she had dropped, a thin leather-bound volume that looked not old, but well-read. Nodding her thanks, she stretched out her hand so he could lay it on her palm.

"What are you reading?" he asked instead, lifting the cover with his thumb.

"Something really very horrid, you may be sure," she answered as she tried to snatch the book from his grasp before he saw.

"A gothic tale?" He tightened his fingertips around the book's spine, refusing to relinquish it. "Are you a devotee of Mrs. Radcliffe's, then?"

"Not particularly." She wrenched the book from his hand and tucked it against her bosom. "If you must know, this is Miss Wollstonecraft."

"Ah." Even a man who had spent years roaming the Atlantic could not remain ignorant of the controversy surrounding Miss Wollstonecraft and her books, with their support of the revolution in France and outspoken demands for women's rights. So Miss Holderin was a radical? It was of a piece with the rest of what he had heard.

And none of it inclined him toward Edward Cary's mad scheme. Six weeks at sea with a bluestocking who spouted Wollstonecraft? Not if he could help it. " 'Really very horrid,' indeed," he murmured.

Evidently suspecting she was being mocked, she parted her lips to reply. Before words could slip past them, Cary interjected. "Go home, Tempest," he urged, walking with her toward the doorway, his hand resting at the small of her back. The gesture might have been permitted under the guise of brotherly affection, but to Andrew it looked more like staking a claim. "I'll join you for supper, if I may."

The offer of his company seemed to mollify her somewhat. "Like old times. I'll have Mari make one of your favorites. But you won't forget about the mill?"

"I won't forget."

The monkey shot one leering grin behind him as they left, sending Caliban into another flurry of barks and forcing Andrew to squat beside him to contain him.

"Hush, Cal," he murmured, his heart not in the command.

"I haven't much patience for Jasper, either, old boy," Cary acknowledged when he reentered the room, casting the dog a sympathetic look. "But that little monkey is a long way from home. A sailor on a slave ship captured him in Africa, intending him for a pet," he explained to Andrew, who was rising to his feet. "When Tempest saw how cruelly the animal was being treated, she rescued him. It's what the Holderins do," he added, almost as an afterthought.

With such a fortune at her disposal, Andrew had imagined the sugar princess would prove pampered and elegant and probably cruel. He had not anticipated a chalk-streaked dress, radical sympathies, and a monkey. Tempest Holderin was not the sort of woman who ran away from trouble—she ran toward it with open arms. He had been wrong. And Cary was wrong. She didn't need to be rescued from this Lord Nathaniel character.

She needed to be rescued from herself.

Cary returned to the desk and riffled through the stack of papers he had set to rights mere moments ago. Selecting one sheet, he dipped a pen and said, "Name your price."

Andrew shook his head. He had not been to England—*home*, some would say, although it would never be so to him—in more than ten years. A man in Cary's position could never offer enough to send him back now. "I draw the line at kidnapping."

Undeterred, Cary scratched something on the paper. "Then think of it as a rescue."

But if abduction was not Andrew's game, neither was salvation. For much of his life, in fact, he had been bent on destruction instead.

And whatever amount Cary offered, the encounter with Miss Holderin left him even more determined to refuse it. Oh, she was tempting in her way, it was true, with that riot of red curls and those stormy eyes.

That, he feared, was the problem.

"Half now," Cary said, thrusting the note toward him. "The rest upon her safe delivery to her grandfather."

Reluctantly, Andrew took it, at the same time raising his free hand to his eyes, some part of him hoping he could rub them hard enough to erase the afternoon entirely—hard enough, at least, to render the figures on the paper an illegible blur.

He must have been staring at the number longer than he realized, for Caliban gave a troubled sort of whimper and nudged his wet nose against his hand, confused by his master's unusual stillness. The paper trembled.

He could not begin to imagine where Cary could have acquired such a sum. Was he somehow stealing from Miss Holderin's personal fortune to subsidize her abduction? For his own part, it still would not have been enough. But harder, much harder, to refuse it on behalf of his crew. Certainly Bewick and some of the others would be glad enough to glimpse old London town once more.

"Well?" Cary prompted.

The man had persuaded himself that he needed someone who was willing to break the rules, to save a woman who seemed quite indifferent to them herself.

Had he fully considered what might happen between his Tempest and such a man?

"Six weeks at sea. She will be ruined, you know."

A muscle ticked along Cary's jaw. "Only her reputation, I trust. And far more than that could be lost if she stays," he added, sounding resigned.

Andrew's fingers curled around the paper, crumpling it into a tight ball. Against his better judgment, he jerked his chin in a single nod. "I'll do it."

A love affair with historical romances led **Susanna Craig** to a degree (okay, three degrees) in literature and a career as an English professor. When she's not teaching or writing academic essays about Jane Austen and her contemporaries, she enjoys putting her fascination with words and knowledge of the period to better use: writing Regency-era romances she hopes readers will find both smart and sexy. She makes her home among the rolling hills of Kentucky horse country, along with her historian husband, their unstoppable little girl, and a genuinely grumpy cat. Find her online at www.susanna craig.com.

CPSIA information can be obtained at www.ICGtesting.com
Printed in the USA
LVOW10s1636110816

499998LV00001B/209/P